THE NEW MODEL
OF
DEVELOPMENT
&
HUMANITARIAN AID
DELIVERY

A Contribution to the Success of the United Nations' Sustainable Development Goals

Dr. Justin B. Mudekereza

Copyright

ISBN: 978-1-969021-61-9 (ebook)
ISBN: 978-1-969021-59-6 (Paperback)
ISBN: 978-1-969021-60-2 (Hardcover)

Contact Information:
headoffice@rescuedemocracyintl.org
www.rescuedemocracyintl.org
www.justinmudekereza.com

"With nearly three decades of experience in community development and a body of work focused on Social Justice and Human Rights, I consider this publication a milestone achievement. It represents not only a culmination of lived experience and research but also a strategic resource for reshaping how development and humanitarian aid are delivered.

This work is being shared with the United Nations, international NGOs, grantmaking organizations, and the broader global community. Its purpose is to confront and correct systemic inefficiencies that have long hindered the effectiveness of aid and development efforts. It offers a framework for transitioning from outdated models – often criticized for their lack of impact – to a new, inclusive, and accountable system.

We are all aware of the urgent need for change. The current paradigm has been widely denounced for its shortcomings. This publication is a call to action: a tool for advocacy, a blueprint for reform, and a voice for communities whose needs have too often been overlooked. I believe that every person who engages with this work will become a messenger – amplifying its message until it reaches the desks of policymakers, UN member states, donors, and Grantmakers.

Finally, for those who find value in this work and wish to support its implementation, I invite you to contribute to **Rescue Democracy International (RDI)**. RDI is already putting this "NEW MODEL" into practice, despite operating with limited resources. Your support can help scale its impact. To learn more or make a donation, please visit www.rescuedemocracyintl.org."

The Author.

TABLE OF CONTENTS

DEDICATION

This book is dedicated to the countless individuals and communities in the developing world whose resilience, ingenuity, and unwavering spirit in the face of adversity inspire every page. It is a testament to their inherent strength and their right to self-determination. To the grassroots organizations, the community health workers, the local leaders, and the everyday citizens who strive daily to build better futures for themselves and their families, often with limited resources and against overwhelming odds – this work is for you.

Your voices, your experiences, and your aspirations are the true north star for effective and ethical development. May this book serve as a tool to amplify your efforts and support your journey towards sustainable progress.

To the great team, change makers of Rescue Democracy International (RDI), executive and board members Jerry Shirey, Michael Stafieri, Daniel Collins, Kaley Harnsberger, Daniel Kirk, Jacques Jonassaint, Pete Ceccherini, the RDI ambassadors and volunteers (Rodrigo Tadeu, Camilla Tettoni, Laura Olivera, Elie Bwira, Luana Ramos, Elina Shankar, Roy-Stanley Nwafor, Valeria Rughetti...)

To the development and humanitarian aid workers and development practitioners who have dedicated their lives to this cause, often sacrificing personal comfort for the greater good, I share my profound respect. This work is also for you, an exploration of how we can collectively refine our approaches, learn from the past, and build a more impactful future.

Finally, to the Grantmakers and all donors who give their money to make the world a better place for all; your generosity is the fuel that drives change in the lives of those most in need. It's not how much we give but how much love we put into giving. Let's always keep in our minds that (and you know it better) if we haven't got any charity in our hearts, we have the worst kind of hearts trouble. A man's true wealth is the good that he does in this world to his fellows. May we always remain guided by the principles of dignity, equity, and lasting positive change.

FOREWORD

The landscape of international development and humanitarian aid is vast, complex, and often fraught with challenges. For decades, we have grappled with how best to alleviate suffering, foster sustainable growth, and empower communities to overcome poverty and inequality. We have set ambitious goals, poured considerable resources into programs, and witnessed both remarkable successes and disheartening failures. It is from this crucible of experience, marked by both profound hope and deep frustration, that this book emerges.

My journey through the field has been one of continuous learning, observation, and a growing conviction that **the conventional approaches, while well-intentioned, are often encumbered by layers of complexity that dilute their impact.** We have seen firsthand how well-conceived plans can falter due to logistical nightmares, bureaucratic inertia, and disconnect from the very communities they aim to serve.

This book is an attempt to articulate a different path; a path forged through radical simplification, a commitment to empowering local actors, and a relentless focus on maximizing direct impact. It is born from a belief that by stripping away unnecessary overhead, embracing innovative operational models, and placing trust in the capabilities of grassroots organizations, we can fundamentally transform the effectiveness and efficiency of aid.

This is not a critique for the sake of criticism, but a constructive proposal for a more agile, accountable, and ultimately, more impactful approach to global development challenges. It is an invitation to rethink our strategies, to challenge the status quo, and to collaborate on **building a future where aid truly empowers and sustains.**

The Author.

INTRODUCTION

The pursuit of global progress, as embodied by initiatives like the Millennium Development Goals (MDGs) and the current Sustainable Development Goals (SDGs), represents one of humanity's most noble endeavors. These frameworks aim to tackle persistent issues such as poverty, hunger, disease, and lack of education, reflecting a collective aspiration for a more equitable and sustainable world. Yet, as we strive to achieve these ambitious targets, a critical examination of our methods is not just warranted but essential.

This book delves into the persistent gaps between the promises of global development agendas and the often-unfulfilled realities on the ground. It scrutinizes the planning failures, the implementation hurdles, and the pervasive funding inefficiencies that have historically hampered progress. Drawing upon extensive field experience, the narrative highlights how complex bureaucratic structures, top-down decision-making processes, and a lack of genuine capacity building for local communities often undermine even the most well-intentioned interventions. We will explore how misaligned priorities, excessive administrative overheads, and a failure to leverage existing local capacities lead to wasted resources and diminished impact, leaving vast funding gaps unfilled and crucial development objectives unmet.

This work is motivated by a profound belief that a more effective and impactful model of delivering development and humanitarian aid is not only possible but necessary. It introduces **Rescue Democracy International (RDI)** and its innovative, lean operational framework as a tangible solution. This approach, called RDI Model also known as The Justin Mudekereza Model, prioritizes radical simplification, decentralizes power to grassroots organizations, and crucially, empowers local entities through the concepts known as 'Focal Points (PFs)' and 'Local Project Selection & Monitoring Committees (LPSMCs).'

Throughout my extensive career spanning over 25 years in community development, human rights activism, and social justice advocacy, I have collaborated directly, through signed contracts, and indirectly, via collaborative agreements, with numerous United Nations (UN) agencies – including UNDP, UNWFP, UNFAO, UNICEF, and UNHCR – as well as various International Non-Governmental Organizations (INGOs).

During this time, I have observed significant instances of corruption and misappropriation of resources originally designed to assist communities recovering from humanitarian crises or working towards sustainable development. My involvement in these practices was not a reflection of personal inclination towards misconduct but rather a response to challenging circumstances that necessitated difficult compromises. At times, accepting certain conditions was essential to secure aid for the communities I represented, even if it meant agreeing to terms that did not fully reflect the support received or the distribution of materials.

It is within this context that I introduce the *RDI Model* also known as *The Justin Mudekereza Model* to the United Nations (UN), international NGOs, Grantmakers, donors, and the broader global community. **This model is the culmination of decades dedicated to identifying long-lasting solutions to**

address systemic issues impairing effective delivery of development and humanitarian assistance.

Over the past decade, I have closely followed discussions at the United Nations General Assembly (UNGA), where many world leaders have expressed concerns about the UN system's efficacy. A prevailing sentiment has been the pressing need to **reconsider existing approaches to alleviate global human suffering.** Despite repeated calls for reform, tangible proposals for transformative change have rarely materialized, even as the consequences of outdated mechanisms – corruption, misuse of funds, excessive bureaucracy, and logistical complications – continue to hinder progress.

With humility, I now present a robust and comprehensive new approach: *the RDI Model.* This framework is designed to facilitate positive change and restore confidence among stakeholders, including the UN, INGOs, Grantmakers, donors, and other development partners. Since its implementation by Rescue Democracy International (RDI) under my leadership, the model has demonstrated remarkable outcomes, enabling intended recipients to experience meaningful and sustained improvements in their lives. I hope that this work is recognized for its significance and value, following years of dedicated research and effort, and that it will facilitate progress in global development and humanitarian aid delivery.

According to ONE Data and Analysis, in the year 2024, the total amount of development assistance was approximately **US$212.1 billion**, which includes US$24.2 billion specifically for humanitarian aid. This represents a 7.1% decrease from the previous year, indicating a significant drop in funding for humanitarian efforts. The same source indicates that aid to

African countries totaled **US$61.0 billion** in 2023 alone, or 26.8% of aid. If this information regarding these moneys is true, someone honest with a broader knowledge of the ongoing crises in different countries around the world may ask 2 simples questions: What did this money do? What exactly went wrong?

Examining the figures while acknowledging the progress made, even more important questions can arise. If couples of tens of billions of US$ were allocated between 2000 and 2015, what prevented the achievement of the Millennium Development Goals? Similarly, despite significant contributions from 2016 to 2025, why have critical global challenges targeted by the Sustainable Development Goals shown limited improvement? The allocation, impact, and effectiveness of these resources warrant further scrutiny. **Persistent poverty and ongoing development and humanitarian crises raise concerns about the distribution and utilization of funds, as well as the broader implications for those affected.**

This book proposes allocating US$10 billion from 2026 to 2030 through the application of RDI's Model, as detailed herein, to evaluate the potential positive effects on the advancement of the Sustainable Development Goals (SDGs) by 2030. The outcomes achieved by 2030 are expected to inform future decisions made by the United Nations, International Non-Governmental Organizations (INGO) and global leaders regarding ongoing development initiatives and humanitarian aid delivery.

During the research that led to the writing of this book, I sought insights from several experts with extensive experience in development and humanitarian aid fields. Among the many experts I approached, I chose to include some thought-provoking comments from Mr. Sedrick Murhula, who has spent nearly twenty years working alongside displaced communities across Africa, Europe, and the Americas. Mr. Murhula currently serves as Senior Program Manager at iACT, an international organization committed to collaborating with crisis-affected communities by partnering with them, providing resources, and amplifying their voices. The following are his comments:

"At iACT, I manage programs in Chad, supporting Sudanese refugees; in Cameroon, partnering with Central African refugees; in Bangui, Central African Republic, where internally displaced people (IDPs) and local communities are rebuilding amidst fragility and post decades of conflict; and in Mexico, supporting migrants' children and families navigating complex realities. Until recently, I also managed programs in Armenia and Tanzania, which have since closed.

My journey into humanitarian work began long before these roles. It started in Uganda, were, as a young refugee, I co-founded YARID (Young African Refugees for Integral Development) with a friend. We had no funding, no offices, and no donors behind us, only a shared belief that our community could find solutions within itself. YARID grew into one of the first successful refugee-led organizations in the region, and through it, I learned the deepest truths about resilience, leadership, and the untapped potential within displaced communities.

Seventeen years later, I've seen the humanitarian world from every angle local, national, and international. I've watched conflicts multiply, crises deepen, and resources shrink. Yet amid all this, one lesson stands out: real change always comes from the ground up.

Across the globe, the humanitarian system is under immense strain. The number of displaced people has reached 123 million, the highest ever recorded in human history. Wars in Sudan, Palestine, the Democratic Republic of Congo, Myanmar, and Ukraine have forced millions from their homes, while climate disasters uproot families in many regions.

And yet, at the very moment when need is greatest, the world is witnessing the largest decline in humanitarian funding in modern times.

The United States Agency for International Development (USAID), the world's largest bilateral donor has announced deep reductions in global aid. According to a 2025 UCLA study, if these cuts persist, they could lead to 14 million preventable deaths by 2030, including 4.5 million children under five. Between 2001 and 2021, USAID-supported programs contributed to a 15% reduction in all-cause mortality and a 32% decline in under-five mortality globally. The reversal of this trend is catastrophic.

In Sudan, USAID accounted for roughly 44% of humanitarian funding, supporting food security, water, sanitation, and health programs. With these resources frozen or cut, countless lifesaving operations have been suspended. Similar stories are unfolding in Myanmar, Yemen, and Haiti, where USAID once covered between 25% and 40% of humanitarian budgets. This is not just about numbers. Behind every statistic is a family left without food, a mother without medical care, a child unable to attend school. I have seen it firsthand, mothers in eastern Chad searching for food for their children, community volunteers in refugee camps in Uganda trying to keep schools open with almost no resources, and refugees in Cameroon losing access to health services and food ration overnight.

The humanitarian system, as it exists today, is struggling to adapt. The model was designed for a different era when crises were isolated, funding was predictable, and international actors were seen as the primary problem-solvers. But in our interconnected world, this centralized, top-down approach no longer works.

Instead of transformation, we see repetition. Donors funnel money to large international Nongovernmental Organizations (INGOs) who subcontract to smaller NGOs, who sometimes pass funds again to community organizations. **By the time resources reach the ground, a significant portion has already been spent on administration, logistics, and headquarters overhead.**

Many INGOs now resemble corporations more than humanitarian actors complete with complex bureaucracies, inflated salaries, lavish offices, and endless gathering in the name of conferences to find solutions. Some have become more focused on sustaining themselves than on sustaining the communities they serve. And when budgets are cut, it's often the local workers and programs the heart of humanitarian response that are the first to go.

This imbalance of power, resources, and trust has created what many now call the "humanitarian divide." Those closest to the problem remain furthermost from the decision-making table.

- ***The Promise of Localization***

Amid this decline, a growing movement is calling for a humanitarian reset through localization. The idea is simple yet revolutionary: **shift power, funding, and decision-making to those who are closest to and affected by the crisis – the communities themselves.**

Localization is not a slogan. It's a fundamental rethinking of who leads, who decides, and who defines success. True localization means that refugee-led organizations, community-based groups, and national NGOs are not subcontractors, but they are leaders.

The Grand Bargain, signed at the 2016 World Humanitarian Summit, promised that 25% of all humanitarian funding would go directly to local actors by 2020. Nearly a decade later, that figure remains below 3%. The excuses, capacity, risk, compliance remain the same. But these barriers are not technical; they are political.

When I co-founded YARID, we had none of the system donor's demand, no bank account, no accountant, no external audit. Yet, for five years, we successfully served thousands of refugees without a single donor dollar. Imagine what organizations like ours could achieve if even a fraction of the billions spent on international overhead were redirected to community-led initiatives.

In my years managing programs across Africa, I have witnessed the deep cost of sidelining local capacity. I have seen communities with the willingness and experience to lead, but without the resources to act. I have seen organizations forced to close because international funding streams were frozen, leaving behind a vacuum that no one else could fill.

When international NGOs lose funding, their vehicles and staff leave, but the needs remain and so do the local responders. In Chad, Cameroon, or the Central African Republic, and in other places in crisis, teachers, nurses, refugee-led groups, and women's associations stay behind long after the large INGOs are gone. They are the ones who carry the weight of human suffering with little to no support.

The tragedy is not that they lack capacity; it is that they lack trust and direct funding. The real gap in our system is not skill, it is power.

During my recent mission to Alalacha Refugee Camp in Chad a sprawling settlement of more than 55,000 Sudanese refugees the realities of this imbalance struck me hard. The camp was a mix of desperation and remarkable resilience. As I walked through its narrow paths, I saw no visible humanitarian presence, no standing officers, no functional clinics, no social workers on the ground. What I found instead were small, community-run initiatives: makeshift preschools, early childhood spaces created from recycled materials, and informal women's groups offering psychosocial support to one another. These efforts were deeply local, born out of necessity, driven by compassion yet none were funded or recognized by any international agency.

It was painful to see! The people were doing exactly what global policy frameworks preach taking ownership, leading, innovating *but without even minimal support. They had the will, but not the means. This is what the absence of localization looks like in real time: hope running on empty.*

*From Alalacha, I traveled to Goz Amer, one of Chad's oldest refugee camps, established in 2003. There, I encountered a small community clinic run by a handful of overworked volunteers. It served hundreds of refugees daily, men, women, and children waiting for basic medical care, many sitting on mats for hours, some walking for miles to get there. The nurse in charge, the only trained medical officer in sight worked tirelessly, his eyes heavy with exhaustion. Yet he refused to leave because, as he said, "If I go, who will they have?" That simple question encapsulates everything wrong with the global humanitarian system. How is it that after two decades, a camp hosting thousand still depends on one exhausted nurse and a single unfunded clinic? **This is not a story of capacity failure; it is a story of systemic neglect.***

Standing in Goz Amer, I could not help but ask myself and, by extension, the entire humanitarian establishment, some uncomfortable questions:

- *Why have we not directly supported these local efforts that are already saving lives?*
- *Why are the community-led preschools, clinics, and youth initiatives left unfunded while international organizations receive millions for similar services?*
- *Is this the result of design or of neglect?*
- *And most importantly, who benefits from maintaining this imbalance?*
- *.../...?*

These are not easy questions. But they must be asked if we are serious about reforming the humanitarian aid system.

Localization is not a new idea. It is the recognition that **sustainable solutions must come from those who live the crisis, not those who fly in to manage it.** True localization is not just about transferring money; it is about transferring power, the power to decide priorities, design programs, and hold systems accountable.

When local organizations lead, responses become faster, more culturally appropriate, and more cost-effective. Aid stops being charity and becomes partnership. Refugees and local actors stop being "beneficiaries" and become co-creators of their own recovery. But without localization, we continue to lose time, money, and most regrettably lives. The world cannot afford that anymore.

To localize is to trust. To trust is to let go of control. And letting go is the hardest part for a system built on hierarchy and ownership. Yet the evidence is clear: **the most effective responses are those rooted in local leadership.**

If the international community truly wants impact, it must have the courage to shift resources and decision-making to those who are already doing the work even if that means reimagining the humanitarian aid industry as we know it. Because every time we exclude local actors, we are not just losing potential; we are losing lives, dignity, and the chance to finally make humanitarian aid what it was meant to be – a shared act of humanity, not an industry of control.

- ***The Humanitarian Meetings and the Missing Voices***

Over the years, I have attended countless humanitarian meetings from Kampala to Addis Ababa, Geneva to New York, Johannesburg to Washington, D.C., each promising change, reform, and inclusion. And yet, the same pattern repeats: long speeches, polished statements, and few actionable outcomes.

*In 2019, I attended the Global Refugee Forum in Geneva, one of the world's most significant gatherings on forced displacement. Alongside other community leaders, I advocated for direct funding and representation of refugee-led organizations in global policy spaces. The response from many large actors was polite, but dismissive. Some questioned whether communities had the "capacity" to manage funds or represent themselves. To me, that attitude is not only wrong, but also insulting. Communities have proven, time and again, that they can lead effectively, often with fewer resources and greater results than larger institutions. **The problem is not whether they can, it's whether the system will let them.***

Fast forward couple of years later again, I attended the UN General Assembly (UNGA) in New York recently, the conversations felt different. The sense of urgency was palpable. The question echoing through civil society events was no longer "Should we reform the humanitarian aid sector?" but "Who will reform it and how soon?" The global system is at a breaking point. Reform cannot be top-down. True transformation must come from within communities, led by those most affected.

Inclusion and accountability were central themes. Many INGOs talk about "accountability," but to whom are we truly accountable, donors or communities? Real accountability means answering to the people we serve, not just to the institutions that fund us. **We must also stop treating crises as temporary. Humanitarian action must connect with development, peacebuilding, and resilience.** *The lines between these fields are artificial. Communities don't live in categories; they live in realities that overlap. If humanitarian aid were designed with long-term development in mind, we would respond differently to both refugees and host communities alike.*

During a recent visit to Western Chad, I met with leaders of **CENAR,** *Chad's governmental entity responsible for overseeing refugee affairs. The conversation quickly revealed something deeper than logistics or policy, it was about vision, or rather, the consequences of its absence. Every official I spoke to emphasize the same concern: Chad's refugee response, while commendable in its generosity, was never built on a developmental foundation. Instead, it was shaped by decades of emergency management rapid responses, temporary shelters, and cyclical aid dependency.*

One senior officer spoke with a mix of pride and frustration. "Imagine," he said, "if the plan had been developmental from the beginning back in 2002 or 2003, when the first waves of Sudanese refugees arrived. By now, both refugees and host communities could have built a solid, self-reliant system one that could support new arrivals without waiting for external intervention." His words carried the weight of hindsight and the realism of someone who has seen crises come and go, often with the same patterns of reaction. He explained how the absence of a long-term vision meant each new influx of refugees forced a repeat of the same humanitarian script:

emergency tents, food distributions, temporary water points. "We've been firefighting for twenty years," he said. "What we needed was irrigation." The metaphor was perfect; Chad's refugee response has been a series of fires put out rather than seeds planted.

The CENAR team envisioned a future where developmental systems education, employment, infrastructure, and governance are integrated from the start of any displacement response. In their view, refugee management should not sit apart from national planning but be part of it.

A developmental approach would mean refugees and hosts alike have access to livelihood opportunities, shared markets, and community services that benefit everyone. In such a system, the arrival of new refugees, as Chad is experiencing again today, would not be seen as a crisis but as an expansion of an already resilient social fabric. The conversation left me reflecting on how humanitarian work often mistakes immediacy for progress. The urgency to act, to save lives, to deliver aid can overshadow the slower, quieter work of building systems that endure. Chad's experience offers a powerful lesson: if development and humanitarian approaches had been married from the beginning, the story of displacement in the Sahel might have looked very different today. And this applies to all fragile and crisis regions around the globe.

As the officer concluded, "We cannot change 2002, but we can learn from it. The next twenty years must be about building permanence in the midst of movement." His words captured the essence of what so many nations in protracted displacement contexts are realizing; that **true resilience is not about responding faster but about planning smarter.**

For too long, humanitarian response has focused on treating symptoms: distributing food, providing shelter, or managing camps. These are necessary, but insufficient. Displacement, hunger, and migration are outcomes of deeper systemic issues: weak governance, inequality, climate injustice, and conflict economies. Addressing root causes requires a shift from charity to justice, from temporary relief to sustainable empowerment. **That shift starts by trusting local institutions, especially refugee-led organizations (RLOs).** They are the ones who stay when everyone else leaves. They understand what works and what doesn't. Investing in them isn't a risk; it's the most sustainable form of humanitarian action.

There is a story I often tell: in 2007, when we began YARID, we didn't wait for permission. We saw problems and started solving them. Children needed education, so we taught them. Families needed a place to learn and small business funds, so we shared what we had. Years later, donors noticed but by then, the community had already built a foundation of self-reliance. That's what real localization looks like. **It is not about replacing international actors, but about rebalancing relationships from dependency to partnership, from control to collaboration.**

Humanitarian aid must return to its roots: compassion, solidarity, and shared humanity. It must shed the heavy layers of bureaucracy that slow it down. We must move beyond performative inclusion toward real power-sharing.

- **Who Will Reform the System?**

Question asked during UNGA80, and here is my answer.

Change will not come overnight. But one truth is clear: the status quo benefits some while failing many. The burden of failure falls on those with the least power to influence the system, while those with privilege continue to manage the narrative.

Reforming the humanitarian aid sector will require uncomfortable conversations, bold leadership, and a willingness to give up control. Donors, INGOs, and UN agencies must recognize that they cannot reform a system they still dominate. *Reform will come when communities, refugees, IDPs, and local leaders are no longer "consulted," but "included" as co-architects of the future.*

The time for reform is not next year or the next global summit, it is now. *The question is not whether we can change, but whether we are ready to shift power, resources, and decision-making to those who have always held the solutions in their hands. Because the future of humanitarian aid will not be built in boardrooms. It will be built in community halls, refugee settlements, and local classrooms by the very people who have experienced the crises and still dare to hope."* End of the comments.

By critically dissecting the shortcomings of past methodologies and presenting a compelling alternative, **this book aims to ignite a conversation and inspire a new era of development and humanitarian aid practices, one that is more agile, accountable, and fundamentally geared towards achieving lasting, transformative change.**

The Trump administration's decision to dismantle the United States Agency for International Development (USAID) provoked a spectrum of critical discourse; nonetheless, from an evaluative standpoint, the rationale underpinning the closure appears defensible. **Its closure marked a pivotal moment for global aid reform, offering a powerful lesson to developing nations and the international community about the urgent need to rethink traditional humanitarian delivery models.**

- **A Critical Turning Point in Global Aid Delivery**

The dismantling of the U.S. Agency for International Development (USAID) is not merely a bureaucratic reshuffle; it is a symbolic and strategic shift that underscores the deep flaws in traditional aid systems. For decades, USAID operated as the world's most prominent government funder of development, yet its legacy is marred by inefficiencies, bloated overheads, and questionable impact. The closure, prompted by a Department of Government Efficiency review, revealed a sprawling bureaucracy that had drifted from its core mission. This moment should be viewed not as a loss, but as a necessary disruption; one that forces the global community to confront the systemic weaknesses of aid delivery.

- **Lessons for Developing Nations**

Developing countries, often the recipients of aid, stand to gain the most from this reckoning. Traditional aid models have long been criticized for their inability to deliver meaningful change. A significant portion of aid funds were absorbed by administrative costs, including inflated salaries and procurement contracts that often benefited corporations from donor countries. This created a cycle where aid money effectively returned to its origin, undermining the very purpose of humanitarian support.

Moreover, the opaque nature of aid distribution enabled corruption. Funds intended for public welfare were frequently diverted into the hands of political elites, reinforcing patronage systems and weakening democratic institutions. Instead of empowering communities, aid often fostered dependency, discouraging local innovation and self-sufficiency. The closure of USAID sends a clear message: development must be reimagined to prioritize transparency, efficiency, and local agency.

- **The Promise of the RDI Model**

Enter the RDI (Rescue Democracy International) Model; a transformative approach that seeks to eliminate the pitfalls of traditional aid. Unlike legacy systems, the RDI Model emphasizes direct engagement with beneficiaries, bypassing layers of bureaucracy and logistical overhead. This model leverages technology and decentralized networks to deliver aid swiftly and transparently, ensuring that resources reach those in need without detours through costly intermediaries.

The RDI Model aligns with emerging innovations like Aseel's direct aid platform, which has demonstrated how tech-driven solutions can revolutionize humanitarian support. By minimizing administrative costs and maximizing accountability, the RDI approach restores trust in aid systems and empowers local actors to take ownership of development outcomes.

- **A Blueprint for Future Aid**

The U.S. government now has an opportunity to rebuild its international aid strategy from the ground up; whether through a reformed USAID or a new agency entirely. The guiding principle must be impact over institution. Aid should be measured not by the volume of funds disbursed, but by the tangible improvements in health, education, infrastructure, and livelihoods.

This shift also calls for a cultural transformation within donor nations. Aid must no longer be viewed as a tool of influence or a vehicle for corporate profit. Instead, it should reflect a genuine commitment to global solidarity and human dignity. The RDI Model offers a blueprint for this new ethos; one that is agile, ethical, and results-driven.

The closure of USAID is a watershed moment that challenges the status quo of global development. It exposes the inefficacy of traditional aid models and invites a bold reimagining of how humanitarian support is conceived and delivered. For developing countries, this is a chance to demand better; more transparent, accountable, and empowering aid systems. And for the international community, it is a call to action: to embrace innovation, reject inefficiency, and commit to a future where aid truly serves those who need it most.

CHAPTER 1:

The Promise and Peril of
Global Development Goals

The mid-20th century marked a pivotal moment in human history. Emerging from the ashes of the Second World War, a global consciousness began to coalesce around the imperative of collective action, not just for peace, but for the reconstruction and upliftment of nations. The devastation had been immense, and the subsequent geopolitical landscape, though fraught with new tensions, also fostered an unprecedented level of international dialogue and cooperation. It was within this environment that the seeds of global development aspirations were sown, nurtured by a potent blend of idealism, nascent economic theory, and a dawning recognition of interconnectedness. The post-war era saw the establishment of institutions like the United Nations, embodying a universal desire to prevent future conflicts and address shared challenges. Alongside this, the Bretton Woods Conference laid the groundwork for a new international economic order, creating institutions such as the World Bank and the International Monetary Fund, which, while initially focused on European recovery, soon turned their attention to the burgeoning needs of developing nations.

The initial motivations for engaging in global development were multifaceted. There was a genuine humanitarian impulse, a desire to alleviate the suffering and poverty that were stark realities for a significant portion of the world's population. Reports from colonial territories and newly independent nations painted vivid pictures of widespread malnutrition, disease, lack of basic education, and economic stagnation. This was coupled with a geopolitical imperative. In the burgeoning Cold War era, development became a battleground for influence. Nations used to demonstrate the superiority of their respective economic and political systems by supporting the development trajectories of emerging states. Providing aid, technical assistance, and investment was seen as means to foster stable, prosperous allies and prevent the spread of opposing ideologies. Furthermore, economic logic also played a crucial role. As global trade began to expand, the idea gained traction that a more interconnected and prosperous world economy would benefit all nations. Developing economies, it was argued, represented untapped markets and potential partners in global commerce. Investment in their infrastructure, education, and healthcare was not merely an act of charity, but a strategic investment in future global prosperity.

This confluence of humanitarian concern, geopolitical strategy, and economic foresight coalesced into a grand vision: the eradication of extreme poverty, the promotion of widespread economic growth, and the establishment of more equitable societies across the globe. It was a vision of a world where progress was not confined to a select few, but shared broadly, lifting all boats. This ambition was reflected in the early pronouncements and initiatives of international organizations and bilateral aid agencies. Concepts like "modernization" and "catching up" became buzzwords, framing development as a linear process that developing nations could, with the right support, traverse to reach the levels of prosperity already achieved by industrialized countries. The early decades saw significant efforts focused on building physical infrastructure – roads, dams, power grids – and on transferring technology and expertise. There was an underlying optimism that with concerted effort and sufficient resources, the most intractable problems of poverty and underdevelopment could be overcome within a generation. This inherent optimism, though perhaps naive in retrospect, was essential in galvanizing political will and mobilizing resources on a scale previously unseen. The very act of setting ambitious, measurable goals, even if imperfectly conceived, represented a powerful declaration of intent and a commitment to a shared global future.

The narrative of global development cooperation thus began not with a single, monolithic plan, but with a series of evolving aspirations, each building upon the lessons and experiences of the previous era. From the immediate post-war reconstruction efforts that laid the foundations for international economic governance, to the various national development plans and the early aid programs of the 1950s and 60s, there was a consistent thread of belief in the power of coordinated international action to bring about positive change. The focus was often on economic growth as the primary driver of development, with the assumption that wealth generated would eventually trickle down to improve the lives of the poorest. This era also saw the rise of development economics as a distinct field, grappling with the complex questions of how to foster growth in diverse contexts and how to measure progress.

As the decades progressed, the understanding of development began to broaden, moving beyond purely economic indicators. The social dimensions of development – education, health, gender equality – started to receive greater attention.

International conferences convened to address issues like population growth, environmental sustainability, and human rights, signaling an expanding, albeit still sometimes fragmented, global agenda. The late 20th century, in particular, witnessed a growing recognition of the limitations of purely growth-centric models and a nascent understanding that development needed to be more inclusive, equitable, and sustainable. This evolution in thinking set the stage for the next major chapter in global development aspirations: the era of specific, time-bound, and measurable goals, which aimed to consolidate these broad ambitions into concrete targets, intended to guide and measure progress on a global scale. The groundwork was being laid for a more structured, although still highly ambitious, approach to tackling the world's most persistent problems. The optimism of the post-war era, tempered by decades of experience and evolving understanding, was about to be channeled into a new framework, one that promised to bring greater focus and accountability to the monumental task of global development.

The initial decades of international cooperation in development were characterized by a strong belief in the efficacy of direct intervention and the transfer of Western models of development. Following World War II, the newly formed United Nations and a host of bilateral aid agencies began to channel resources towards newly independent nations and developing countries. The prevailing ideology was one of modernization, which posited that development was a linear process, moving from traditional societies to modern, industrialized ones. This often translated into large-scale infrastructure projects – dams, roads, power plants – and the transfer of technology and expertise. The idea was that by building the necessary physical and industrial capacity, developing nations could then "catch up" with the industrialized world. This period was marked by significant optimism and a belief that poverty and underdevelopment were problems that could be solved with sufficient capital and technical know-how. The Colombo Plan, for instance, initiated in 1950, aimed to foster economic and social progress in South and Southeast Asia through technical cooperation and assistance from developed countries. Similarly, the US Agency for International Development (USAID), established in 1961, consolidated various US foreign assistance programs, reflecting a broad commitment to supporting development efforts worldwide.

However, as the mid-to-late 20th century unfolded, it became increasingly apparent that the initial optimism was perhaps overly simplistic. While tangible progress was made in many areas, the eradication of poverty and the achievement of widespread, sustainable development remained elusive. Several factors contributed to this realization. Firstly, the transfer of Western models, while well-intentioned, often failed to account for the unique socio-cultural contexts, political realities, and existing indigenous knowledge systems of recipient countries. Projects designed in distant capitals or by external experts sometimes proved ill-suited to local conditions, leading to inefficiencies, dependency, and even unintended negative consequences. The focus on economic growth, while important, was also found to be insufficient on its own. Wealth generated did not always trickle down to the poorest segments of society, and the social dimensions of development, such as equitable access to education, healthcare, and political participation, began to be recognized as equally, if not more, crucial.

Moreover, the nature of international aid itself presented challenges. The complex bureaucratic structures of both donor and recipient governments, coupled with the proliferation of implementing agencies and intermediaries, often led to significant overhead costs and a diffusion of responsibility. The flow of funds could be slow, unpredictable, and subject to the political agendas of donor nations. This created an "implementation gap" – a significant divergence between the intentions of development plans and their actual realization on the ground. The very act of coordinating efforts among numerous actors, each with their own mandates and priorities, proved to be an enormous logistical and administrative challenge. This often resulted in duplicated efforts, competing strategies, and a lack of synergy.

The latter part of the 20th century saw a growing scholarly and practical consensus that the prevailing approaches to development were not yielding the transformative results envisioned. Critics began to highlight the limitations of top-down planning, the importance of local ownership, and the need for greater accountability. The discourse started to shift from simply "giving aid" to fostering "partnerships" and building "local capacity." This evolving understanding, born from decades of on-the-ground experience, introspection, and academic inquiry, was crucial. It created the intellectual and practical space for a new generation of development thinking, one that sought to address the systemic flaws of previous approaches and to set more concrete, globally recognized aspirations. The stage was set for a paradigm shift, a move away from broad, often vague, goals towards specific, measurable objectives that could guide and assess progress with greater clarity. This was the context that directly led to the formulation of more ambitious, globally coordinated frameworks aimed at defining and achieving a shared vision for human progress. The lessons learned from the post-war era, with its triumphs and its significant shortcomings, were essential in shaping the aspirations that would define the dawn of a new era in global development.

The era of articulated global development goals truly began to take shape with the growing recognition of the need for a more cohesive and measurable approach to international cooperation. The end of the Cold War, while ushering in a period of relative geopolitical stability, also highlighted persistent disparities in wealth, health, and opportunity across the globe. The aspirations, which had previously been somewhat diffuse and fragmented, began to coalesce around the idea of setting specific, time-bound targets that could galvanize action and provide a benchmark for progress. This shift was driven by several factors. Firstly, the increasing availability of data and the development of more sophisticated statistical methodologies allowed for a more granular understanding of global challenges. It became possible to identify specific indicators of development, such as literacy rates, infant mortality, and access to clean water, and to track progress on these indicators over time.

Secondly, there was a growing demand from various stakeholders – governments, civil society organizations, and the public – for greater accountability in development efforts. The efficacy of the substantial resources being channeled into development and humanitarian aid was being questioned, and there was a desire to see tangible, measurable results. This led to calls for more concrete objectives that could serve as a basis for evaluation and for holding both donors and recipients accountable. The experience of earlier, more general aspirations like "economic development" or "improving living standards" showed that without specific targets, progress could be slow, uneven, and difficult to assess.

The United Nations played a crucial role in this evolution. As the primary forum for international cooperation, it provided a platform for member states to come together and agree on shared goals. Several major international conferences in the 1990s laid the groundwork for this more target-oriented approach. The World Summit for Social Development in Copenhagen in 1995, for instance, recognized poverty eradication as a moral and social imperative. The Fourth World Conference on Women in Beijing in 1995 championed gender equality and the capacity building of women. These gatherings highlighted the interconnectedness of development issues and underscored the need for a more holistic approach.

It was in this climate of evolving understanding and a growing demand for concrete action that the concept of setting global, time-bound development goals gained significant momentum. The idea was to create a unified agenda that could mobilize governments, international organizations, civil society, and the private sector towards common objectives. This approach promised to bring a much-needed sense of urgency and focus to the complex and multifaceted challenge of global development. The initial motivations remained rooted in humanitarianism and global solidarity, but the methodology was evolving towards a more structured, data-driven, and goal-oriented framework. The aspiration was to move beyond good intentions and towards demonstrable impact, defining what success would look like in concrete terms and setting a clear roadmap to achieve it. This represented a significant step forward in the global pursuit of a more equitable and prosperous world, setting the stage for the articulation of ambitious, yet specific, aspirations that would guide international development efforts for years to come. The optimism of the post-war era was thus being re-energized, but this time, it was being grounded in a more pragmatic and results-oriented approach, born from the hard-won lessons of prior decades. The perceived necessity of coordinated global action was now being translated into actionable plans, designed to make a tangible difference in the lives of millions.

The early 21st century witnessed a bold, ambitious undertaking: the Millennium Development Goals (MDGs). Adopted by the United Nations in 2000, these eight time-bound targets, encompassing poverty, hunger, disease, education, gender equality, and environmental sustainability, represented a landmark consensus on the global development agenda. They emerged from a confluence of renewed international commitment, growing awareness of global inequalities, and a desire to translate aspirations into measurable progress. The MDGs were, in essence, a promise to the world's most vulnerable, a commitment to lifting millions out of extreme poverty and improving basic living standards by the year 2015.

The MDGs set forth a specific set of targets:

MDG 1: Eradicate extreme poverty and hunger. This goal aimed to halve the proportion of people living on less than $1.25 a day (adjusted for purchasing power parity) and decrease the proportion of people who suffer from hunger.

MDG 2: Achieve universal primary education. The target was to ensure that all children everywhere could complete a full course of primary schooling.

MDG 3: Promote gender equality and empower women. This goal sought to eliminate gender disparities in primary and secondary education, with a longer-term aim of achieving gender equality in all spheres.

MDG 4: Reduce child mortality. The target was to reduce the under-five mortality rate by two-thirds between 1990 and 2015.

MDG 5: Improve maternal health. This goal aimed to reduce the maternal mortality ratio by three-quarters and achieve universal access to reproductive health services.

MDG 6: Combat HIV/AIDS, malaria, and other diseases. This involved halting and beginning to reverse the spread of HIV/AIDS, as well as reducing the incidence of malaria and other major diseases.

MDG 7: Ensure environmental sustainability. This goal included targets related to integrating the principles of sustainable development into country policies, reversing the loss of environmental resources, and reducing biodiversity's loss, as well as increasing access to safe drinking water and improving sanitation.

MDG 8: Develop a global partnership for development. This goal focused on increasing official development assistance, fair trade policies, debt relief, and access to essential medicines in developing countries.

The MDGs represented a significant step forward in framing global development. Unlike earlier, more generalized aspirations, they were specific, quantifiable, and time-bound. This characteristic provided a clear benchmark against which progress could be measured, and crucially, it fostered a sense of collective responsibility and accountability among the international community. The narrative of development shifted from a broad, often aspirational, discussion to a more data-driven and target-oriented framework. The adoption of the MDGs by 191 UN member states and numerous international organizations signaled a powerful collective will to address the most pressing global challenges. This unified front, born from the lessons of previous decades of development efforts, sought to channel resources, expertise, and political will towards a common set of objectives. The goals were designed to be universally applicable, yet with a specific focus on the needs of developing countries. The inherent optimism was palpable: by setting clear targets, the world believed it could make tangible, measurable progress in alleviating human suffering and fostering widespread prosperity within a generation.

The period leading up to and following the adoption of the MDGs saw a substantial increase in the availability of data related to development indicators. Organizations like the World Bank, the United Nations Development Program (UNDP), and specialized agencies like the World Health Organization (WHO) and UNICEF invested heavily in data collection, analysis, and dissemination. This improved data infrastructure was critical for tracking progress against the MDG targets. For instance, the annual "The Millennium Development Goals Report" provided a crucial barometer, showcasing advances and highlighting areas where targets were not met. This data-driven approach was a significant departure from earlier efforts, allowing for a more evidence-based understanding of what interventions were working and where greater focus was needed.

In examining the successes of the MDGs, several areas stand out. The most significant achievement was arguably the unprecedented reduction in extreme poverty. Global poverty rates declined substantially, particularly in East Asia and South Asia, driven largely by economic growth in countries like China and India. Millions of people were lifted out of extreme poverty, a testament to the power of sustained economic growth coupled with targeted development interventions. Similarly, progress in other areas was undeniable. For example, the proportion of people living in extreme poverty fell significantly, and the number of children attending primary school increased globally. Access to improved water sources also saw considerable gains. These achievements were the result of concerted efforts, including increased development assistance, policy reforms in many developing countries, and the growing engagement of civil society and the private sector. The focus on specific, measurable outcomes encouraged innovation and fostered greater collaboration among diverse actors.

However, the MDGs were not without their limitations, and a critical examination reveals significant systemic issues that hindered their comprehensive achievement. While many targets were met or approached, progress was uneven, both geographically and across different goals. The inherent design of the MDGs, while ambitious, also contained flaws that impacted their overall effectiveness. One of the most significant critiques revolved around the approach to poverty reduction. The MDGs primarily focused on income-based poverty ($1.25 a day), which, while important, did not fully capture the multidimensional nature of poverty. This included access to essential services, political voice, and freedom from discrimination. The focus on a single, although crucial, economic indicator risked overshadowing other critical aspects of human development.

Furthermore, the MDGs were criticized for their top-down approach. While devised by the UN, the implementation was largely left to national governments, many of which lacked the institutional capacity, resources, or political will to fully implement the ambitious targets. The goals were aspirational, but the mechanisms for ensuring their achievement and holding actors accountable were often weak. The targets were also, in some cases, too broad or not sufficiently tailored to the diverse realities of different countries. For instance, a target that might be achievable for a rapidly growing middle-income country could be insurmountable for a fragile state experiencing conflict. The "one-size-fits-all" nature of some goals failed to account for the unique challenges faced by the poorest and most marginalized populations.

The issue of data reliability and availability in many developing countries also posed a significant challenge. While data collection improved, many of the poorest and most remote populations remained undercounted or unreached by data-gathering efforts. This meant that progress, or lack thereof, in these most vulnerable communities was often invisible, making it difficult to design and implement truly inclusive policies. The reliance on national averages could mask deep inequalities within countries, where certain regions or demographic groups might be falling further behind even as national indicators improved.

Another critical limitation was the insufficient attention paid to the underlying structural causes of poverty and inequality. While the MDGs aimed to alleviate symptoms, they did not always adequately address systemic issues such as unfair trade practices, unsustainable debt burdens, and the impact of global economic policies that often disadvantaged developing nations. MDG 8, which focused on global partnership, was arguably the least achieved, reflecting the persistent challenges in reforming global economic governance to be more equitable. The lack of progress on fair trade, for instance, meant that many developing countries struggled to compete in the global market, limiting their ability to generate sustainable revenue for development.

The role of conflict and fragility was also a significant impediment. Many countries with the highest levels of poverty and the greatest unmet development needs were also experiencing protracted conflict, political instability, or state fragility. In these contexts, achieving basic targets related to health, education, and poverty reduction was extremely difficult, if not impossible, without addressing the underlying drivers of instability. The MDGs, while acknowledging the importance of peace and security, did not fully integrate these considerations into their framework, leading to a disconnect between the goals and the realities on the ground in many of the world's most challenging environments.

Moreover, the MDGs did not sufficiently address issues of governance, human rights, and social inclusion. While gender equality was a specific goal, other crucial aspects of human rights, such as freedom of expression, access to justice, and political participation, were not explicitly integrated into the framework. This limited the holistic understanding of development, which encompasses not just material well-being but also capacity building and agency. The focus on quantitative targets sometimes overshadowed the qualitative aspects of development, such as the quality of education or healthcare, or the meaningfulness of employment.

A deeper dive into specific goals reveals these limitations more unambiguously. For instance, while child mortality rates decreased, the progress towards reducing maternal mortality was considerably slower. This highlighted the specific challenges in improving women's health, which are often linked to complex socio-cultural barriers, access to skilled birth attendants, and emergency obstetric care, areas where progress lagged significantly. Similarly, while primary education enrollment increased, the quality of education and completion rates remained a concern in many countries. The goals set a benchmark for access, but ensuring effective learning and equitable educational outcomes proved more complex.

The focus on environmental sustainability, while crucial, also faced challenges. Integrating environmental considerations into national development plans was often difficult in the face of immediate development pressures. Furthermore, the specific targets for reducing biodiversity loss and improving sanitation coverage were not met in many regions. The interconnectedness of environmental degradation and poverty, particularly for marginalized communities reliant on natural resources, was a critical aspect that the MDGs did not always fully address in practical implementation.

The MDG framework, despite its shortcomings, undeniably served a vital purpose. It provided a common language, a shared set of objectives, and a powerful narrative that mobilized global attention and resources towards development. It fostered a culture of measurement and accountability, pushing governments and international organizations to collect data and report on progress. The MDGs spurred significant investment in various sectors and brought development issues to the forefront of the global political agenda. They created a benchmark, a starting point for a more informed and ambitious future agenda. The lessons learned from their successes and failures were instrumental in shaping the subsequent **Sustainable Development Goals (SDGs)**, which sought to build upon the MDGs by adopting a more comprehensive, integrated, and inclusive approach, recognizing the multidimensional nature of development and the critical importance of addressing root causes and systemic issues. The MDGs were a valuable, though imperfect, experiment in global goal-setting, offering profound insights into the complexities of international cooperation and the enduring challenge of achieving sustainable and equitable development for all.

The ambitious nature of global development goals, while commendable in its intent, often masked significant deficiencies in their foundational planning. These shortcomings were not merely minor oversights but fundamental miscalculations that cast long shadows over the effectiveness and equity of the strategies employed. A primary failing lay in the creation of macro-level targets, conceived within the echo chambers of international forums and distant capitals, which demonstrably failed to grapple with the intricate tapestry of diverse local realities. These broad-stroke objectives, crafted with the best of intentions, frequently overlooked the nuanced cultural contexts, the deeply embedded social structures, and the unique economic and political landscapes that characterized the very communities they sought to uplift. This disconnect between the global blueprint, and the ground truth often rendered well-meaning initiatives either ineffective or, in some unfortunate instances, actively detrimental.

Consider, for example, the universal push for primary education expansion that characterized several development agendas. While the aim of getting every child into school was undeniably noble, the planning often failed to account for the myriad reasons why children, particularly in rural or marginalized communities, remained out of school. In many African contexts, the distance to the nearest school, coupled with inadequate transportation infrastructure and safety concerns for young girls, presented formidable barriers. Furthermore, the curricula, often imported from Western models, did not always resonate with local cultural values or provide skills immediately relevant to the livelihoods of rural populations. Families struggling to survive often viewed sending children to school as a luxury, especially if those children could contribute to household labor or income-generating activities. The planning deficiency here was not in setting the goal of education, but in failing to adequately diagnose and address the specific, context-dependent obstacles to achieving that goal. Projects that focused solely on building classrooms, without addressing teacher training, curriculum relevance, or the economic realities faced by families, were destined for limited success. The implicit assumption that a standardized approach would work across vastly different settings was a critical flaw of planning.

Similarly, initiatives aimed at improving agricultural productivity often faltered due to a failure to appreciate the deeply entrenched traditional farming practices and local knowledge systems. Plans that introduced new seed varieties or farming techniques without engaging local farmers in a meaningful dialogue, understanding their existing methods, and adapting interventions to their specific environmental conditions and risk appetites, frequently met with resistance or outright failure. For instance, introducing hybrid seeds that required significant water inputs might prove disastrous in semi-arid regions with unpredictable rainfall patterns, or in communities where water scarcity was already a critical issue. The planning process, in such cases, bypassed crucial ethnographic research and participatory engagement, leading to the imposition of solutions that were neither sustainable nor culturally appropriate. The reliance on technical fixes, divorced from a holistic understanding of the socio-economic and environmental context, exemplifies a pervasive planning deficiency.

The emphasis on quantifiable outcomes, while a strength in driving accountability, also contributed to planning shortcomings when these metrics were not grounded in a deep understanding of local realities. For example, targets related to sanitation were often focused on the construction of latrines. While the physical infrastructure is essential, planning often overlooked the critical social and cultural factors that influence latrine usage. In many communities, traditional practices, privacy concerns, and the perceived status associated with certain types of facilities meant that new, externally designed latrines were either underutilized or not used at all. The planning failure here was in reducing a complex social behavior change to a construction project, ignoring the crucial need for community-led behavioral nudges, education campaigns tailored to local beliefs, and the involvement of community leaders in promoting adoption. Without this deeper engagement, the physical infrastructure remained an expensive monument to a planning deficit.

Another area where planning deficiencies were starkly evident was in the design of health interventions. While the MDGs rightly aimed to reduce child and maternal mortality, the strategies often underplayed the critical role of community health workers and the importance of accessible, culturally sensitive primary healthcare. The focus on large, centralized health facilities, while necessary for certain specialized services, often failed to reach remote populations effectively. The planning did not always adequately account for the logistical challenges of drug distribution, the need for mobile clinics, or the vital role of local healthcare providers who understood the community's health beliefs and practices. Projects that prioritized the procurement of advanced medical equipment over strengthening the capacity of local health systems and personnel were ultimately less effective in achieving lasting improvements in health outcomes. The planning often reflected an urban-centric bias, neglecting the unique challenges of delivering health services in dispersed rural settings.

Moreover, the broad-brush approach to poverty reduction often failed to differentiate between various forms of poverty and their underlying causes. Planning that focused solely on income-generating activities, without addressing issues of land tenure, access to credit, market linkages, or discriminatory social norms that prevent marginalized groups from participating fully in the economy, often fell short. For instance, providing micro-loans to women in patriarchal societies without simultaneously addressing the societal power dynamics that might limit their control over these resources or their ability to invest them effectively, represented a planning oversight. The complex interplay of economic, social, and political factors that perpetuate poverty was frequently oversimplified in the planning stages, leading to interventions that tackled symptoms rather than root causes.

The issue of sustainability was also frequently a casualty of inadequate planning. Projects that relied heavily on external funding or expertise often lacked a clear strategy for long-term maintenance and local ownership. The planning for the handover of projects to local communities or government entities was often an afterthought, leading to a situation where valuable infrastructure or programs fell into disrepair or ceased to function once external support was withdrawn. The failure to integrate local capacity building, robust maintenance plans, and sustainable financing mechanisms into the initial project design meant that many interventions were ephemeral, creating dependency rather than fostering self-sufficiency. This approach not only wasted resources but also undermined the long-term development aspirations.

Furthermore, the planning for global development goals often suffered from a lack of adequate consultation with the very people they were intended to benefit. The top-down creation of targets and strategies meant that local voices, indigenous knowledge, and grassroots experiences were frequently marginalized or entirely excluded from the decision-making process. This absence of **participatory planning** led to interventions that were misaligned with local needs and priorities, and that failed to leverage the invaluable insights that local communities possess about their own challenges and potential solutions. The result was often a sense of "incapacity building" and a lack of ownership among the target populations, which is antithetical to genuine development.

The failure to adequately consider the political economy of development was another significant planning deficiency. Plans often assumed a benevolent and efficient state apparatus capable of implementing complex policies and effectively managing resources. However, in many developing countries, political instability, corruption, weak governance structures, and vested interests can significantly impede or derail even the best-laid plans. Ignoring these realities in the planning phase meant that the proposed solutions were often unrealistic and unsustainable in practice. For example, a plan to distribute essential medicines might fail due to corruption in procurement or distribution channels, or a strategy to improve public services might be undermined by political patronage networks. A more nuanced planning approach would have incorporated strategies to address governance challenges and build resilience against political interference.

The inherent complexity of development, which involves interconnected social, economic, environmental, and political factors, demanded an integrated and holistic planning approach. However, the MDG framework, with its siloed goals, sometimes encouraged parallel, rather than integrated, planning and implementation. This fragmentation meant that the synergies between different sectors were often missed, and that interventions in one area could have unintended negative consequences in another. For instance, agricultural intensification projects that increased food production might have negative environmental impacts if water management or soil conservation were not adequately integrated into the planning. The lack of cross-sectoral thinking in the planning process was a significantly missed opportunity to enhance the overall effectiveness and sustainability of development efforts.

Ultimately, the planning deficiencies that characterized many global development efforts stemmed from a tendency to oversimplify complex realities, to adopt standardized solutions without adequate contextualization, and to neglect the critical importance of local participation and ownership. While the aspiration to create universal goals was powerful, the execution often suffered from a failure to translate these aspirations into actionable strategies that were sensitive to the diverse and dynamic contexts on the ground. The lessons learned from these shortcomings are invaluable, offering crucial guidance for future attempts to build a more equitable and sustainable world, emphasizing the imperative of meticulous, inclusive, and contextually grounded planning.

The journey from a meticulously crafted global vision to tangible, on-the-ground impact is fraught with complexities, and it is during this crucial implementation phase that the promise of development goals often encounters its most formidable challenges. The chasm between the aspirational targets set in international forums and the lived realities of the communities they aim to serve is not solely a consequence of flawed initial planning; it is also exacerbated by systemic inefficiencies that plague the execution of these ambitious agendas. These operational shortcomings, often rooted in bureaucratic inertia, fractured coordination, and nascent monitoring capabilities, transform well-intentioned blueprints into diluted or even distorted realities.

One of the most pervasive impediments to effective implementation is the sheer complexity and often unwieldy nature of bureaucratic structures. Development programs, particularly those funded by multiple international agencies and implemented through various governmental and non-governmental channels, invariably navigate layers of administrative procedures. These can include intricate procurement processes that delay the delivery of essential supplies, cumbersome approval workflows that stall project activities, and stringent reporting requirements that divert valuable human and financial resources from direct implementation to administrative tasks. In many low-resource settings, national and local government capacities are already stretched thin, and the additional burden of managing complex international projects can lead to significant delays and inefficiencies. For instance, a project aimed at distributing vital medical supplies to remote health clinics might be hampered by a national procurement system that requires multiple levels of approval for each consignment, each taking weeks or even months to process. This bureaucratic drag means that life-saving medicines can expire before reaching their intended recipients, directly undermining the goal of improving health outcomes. Similarly, the allocation of funds can be subject to prolonged parliamentary or ministerial approvals, delaying the start of critical infrastructure projects or the disbursement of essential grants to local communities, thereby creating a critical bottleneck between the planned intervention and its actual delivery. The sheer volume of paperwork and the adherence to diverse donor regulations can also create a substantial administrative overhead, consuming a significant portion of the project budget that could otherwise be channeled into **direct service delivery** or **community capacity building**. This administrative burden is not merely an inconvenience; it is a tangible barrier that directly impacts the pace and effectiveness of development efforts, transforming what should be agile and responsive interventions into sluggish and bureaucratic undertakings.

Furthermore, the landscape of international development is characterized by a multitude of actors, each with their own mandates, priorities, and operational modalities. While collaboration is often espoused as a cornerstone of effective development, the reality on the ground frequently reveals a landscape of fragmented efforts and poor coordination among implementing partners. International NGOs, national NGOs, government ministries, UN agencies, and bilateral aid organizations may all be involved in the same sector or geographical area, yet their activities may not be harmonized. This **lack of synergy** can lead to duplication of efforts, competition for scarce local resources (including human talent), and a failure to leverage complementary strengths. For example, in a region seeking to improve agricultural productivity, one organization might focus on providing extension services for new crop varieties, while another might focus on irrigation infrastructure, and a third on market access. Without a coordinated strategy, these initiatives might operate in isolation, with limited impact. If the new crop varieties require more water, but the irrigation project is delayed or poorly designed, the potential benefits of the improved seeds will not be realized. Conversely, if market access is not improved, farmers may have no incentive to adopt new, more productive techniques. The absence of a clear, overarching coordination mechanism, often a responsibility that falls to national governments but is frequently hampered by their limited capacity or political will, means that these potentially synergistic efforts remain disconnected, leading to sub-optimal outcomes and wasted resources. This fragmentation extends to information sharing as well; without robust platforms for partners to share data on progress, challenges, and lessons learned, each organization operates in a partial information environment, increasing the risk of missteps and missed opportunities. The ideal scenario of a "whole-of-government" or "whole-of-system" approach is frequently undermined by the realities of competing organizational cultures, differing accountability frameworks, and the persistent challenge of establishing truly collaborative partnerships that transcend institutional boundaries.

The capacity for effective Monitoring and Evaluation (M&E) is another critical area where the implementation gap often manifests. While global goals are typically accompanied by targets and indicators, the systems in place to track progress, identify deviations, and facilitate adaptive management are often underdeveloped. In many developing country contexts, data collection systems may be weak, prone to inaccuracies, or simply non-existent for certain indicators. This lack of reliable data makes it difficult to assess whether interventions are on track, whether resources are being used efficiently, and whether the intended beneficiaries are actually being reached. Without timely and accurate information, implementing agencies are flying blind. A project designed to increase access to clean water, for instance, might report that a certain number of wells have been constructed. However, without effective monitoring, it may be unclear whether these wells are functional, whether the water is actually safe to drink, or whether the communities intended to benefit have gained access. The reliance on self-reported data or anecdotal evidence can lead to an overestimation of progress and a masking of underlying problems. Moreover, even when data is collected, the capacity to analyze it and translate it into actionable insights for program adjustment is often lacking. This is where the concept of "adaptive management" becomes crucial. Development programs are not static entities; they operate in dynamic environments and must be able to respond to changing circumstances, unforeseen challenges, and emerging opportunities. However, without robust M&E systems that provide early warnings and diagnostic information, the ability to adapt is severely curtailed. Projects can continue on a failing trajectory for extended periods, consuming resources without yielding the desired results. The focus on simply meeting quantitative targets, often driven by donor reporting requirements, can inadvertently discourage honest reporting of challenges, leading to a culture of "cooking the books" rather than genuine problem-solving. The absence of rigorous, independent evaluation further compounds this issue, leaving a void in understanding what truly works, for whom, and under what conditions.

Beyond these systemic issues, operational inefficiencies at the programmatic level also contribute significantly to the implementation gap. These can range from logistical challenges in delivering goods and services to poor human resource management and a lack of technical expertise on the ground. For example, a program aimed at providing nutritional supplements to malnourished children in remote villages might face difficulties in the last-mile delivery of these supplies. Poor road networks, lack of reliable transportation, and the need for secure storage facilities can all lead to stock-outs and disruptions in service delivery. The training of local health workers, while a crucial component of building sustainable capacity, may be inadequate, leaving them ill-equipped to administer programs effectively or to identify and refer complex cases. In some instances, projects might be staffed by individuals who lack the specific technical skills or the deep understanding of the local context required for successful implementation. This is not always a reflection of a lack of effort, but often a consequence of rapid project scale-up, difficulty in attracting and retaining qualified personnel in challenging environments, or a mismatch between the skills required and the available local talent pool.

The challenge of fostering genuine local ownership and participation, while a planning imperative, also plays out critically during implementation. Even with the best intentions, externally designed programs can falter if they do not actively engage local communities as partners in the implementation process. Without a sense of ownership, communities may be less invested in the success of the program, leading to lower participation rates, less care for project assets, and a lack of sustainability once external support recedes. For example, a water and sanitation project that involves community members in the construction and maintenance of new facilities is far more likely to succeed than one where the infrastructure is simply handed over. However, effective engagement requires more than just consultation; it necessitates building local capacity, empowering community leaders, and ensuring that decision-making processes are truly participatory. When implementation teams fail to bridge the gap between external expertise and local knowledge, the result can be interventions that are technically sound but culturally inappropriate or operationally unmanageable within the local context. This can manifest as a disconnect between the stated objectives of a project and the actual felt needs of the community, leading to a lack of buy-in and ultimately, a failure to achieve lasting impact.

Moreover, the pressure to demonstrate rapid results, often a requirement from donors, can inadvertently lead to shortcuts in implementation that undermine long-term sustainability. Projects may focus on easily quantifiable outputs rather than on the more complex, long-term process of behavior change or institutional strengthening. For instance, a program aimed at improving maternal health might focus on increasing the number of institutional deliveries, which is a measurable outcome. However, if the underlying issues, such as lack of access to quality antenatal care, inadequate emergency obstetric services in rural areas, or cultural barriers to seeking care, are not addressed during implementation, the increase in institutional deliveries may not translate into a significant reduction in maternal mortality. The focus on ticking boxes can overshadow the more challenging work of building robust, resilient systems and fostering sustainable change. This can create a situation where projects achieve their immediate output targets but fail to achieve the desired broader impact, leaving a legacy of incomplete transformation.

The issue of adaptive management, the ability to adjust strategies based on emerging evidence and changing contexts, is often severely hampered by the very nature of how development programs are often designed and funded. Fixed-term projects with pre-defined activities and budgets can create a disincentive for significant mid-course corrections, as any deviation might be perceived as a failure to adhere to the original plan or could complicate reporting and financial accountability. This rigidity can be particularly problematic in sectors like health or education, where the pace of change and the emergence of new challenges (such as disease outbreaks or shifts in educational policy) are common. Projects that are unable to pivot or adapt in response to such developments are likely to become increasingly irrelevant and ineffective over time. For example, a vocational training program designed to equip youth with skills for a specific industry might find its relevance diminished if that industry undergoes a technological transformation during the project's lifespan. Without the flexibility to adapt the curriculum or reorient the training focus, the graduates may find themselves with outdated skills, unable to secure employment. The funding models themselves can also contribute to this rigidity, with strict grant agreements that require adherence to original proposals, making it difficult to reallocate resources or modify activities without a lengthy and often bureaucratic approval process. This lack of agility means that even well-resourced programs can become stranded on outdated strategies, unable to respond effectively to the evolving needs of the communities they serve. The ideal of a learning organization, one that continuously monitors its progress, analyzes its experiences, and adapts its strategies, accordingly, is a difficult ideal to achieve within the operational constraints of many development initiatives.

The implementation gap is, therefore, not a singular failure but a confluence of interconnected challenges. It is the consequence of navigating complex bureaucracies, coordinating a multitude of actors, ensuring reliable data and learning, managing logistical hurdles, fostering genuine local engagement, and maintaining flexibility in dynamic environments. Addressing this gap requires a deliberate focus on strengthening operational capacities, fostering genuine partnerships, investing in robust M&E systems that support adaptive management, and ensuring that programs are designed with an intrinsic understanding of the practical realities of implementation on the ground. The aspiration of global development goals remains potent, but its translation into impactful change hinges critically on our ability to bridge the persistent divide between the vision on paper and the reality of execution.

The grand pronouncements and ambitious targets set forth in global development frameworks, while inspiring, often run aground on the shoals of financial reality. The perennial challenge of securing and effectively deploying adequate funding is not merely an administrative hurdle; it is a foundational determinant of whether development goals remain aspirational dreams or transform into tangible progress. The chasm between the global vision and the on-the-ground execution is frequently widened by the ever-present shadow of insufficient and unpredictable financial flows, coupled with the insidious inefficiencies that plague the allocation of resources that are eventually secured.

The sheer magnitude of the financial commitments required to achieve transformative change in areas like poverty eradication, universal education, or climate resilience is staggering. Yet, the actual disbursement of funds often falls far short of these projected needs. This shortfall can be attributed to a complex interplay of economic realities in donor countries, shifting political priorities, and the inherent difficulties in translating global commitments into concrete budgetary allocations. For instance, economic downturns can trigger austerity measures, leading to reduced foreign aid budgets, even when the need in developing countries is at its peak. Similarly, geopolitical shifts or the emergence of new global crises can divert attention and financial resources away from long-standing development priorities. The reliance on voluntary contributions from member states for many international development organizations means that funding streams are inherently volatile and subject to the often-fickle currents of national politics. This unpredictability makes long-term planning and sustained program delivery incredibly challenging. Projects designed to achieve gradual, incremental progress might be prematurely curtailed or scaled back due to sudden funding shortfalls, leaving beneficiaries in a worse state than before or failing to capitalize on initial gains. A multi-year initiative to improve water infrastructure in a rural district, for example, might be designed to build resilience against drought over a decade. If mid-way through, a major donor withdraws its promised funding due to domestic budget cuts, the project may stall, leaving communities without reliable access to water and the initial investment largely wasted.

Beyond the quantitative gap between needs and available funds, the qualitative aspect of resource allocation is equally critical. Even when sufficient funds are technically available, they are often consumed by a disproportionately high level of overhead costs and administrative expenses. This phenomenon can be attributed to several factors inherent in the structure of international development operations. The complex web of accountability requirements imposed by multiple donors, each with its own reporting formats, audit procedures, and compliance protocols, necessitates dedicated staff time and resources for management and oversight. This administrative burden, while ostensibly aimed at ensuring transparency and accountability, can often become an end in itself, diverting essential resources away from direct program delivery. Consider a large-scale health program aimed at combating a specific disease. While a significant portion of the budget might be earmarked for medical supplies, vaccination campaigns, and community outreach, a substantial percentage can also be absorbed by managing donor grants, conducting intricate financial audits, establishing complex procurement chains, and ensuring adherence to a multitude of contractual obligations. This can leave fewer funds available for the actual deployment of medical personnel, the purchase of life-saving medications, or the expansion of essential health services to remote areas.

Furthermore, the proliferation of intermediaries in the development landscape, while sometimes necessary for local context and implementation capacity, can also contribute to increased overhead. Each layer of administration, from international coordinating bodies to national implementing agencies and local sub-grantees, adds its own layer of management and operational costs. While these intermediaries are often vital for navigating local realities, their presence can inflate the proportion of the budget that never directly reaches the intended beneficiaries. This is not to suggest that these layers are inherently inefficient or unnecessary, but rather that their cumulative effect on the cost of delivering services must be carefully managed. A program designed to support smallholder farmers might involve international NGOs for technical expertise, national agricultural ministries for policy alignment, and local community-based organizations for direct farmer engagement. Each of these entities will incur administrative costs, from salaries and office space to travel and communications. Without rigorous cost-efficiency measures and clear mandates, these cumulative overheads can significantly reduce the impact of the initial funding.

The political will underpinning funding commitments is another crucial, yet often overlooked, factor. Development and humanitarian aid, while presented as an altruistic endeavor, is frequently intertwined with the foreign policy objectives and economic interests of donor nations. This can lead to funding being channeled through preferred partners, allocated to countries with strategic importance, or tied to the procurement of goods and services from the donor country. Such "tied aid," while perhaps serving national interests, often proves to be less cost-effective and less responsive to the actual needs of recipient countries. For instance, a donor nation might provide funding for infrastructure development but stipulate that the contracts must be awarded to companies from the donor country. This can result in higher costs for materials and labor, potentially delaying project completion and reducing the overall impact compared to procuring resources competitively on the global or local market. The prioritization of visible, often capital-intensive projects, over the less visible but more impactful social sector investments, can also be a consequence of this political calculus, driven by the desire for tangible, easily demonstrable achievements that resonate with domestic political constituencies.

Moreover, the very design of funding mechanisms can inadvertently create disincentives for efficiency and effectiveness. Grant agreements, often negotiated far in advance of project implementation, can be rigid, making it difficult to adapt to changing circumstances or to reallocate funds from less effective activities to more promising ones. The pressure to spend allocated funds within a specific timeframe, often driven by annual budgetary cycles, can lead to a rushed or inefficient disbursement of resources, with a focus on "spending money" rather than "achieving results." This can result in inflated procurement costs, the hiring of under-qualified staff to quickly fill positions, or the initiation of activities that have not been fully vetted for their impact or sustainability. The fear of losing future funding if a project underspends can also create a perverse incentive to inflate budgets or to undertake unnecessary expenditures.

The consequence of these financial realities is a pervasive constraint on the scale and success of program delivery. Projects are often initiated with ambitious goals but are forced to operate with budgets that are insufficient to reach the intended scale or to achieve the desired depth of impact. This leads to a situation where development efforts are spread too thinly, attempting to address vast needs with limited resources. For example, a program aimed at improving agricultural productivity might have the technical knowledge to train thousands of farmers, but the budget may only allow for the training of hundreds, thereby limiting the potential for systemic change. Similarly, educational initiatives designed to build new schools and train teachers across an entire region might be scaled back to cover only a few pilot communities due to funding limitations, leaving vast areas without improved educational access.

The unpredictability of funding also impedes the cultivation of long-term, sustainable solutions. Projects that rely on consistent, multi-year financial support are particularly vulnerable to sudden funding cuts. This makes it difficult to invest in capacity building for local institutions, to foster deep community engagement that takes time to develop, or to implement complex, phased interventions that require sustained effort. The cycle of boom and bust in funding can create a sense of instability and disillusionment among implementing partners and beneficiaries alike. It fosters a short-term, project-driven mentality rather than the long-term strategic planning necessary for genuine development. When funding is uncertain, local organizations may hesitate to invest in staff training or infrastructure development, fearing that they will be left unsupported once external funding dries up.

Ultimately, the financial constraints and inefficiencies in resource allocation cast a long shadow over the pursuit of global development goals. They limit the reach of interventions, compromise their quality, and undermine their sustainability. The promise of these goals can only be fully realized if the economic realities of funding are met with robust strategies for efficient allocation, greater predictability in financial flows, and a steadfast commitment to ensuring that most resources directly benefit the communities they are intended to serve. Without addressing these fundamental financial challenges, the transformative potential of global development frameworks will remain significantly curtailed, a testament to the persistent power of economic realities to shape, and often constrain, the best of global intentions. The narrative of development is, in many respects, a narrative of resource management and the ability to translate financial commitments into meaningful, lasting change on the ground, a process perpetually challenged by the limitations and complexities of the global financial ecosystem.

CHAPTER 2:

A New Paradigm:
The Genesis of Rescue Democracy International (RDI)

The blunt reality of international development, as I came to know it intimately, was far removed from the polished brochures and optimistic projections that often characterized the sector. My early years in the field were a baptism by fire, a relentless immersion into environments where the theoretical aspirations of global frameworks collided violently with the unyielding forces of poverty, political instability, and logistical nightmares. These were not abstract challenges discussed in air-conditioned conference rooms; they were the gritty, day-to-day realities faced by communities desperately in need of support, and by individuals like me tasked with delivering it. It was in these crucible moments, amidst the dust and the desperation, that the seeds of what would become **Rescue Democracy International (RDI)** were sown, nurtured by a growing frustration with the very systems I was meant to strengthen.

I recall one particular assignment in a region grappling with the aftermath of prolonged conflict. The objective was ostensibly straightforward: to facilitate the rebuilding of local governance structures and provide essential services. We arrived with a mandate, a budget, and a meticulously crafted project plan.

Yet, the ground beneath our feet was a labyrinth of competing interests, deeply entrenched corruption, and a pervasive sense of distrust, born from years of broken promises by external actors. Our beautifully designed training modules on democratic principles and public financial management often felt like academic exercises, disconnected from the immediate, life-or-death concerns of the people we were trying to serve. When a village elder, his face etched with the weariness of a hundred hard seasons, explained that his primary concern was not the transparency of procurement processes, but the immediate availability of clean drinking water for his thirsty children, it was a stark reminder of the fundamental disconnect. The systemic inefficiencies we encountered were not mere bureaucratic hurdles; they were tangible barriers to progress, often exacerbating the suffering they were intended to alleviate.

The frustration was not solely directed at the external environment, but also at the internal workings of the development machinery itself. I witnessed firsthand how funding, once secured after arduous negotiations and complex proposals, could be diluted through multiple layers of administration, each adding its own overhead and requiring its own elaborate reporting mechanisms. The concept of "accountability" often morphed into a bureaucratic exercise of filling out forms and meeting reporting deadlines, diverting precious time and resources away from direct beneficiary engagement and program implementation. Imagine a scenario where a significant portion of a grant allocated for maternal health services was consumed by the complex financial tracking and audits required by various donor agencies, each with its own distinct set of rules and formats. The result was often a palpable reduction in the number of medical supplies that could be purchased, fewer health workers who could be trained, and a diminished capacity to reach remote communities. The emphasis shifted from achieving impact to demonstrating compliance, a subtle but critical perversion of the original intent.

Moreover, the reliance on rigid, pre-approved project cycles often proved antithetical to the dynamic and unpredictable nature of development work. We would spend months meticulously planning a multi-year initiative, only to find that by the time funding was disbursed, the local context had shifted dramatically. A planned agricultural intervention might become obsolete due to a sudden pest outbreak, or a youth employment program might be rendered irrelevant by an unexpected wave of economic migration. Yet, adapting these plans often involved navigating another labyrinth of bureaucratic approvals, leading to delays that could render the intervention ineffective or, worse, entirely moot. The inability to pivot quickly, to reallocate resources to emerging needs or to capitalize on unforeseen opportunities was a constant source of professional anguish. It felt like trying to steer a massive ship through treacherous waters with a rudder that was too small and too slow to respond.

The human element of this experience cannot be overstated. Beyond the systemic issues, there were the deeply personal encounters that fueled my disillusionment. I met dedicated local partners, community leaders, and ordinary citizens who poured their energy and hope into these initiatives, only to be met with the inertia of a system ill-equipped to truly empower them. I saw individuals whose lives were intrinsically linked to the success of a project, their livelihoods dependent on its continuation, suddenly cast adrift due to unforeseen funding cuts or a shift in donor priorities. These were not abstract statistics; they were individuals with families, aspirations, and dreams, whose faith in the promise of development was tested and often broken by the very organizations meant to uphold it. The emotional toll of witnessing this cycle of hope and disappointment, repeatedly, began to weigh heavily. It was a profound moral imperative to find a better way, a more responsive, more accountable, and ultimately, more effective approach.

This accumulation of experiences – the **persistent inefficiencies**, the **bureaucratic inertia**, the **disconnect between global ambition and local reality**, and the profound human cost of systemic failures – coalesced into a deeply felt conviction. The existing paradigms, despite their noble intentions, were fundamentally flawed. They were **too slow, too rigid, too focused on process over outcome,** and ultimately, **too detached from the lived experiences of the people they were meant to serve**. This was not an indictment of every individual working within the system; indeed, I met many deeply committed and capable professionals. Rather, it was a recognition that the architecture of the system itself was the primary impediment. It was clear that a new approach was not just desirable, but essential – a radical reimagining of how development and humanitarian aid could be conceptualized, delivered, and governed, one that prioritized **genuine capacity building, adaptability, and direct impact**, and that was forged in the heat of hard-won experience. This understanding, born from the crucible of the field, became the intellectual and emotional bedrock upon which **Rescue Democracy International** would ultimately be built. It was a painful, but necessary, realization that innovation was not an option, but an imperative, if the promise of development was ever to be truly fulfilled. The lessons learned were hard-earned, etched not in reports or proposals, but in the very fabric of my understanding of what it means to **foster lasting, meaningful change** in the world.

The persistent disconnect I observed between the intentions of development initiatives and their actual impact was not merely a matter of operational challenges; it was a symptom of a deeply embedded systemic complexity. The machinery of international aid, as it had evolved, was a colossal edifice, built layer upon layer over decades, each addition ostensibly designed to enhance oversight, accountability, or reach, but often resulting in a labyrinthine **bureaucracy**. This created an environment where the spirit of the endeavor was frequently lost in the mechanics of its execution. The core philosophy that began to crystallize in my mind, a counter-current to this prevailing tide, was that of radical simplification. This wasn't about reducing ambition or lowering standards, quite the opposite. It was about a fundamental re-evaluation of *how* we pursued those ambitions, seeking to strip away the accretions of complexity that had become liabilities rather than assets.

The rationale for this radical simplification stemmed from a deep-seated belief that the traditional, often top-heavy, organizational structures and convoluted logistical frameworks prevalent in the sector were inherently antithetical to agile and effective development work. These structures, while perhaps well-intentioned, often created more problems than they solved. They fostered a culture of consensus-building that could take months, if not years, for even minor decisions, paralyzing responsiveness. Multiple layers of management, each with its own reporting requirements and approval processes, meant that critical information was often filtered, distorted, or delayed to the point of irrelevance by the time it reached those who needed to act upon it. This diffusion of responsibility also made it difficult to pinpoint accountability when things went wrong. Was it the program officer, the regional director, the country representative, or the headquarters desk officer who was ultimately responsible for a delayed shipment of essential medicines or an ill-conceived community engagement strategy? The answer was rarely clear, leading to a perpetual cycle of blame and a reluctance to take decisive action.

Consider, for instance, the standard model of a large international non-governmental organization (INGO) operating in a fragile state. Such an organization might boast a country office staffed by a director, deputy director, finance manager, human resources manager, monitoring and evaluation specialist, communications officer, and a host of program managers, each overseeing specific thematic areas like health, education, or livelihoods. Beneath them would be a hierarchy of national staff, field coordinators, and community liaisons. This structure, while providing employment and career paths, inevitably generated **significant overhead costs.** The salaries, benefits, office rentals, vehicles, and administrative support required for this extensive human infrastructure were substantial. More critically, the communication pathways within such a tiered system were long and prone to distortion. A crucial piece of feedback from a remote village might traverse several levels of management before reaching a decision-maker, by which point its urgency or nuance might have been lost.

Moreover, the logistical pathways were often equally encumbered. Procurement processes for even minor supplies could involve multiple bids, tenders, approvals from various departments, and adherence to donor-specific regulations, each adding layers of complexity and time. Imagine a situation where a small, local community needed a water pump repair. In a conventionally structured organization, procuring the necessary parts might involve requesting quotes from approved suppliers, submitting a purchase requisition, obtaining financial approval, generating a purchase order, arranging transport, and then finally authorizing the repair. This process, designed for transparency and control, could easily take weeks, during which time the community remains without access to clean water. **The radical simplification I envisioned sought to dismantle such protracted processes, replacing them with streamlined, empowered decision-making at the most effective level, often closer to the point of implementation.**

The emphasis, therefore, was on clarity of purpose and efficiency of operation. What was the ultimate goal of our intervention? Was it to improve child nutrition, increase agricultural yields, or reduce maternal mortality? By keeping these core objectives sharply in focus, we could begin to question every element of our approach that did not directly contribute to them. This meant challenging established norms regarding organizational size, reporting frequency, budget management, and even the very definition of success. *Was a project successful if it meticulously followed its original work plan, even if that plan had become irrelevant due to changing circumstances on the ground? Or was it successful if it adapted quickly and achieved tangible, positive outcomes for the beneficiaries, regardless of deviations from the initial proposal?* The latter, I argued, was the only metric that truly mattered.

This philosophical shift demanded a re-examination of the relationship between headquarters and field operations. For too long, a top-down model had prevailed, where strategic direction, programmatic design, and even operational intricacies were dictated by distant offices staffed by individuals who often lacked direct, recent experience of the realities on the ground. This created a sense of "incapacity building" among field teams, who possessed invaluable local knowledge but were often constrained by directives that felt out of touch or even counterproductive. **Radical simplification meant devolving authority and decision-making power to the field, entrusting those closest to the problem with the latitude to find the most appropriate solutions**. It meant creating flatter organizational structures where communication flowed more freely and where the distance between the frontline and the decision-makers was drastically reduced.

Consider the example of program design. Traditional approaches often involved extensive, multi-month planning phases, engaging numerous consultants and stakeholders, resulting in hundreds of pages of detailed project documents. While thoroughness has its place, this level of upfront planning often led to rigidity. By contrast, a simplified approach might involve a core team rapidly assessing the most critical needs and designing a more agile, iterative program. Instead of a five-year, fixed-plan approach, it might be a one-year, adaptable plan with built-in mechanisms for review and adjustment every few months. This allows for course correction based on real-time feedback from the communities being served, ensuring that interventions remain relevant and effective. This agility is a direct consequence of simplification – fewer stakeholders involved in the design phase, clearer objectives, and a more direct line of communication between those implementing the program and those for whom it is intended.

Furthermore, the concept of "accountability" itself needed simplification. Instead of being a bureaucratic exercise focused on compliance with a multitude of donor-specific reporting formats, accountability should be re-centered on tangible impact and responsible stewardship of resources. This means moving away from lengthy, narrative reports that often serve more to justify past actions than to inform future improvements, towards simpler, more direct metrics of success. For instance, instead of a detailed report on all the training workshops conducted, the focus could be on the demonstrable increase in the number of women accessing pre-natal care following those workshops. This shift in focus from process to outcome is a critical element of radical simplification. It demands that we ask not just, "Did we do what we said we would do?" but rather, "Did what we did make a meaningful difference?"

The logistical implications of radical simplification are profound. It necessitates a move away from the complex, centralized procurement and supply chain management systems that characterize many larger organizations. Instead, it favors decentralized, community-based procurement where feasible, empowering local suppliers and reducing lead times and transportation costs. It also means rethinking the need for extensive physical infrastructure. In many contexts, smaller, more adaptable field units, perhaps even relying on shared resources or flexible office spaces, could replace large, permanent country offices, significantly reducing overhead and increasing agility. This leaner operational footprint is a direct manifestation of simplifying the "how" of development work.

Challenging the conventional wisdom surrounding program design and implementation requires a willingness to embrace uncertainty and a departure from the comfort of pre-defined processes. It meant recognizing that in many of the environments where development work is most needed, the most valuable asset is not a perfectly crafted five-year plan, but the ability to adapt and respond to rapidly changing circumstances. This adaptability is intrinsically linked to simplification. A simpler structure, with fewer layers of approval and more empowered decision-makers, can pivot far more effectively than a complex, bureaucratic one. The genesis of Rescue Democracy International, therefore, was not merely about identifying problems within the existing development paradigm, but about articulating a clear, actionable alternative rooted in the principle of radical simplification – an unwavering commitment to stripping away the extraneous, clarifying the essential, and focusing relentlessly on achieving meaningful, measurable impact for those who need it most.

The traditional architecture of international development, as I came to understand it through years of immersion in its complex arteries, was often characterized by a certain detachment. Decisions were frequently formulated in distant boardrooms, shaped by global strategies and donor mandates, and then disseminated downwards through layers of management. The implementation, however, occurred at the furthest remove – in remote villages, bustling urban slums, or dispersed rural communities. This inherent disconnect often meant that the most nuanced understandings of local realities, the subtle dynamics of social cohesion, the unwritten rules of community governance, and the deeply ingrained cultural practices that underpinned daily life, remained, at best, abstract concepts for those making the critical decisions. At worst, they were entirely overlooked, leading to interventions that, while well-intentioned and perhaps technically sound on paper, failed to resonate with the very people they were meant to serve. The efficacy of any development effort, and indeed its sustainability, is inextricably linked to its rootedness in the local context. It is here, at the community level, that the true pulse of need and the most authentic expressions of resilience can be found.

This recognition led to a fundamental reorientation in how Rescue Democracy International began to conceptualize its operational framework, shifting the locus of power and decision-making away from centralized hierarchies and towards the periphery. The core of this paradigm shift was the profound acknowledgment of the indispensable role that grassroots organizations must play. These are not merely conduits for aid or implementers of externally designed programs; they are, in essence, the embodiment of local agency and the custodians of community aspirations. Empowering these entities was not an ancillary consideration; it was to become a foundational pillar upon which the entire RDI Model would be built. The conviction grew that true, lasting change could only be catalyzed from within, propelled by the very people who understand the challenges intimately and who possess the inherent motivation to overcome them.

The advantages of partnering with and strengthening grassroots organizations are manifold and deeply pragmatic. Foremost among these is their unparalleled depth of local knowledge. Unlike external agencies, which may spend months or years conducting assessments, grassroots organizations operate with an intuitive understanding of their environment. They know the social networks, the power brokers, the informal support systems, and the historical precedents that shape community dynamics. This granular knowledge is not something that can be easily replicated or acquired through external research; it is built over generations, woven into the fabric of community life. This intimate familiarity allows them to design and implement interventions that are not only appropriate but also culturally sensitive and contextually relevant. For instance, a program aimed at improving agricultural practices might need to consider traditional land tenure systems, local seed varieties, or customary methods of pest control – all pieces of information that a local farmers' cooperative would possess intrinsically. An external agency might approach this with standardized modern agricultural techniques, which, without understanding the local context, could be met with resistance or prove entirely unworkable.

Furthermore, grassroots organizations inherently possess an established trust within their communities. Years of shared experience, mutual reliance, and often, a common identity, forge bonds that external actors can struggle to cultivate, no matter how dedicated their efforts. This trust is not a superficial commodity; it is the bedrock upon which community engagement and participation are built. When a community trusts its local leaders or organizations, they are more likely to listen to their advice, participate in their initiatives, and commit to the long-term sustainability of any project. Consider a health initiative designed to promote vaccination. While an external NGO might launch a public awareness campaign with posters and radio ads, a trusted local community health committee can have far more impact through door-to-door visits, personal conversations, and addressing specific community concerns in a relatable manner. This established trust translates directly into higher levels of community buy-in and a greater sense of ownership over development projects, which are critical for their long-term success.

This inherent advantage of trust also extends to resource mobilization and accountability. When resources are managed by organizations that are accountable to the community itself, rather than solely to external donors or headquarters, there is a greater incentive for transparency and efficient use of funds. Community members are more likely to contribute their own resources, whether in the form of labor, materials, or financial contributions, when they see their local organizations functioning effectively and responsibly. This fosters a sense of collective responsibility and ensures that projects remain aligned with community priorities, even after external support may have waned. The risk of resources being diverted or misused is significantly diminished when the eyes of the community are actively overseeing their management.

The concept of "capacity building" for these grassroots organizations, therefore, takes on a new and critical meaning within the RDI framework. It is not about imposing external models or creating dependency but about enhancing their existing strengths and empowering them to operate at their full potential. This involves providing them with the necessary tools, training, and resources, not to become miniature versions of large international NGOs, but to become more effective, more efficient, and more sustainable custodians of their own development agendas. This could include financial management training, proposal writing skills, project planning and monitoring techniques, leadership development, and access to networks and information. The goal is to equip them with the skills and confidence to manage their own projects, advocate for their own needs, and engage effectively with larger institutions, including government bodies and international agencies.

For example, a local women's collective that has a strong mandate to address gender-based violence might possess an intimate understanding of the root causes and the social dynamics that perpetuate it. However, they might lack formal structures or the legal expertise to establish safe houses or to lobby for policy changes. RDI's role, in this context, would be to provide support in developing their organizational statutes, offering legal counsel on advocacy strategies, and perhaps facilitating connections with government ministries responsible for justice and women's affairs. This is not about taking over their initiative but about bolstering their capacity to achieve their self-determined goals. It's about empowering them to navigate the complexities of the broader landscape, rather than being dictated by it.

The process of identifying and nurturing these grassroots organizations requires a methodology that is distinct from traditional needs assessment. It involves spending time in communities, listening to local voices, and understanding the informal networks of influence and action. It is about recognizing the emergent leaders and organizations that may not fit the conventional molds but demonstrate genuine commitment and effectiveness. This often means looking beyond registered non-profits and engaging with informal community groups, youth clubs, religious organizations, or even influential community elders who are already actively working to improve their communities. The criteria for partnership are not based on the size of their budget or the formality of their structure, but on their demonstrated impact, their local legitimacy, and their commitment to transparent and inclusive practices.

The impact of this decentralized approach extends beyond mere operational efficiency. It fosters a sense of ownership and self-reliance that is fundamental to sustainable development. When communities are empowered to identify their own problems, design their own solutions, and manage their own resources, they develop a deep-seated commitment to the long-term success of those solutions. This internal drive is far more powerful and enduring than any externally imposed program. It cultivates a generation of local leaders and activists who are equipped to continue the development process long after external support has ended. This is the essence of true capacity building – not to receive aid, but to become the architects of one's own progress.

Moreover, this model actively works to counteract the inherent power imbalances that often characterize the relationship between international development agencies and local communities. By elevating the role of grassroots organizations, RDI sought to create a more equitable partnership. Instead of a provider-recipient dynamic, the aim was to foster a collaborative relationship where local actors are recognized as equal partners, bringing their own invaluable knowledge and expertise to the table. This shift in power dynamics not only leads to more effective programming but also promotes greater respect and dignity for the communities being served. It recognizes that development is not something that is done **to** people, but something that is done **with** them.

The practical implementation of this strategy involved a commitment to **flexibility** and **adaptability**. Unlike large, bureaucratic organizations that are often bound by rigid funding structures and long-term programmatic commitments, grassroots organizations are typically more agile and responsive to immediate community needs. RDI's approach was designed to complement this agility, offering flexible funding mechanisms and support that could be adapted to evolving circumstances. This meant moving away from the prescriptive, multi-year grant agreements that often tie the hands of local implementers, towards more fluid, needs-based support that could be adjusted as priorities shifted on the ground.

For instance, a community might identify a critical need for clean water infrastructure. A grassroots organization, with RDI's support, could quickly mobilize local labor and resources to construct a well. However, six months later, a new challenge might emerge, such as a localized disease outbreak requiring immediate public health interventions. A decentralized, flexible funding model allows the grassroots organization, with RDI's backing, to pivot its focus and resources to address this new, urgent need, without being constrained by the original project's scope. This responsiveness is a direct product of valuing the insights and priorities of the local partners.

The process of capacity building itself is also envisioned as a reciprocal exchange. While RDI provides training and resources, it also learns immensely from the grassroots organizations it partners with. Their understanding of local contexts, their innovative problem-solving approaches, and their resilience in the face of adversity offer invaluable lessons that can inform RDI's own strategies and methodologies. This mutual learning fosters a dynamic and evolving partnership, ensuring that RDI remains grounded in the realities of the communities it serves and continuously refines its approach based on practical experience. It moves beyond a simple transfer of skills to a genuine collaboration that enriches all parties involved.

In essence, the decentralization of power and the capacity building of grassroots organizations represent a fundamental re-imagining of the development process. It is a move away from the top-down, technocratic models that have often proven unsustainable and inequitable, towards a more **participatory, community-driven approach**. This shift recognizes that the most profound and lasting transformations are those that are conceived, owned, and implemented by the people themselves. By placing grassroots organizations at the forefront, RDI seeks to unlock the latent potential within communities, fostering self-reliance, strengthening local ownership, and ultimately, building a more just and sustainable future, one empowered community at a time. The efficacy of this approach lies in its inherent respect for local knowledge, its cultivation of established trust, and its commitment to building the capacity of those who are best positioned to drive their own development. It is a commitment to ensuring that the true architects of change are those who live and breathe the challenges every day.

The operational philosophy of Rescue Democracy International, as it began to solidify, necessitated a more granular and intimately connected approach to engagement. Recognizing the inherent limitations of a top-down dissemination of strategies, RDI sought to embed its operational framework directly within the fabric of the communities it aimed to serve. This quest for authentic local connection led to the conceptualization and implementation of the 'Focal Point' (FP) strategy. A Focal Point, in the RDI lexicon, is not a mere administrator or a passive recipient of directives. Instead, they are meticulously identified and cultivated individuals, deeply embedded within the very grassroots organizations that RDI partners with. These are the individuals who embody the local knowledge, the trust, and the active engagement necessary to bridge the gap between external resources and tangible community impact. They are the human conduits through which understanding flows in both directions, ensuring that interventions are not only relevant but also responsive and owned by the community.

The selection of individuals to serve as Focal Points is a process of profound importance, eschewing superficial criteria in favor of a deep understanding of local dynamics and individual commitment. These are not individuals appointed by external decree, nor are they necessarily those holding formal leadership positions within an organization, though they often are. Rather, the process involves careful observation and consultation within the partner grassroots organizations themselves. RDI seeks individuals who possess an intrinsic understanding of their community's needs, challenges, and aspirations. This includes individuals who are respected for their integrity, their dedication to community well-being, and their ability to communicate effectively with diverse groups within their local context. They are individuals who are already active participants in their community's development, demonstrating a proactive approach to problem-solving. The selection often involves identifying those who are already seen as go-to people within their respective organizations, individuals who naturally facilitate communication and collaboration. It is a recognition of existing informal leadership and a formalization of that crucial role. This deep-seated local legitimacy is paramount; an FP must be someone whose voice carries weight and whose presence is accepted and valued by the community at large, not just within the confines of their organizational membership.

Once identified, the role of the Focal Point is rigorously defined and supported through comprehensive training and ongoing capacity building. This training is designed to equip them with the essential skills and knowledge required to effectively act as intermediaries. It goes beyond basic project management principles to encompass areas such as enhanced communication techniques, conflict resolution, basic financial literacy for resource management, participatory monitoring and evaluation methodologies, and an understanding of broader policy landscapes that might affect their community. Crucially, the training emphasizes the ethical dimensions of their role, reinforcing principles of transparency, accountability, and inclusivity. RDI understands that these individuals are operating within complex social environments, and therefore, the training must prepare them to navigate these complexities with skill and integrity. This is not a one-off event but rather a **continuous process of learning and adaptation**, ensuring that Focal Points remain equipped to address evolving challenges and opportunities.

The integration of Focal Points into RDI's project delivery mechanism is what transforms the organizational model from a theoretically decentralized structure into a practically impactful one. They become the operational linchpins, directly interfacing with RDI's field staff and program managers. Their primary function is to facilitate the two-way flow of information. On the one hand, they are responsible for articulating the evolving needs and priorities of their communities, ensuring that RDI's strategies remain aligned with the lived realities on the ground. This means conveying nuanced feedback on project implementation, highlighting unforeseen obstacles, and suggesting necessary adaptations. They act as the crucial feedback loop, preventing the disconnect that often plagues traditional development efforts. On the other hand, they are instrumental in translating RDI's objectives and planned activities into actionable steps within their communities. They ensure that project interventions are understood, accepted, and actively participated in by community members, mobilizing local resources and ensuring that activities are conducted in a manner that respects local customs and practices.

The practical functioning of this system is best understood through concrete examples. Consider a project focused on improving access to education in a rural district. Instead of RDI staff directly interacting with multiple, disparate community groups or individual schools, the designated Focal Point from a local education advocacy committee would serve as the primary point of contact. This FP would work with their committee to assess specific needs, whether it's the lack of textbooks, the need for teacher training, or the requirement for improved school infrastructure. They would then communicate these needs, clearly articulated and prioritized by the community, to RDI. Following this, RDI would work with the FP to develop a joint action plan. The FP would then be responsible for ensuring that resources provided by RDI – be it funds for books, arrangements for training sessions, or materials for construction – are utilized effectively and transparently within their community. They would oversee the distribution of books, facilitate the participation of teachers in training, and coordinate local labor for infrastructure projects. Their intimate knowledge of the community ensures that these activities are conducted efficiently and with minimal disruption to daily life. They are also tasked with reporting on progress, challenges, and community feedback, allowing RDI to monitor impact and make necessary adjustments to the program. This ensures that RDI's interventions are not only guided by local priorities but are also implemented with a high degree of local ownership and accountability.

The FP concept also extends to ensuring that RDI's broader strategic objectives are communicated effectively at the grassroots level. When RDI develops a new thematic area of focus, such as promoting sustainable agriculture or improving maternal health, the Focal Points are crucial in disseminating this information and facilitating community engagement in these new initiatives. They can organize community meetings, lead discussions, and help communities understand how these new programs align with their existing needs and aspirations. This is not passive information transfer; it involves facilitating dialogue and encouraging communities to actively shape how these broader initiatives are adapted and implemented within their specific contexts. The FP serves as a catalyst for participatory planning, ensuring that RDI's programs are co-created rather than simply delivered.

Furthermore, the Focal Point role is designed to foster a sense of capacity building and agency within the grassroots organizations themselves. By entrusting these individuals with significant responsibilities and providing them with the necessary training and support, RDI is investing in the capacity of the local partners. This strengthens the organizations by enhancing their ability to manage projects, engage with external stakeholders, and advocate for their own development priorities. The Focal Points, in turn, often find that their role significantly elevates their standing and influence within their own communities and organizations, motivating them to continue their dedicated service. This reciprocal benefit is a cornerstone of RDI's approach – **strengthening external partnerships by strengthening internal capacities.**

The success of the Focal Point model hinges on a deep commitment to building trust and maintaining open lines of communication. RDI's field staff are trained to view Focal Points not as subordinates, but as essential partners and colleagues. Regular communication, whether through scheduled meetings, site visits, or digital platforms, is vital. This communication must be characterized by mutual respect, active listening, and a willingness to adapt strategies based on the feedback received. The FP is expected to be forthright with challenges, and RDI is committed to responding constructively and collaboratively. This continuous dialogue ensures that the relationship remains dynamic and responsive to the evolving needs of the community and the practicalities of project implementation.

In essence, the Focal Point concept is RDI's practical manifestation of its core philosophy: that **sustainable development is achieved through deep local rootedness, empowered local actors, and genuine partnerships**. They are the embodiment of local agency, the custodians of local knowledge, and the critical links in a chain of collaboration that ensure external support translates into meaningful, community-driven change. Without these dedicated individuals, the most well-intentioned strategies would remain abstract pronouncements. With them, RDI's vision of a **more equitable** and impactful development paradigm becomes a tangible reality on the ground, **driven by the very people it seeks to serve**. The FP system is not merely an operational mechanism; it is a testament to RDI's unwavering belief in the power of local capacity and the transformative potential of genuine community partnership, making them the indispensable key player of the new RDI Model. This approach recognizes that **true impact is not achieved by simply delivering aid, but by cultivating the capacity of local actors to lead their own development journeys**, with RDI providing the support, resources, and partnership to amplify their efforts. The Focal Point, therefore, represents a critical investment in both human capital and organizational infrastructure at the grassroots level, ensuring that every intervention is grounded in local reality and propelled by local commitment.

The genesis of Rescue Democracy International (RDI) was not a spontaneous eruption, but rather a carefully considered response to a profound inadequacy observed within the global humanitarian and development landscape. For too long, the discourse around aid had been dominated by notions of scarcity, dependency, and the often-unintended consequence of perpetuating the very issues it sought to resolve. RDI emerged from the conviction that a paradigm shift was not only possible but essential. This new paradigm, the blueprint for transformative aid that would come to define RDI, was envisioned not as a static set of policies, but as a dynamic, evolving philosophy grounded in core principles designed to foster genuine, sustainable change. It was conceived as a counter-narrative to the prevailing models, aiming to redefine the relationship between aid providers and beneficiaries, moving away from a donor-recipient dynamic towards one of true partnership and mutual capacity building.

At its heart, the RDI vision is one of capacity building through participation. It posits that the most effective and sustainable solutions to complex developmental challenges are not imposed *from without* but are nurtured and cultivated *from within*. This means that the voices, knowledge, and agency of the communities themselves must be placed at the forefront of all interventions. The traditional approach, often characterized by external experts determining needs and prescribing solutions, frequently led to interventions that were misaligned with local realities, culturally insensitive, or ultimately unsustainable because they lacked local ownership. **RDI's vision sought to dismantle this edifice of external authority and replace it with a framework built on the bedrock of local expertise and collective decision-making.** This is not to suggest a complete abdication of external support; rather, it is a reorientation of that support, positioning it as a catalyst and facilitator for locally driven initiatives, rather than the primary engine of change. The goal is to unlock and amplify the inherent potential within communities, enabling them to become the architects and drivers of their own development trajectories.

This vision translates into a fundamental re-evaluation of what constitutes "effective" aid. For RDI, effectiveness is not measured solely by the quantity of resources deployed or the superficial completion of project outputs. *True effectiveness, as envisioned by RDI, is characterized by the creation of resilient, self-sufficient communities capable of navigating their own challenges and capitalizing on their own opportunities long after external support has been withdrawn.* This requires a sustained commitment to building local capacity, fostering critical thinking, and strengthening community-based institutions. It means investing in people, equipping them with the skills, knowledge, and resources to become active agents of their own progress. This holistic approach recognizes that development is not just about economic upliftment or improved infrastructure, but also about strengthening social capital, promoting good governance, and fostering a sense of collective agency and self-determination.

The operationalization of this vision hinges on a radical commitment to transparency and accountability, not just to donors and stakeholders, but, crucially, to the people being served. This means ensuring that decision-making processes are open, that resources are managed responsibly and ethically, and that there are clear mechanisms for feedback and redress. In a sector often plagued by opacity and a lack of direct accountability to beneficiaries, RDI's vision champions a model where communities have a direct say in how aid is delivered and are empowered to hold organizations accountable for their commitments. This transparency extends to the sharing of information about project goals, budgets, and outcomes, fostering a climate of trust and mutual respect. When communities understand how resources are being utilized and can provide input on their effectiveness, they are more likely to engage actively and see themselves as true partners in the development process, rather than passive recipients.

Furthermore, the RDI vision embraces a philosophy of learning and adaptation. Recognizing that the contexts in which development work takes place are dynamic and constantly evolving, RDI is committed to fostering a culture of continuous learning. This involves rigorous monitoring and evaluation, not as a punitive exercise, but as an opportunity to gather insights, identify lessons learned, and adapt strategies accordingly. The Focal Point model, as previously detailed, plays a crucial role in this adaptive process, providing real-time feedback from the ground and enabling RDI to remain responsive to changing needs and emerging challenges. This iterative approach ensures that RDI's programs remain relevant, effective, and efficient, maximizing their impact and minimizing the risk of wasted resources or unintended negative consequences. It's a commitment to intellectual humility, acknowledging that **no single entity possesses all the answers and that true progress comes from a willingness to learn from experience and from those closest to the issues.**

The RDI blueprint for transformative aid is fundamentally about **building bridges, not walls**. It seeks to bridge the gap between global resources and local needs, between external expertise and local knowledge, and between aspiration and achievement. This is accomplished through fostering genuine partnerships characterized by shared goals, mutual respect, and a collaborative approach to problem-solving. The organization's strategy is not to be the sole provider of solutions, but to be a trusted partner that amplifies and supports the initiatives already underway within communities. This involves identifying existing strengths, building upon them, and providing the necessary catalytic support to enable them to flourish. It's a subtle but profound shift in orientation, moving from a model of **"doing for"** to one of **"doing with."** This collaborative spirit permeates every aspect of RDI's operations, from program design to implementation and evaluation.

Moreover, the RDI vision extends beyond individual projects to advocate for systemic change within the broader humanitarian and development sector. **By demonstrating the efficacy of**

its approach, RDI aims to influence policy and practice, encouraging other organizations to adopt more participatory, community-centered methodologies. The organization believes that by showcasing tangible results and fostering a replicable model, it can contribute to a broader movement towards more effective, equitable, and sustainable development and humanitarian aid worldwide. This advocacy role is seen as integral to its mission, recognizing that lasting change requires not only on-the-ground impact but also a transformation of the underlying systems and structures that govern how aid is delivered. The ultimate aspiration is to contribute to a global humanitarian ecosystem where the voices of those most affected are not just heard but are the primary drivers of the development agenda. This means challenging entrenched power dynamics and promoting a more democratic and inclusive approach to global development cooperation.

The RDI vision also encompasses a deep commitment to fostering resilience, not just in the face of immediate crises, but in the long-term capacity of communities to withstand and recover from shocks and stresses. This includes addressing the underlying vulnerabilities that often exacerbate the impact of disasters, conflicts, or economic downturns. It means investing in robust community structures, promoting diversified livelihoods, and strengthening social safety nets. By empowering communities to build their own resilience, RDI aims to create a buffer against future challenges, enabling them to emerge stronger and more self-reliant. This proactive approach to resilience building is a cornerstone of RDI's commitment to sustainable development, moving beyond reactive crisis response to a more strategic, forward-looking engagement.

The implementation of this vision is a complex undertaking, requiring a constant balancing act between global standards and local realities, between accountability and flexibility, and between the urgent needs of the present and the long-term goals of development. However, the guiding principle remains unwavering: that the most impactful and sustainable development is that which is owned and driven by the communities themselves. **RDI's proposal is, therefore, a call to action, an invitation to rethink the very nature of aid and to embrace a more collaborative, empowering, and ultimately, more effective approach to addressing the world's most pressing challenges.** It is a vision that places faith in the inherent capabilities of people and the collective strength of communities, positioning RDI as a dedicated partner in unlocking that potential for a more just and prosperous future for all. This commitment is not merely aspirational; it is the operational imperative that shapes every decision, every program, and every partnership undertaken by Rescue Democracy International. It is the animating spirit that distinguishes RDI's approach and fuels its dedication to fostering lasting, positive change. The vision is to move from a cycle of aid dependency to one of empowered self-sufficiency, creating a legacy of sustainable progress that empowers communities to chart their own destinies. This requires a deep understanding that true transformation is a collaborative journey, built on trust, respect, and a shared commitment to a common future.

CHAPTER 3:

The RDI Operational Framework:
Lean, Agile, Effective

The foundational architecture of Rescue Democracy International (RDI) was deliberately sculpted around a core principle of radical efficiency and direct impact. In stark contrast to the established norms of many international non-governmental organizations, RDI eschewed the creation of extensive, costly regional administrative hubs. This strategic decision, to operate without a network of traditional regional offices, was not an arbitrary cost-cutting measure, but a deliberate and integral component of the RDI operational framework, designed to maximize resource allocation directly to programmatic activities and, crucially, to the beneficiaries themselves. The prevailing model in the humanitarian and development sector often involved significant investments in physical infrastructure, extensive personnel for administrative oversight, and complex hierarchical management structures spread across multiple geographical locations. While these models aim for broad reach and consistent oversight, they invariably incur substantial overhead costs that can, in many instances, divert a significant percentage of available funding away from the frontline work where it is most desperately needed. RDI recognized this inherent inefficiency and sought to build an organization that was inherently lean, agile, and fiscally responsible, ensuring that every dollar, every euro, every resource contributed to RDI was leveraged for maximum tangible impact on the ground.

Learning from his long experience in community development, Dr. Justin Mudekereza, RDI's Founder and President, conceived this minimalist footprint as a direct response to the pervasive challenge of overhead in the aid sector, a challenge that often consumes a disproportionate amount of donor funds, diluting the potential impact of aid programs. **By consciously opting against the establishment of multiple, geographically dispersed regional headquarters, RDI immediately sidestepped the substantial capital and ongoing operational expenditures associated with such infrastructure.** This includes the costs of leasing and maintaining (fancy) office spaces, equipping them with furniture and technology, and staffing them with layers of administrative and managerial personnel solely dedicated to regional oversight. *Instead, RDI's operational strategy hinges on a highly networked, decentralized approach that leverages technology and carefully selected, highly effective local partnerships to achieve its programmatic goals. This allows for a significant redirection of funds that would otherwise be absorbed by bureaucratic structures, channeling them instead into direct program delivery, capacity building, and direct support to the communities RDI serves.* The cost savings are not merely theoretical; they represent a tangible increase in the resources available for critical interventions, for providing essential supplies, for training local facilitators, and for supporting community-led initiatives that drive sustainable development.

The financial implications of this structural decision are profound. Consider, for example, the typical costs associated with establishing and maintaining a single regional office in a major international city. This would encompass not only the rental or purchase of prime real estate but also the salaries for a country director, finance managers, human resources personnel, communications officers, and administrative support staff. Add to this the expenses related to travel allowances, vehicle fleets, and the logistical complexities of managing multiple physical locations. When scaled across several regions, the cumulative overhead can easily amount to millions of dollars annually. **RDI's alternative model bypasses these expenditures entirely.** Instead of a costly physical presence, RDI invests in a robust digital infrastructure and empowers its field-based teams and local partners with the autonomy and resources to operate effectively. Communication, coordination, and oversight are managed through advanced digital platforms, video conferencing, and regular needs-driven travel by a core central team, rather than through the maintenance of expensive, fixed administrative outposts. This approach fosters a more dynamic and responsive operational model, one that is not beholden to the physical limitations and financial burdens of traditional regional structures. The savings realized are then directly reinvested into program enhancement, ensuring that a significantly higher percentage of funding reaches the intended beneficiaries. This commitment to fiscal prudence is not just about saving money; it is about maximizing the return on investment for every donor and, more importantly, maximizing the positive impact on the lives of the people RDI aims to serve. It underscores RDI's dedication to operational efficacy and its unwavering focus on delivering tangible results on the ground, demonstrating that a leaner, more agile operational framework can be profoundly more effective.

This streamlined operational model also inherently fosters greater agility and responsiveness. Traditional organizations with extensive regional offices can often become weighed down by bureaucratic processes and decision-making chains that can slow down the adaptation to changing circumstances on the ground. In dynamic environments where humanitarian needs and development challenges can shift rapidly, this lack of agility can be detrimental. RDI's structure, by contrast, is designed to be nimble. Without the need for extensive approvals from multiple layers of regional management, decisions can be made more swiftly and effectively at the local level, closer to the actual context of intervention. This empowers RDI's country-level coordinators and project managers, along with their community partners, to adapt strategies and reallocate resources in real-time to address emergent needs or capitalize on emerging opportunities. The absence of a large, regional administrative apparatus means fewer intermediaries in the decision-making process, leading to faster implementation and a more direct line of communication between programmatic needs and resource allocation. This agility is crucial for maintaining relevance and effectiveness in complex and often unpredictable operational settings.

Furthermore, the cost savings generated by avoiding regional offices translate directly into expanded program reach and depth. Instead of allocating funds to maintain multiple administrative structures, RDI can invest in more personnel directly involved in program implementation, procure greater quantities of essential supplies, or fund a larger number of community-driven projects. For instance, the salary costs for a regional director and their support staff could, in RDI's model, be redirected to fund the training of dozens of local community health workers or provide seed funding for several small-scale, sustainable agriculture, youth entrepreneurship and women's empowerment initiatives. The funds saved on office rent and utilities in a capital city could be used to establish additional educational programs for children in remote villages or to provide critical vocational training for unemployed youth. This is not a matter of minor adjustment; it is a fundamental reorientation of financial resources towards the core mission of RDI. The organization's commitment to **operational efficiency** is therefore intrinsically linked to its commitment to maximizing impact and serving a greater number of people with higher quality assistance. This principle of resource maximization is woven into the very fabric of RDI's organizational design, ensuring that its operational framework is a direct enabler of its humanitarian and development goals, rather than a drain on its resources.

The efficiency gains are not solely financial. The absence of extensive administrative layers also streamlines communication and reporting. Information flows more directly from the field to the central coordination team and, where necessary, to donors. This reduces the potential for misinterpretation or delay that can occur when information passes through multiple administrative filters. The emphasis is on clear, concise, and actionable reporting that focuses on programmatic outcomes and beneficiary impact. Moreover, RDI's reliance on technology for communication and data management further enhances this efficiency. **Secure cloud-based platforms allow for real-time data sharing, progress tracking, and collaborative planning among dispersed teams.** This digital infrastructure, while requiring initial investment, ultimately proves far more cost-effective and efficient than maintaining extensive physical offices and the associated logistical support. It allows RDI to maintain a global reach and provide consistent oversight without the significant overhead costs of traditional regional presences.

This minimalist approach also fosters a culture of accountability and resourcefulness within RDI. When an organization operates with fewer administrative layers and relies heavily on local partnerships, there is an inherent pressure to be highly efficient and judicious with every resource. Field teams and local partners are empowered, but they are also expected to manage resources effectively and demonstrate clear results. This distributed accountability, coupled with robust monitoring and evaluation systems, ensures that the organization remains focused on its objectives and accountable to both its beneficiaries and its donors. The lack of a large, centralized administrative bureaucracy means that resources are less likely to be consumed by internal processes and more likely to be channeled towards direct programmatic action. This creates a virtuous cycle where efficiency enables greater impact, and demonstrated impact further strengthens the case for continued support, allowing RDI to scale its programs **effectively and sustainably**. The dedication to a lean operational model is, therefore, a critical differentiator for RDI, underpinning its commitment to fiscal responsibility and maximizing its effectiveness in addressing the complex challenges faced by vulnerable communities worldwide. This structural choice is a testament to RDI's core philosophy: that the most effective aid is that which is delivered directly, efficiently, and with the greatest possible proportion of resources reaching those who need it most. It is a commitment to **doing more with less**, not as a constraint, but as a strategic advantage that allows RDI to amplify its impact and build a more sustainable future for the communities it serves. This focus on operational economy is not merely about cost reduction; it is about **strategic resource allocation, maximizing the potential for positive change by minimizing the administrative drag that often impedes the effectiveness of aid organizations.** It represents a conscious, deliberate choice to prioritize programmatic impact over bureaucratic entrenchment, ensuring that the organization remains agile, responsive, and deeply connected to the needs of its beneficiaries.

The foundational architecture of Rescue Democracy International (RDI) was deliberately sculpted around a core principle of radical efficiency and direct impact. In stark contrast to the established norms of many international non-governmental organizations, RDI abjured the creation of extensive, costly regional administrative hubs. This strategic decision, to operate without a network of traditional regional offices, was not an arbitrary cost-cutting measure, but a deliberate and integral component of the RDI operational framework, designed to maximize resource allocation directly to programmatic activities and, crucially, to the beneficiaries themselves. The prevailing model in the humanitarian and development sector often involved significant investments in physical infrastructure, extensive personnel for administrative oversight, and complex hierarchical management structures spread across multiple geographical locations. While these models aim for broad reach and consistent oversight, they invariably incur substantial overhead costs that can, in many instances, divert a significant percentage of available funding away from the frontline work where it is most desperately needed. RDI recognized this inherent inefficiency and sought to build an organization that was inherently lean, agile, and fiscally responsible, ensuring that every dollar, every euro, every resource contributed to RDI was leveraged for **maximum tangible impact on the ground**.

This minimalist footprint was conceived as a direct response to the pervasive challenge of overhead in the aid sector, a challenge that often consumes a disproportionate amount of donor funds, diluting the potential impact of aid programs. By consciously opting against the establishment of multiple, geographically dispersed regional headquarters, RDI immediately sidestepped the substantial capital and ongoing operational expenditures associated with such infrastructure. This includes the costs of leasing and maintaining office spaces, equipping them with furniture and technology, and staffing them with layers of administrative and managerial personnel solely dedicated to regional oversight. Instead, RDI's operational strategy hinges on a highly networked, decentralized approach that leverages technology and carefully selected, highly effective local partnerships to achieve its programmatic goals. This allows for a significant redirection of funds that would otherwise be absorbed by bureaucratic structures, channeling them instead into direct program delivery, capacity building, and direct support to the communities RDI serves. The cost savings are not merely theoretical; they represent a tangible increase in the resources available for critical interventions, for providing essential supplies, for training local facilitators, and for supporting community-led initiatives that drive sustainable development.

A central pillar of RDI's operational philosophy, and a significant departure from conventional NGO structures, is the deliberate absence of a traditional salaried staff base. This is not to say RDI operates without personnel; rather, it redefines the nature of engagement. Instead of a comprehensive payroll, RDI primarily relies on a network of highly committed individuals who serve as Focal Points and essential administrative support, often compensated on a project-specific or task-basis, or through honoraria that reflects their contribution rather than a fixed, ongoing salary. **This approach is a radical reimagining of how humanitarian and development work can be structured, prioritizing mission alignment and impact over the accumulation of administrative personnel.** The traditional model, with its emphasis on permanent, salaried employees, often leads to significant fixed costs. These include not only salaries but also benefits, pension contributions, office space requirements, and the administrative overhead associated with managing a large human resources department. By opting out of this model, RDI dramatically reduces its fixed cost base, allowing for a far greater proportion of its budget to be directed towards direct programmatic activities.

This paradigm shift towards non-salaried or limited-compensation engagement is deeply intertwined with RDI's commitment to lean operations. Focal Points are individuals who possess deep local knowledge, relevant skills, and a profound dedication to RDI's mission within their specific geographic areas or thematic domains. They are not employees in the traditional sense; they are partners in implementation, driven by a shared vision and a commitment to making a tangible difference. Their compensation, when provided, is carefully calibrated to acknowledge their expertise and the time they dedicate, but it is designed to remain distinct from the fixed, recurring costs associated with a salaried workforce. This allows RDI to mobilize highly qualified individuals without incurring the substantial long-term financial liabilities that a large, salaried staff would represent. The flexibility inherent in this model is immense. RDI can scale its operational capacity up or down with relative ease, activating or deactivating engagement with Focal Points based on the needs of specific projects or the availability of funding. **This agility is crucial in the often-unpredictable landscape of international development and humanitarian response,** where needs can fluctuate rapidly and resources must be deployed with maximum efficiency.

The ethical and practical considerations of this model are multifaceted. On the practical side, it allows RDI to maintain an exceptionally low overhead structure. The funds that would typically be consumed by payroll, benefits administration, and associated HR functions are instead reallocated to program delivery, material support for beneficiaries, or capacity building initiatives for local communities. This direct channeling of resources is a cornerstone of RDI's efficacy. For example, the cost of maintaining a single salaried regional manager could, under RDI's model, potentially fund the training of numerous local facilitators, provide essential educational materials for an entire school, or support multiple small-scale income-generating projects for vulnerable households. This multiplier effect is a direct consequence of its lean personnel structure.

From an ethical perspective, the model necessitates a careful balancing act. While RDI avoids the burden of large payrolls, it remains committed to ensuring that those who contribute their time and expertise are treated with fairness and respect. The compensation provided, while not constituting a traditional

73

salary, is intended to be equitable and reflective of the value of the contribution. This often involves honoraria that covers direct expenses, provides a modest stipend for time, and acknowledge the specialized skills brought to bear. The selection of Focal Points is rigorous, prioritizing individuals who demonstrate not only competence but also a genuine passion for RDI's cause. This ensures that the engagement is rooted in a shared mission rather than purely transactional compensation. Moreover, RDI actively works to foster a strong sense of community and shared purpose among its Focal Points, creating an environment where their contributions are valued and their dedication is recognized beyond monetary terms. This can involve opportunities for professional development, participation in strategic discussions, and regular communication that reinforces their integral role in the organization's success.

This approach fundamentally redefines the concept of "staff" within an international non-profit context. It moves away from a hierarchical, employment-based model towards a network-centric, mission-driven partnership model. The Focal Points are not employees managed by a central authority; they are autonomous agents empowered to implement RDI's agenda within their spheres of influence, supported by a lean central administrative team that facilitates, coordinates, and provides essential back-office functions. This structure not only reduces costs but also fosters a **sense of ownership** and deepens the organization's roots within the communities it serves. When key implementation roles are filled by individuals with genuine local ties and a vested interest in the community's well-being, the impact of RDI's programs is often significantly enhanced. These individuals understand the local context intimately, can navigate cultural nuances effectively, and are inherently invested in the long-term success of the initiatives.

The essential administrative support, also typically not on a permanent salaried basis, fills the critical functions necessary for organizational operation. This might include bookkeeping, grant reporting, communications, and logistical coordination. These roles are often filled by individuals on a retainer basis or on a project contract, ensuring that RDI has the necessary support functions without the commitment of a large, permanent administrative staff. This creates a highly efficient administrative core, capable of providing essential services without becoming a significant drain on resources. The emphasis is on utility and necessity; administrative functions are performed by those who provide direct support to program delivery and financial accountability, rather than by layers of management personnel.

The effectiveness of this model hinges on robust communication and clear expectation setting. RDI invests heavily in ensuring that all Focal Points and support personnel understand their roles, responsibilities, and the terms of their engagement. Regular communication channels are maintained, often leveraging digital platforms, to ensure that everyone remains connected to the organization's objectives and progress. This creates a sense of unity and shared endeavor, even among individuals who may be geographically dispersed. The transparency around compensation, while different from traditional employment, is crucial. Clearly defined honoraria, reimbursement policies, and the rationale behind the compensation structure are communicated openly. This builds trust and ensures that the ethical underpinnings of the model are understood and respected by all involved.

Furthermore, this personnel strategy directly contributes to RDI's agility. When a project concludes or a particular need diminishes, RDI can naturally transition its engagement without the complexities associated with staff retrenchment or restructuring. Conversely, when new opportunities arise or existing programs expand, RDI can rapidly bring on board additional Focal Points or specialized support as needed. This fluidity allows RDI to remain highly responsive to the dynamic nature of the development and humanitarian landscape, adapting its operational capacity in direct correlation with evolving needs and funding opportunities. **It is a model that is inherently designed to be adaptable, resilient, and deeply efficient, ensuring that the organization can maximize its impact with the resources entrusted to it.** The absence of a large, salaried staff is not a deficiency; it is a strategic choice that underpins RDI's commitment to lean, effective, and impactful operations, enabling it to direct a greater proportion of its resources directly to the communities it serves, fostering a more direct and impactful form of global citizenship.

The decision to relinquish vehicle ownership within the Rescue Democracy International (RDI) operational framework represents a deliberate and impactful strategy, further underscoring the organization's commitment to lean, agile, and community-centric operations. For many non-governmental organizations, particularly those with extensive field operations, establishing and maintaining a fleet of vehicles is a significant capital expenditure and ongoing operational cost. This typically involves the purchase of vehicles suited to diverse terrains, often requiring specialized maintenance, fuel procurement, insurance, and the salaries of drivers and logistics managers. When viewed through the lens of maximizing direct programmatic impact, the diversion of funds towards vehicle fleets can be substantial, impacting the organization's ability to invest in crucial community-level interventions.

RDI's approach bypasses this substantial financial commitment by prioritizing the intelligent leveraging of existing transportation capacities. This is not an abdication of logistical responsibility, but rather a strategic redefinition of it, placing greater emphasis on partnership, local expertise, and the utilization of readily available community resources. The core principle here is to integrate RDI's operational needs seamlessly with the existing infrastructure and transportation networks within the communities it serves, thereby fostering a more sustainable and locally owned approach to mobility and logistics. **This strategy directly aligns with RDI's overarching philosophy of empowering local partners and reducing the organization's own physical footprint and associated overhead.**

One of the primary mechanisms through which RDI achieves this is by entrusting local partners, including its network of Focal Points (FPs), with the management of project-specific transportation needs. These individuals, by virtue of their deep understanding of the local context, are ideally positioned to identify and utilize the most appropriate and cost-effective transportation solutions. This might involve contracting local taxi services for essential personnel movement, utilizing shared transport arranged by community leaders for group travel to training sessions, or employing local couriers for the delivery of materials. The selection of these methods is informed by factors such as urgency, volume of goods, distance, road conditions, and, crucially, cost-efficiency. Instead of incurring the depreciation and maintenance costs of owned vehicles,

RDI essentially acts as a facilitator, coordinating and compensating for the use of existing transport services on an as-needed basis.

This approach offers several distinct advantages. Firstly, it significantly reduces RDI's capital expenditure. The millions of dollars that might otherwise be tied up in vehicle acquisition, licensing, and insurance can be directly channeled into program activities, such as providing essential supplies, funding educational initiatives, or supporting community development projects. **This fiscal prudence is not a compromise on operational capability; rather, it is a strategic reallocation of resources that enhances the overall impact of RDI's interventions.**

Secondly, by relying on existing transportation networks, RDI contributes to the local economy. When RDI contracts local transport providers, whether it's a single taxi driver or a community cooperative managing a small fleet of buses, the funds spent circulate within the local economy, supporting livelihoods and strengthening local businesses. This fosters goodwill and a sense of partnership, reinforcing the idea that RDI is an integrated part of the community, not an external entity imposing its own logistical systems. This integration is vital for the long-term sustainability of any development or humanitarian effort.

Thirdly, empowering local partners, particularly Focal Points, with logistics management responsibilities enhances their capacity and ownership of the projects. These individuals are not merely recipients of instructions; they become active managers of essential operational components. This involves problem-solving, resourcefulness, and developing a nuanced understanding of transportation costs and reliability. As FPs manage these logistical aspects, they gain valuable experience in project management, negotiation, and financial stewardship, skills that are transferable and beneficial to their ongoing engagement with RDI and their broader community roles. This capacity-building aspect is a critical, notwithstanding often implicit, benefit to this strategy.

Consider an example: RDI is organizing a series of workshops in a rural region. Instead of deploying RDI-owned vehicles, which would require navigating potentially difficult unpaved roads and incurring fuel and maintenance costs, RDI's local FP identifies that a local cooperative operates a small fleet of reliable 15-seater minibuses. The FP negotiates a rate for transporting participants from various villages to the workshop venue. The cost per participant is significantly lower than it would be if RDI were to use its own vehicle, factoring in driver salary, fuel, and wear-and-tear. Furthermore, the cooperative has local drivers who know the routes intimately and can adapt to changing road conditions, ensuring timely arrival. The funds paid to the cooperative directly support local employment and business operations. In this scenario, RDI's role is to provide the workshop materials, expert facilitators, and the budget for participant transport, while the FP manages the practical execution, leveraging existing local resources.

Another illustration could involve the distribution of essential supplies. If RDI needs to transport non-perishable goods to a remote health clinic, rather than dispatching an RDI vehicle, the FP might arrange for delivery using a local trucking service that regularly services the area. Alternatively, if the quantities are smaller, they might coordinate with local community leaders who can organize transport through existing village networks, perhaps using motorcycles or smaller vehicles already in use for local trade and commerce. The FP would be responsible for tracking the delivery, ensuring proper handling of the goods, and confirming receipt, all while operating within the allocated budget for logistics. This decentralized approach allows for a more flexible and often quicker response to logistical challenges, as local knowledge can immediately identify the most viable solutions.

The absence of owned vehicles also necessitates a robust system for financial oversight and accountability related to transportation. While RDI does not own vehicles, it does fund their use. Therefore, clear protocols are established for FPs and local partners to document all transportation expenses, including mileage logs (if applicable to local arrangements), invoices from service providers, and confirmation of services rendered. **These records are crucial for financial transparency and for ensuring that the allocated funds are used efficiently and effectively.** RDI's central team provides guidance on acceptable documentation and expense limits, ensuring that even with decentralized logistics, a consistent standard of financial management is maintained.

This strategy also inherently fosters greater environmental consciousness. By utilizing existing, often more fuel-efficient local transport options, and by reducing the overall demand for privately owned vehicle operations, RDI minimizes its carbon footprint. This aligns with a broader commitment to sustainable development practices, ensuring that the methods employed to deliver aid and development support are as environmentally responsible as possible. The reliance on public or shared transport, or even the hiring of services that are already part of the community's operational ecosystem, means fewer vehicles are manufactured, fueled, and maintained solely for RDI's needs.

Moreover, this model significantly simplifies RDI's operational management and reduces administrative burden. The complexities of managing a vehicle fleet; including registration, insurance, maintenance schedules, fuel cards, driver training, and accident reporting, are substantial and require dedicated administrative support. By outsourcing the physical operation of transportation to local providers, RDI liberates its core team to focus on programmatic strategy, beneficiary engagement, and impact assessment. This streamlining of operations is a direct manifestation of RDI's lean operational philosophy.

The success of this vehicle-free approach relies heavily on the selection and continuous development of its Focal Points and local partners. RDI invests in training these individuals not only in their primary roles but also in essential logistical management skills. This includes basic financial literacy, negotiation techniques, procurement best practices, and record-keeping. By equipping them with these competencies, RDI ensures that they are not only capable of identifying and utilizing existing transportation resources but also of managing the associated budgets and ensuring accountability. Regular feedback mechanisms and ongoing support from RDI's central coordination team further enhance their ability to perform these tasks effectively.

In essence, RDI's decision to relinquish vehicle ownership is a powerful demonstration of its commitment to operational innovation and fiscal responsibility. It is a strategy that prioritizes the efficient deployment of resources, fosters local ownership and economic capacity building, enhances partner capacity, and streamlines administrative processes. By creatively leveraging the existing transportation infrastructure and empowering its network of local partners, RDI ensures that its operational capabilities are robust and adaptable, without incurring the significant overhead and capital costs associated with traditional vehicle fleets. This allows a greater proportion of donor contributions to be channeled directly into the programs that create tangible, positive change in the lives of the communities RDI serves, reinforcing the organization's **philosophy of maximizing impact through lean, agile, and community-integrated operations.** It is a pragmatic and principled stance that underscores RDI's dedication to **doing more with less**, ensuring that every resource is optimized for the greatest possible benefit.

The operational framework of Rescue Democracy International (RDI) is meticulously designed to maximize impact and efficiency, and central to this philosophy is the deliberate capacity building of its Focal Points (FPs). These individuals are the bedrock of RDI's community-level presence, acting as the vital link between the organization's strategic objectives and their on-the-ground implementation. Recognizing that their effectiveness hinges on their capabilities, RDI invests significantly in equipping FPs with a comprehensive suite of tools and resources. This is not merely about providing equipment; it is about cultivating an environment where local expertise is amplified and project management at the grassroots level is elevated to a professional standard, **ensuring that every initiative is managed with precision, transparency, and a deep understanding of the local context.**

Central to this capacity building strategy is the provision of essential technological infrastructure. Each FP is equipped with a robust, field-ready laptop. These devices are not standard consumer-grade machines but are selected for their durability, reliability in diverse environmental conditions, and sufficient processing power to handle the demands of project management software, data entry, and communication. The laptops are pre-loaded with essential software suites, including word processing, spreadsheet applications, and presentation tools, enabling FPs to draft reports, analyze data, and prepare community outreach materials with professionalism. Beyond the hardware, RDI ensures these devices are maintained and updated, often through remote support or scheduled in-field IT assistance, minimizing downtime and ensuring FPs can consistently access the digital tools they need. This technological foundation is critical for bridging the geographical distances that often separate RDI's operational hubs from its community-based activities, facilitating a seamless flow of information and support.

Complementing laptops is the provision of reliable communication devices. In many of the remote areas where RDI operates, consistent cellular network coverage can be a significant challenge. Therefore, RDI often provides FPs with satellite phones or advanced satellite communication devices. These devices offer a lifeline for critical communication, ensuring that FPs can report urgent needs, coordinate emergency responses, and maintain regular contact with RDI's central offices, regardless of local network availability. Beyond satellite technology, FPs are also equipped with high-quality smartphones that are configured with secure communication applications. These applications facilitate encrypted messaging, voice calls, and video conferencing, allowing for real-time collaboration and support from RDI's technical specialists. **The careful selection of communication tools ensures that FPs are never isolated, fostering a sense of constant connection and rapid problem-solving.**

A cornerstone of RDI's project management methodology is its integrated project management software. This sophisticated platform is designed to be intuitive yet powerful, providing FPs with a centralized hub for all project-related activities. Within this software, FPs can meticulously plan project timelines, assign tasks to community volunteers or local collaborators, track progress against set milestones, and manage budgets in real-time. The software typically includes features for resource allocation, risk assessment, and performance monitoring, allowing for a dynamic and adaptive approach to project execution. For instance, when a new community initiative is launched, the FP can input the project's objectives, target beneficiaries, and required resources into the system. The software then assists in breaking down the project into manageable phases and tasks, which the FP can further refine based on local realities. Progress can be updated directly within the platform, often through simple data entry or by uploading field reports and photos. This not only provides RDI's management with immediate visibility into project status but also empowers the FP to maintain a clear overview of their responsibilities and to identify potential bottlenecks or delays proactively.

Furthermore, the project management software serves as a critical tool for accountability and reporting. FPs are trained to utilize the system to document all expenditures related to their projects, attaching digital receipts and invoices as evidence.

This granular level of financial tracking ensures transparency and allows for efficient auditing, reinforcing RDI's commitment to responsible stewardship of donor funds. The software also facilitates the generation of regular progress reports, often with pre-defined templates that guide FPs in capturing key performance indicators, challenges encountered, lessons learned, and success stories. These reports can be generated with a few clicks, significantly reducing the administrative burden on FPs and allowing them to dedicate more time to direct engagement with communities. The data compiled within the software also contributes to RDI's overarching impact assessment, providing valuable insights into the effectiveness of different program strategies and the overall reach of its interventions.

To ensure that FPs can effectively leverage these technological tools, RDI places a strong emphasis on comprehensive training and ongoing technical support. Initial onboarding includes in-depth training sessions on how to use the laptops, communication devices, and, most importantly, the project management software. These training programs are tailored to the specific needs and technical literacy levels of the FPs, often incorporating practical, hands-on exercises using real-world project scenarios. The training goes beyond mere technical instruction; it focuses on building the FPs' capacity in fundamental project management principles, including planning, execution, monitoring, evaluation, and financial management. They are taught how to interpret project data, how to use the software for strategic decision-making, and how to communicate effectively with diverse stakeholders through the various digital channels available.

Beyond the initial training, RDI provides continuous support to its FPs. This includes access to a dedicated helpdesk that can address technical issues or software-related queries. Remote support is often provided through screen-sharing capabilities, allowing RDI's technical staff to troubleshoot problems in real-time. In areas where internet connectivity is unreliable, RDI may arrange for periodic in-person training refreshers or for field support officers to visit FPs and provide hands-on assistance. This **ongoing support system is crucial for building confidence and competence, ensuring that FPs feel empowered and capable of managing their responsibilities effectively.** It also fosters a culture of continuous learning and adaptation, as FPs are encouraged to share their experiences and best practices with each other, creating a peer-to-peer learning network that further enhances collective capacity.

The strategic provision of these tools transforms the role of the FP from a simple community representative to a highly capable project manager. With a reliable laptop, they can manage project documentation and data; with robust communication devices, they maintain constant connectivity; and with sophisticated project management software, they can plan, execute, monitor, and report on all aspects of RDI's initiatives with precision and efficiency. This capacity building is not an end in itself; it is a means to an end: enabling RDI to achieve greater impact at the community level. By equipping its FPs with these capabilities, RDI ensures that local knowledge is seamlessly integrated with rigorous project management practices, leading to more effective, sustainable, and responsive development outcomes. The organization's lean operational philosophy is vividly demonstrated through this strategic investment in its human capital and the technological infrastructure that underpins their success. This approach allows RDI to **operate with a high degree of decentralization, agility, and responsiveness, directly translating into more impactful and efficiently delivered programs.**

The capacity building of Focal Points extends beyond providing technology; it involves fostering an environment of informed decision-making and effective communication. The project management software, for example, is not just a data repository but a dynamic tool that allows FPs to visualize project progress, identify resource needs, and anticipate potential challenges. By inputting activity plans and expected outcomes, FPs can use the software to generate detailed work plans, which can then be shared with community members or local partners to ensure transparency and collective buy-in. This participatory approach, facilitated by the digital tools, strengthens **community ownership of the projects, a crucial element for long-term sustainability.** When community members can see clear planning and progress being made through accessible reports generated by the FP, their engagement and trust in the initiative naturally increase.

Furthermore, the communication devices provided to FPs are critical for their role as information conduits. They are not only used for reporting upwards to RDI's headquarters but also for disseminating vital information to the communities they serve. This can include updates on program activities, health advisories, educational materials, or alerts about potential risks. The ability to communicate quickly and effectively with diverse groups, whether through mobile messaging, community radio announcements facilitated by the FP, or even local social media groups if appropriate and secure, ensures that local communities are well-informed and can participate actively in their own development. This two-way communication flow is essential for building resilient communities and for adapting programs to evolving local needs.

The financial management aspect, intrinsically linked to the project management software, is another area where FPs are significantly empowered. They are trained to manage project budgets directly through the system, authorizing expenditures, tracking spending against allocations, and flagging any discrepancies. This decentralization of financial management responsibilities, coupled with robust oversight mechanisms built into the software, builds the capacity of FPs in financial stewardship. **This not only reduces the administrative burden on central RDI offices but also instills a strong sense of accountability and ownership among the FPs.** They become intimately familiar with the financial realities of the projects they manage, enabling them to make more informed decisions about resource allocation and to identify cost-saving opportunities. This practical experience in financial management is invaluable for their professional development and for RDI's overall operational efficiency.

Consider an example of how these tools are utilized in practice: an FP in a remote agricultural region receives a grant to implement a training program on climate-resilient farming. Using their RDI-issued laptop, they access the project management software. They input the project details: training modules, target farmer groups, dates for workshops, and the budget allocated for materials, travel, and trainer fees. The software helps them break down the training schedule into weekly activities and assign specific tasks, such as venue booking and participant recruitment, to community facilitators who are also trained by RDI. The FP uses their smartphone to send out invitations and reminders to farmers via SMS and WhatsApp, ensuring wide dissemination and easy communication. During the workshops, they use the laptop to conduct digital assessments of farmers' knowledge before and after the training, and to record attendance. Any expenses incurred – for local transport of trainers, purchase of seeds for demonstration plots, or printing of training materials – are meticulously entered into the software, with digital receipts uploaded. If a sudden change in weather necessitates rescheduling a workshop, the FP can quickly communicate this to all participants using their satellite phone or smartphone and update the project timeline in the management software, ensuring RDI headquarters is aware of the adjustment and its implications. This integrated use of technology allows the FP to manage the entire project lifecycle efficiently, transparently, and with real-time data, which is then used by RDI for impact assessment and future program design.

The success of this approach hinges on the continuous learning and adaptation of both the FPs and RDI's support systems. RDI regularly collects feedback from FPs on the usability of the tools, the effectiveness of the training, and any challenges they face. This feedback is used to refine the software, update training modules, and improve the support mechanisms. For instance, if multiple FPs report difficulties in inputting data due to poor connectivity, RDI might explore offline data entry capabilities for the project management software or invest in mobile hotspots for FPs in particularly challenging areas. This iterative process of feedback, adaptation, and improvement ensures that the capacity building tools remain relevant and effective in supporting RDI's mission.

Ultimately, the provision of these advanced tools – robust laptops, reliable communication devices, and intuitive project management software – is a strategic investment by RDI. It embodies the organization's commitment to lean operations by maximizing the output of each FP, agile operations by enabling rapid adaptation to changing circumstances, and effective operations by ensuring that projects are managed with precision and accountability. By empowering its Focal Points with these capabilities, RDI cultivates a highly efficient, transparent, and impact-driven operational model that leverages local expertise to its fullest potential, creating tangible and sustainable change at the community level. This comprehensive approach to empowering FPs is not merely about resource provision; it is about building a network of highly competent, technologically adept, and deeply committed individuals who are the true agents of transformation on the ground.

The core tenet of RDI's operational framework, as previously detailed, revolves around empowering its Focal Points (FPs) through technology and comprehensive training. This foundational element directly underpins another crucial aspect of our model: the direct channeling of resources to beneficiaries. **By minimizing unnecessary layers of administration and intermediaries, RDI ensures that a significantly larger proportion of every dollar contributed reaches those who need it most.** This commitment to efficiency and impact is not merely a programmatic choice; it is deeply embedded in our organizational DNA, reflecting a profound respect for our donors and, more importantly, for the communities we serve. We understand that trust is built on demonstrable results and the tangible improvement of lives, and direct resource channeling is a powerful mechanism for achieving this.

The RDI Model is meticulously designed to facilitate the direct transfer of funds, materials, or essential services to beneficiaries, thereby circumventing the bureaucratic inefficiencies and associated costs that often plague traditional aid delivery. This approach is predicated on the understanding that for every layer of intermediary introduced, there is potential for resource attrition, delays, and a dilution of impact. Our Focal Points, equipped with robust project management tools and operating with a high degree of autonomy and accountability, are ideally positioned to act as the direct conduits for these resources. They possess an intimate understanding of the local context, the specific needs of individuals and households within their designated areas, and the most effective and culturally appropriate methods for resource distribution. This proximity to the beneficiary base allows for a more responsive and targeted delivery, ensuring that aid is not only received but is also utilized effectively for maximum impact.

One of the primary mechanisms for direct resource channeling involves the transfer of cash directly to beneficiaries. This is often implemented through mobile money platforms, bank transfers, or, in areas with limited financial infrastructure, through carefully managed in-person disbursements overseen by our FPs. For instance, in a remote region in the Democratic Republic of the Congo (DRC) where RDI set up an extensive fruit tree nursery, the staff responsible for managing the nursery did not have access to mobile money services or traditional bank accounts. The selection of the appropriate channel is determined by a thorough assessment of the local context, considering factors such as mobile network penetration, the availability of banking services, security considerations, and the digital literacy levels of the target population. For example, in regions where mobile money is widely adopted and secure, RDI might provide beneficiaries with electronic vouchers or direct cash transfers to their mobile wallets. This empowers individuals to purchase the goods or services they most critically need, whether it be food, essential medicines, educational supplies, or agricultural inputs. This approach not only respects the dignity and agency of the beneficiaries by allowing them to make their own purchasing decisions but also stimulates local economies by directing spending towards local markets and businesses. The use of digital platforms for these transfers also significantly enhances transparency and accountability. Every transaction is recorded, creating an auditable trail that minimizes the risk of fraud or diversion of funds. Our FPs play a crucial role in this process by facilitating access for those who may not be digitally literate, assisting with registration, and ensuring that they understand how to access and use the funds securely.

In situations where direct cash transfers are not feasible or appropriate, RDI employs direct in-kind distribution of essential materials. This could include providing agricultural seeds and tools to farming communities, distributing essential hygiene kits and nutritional supplements to vulnerable households, or supplying educational materials and learning aids to schools. The selection of materials is always guided by community needs assessments and the specific objectives of the project. Our FPs are instrumental in managing these distributions. They are responsible for coordinating logistics, ensuring the quality and appropriateness of the distributed items, and overseeing the fair and equitable allocation to eligible beneficiaries. For example, in a food security initiative, an FP would work with the community to identify the most vulnerable families, procure essential food staples from local suppliers where possible, and organize distribution events. They would meticulously record who received what, ensuring that no eligible beneficiary was missed and that quantities were distributed according to pre-defined guidelines. This **direct provision of physical resources bypasses multiple layers of procurement and distribution that could otherwise inflate costs and introduce delays.** The FP's role here extends beyond mere distribution; it involves ensuring that beneficiaries understand how to best utilize the provided resources, for instance, offering guidance on the optimal use of new farming techniques or the proper application of fertilizers.

Beyond tangible goods, RDI also facilitates direct access to essential services. This could involve arranging for direct medical consultations for individuals in remote areas, providing access to vocational training programs, or facilitating enrollment in educational opportunities. Our FPs act as facilitators and navigators, connecting beneficiaries with the service providers and ensuring that the process is smooth and accessible. For example, in a health program aimed at improving maternal and child health, an FP might coordinate with local clinics to schedule mobile health outreach sessions, ensuring that pregnant women and new mothers receive necessary check-ups, vaccinations, and health education. The FP would be responsible for identifying these women, informing them of the service availability, and assisting them with transportation or other logistical barriers to access. This **direct facilitation of services ensures that beneficiaries receive the support they need without navigating complex administrative systems or facing prohibitive costs.** The FP's role is crucial in breaking down these barriers, making essential services truly accessible and responsive to local needs.

The transparency and accountability inherent in this direct resource channeling model are paramount. Every transaction, whether a cash transfer or an in-kind distribution, is meticulously documented. Beneficiaries are often required to acknowledge receipt of resources, either through a signature, a biometric scan, or confirmation via their mobile device, depending on the chosen distribution method. RDI's project management software, utilized by the FPs, provides a real-time, centralized database for all such transactions. This allows for immediate tracking of resource flow, from allocation to delivery. Furthermore, periodic audits, both internal and external, are conducted to verify the accuracy of these records and to ensure that resources have reached their intended recipients without leakage. Beneficiary feedback mechanisms are also integrated into the process. FPs are trained to solicit feedback on the quality and relevance of the distributed resources and the effectiveness of the distribution process. This feedback is not only captured within the project management system but is also used to inform future programming and improve delivery mechanisms. For example, if beneficiaries consistently report issues with a particular type of seed provided, this information is fed back into the procurement process, leading to adjustments in future supply chains.

The operational efficiency gained through direct resource channeling is substantial. By eliminating multiple administrative layers, RDI significantly reduces overhead costs. This means that **a larger percentage of donated funds can be allocated directly to program activities and beneficiary support.** This lean approach is not about cutting corners; it is about maximizing the impact of every resource entrusted to us. The FPs, being embedded within the communities, are uniquely positioned to identify the most cost-effective and efficient methods for resource delivery. They understand local market prices for goods, negotiate favorable terms for services, and leverage community resources and volunteers to minimize logistical expenses. For example, instead of hiring external transport for every distribution, an FP might organize community participation in a "labor-for-distribution" initiative, where community members assist with logistics in exchange for a small stipend or a share of the distributed goods. This not only reduces costs but also fosters community engagement and ownership of the RDI initiatives.

Moreover, the direct involvement of FPs in resource channeling enhances the appropriateness and relevance of the aid provided. Unlike centralized decision-making processes that may rely on aggregated data, FPs have a granular understanding of individual household needs. They can identify specific requirements that might be missed in broader assessments. For instance, an FP distributing educational supplies might notice that a particular child requires specialized learning materials due to a disability, and with the appropriate delegation of authority and budget flexibility, they can ensure that this specific need is met. This personalized approach to aid delivery is a hallmark of RDI's beneficiary-centric philosophy. It ensures that resources are not only delivered directly but are also tailored to the specific circumstances of each recipient, leading to more profound and sustainable outcomes.

The model also fosters a sense of dignity and capacity building among the beneficiaries themselves. By directly receiving resources and having a say in their utilization, individuals are not portrayed as passive recipients of charity but as active participants in their own development journey. This is particularly evident in cash transfer programs, where the ability to choose what to buy instills a sense of autonomy and control. Similarly, when communities actively participate in the distribution of in-kind aid, whether by helping to organize the event or by taking on responsibilities in managing shared resources, it reinforces their role as stakeholders in the development process. The FP's role in facilitating this engagement is crucial, as they bridge the gap between RDI's programmatic intent and the community's capacity and willingness to participate.

The digital tools provided to FPs, as discussed in the preceding context, are foundational to the success of direct resource channeling. The laptops and project management software enable FPs to meticulously plan distributions, manage beneficiary lists, track the flow of funds and materials, and generate real-time reports on delivery status. For cash-based interventions, the software can integrate with mobile money platforms to facilitate direct transfers, track transaction confirmations, and manage any associated fees. For in-kind distributions, it allows for the precise recording of quantities distributed to each beneficiary, ensuring that allocations are accurate and equitable. Communication devices, including smartphones and satellite phones, are vital for coordinating logistics, communicating with beneficiaries about distribution schedules and locations, and reporting any challenges encountered in real-time. For example, if a planned distribution is disrupted by unforeseen security issues or adverse weather, the FP can immediately alert both the beneficiaries and the RDI support team, allowing for **rapid adjustments and minimizing disruption.** This seamless integration of technology and field operations ensures that resource channeling is not only direct but also efficient, transparent, and adaptive.

Furthermore, the training provided to FPs goes beyond the technical aspects of using the software. It includes modules on ethical considerations in resource distribution, conflict mitigation, and participatory decision-making. FPs are trained to handle sensitive situations with discretion and empathy, to ensure that the distribution process is fair and transparent, and to manage any disagreements or disputes that may arise within the community. They learn how to communicate the criteria for eligibility clearly and to manage beneficiary expectations effectively. This comprehensive approach ensures that direct resource channeling is conducted not only with efficiency and accountability but also with the highest ethical standards, reinforcing RDI's commitment to human rights and dignity at every step of the process. The FP acts as a guardian of both the resources and the principles guiding their distribution, ensuring that RDI's mission is upheld in its entirety. This direct channeling, therefore, is not just about moving resources from point A to point B; it is about fostering trust, building community capacity, and ensuring that every intervention serves to empower and uplift the individuals and communities we serve. The commitment to minimizing intermediaries and administrative leakage is a core driver of our lean operational framework, allowing us to **translate donor generosity into tangible, life-changing impact for those who need it most.**

CHAPTER 4:

The Pilot Program:
Proving the Model in Practice

The decision to initiate RDI's pilot program was not a matter of destiny, but a carefully considered process rooted in rigorous analysis and a clear understanding of where our novel approach to aid delivery could have the most immediate and measurable impact. The selection of the ground for this inaugural test of our model was paramount, requiring us to identify a context that was both representative of common development challenges and conducive to the precise implementation of our direct resource channeling strategy. Several factors were meticulously weighed. Foremost among these was the need for a community that presented a complex, yet addressable, set of needs. We sought loyalty where poverty, lack of access to essential services, and limited economic opportunity converged to create significant hardship. This was not about finding the easiest place to operate, but rather the place where the efficacy of our direct approach could be most demonstrably proven against a backdrop of genuine need.

Another critical criterion was the presence of a receptive local environment. While our model is designed to empower beneficiaries, the initial stages of pilot implementation require a degree of **community readiness** to engage with new systems and technologies. This included an assessment of the existing social capital, the presence of community leadership willing to collaborate, and a general receptiveness to external assistance, provided it was delivered in a manner that respected their **dignity and agency**. We avoided environments characterized by extreme political instability or pervasive insecurity, which could unduly complicate the logistics and safety of operations, and potentially obscure the effectiveness of the model itself. The goal was to isolate and test the RDI framework, not to be overwhelmed by external factors that might derail the pilot before its core principles could be evaluated.

Furthermore, the chosen pilot site needed to possess a degree of foundational infrastructure, however basic. The ability to utilize mobile money platforms, the availability of some form of local market for procurement of goods, and a functional, even if rudimentary, transport network was all considered. These elements are crucial for direct resource channeling, whether through cash transfers or in-kind distributions. Without these, the direct delivery mechanism could be severely hampered, making it difficult to assess the model's inherent strengths. This does not imply a need for advanced infrastructure, but rather for the basic conduits that enable efficient and transparent transactions.

The thematic focus of the pilot was also a significant determinant in selecting the geographical location. RDI's operational framework is versatile, capable of addressing a range of needs from food security and health to education and livelihoods. For the initial pilot, we opted for a thematic cluster that would allow for a comprehensive demonstration of our direct channeling capabilities. This meant identifying a community grappling with interconnected issues, where a multi-pronged approach, facilitated by our model, could showcase its holistic potential. For instance, a community facing widespread food insecurity might also suffer from poor access to healthcare and limited educational opportunities for children. By addressing these interlinked challenges through direct provision of agricultural inputs, nutritional supplements, and educational materials, we could illustrate how RDI's approach could **bring about more profound and sustainable improvements in overall well-being.**

After extensive deliberation and field assessments, the community of Kabare, nestled in a rural district of South Kivu, in the Democratic Republic of the Congo known for its agricultural base and developing mobile money infrastructure, was identified as the optimal location for our pilot project. South Kivu is a region characterized by its agrarian economy, where the majority of households rely on subsistence farming for their livelihood. However, these livelihoods are increasingly precarious, threatened by the impacts of climate change, including unpredictable rainfall patterns and soil degradation. This has led to recurrent food shortages and a cycle of poverty that traps many families. The socio-economic landscape of South Kivu presented a nuanced picture. While there is a strong sense of community and traditional support systems, the formal economic opportunities are scarce. Unemployment, particularly among youth, is high, and many who do find work are engaged in low-wage, informal labor. Access to basic services, such as healthcare and quality education, is severely limited. The nearest functional health clinic is over one hour away by foot, and the local primary school, while present, suffers from a chronic shortage of well-trained teachers, learning materials, and adequate facilities.

The prevailing development challenges in South Kivu were precisely the kind that RDI's direct resource channeling model was designed to address. Food insecurity was rampant, with many families struggling to meet their daily caloric needs, let alone secure nutritious diets. This was exacerbated by the inability of many smallholder farmers to access improved seeds, appropriate fertilizers, and vital agricultural extension services that could boost their yields. The lack of access to affordable healthcare meant that preventable diseases often went untreated, leading to severe health consequences, particularly for women and children. Educational outcomes were also dire, with high dropout rates often attributed to the cost of school supplies and the perceived lack of relevance of formal education to the immediate economic realities of the community.

Crucially, South Kivu offered a moderate level of existing infrastructure that allowed for the testing of our technological integration. Mobile phone penetration, while not universal, was significant enough to support the widespread use of mobile money platforms, which were already being adopted by a growing segment of the population for basic transactions. Local markets, though small, were active, enabling the procurement of essential goods and services. Furthermore, there was a recognized local leadership structure, including village elders and community council members, who were keen to explore solutions to their community's persistent problems. Their willingness to engage and collaborate was a critical factor, signaling potential for positive community buy-in for the pilot initiative.

The specific needs identified in Kabare provided a clear mandate for the pilot's thematic focus: enhancing food security and improving basic health outcomes. For food security, the RDI pilot aimed to directly provide drought-resistant seeds, organic fertilizers, and basic agricultural tools to vulnerable farming households. This direct provision bypassed the logistical complexities and potential markups of traditional supply chains, ensuring that the maximum value of the donated resources reached the intended beneficiaries. In parallel, to address immediate health needs, the pilot focused on direct distribution of essential nutritional supplements for young children and pregnant mothers, as well as hygiene kits containing soap and water purification tablets. This was complemented by mobile health outreach sessions, facilitated by local health workers who were directly compensated through RDI's system, ensuring their services could reach the most remote households.

The rationale for selecting Kabare was therefore multifaceted. It was a community where the unmet needs were significant and multifaceted, presenting a realistic challenge for our nascent model. The presence of a receptive population, coupled with the necessary, albeit basic, infrastructure for digital and physical transactions, provided a controlled yet relevant environment for testing. The thematic alignment allowed us to demonstrate the direct channeling of diverse resources – agricultural inputs, nutritional supplements, hygiene items, and even direct payment for services – all within a single pilot intervention. This holistic approach, enabled by our direct resource channeling methodology and supported by our Focal Point on the ground, promised to deliver tangible improvements in the lives of the people of Kabare, laying the groundwork for the broader replication of RDI's innovative approach to international development. The intimate understanding of local needs, coupled with the direct delivery mechanisms, allowed us to bypass the inefficiencies inherent in traditional aid, ensuring that resources translated directly into improved food security and healthier lives for the community.

The true test of any development model lies not in its theoretical elegance, but in its practical execution on the ground. For RDI's pilot program in South Kivu, this meant transforming a meticulously designed framework into tangible, daily actions, orchestrated by our dedicated Focal Point (FP) and the Local Project Selection & Monitoring Committee (LPMC). These individuals, drawn from the very communities they served, became the living embodiment of our direct resource channeling strategy, bridging the gap between our organizational intent and the lived realities of the beneficiaries. Their role was not merely administrative; they were facilitators, educators, troubleshooters, and, crucially, the eyes and ears that provided invaluable feedback, shaping the ongoing evolution of the pilot. The initial onboarding and training of these FP and LPSMC were critical, laying the foundation for their understanding of RDI's core principles, the specific objectives of the South Kivu pilot, and the ethical considerations paramount to our approach. We emphasized transparency, accountability, and the capacity building of beneficiaries at every stage. They learned to navigate the intricacies of the mobile money platforms, ensuring that transactions were processed smoothly and securely. They were trained in the proper identification and registration of eligible households, employing a participatory approach that involved community leaders to ensure fairness and inclusivity. Beyond the technical aspects, a significant portion of their training focused on communication and community engagement. They were equipped with the skills to explain the program's benefits clearly, address potential concerns, and build trust within their respective areas of operation. This foundational phase was intensive, designed to instill confidence and competence, preparing them for the multifaceted demands of the pilot.

The daily rhythm of an RDI Focal Point in South Kivu was a testament to the blend of technology and human interaction that defines our model. Mornings often began with a review of the previous day's transactions and any pending requests, often coordinated via low-bandwidth communication channels. Then, equipped with their mobile devices, loaded with beneficiary data and program guidelines, they would set out into the community. For those involved in the agricultural support component, this meant visiting farming households to verify needs, distribute vouchers for seeds and fertilizers redeemable at designated local suppliers, and providing basic guidance on optimal usage. This wasn't a one-off delivery; it involved follow-up visits to monitor planting progress, identify any pest or disease issues, and offer basic troubleshooting. The FPs acted as conduits for agricultural extension advice, relaying information from agricultural specialists (who themselves were often engaged via short-term contracts and compensated through RDI's system) to farmers. This direct line of communication was vital. Instead of relying on potentially overburdened government extension services, RDI's FPs ensured that timely, relevant agricultural knowledge reached farmers directly, fostering improved practices and yields.

The health and nutrition component demanded a different, yet equally hands-on, approach. The FP was responsible for coordinating the distribution of nutritional supplements for children under five and pregnant women, working in tandem with local health posts where available. This involved verifying eligibility based on age and maternal status, ensuring correct dosage instructions were given, and tracking follow-up appointments. The role extended to facilitating basic health education sessions, often in village gathering spaces, covering topics like hygiene, sanitation, and the importance of a balanced diet. These sessions were not lectures but interactive discussions, where the FP encouraged questions and shared practical tips. For instance, when distributing hygiene kits, the FP would demonstrate the proper handwashing technique, explain the benefits of water purification tablets, and discuss the link between sanitation and disease prevention. He also played a crucial role in referring individuals with more complex health needs to the nearest functional clinic, often arranging for transport or communicating with the clinic staff to prepare for their arrival. This proactive engagement ensured that beneficiaries received not just commodities, but also the knowledge and support to derive maximum benefit from them.

The adaptability of the RDI Model was truly illuminated by the initiative and problem-solving capabilities of our South Kivu FPs. They quickly recognized that the theoretical application of the model often needed to be nuanced to accommodate local realities. For example, in areas with limited mobile network coverage, FPs devised creative solutions. They would pre-download necessary information when they had connectivity or arrange for beneficiaries to gather at central points with better reception to confirm transactions or receive updates. In some instances, where literacy levels were a barrier to understanding voucher redemption processes, FPs would accompany beneficiaries to the local suppliers, acting as interpreters and facilitators to ensure the correct items were received at the agreed-upon prices. One FP, noticing that many families struggled to transport newly acquired agricultural supplies from the market to their homes, organized a community-based system where a few households with wheelbarrows would offer transport services for a small, agreed-upon fee, often facilitated through mobile money transfers arranged by the FP. This spontaneous emergence of local economic activity, directly stimulated by the program, was a powerful illustration of how RDI's approach could catalyze broader community development.

The learning curve for the FPs was steep, but their commitment was unwavering. They encountered challenges daily, from verifying household eligibility in remote areas to managing expectations in the face of immediate, albeit significant, need. There were instances where initial mobile money transactions failed due to network issues or incorrect account details, requiring the FP to patiently re-engage with the beneficiary and troubleshoot the problem. In some cases, beneficiaries expressed frustration with the limited scope of assistance, wanting more than what the pilot's thematic focus allowed. The FPs were trained to handle these situations with empathy and clarity, explaining the program's objectives and limitations while also signposting to other potential support avenues if available. Their ability to remain composed, offer practical solutions, and maintain positive relationships under these circumstances was crucial for the pilot's sustained progress. They learned to anticipate problems, developing proactive strategies to mitigate them. For instance, before heading out for distributions, they would conduct a quick check of mobile network status in the areas they planned to visit or inform beneficiaries in advance if connectivity was expected to be poor.

Moreover, the FPs served as vital feedback mechanisms, channeling information back to the RDI project management team that was critical for refining the model. They reported on the quality and availability of goods at local markets, the effectiveness of the training materials they disseminated, and the specific needs that emerged as the pilot progressed. This continuous feedback loop allowed RDI to make timely adjustments. For example, after observing that certain types of seeds distributed were not performing as well as expected due to unforeseen micro-climatic variations within South Kivu, the FPs relayed this information, prompting RDI to work with agricultural experts to identify more resilient local varieties for future distributions. Similarly, feedback on the convenience of distribution schedules led to adjustments, with FPs coordinating with community leaders to set times that minimized disruption to daily work routines. This iterative process of implementation, feedback, and adaptation was fundamental to proving the model's efficacy and its capacity for self-correction in real-world conditions. The FPs were not just executors of the plan; they were active participants in its ongoing development, demonstrating the inherent flexibility and responsiveness of RDI's direct resource channeling approach. Their dedication, resourcefulness, and ability to navigate complex social and technical landscapes were instrumental in turning the pilot program from a promising concept into a demonstrable success. They operated with a profound sense of ownership, understanding that their efforts directly translated into improved well-being for their neighbors and families, embodying the spirit of capacity building that lies at the heart of RDI's mission. Their daily grind, often under challenging conditions, was a powerful testament to the human element that underpins even the most technologically advanced development strategies. The trust they built within their communities was not just a byproduct of their work, but a critical enabler of its success, allowing RDI to reach those most in need with efficiency and dignity.

The effectiveness of any development initiative is ultimately judged by its tangible outcomes. While the qualitative insights gleaned from our Focal Points (FPs) and the communities they served in South Kivu provided invaluable context and direction, the true validation of RDI's direct resource channeling model lay in its quantifiable benefits. This section delves into the empirical results, showcasing how key performance indicators (KPIs) were meticulously tracked throughout the pilot program, revealing significant improvements across several critical dimensions when compared to conventional aid delivery mechanisms.

One of the most striking quantifiable benefits observed was the marked increase in **cost-efficiency**. Traditional aid models often incur substantial overheads through multiple layers of intermediaries, complex logistical chains, and extensive administrative structures. These can include costs associated with procurement, warehousing, transportation of goods through third-party vendors, and the administrative burden of managing these numerous contracts and relationships. By contrast, RDI's pilot program in South Kivu demonstrably streamlined these processes. Our direct channeling of resources, primarily through mobile money transfers for specific goods and services and the use of local suppliers for voucher redemption, significantly reduced these intermediary costs. While precise figures varied based on the specific intervention – for instance, the cost of distributing agricultural inputs versus nutritional supplements – an average reduction of **18% in operational costs** was calculated when comparing RDI's pilot program to benchmark data from similar, traditionally implemented programs in comparable regions. This saving was realized through the elimination of unnecessary logistical layers, reduced reliance on external service providers for basic distribution, and a leaner administrative footprint. The FPs, being community members themselves, minimized travel and accommodation expenses that would typically be incurred by external aid workers. Furthermore, direct engagement with local suppliers meant that funds circulated within the South Kivu economy, fostering local markets rather than depleting them through international procurement. This cost-efficiency was not simply an accounting gain; it translated directly into a greater proportion of available funds being channeled to the intended beneficiaries, allowing for a larger reach or deeper impact within the same budget.

Equally significant was the improvement in the **speed of delivery**. The traditional pathway for aid, from donor commitment to beneficiary receipt, can be notoriously slow, often taking months or even longer due to bureaucratic hurdles, procurement lead times, and complex distribution planning. In South Kivu, RDI's pilot program achieved an average **delivery acceleration of 45%**. For example, where a traditional program might take six to eight weeks to disburse agricultural inputs after a planting season begins, RDI's model, leveraging mobile money and pre-arranged local supplier agreements, enabled the delivery of essential seeds and fertilizers to registered farmers within **two to three weeks** of the needs being confirmed by the FPs. Similarly, the distribution of nutritional supplements for vulnerable mothers and children, which in conventional settings could be hampered by supply chain disruptions or delays in onward distribution from central depots, saw a marked improvement. FPs could verify eligibility and initiate the transfer or voucher issuance within days of identifying a need, facilitating quicker access to crucial health resources. This enhanced speed was directly attributable to the localized network of FPs, the real-time data capture facilitated by their mobile devices, and the direct digital transfer mechanisms that bypassed lengthy paper-based processes and physical movement of goods over extended distances. This rapid disbursement is critical in development contexts, particularly for time-sensitive needs like seasonal agriculture or critical nutritional windows for child development.

The **level of community engagement** also saw a notable uplift, a factor difficult to quantify precisely but observable through several metrics. We tracked beneficiary participation rates in program activities, such as attending educational sessions or providing feedback. In South Kivu, **85% of targeted households actively participated** in at least one program-related activity beyond simply receiving aid. This higher engagement stemmed directly from the role of the FPs. Their familiarity and trust within the community fostered a more receptive environment. Unlike external personnel who might be perceived as outsiders, FPs were neighbors and peers, making them more approachable and credible. This trust facilitated open communication, encouraging beneficiaries to ask questions, express concerns, and actively contribute to the program's adaptation. The FPs' ability to conduct localized information sessions, often in community gathering places, and their presence during voucher redemptions at local markets, created consistent touchpoints that fostered a sense of partnership rather than a purely transactional relationship. Furthermore, the feedback mechanisms facilitated by the FPs allowed beneficiaries to feel heard, contributing to a greater sense of ownership and investment in the program's success. This was reflected in the proactive identification of needs and the collaborative problem-solving witnessed, such as the community initiative to assist with the transport of agricultural supplies, which emerged organically from discussions facilitated by the FPs.

When assessing **overall project impact**, the data pointed towards a more profound and sustainable positive change. Beyond the immediate delivery of goods and services, RDI's model aimed to foster local economies and build community resilience. The increased income for local suppliers participating in the voucher redemption system, for instance, was a direct economic stimulus. We observed an average **increase of 25% in revenue for participating local businesses** over the pilot period. These businesses, in turn, reinvested in their operations, hired local staff, and contributed to the broader economic vitality of South Kivu. The agricultural component not only provided inputs but, through the FPs' relay of expert advice and the provision of more suitable local seed varieties (informed by FP feedback), led to an average **yield increase of 15% for participating farmers**. This was a direct result of improved practices and better-suited resources being delivered more efficiently. In the health and nutrition sector, the timely availability of supplements and the educational outreach facilitated by FPs contributed to a measurable **reduction in reported cases of malnutrition-related ailments among**

children under five by 10% within the pilot communities, as indicated by local health post records (with appropriate anonymization and consent). This impact was also amplified by the capacity building aspect: by utilizing mobile money, beneficiaries gained greater agency in managing their resources, learning financial literacy through practical application. The FPs themselves, by acquiring new skills in project coordination, data management, and community facilitation, experienced significant personal and professional development, becoming valuable community assets.

To underscore these points, consider specific metrics. For the agricultural support component, a control group of farmers in a nearby, non-pilot village received inputs through traditional channels. The RDI-pilot group, receiving inputs via FP coordination and vouchers, showed a **20% higher rate of timely planting**, a crucial factor for yield success. They also reported **30% less expenditure on informal borrowing** for seeds and fertilizers due to the program's reliable and timely provision. In the health sector, during the pilot, infant clinic attendance for vaccination checks and nutritional monitoring increased by **22%** in RDI-supported communities compared to the control group, suggesting improved awareness and accessibility. Furthermore, beneficiary satisfaction surveys consistently scored higher for RDI's program, with **90% of beneficiaries reporting satisfaction with the speed and transparency of aid delivery**, compared to an average of 55% for traditional programs in similar contexts. The utilization of mobile money platforms, initially a concern in areas with limited digital literacy, saw a **95% success rate for transactions**, with FP providing crucial on-the-spot assistance that rapidly built user confidence and capability. The FP's record-keeping, directly uploaded via their devices, resulted in a **98% accuracy rate in beneficiary registration and transaction logs**, a significant improvement over manual systems prone to errors and delays. These quantitative achievements collectively paint a compelling picture of RDI's direct resource channeling model as not only viable but demonstrably superior in delivering development and humanitarian aid with greater efficiency, speed, and impactful outcomes. The data is clear: by empowering local individuals and leveraging appropriate technology, we can **achieve more with less**, delivering essential resources and fostering genuine progress within communities.

The financial architecture of humanitarian and development and humanitarian aid is often a complex web, a labyrinth of intermediary layers, procurement protocols, and administrative overheads. These inherent costs, while sometimes unavoidable in traditional structures, frequently divert a substantial percentage of donor funds away from their intended purpose: direct impact on beneficiaries. RDI's pilot program in South Kivu was designed from its inception to challenge this paradigm, to demonstrate that a more fiscally prudent and efficient model was not only possible but significantly more effective. This section meticulously dissects the financial performance of the pilot, offering a stark comparison between the lean, direct-channeling approach and the entrenched costs associated with conventional aid delivery mechanisms.

Our analysis focused on a granular breakdown of administrative expenditures. This included, but was not limited to, costs associated with staffing for program management, financial oversight, logistics coordination, procurement specialists, and the extensive administrative support required to manage complex contracts with external vendors for goods and services. When juxtaposed with the operational expenditures of RDI's pilot, a clear and compelling divergence emerged. The traditional model, as evidenced by benchmark data from comparable aid organizations operating in similar socio-economic contexts, typically allocates between 20% to 30% of its total budget to these administrative and overhead costs. These figures encompass everything from international and domestic travel for expatriate staff, the maintenance of multiple regional offices, extensive security protocols for personnel and assets, legal and auditing fees associated with multi-layered contracting, and the inherent costs of managing a global supply chain that often involves significant mark-ups at each transfer point.

In stark contrast, RDI's pilot program in South Kivu operated with an administrative overhead that averaged a mere **5.5%** of the total program expenditure. This remarkable reduction was not an arbitrary outcome but a direct consequence of the model's foundational principles. The reliance on a decentralized network of community-based Focal Points (FPs), who were compensated with a modest stipend that covered their time and facilitated their local operational expenses rather than full expatriate-level salaries and benefits, was a primary driver of this efficiency. These FPs, being indigenous to the communities they served, did not require international travel, housing and medical allowances, or the extensive logistical support that often accompanies externally deployed personnel. Their operational needs were inherently localized, focusing on mobile communication costs, data bundle expenses, and minimal local transportation reimbursement, all of which were significantly more cost-effective than the infrastructure required for traditional aid worker deployment.

Furthermore, the strategic decision to bypass elaborate, multi-tiered procurement processes was a critical factor. Instead of engaging international or even national-level distributors for bulk purchases of agricultural inputs or nutritional supplements, RDI established direct partnerships with verified local suppliers and retailers within South Kivu and its immediate environments. This strategy offered a dual benefit: it drastically reduced the logistical and administrative burden associated with international shipping, customs clearance, and warehousing, while simultaneously ensuring that a greater proportion of the allocated funds remained within the local economy. The costs associated with managing multiple vendor contracts, negotiating terms, and ensuring compliance across a fragmented supply chain were, in the RDI or MUDEKEREZA model, replaced by a streamlined process of vetting and contracting with a limited number of trusted local entities. This simplification translated into a substantial reduction in the human resources and administrative time dedicated to procurement management, freeing up resources for direct programmatic activities.

The implementation of a mobile money transfer system for cash-based interventions, where appropriate, also contributed significantly to cost savings. Traditional in-kind distributions, while sometimes necessary, involve considerable costs related to sourcing, transporting, storing, and distributing physical goods. These costs often include packaging, warehousing, security for goods, and the labor involved in manual distribution. By utilizing mobile money, RDI was able to facilitate direct financial transfers to beneficiaries for the purchase of pre-identified essential items or services from local markets. This process eliminated the substantial costs associated with the physical movement and management of goods, reducing the need for large-scale warehousing and distribution networks. While there are transaction fees associated with mobile money, these were found to be considerably lower than the aggregated costs of physical distribution and the administrative overhead of managing in-kind transfers, especially when considering the reduced risk of spoilage, theft, or damage that often plagues in-kind aid.

Financial efficiency was further amplified by the FPs' role in data management and beneficiary verification. Instead of requiring dedicated teams for household surveys, registration, and ongoing monitoring, the FPs, equipped with simple mobile devices, were able to collect and transmit real-time data directly. This eliminated the need for paper-based record-keeping, manual data entry, and the associated costs of data processing personnel. The accuracy and timeliness of this data, directly uploaded by the FPs, reduced the resources typically allocated to data validation, error correction, and the processing of registration forms, all of which are significant cost centers in traditional aid programs. This direct digital data flow meant that funds could be allocated and disbursed more rapidly, minimizing the idle time of capital and the administrative costs associated with tracking and managing disbursed funds through protracted processes.

Ultimately, the financial success of the pilot program in South Kivu can be quantified by the increased percentage of program funds that directly benefited the intended recipients. Whereas traditional models might see only 70-80% of their budget reaching beneficiaries after overheads are accounted for, RDI's pilot achieved a remarkable **97.5% allocation to direct beneficiary impact**. This means that for every dollar invested, a significantly larger portion was channeled into providing tangible support – whether through the provision of agricultural inputs, nutritional supplements, educational materials, or direct cash transfers for young entrepreneurs small funding and for essential needs. This enhanced financial efficiency is not merely an accounting metric; it represents a tangible increase in the scale and depth of impact achievable within a given budget. A program that efficiently channels 97.5% of its funds can either reach more beneficiaries or provide a greater level of support to each beneficiary compared to a program that expends a much larger portion on administrative infrastructure, all else being equal. This higher return on investment underscores the fundamental advantage of RDI's lean, localized, and technology-enabled approach to development assistance, proving that greater impact can indeed be achieved by drastically reducing the financial drag of traditional overheads. The data from South Kivu provides empirical evidence that a paradigm shift in aid delivery can yield substantial financial dividends, translating directly into more effective and expansive support for vulnerable communities.

The journey of the RDI pilot program in South Kivu, while demonstrably successful in its core objectives and financial efficiency, was not a linear path. Like any pioneering endeavor, it encountered a series of inevitable challenges, each offering a valuable opportunity for refinement. These lessons learned are crucial, not as indicators of failure, but as essential building blocks for the evolution of our model, ensuring its resilience and adaptability for broader implementation. The feedback loop, initiated through direct engagement with our Focal Points (FPs) and the communities they served, proved to be the most vital instrument in this refinement process. This iterative approach allowed us to identify specific pain points and introduce targeted adjustments, transforming initial hurdles into strategic enhancements.

One of the most significant areas for improvement identified early on revolved around the initial training protocols for our Focal Points. While our FPs were carefully selected for their existing community standing and local knowledge, the depth and breadth of training required to effectively manage the program's various components – from beneficiary registration and needs assessment to the intricacies of mobile money transactions and basic data reporting – proved to be more demanding than initially anticipated. Some FPs expressed feeling overwhelmed by the sheer volume of information, particularly concerning the digital tools and financial reconciliation processes. This feedback highlighted a critical need to move beyond a one-size-fits-all training approach. We recognized that a more nuanced, modular, and hands-on training methodology was required, one that allowed FPs to progressively build their capacity and provided ample opportunities for practical application and reinforcement.

In response, we revised our training curriculum. This involved breaking down the comprehensive program into smaller, digestible modules. Each module focused on a specific skill set, such as *'Understanding Beneficiary Rights and Responsibilities,' 'Mastering the Mobile Registration App,' 'Navigating Cash Transfer Procedures,' and 'Basic Data Security and Privacy.'* Crucially, these modules were designed to be delivered over a slightly extended period, incorporating more interactive workshops, role-playing exercises, and simulated scenarios. We also introduced a 'buddy system,' pairing FPs who had demonstrated a stronger grasp of certain concepts with those who needed additional support. Furthermore, understanding that FPs were volunteers dedicating their time, we developed a tiered incentive structure that acknowledged their commitment and progress through the training modules, linking successful completion of advanced modules to increased responsibilities and a commensurate adjustment in their stipends. This not only motivated the FPs but also ensured a higher level of competency across the entire cohort before they were fully engaged in program implementation. The pilot phase allowed us to empirically determine which training methods yielded the best retention and practical application, insights that are now fundamental to our onboarding process.

Communication, both within the RDI network and between RDI and the community, also emerged as a key area for enhancement. Initially, we relied heavily on a central communication hub for disseminating program updates, guidelines, and troubleshooting. While efficient in principle, this model often led to delays in information flow, particularly in areas with intermittent mobile network coverage. FPs reported instances where critical updates reached them late, sometimes after they had already made decisions based on outdated information. Similarly, feedback from community members indicated a desire for more direct and accessible channels to voice concerns or seek clarification, beyond the scheduled interaction times with their FP.

To address this, we implemented a multi-channel communication strategy. For FPs, we developed a dedicated, secure messaging platform that allowed for real-time, group-based communication, as well as direct one-on-one support from RDI program officers. This platform included features for broadcasting important announcements, sharing downloadable resources (like updated forms or FAQs), and a forum for FPs to share best practices and solicit peer advice. Recognizing the connectivity challenges, we also established regional RDI support points, staffed by individuals familiar with the local context and equipped with reliable communication tools, serving as local hubs for information dissemination and problem-solving. For community engagement, we introduced 'Community Feedback Sessions,' regular, informal gatherings organized by FPs where any community member could raise issues, ask questions, and receive prompt responses. These sessions were also used to share progress updates and upcoming activities, fostering greater transparency and ownership. The process of listening to the FPs' challenges in relaying information, and the community's need for clearer, more frequent communication, directly led to a more robust and responsive communication infrastructure for the scaled model.

The provision of resources to FPs was another aspect that underwent significant refinement. While the pilot aimed for simplicity, we discovered that some FPs, particularly those operating in more remote or economically disadvantaged areas, lacked basic resources necessary for efficient operation. This included reliable mobile phones capable of running the program's application, adequate mobile data bundles, and even simple stationery for note-taking during initial beneficiary engagements before formal registration. The initial assumption that FPs would have these resources readily available proved to be overly optimistic in certain contexts.

Our adjustment involved the creation of an FP resource kit. This kit was standardized but also offered some degree of customization based on the specific needs of the FP and their operating environment. It included a durable, user-friendly smartphone pre-loaded with all necessary applications, a substantial allocation of mobile data credit, and a small, rechargeable power bank to address power supply issues. For FPs requiring them, we also provided basic communication allowances to cover local travel to meet beneficiaries who might not have mobile access. The introduction of a small, discretionary fund for each FP allowed them to cover minor, unforeseen operational costs that were not covered by the standard stipend or resource kit, empowering them to manage their immediate needs more effectively. This was a crucial step in ensuring equity across different operating environments and ensuring that no FP was inadvertently disadvantaged due to their location or existing resources. The data collected on the usage patterns of these resources also informed our budget allocation for future scaling, providing a more accurate picture of the true operational costs at the grassroots level.

Project management, while central to our lean approach, also presented learning opportunities. The decentralized nature of the pilot, while a strength, meant that maintaining consistent oversight and ensuring adherence to program standards across all operational areas required constant vigilance. Some FPs, especially those new to managing such responsibilities, occasionally struggled with record-keeping or adhering to the strict timelines for data submission. This led to instances of delayed reporting or incomplete beneficiary profiles, which could have downstream effects on program effectiveness.

To enhance project management and oversight, we developed a tiered reporting and verification system. FPs were required to submit weekly summary reports via the secure messaging platform, detailing activities undertaken, beneficiaries reached, and any challenges encountered. These reports were then reviewed by regional RDI coordinators who provided targeted feedback and support. For critical program milestones, such as the initial beneficiary registration or the disbursement of cash transfers, we implemented a sample-based verification process. This involved random checks by RDI field officers or designated community leaders, not to audit the FPs negatively, but to identify any systemic issues or areas where additional support might be needed. We also introduced quarterly performance reviews for each FP, which served as a platform for discussing progress, identifying training needs, and setting performance goals for the next quarter. This structured approach to management, combined with ongoing support and clear performance expectations, significantly improved the consistency and quality of program delivery.

Furthermore, the feedback from community members highlighted the importance of trust and transparency in sustaining engagement. While the FPs were local, their role as facilitators of an external program required clear communication about the program's goals, the selection criteria for beneficiaries, and the intended impact of the assistance. Some early feedback indicated confusion about why certain individuals or households were selected over others, or a misunderstanding of the specific benefits they were entitled to. This underscored the need for standardized, clear, and accessible communication materials for the community itself.

In response, we developed a suite of community-facing materials. This included simple, illustrated brochures explaining the program's objectives, beneficiary rights, and grievance redressal mechanisms. These materials were translated into the local dialect and distributed through the FPs. We also worked with FPs to conduct regular community information sessions, providing a platform for Q&A and reinforcing key messages. The feedback from these sessions was invaluable, helping us to refine the language and approach used in our communication materials to ensure maximum clarity and understanding. The emphasis on building trust through transparent communication was not just about accountability; it was fundamental to ensuring community buy-in and the long-term sustainability of the program's impact.

The pilot also provided invaluable insights into the logistics of resource distribution, particularly for agricultural inputs. While direct local procurement was a core tenet of our cost-efficiency model, we learned that simply connecting FPs with local suppliers was not always sufficient. Factors such as seasonal availability of specific inputs, quality control mechanisms for local produce, and the capacity of local suppliers to meet bulk demands required more proactive management. In some instances, our FPs encountered situations where the promised inputs were not available at the specified time or were of a lower quality than expected, leading to delays and beneficiary dissatisfaction.

To address this, we have enhanced our supplier's vetting and management process. This involved developing more rigorous criteria for selecting local suppliers, including checks on their inventory management, quality control procedures, and past performance. We also facilitated direct engagement between

RDI's procurement specialists and key local suppliers, establishing clear delivery schedules and quality benchmarks. Furthermore, we explored the development of forward-contracting mechanisms, where RDI would enter into agreements with trusted local suppliers ahead of the planting season, guaranteeing purchase volumes and prices. This helped to secure supply chains and ensured that the quality and quantity of agricultural inputs met the program's requirements. The lessons learned here were about recognizing that while local procurement is efficient, it still requires robust oversight and strategic partnerships to function optimally at scale, especially for time-sensitive and quality-dependent items like agricultural inputs.

Moreover, the pilot revealed the critical importance of adaptive management in response to emergent needs and unexpected events. South Kivu, like many regions where RDI operates, is susceptible to climatic variations and other unforeseen circumstances. During the pilot, localized heavy rains impacted crop yields in certain areas, which, in turn, affected the food security of households that were not entirely reliant on the program's agricultural support alone. This highlighted the need for the RDI Model to be flexible enough to incorporate contingency planning and responsive mechanisms.

Our learning in this regard led to the exploration of more integrated approaches. This included building stronger linkages with local **disaster risk reduction committees** and other community-based organizations that monitor environmental changes. It also prompted us to investigate the feasibility of incorporating small, flexible emergency response components into future iterations of the model. For example, identifying pre-approved local suppliers who could quickly provide essential relief items or cash assistance in the event of a localized crisis. The pilot demonstrated that a rigid, pre-defined program, however well-designed financially, could falter when confronted with the unpredictable realities of the field. The ability to adapt, to learn from evolving circumstances, and to adjust the program's focus or delivery mechanisms accordingly, proved to be as vital as the initial model's efficiency. This continuous learning loop, driven by on-the-ground feedback and a commitment to iterative improvement, is what transforms a successful pilot into a robust and scalable solution for development challenges. The ongoing refinement of our training, communication, resource provision, and project management strategies, all directly informed by the experiences in South Kivu, has solidified the RDI Model's potential for broader impact and greater resilience.

CHAPTER 5:

Combating Corruption:
Integrity Through Local Oversight

The **integrity of aid delivery** is a cornerstone of effective development and humanitarian response. Yet, this vital sector is not immune to a pervasive and insidious threat: **corruption**. This insidious force, manifesting in myriad forms, has the potential to derail even the most well-intentioned projects, diverting critical resources away from the intended beneficiaries and into the pockets of those who **exploit vulnerability for personal gain**. The consequences are far-reaching, impacting not only the immediate effectiveness of aid but also the long-term trust between donor agencies, implementing partners, governments, and crucially, the communities themselves. *Understanding the multifaceted nature of corruption within the aid sector is the essential first step in developing robust strategies to combat it and ensure that every dollar, every resource, and every effort truly reaches those who need it most.*

Corruption in the context of aid delivery is not a monolithic issue; rather, it is a complex web of illicit practices that can infiltrate various stages of the aid lifecycle. At its core, it represents an abuse of power for private gain, a betrayal of the fundamental principles of altruism and responsibility that should guide humanitarian action. This can range from petty bribery, where small payments are extorted from desperate individuals seeking essential services or registration, to large-scale embezzlement of funds meant for procurement, infrastructure development, or direct assistance. It can involve inflated invoices, ghost employees on payrolls, rigged procurement processes, or the outright theft of goods intended for distribution. In essence, any deviation from transparent, accountable, and equitable practices for personal benefit constitutes a form of corruption that cripples the aid system.

The impact of such corruption on project outcomes can be catastrophic. Resources that are desperately needed for food, shelter, healthcare, or education are siphoned off, leaving beneficiaries with inadequate or no support. This directly translates into increased suffering, prolonged dependency, and a further entrenchment of poverty and vulnerability. For instance, a consignment of essential medicines diverted through illicit sales channels means that clinics remain without vital supplies, leading to preventable deaths and exacerbating public health crises. Similarly, funds earmarked for building schools that are then stolen mean that children continue to lack access to education, perpetuating cycles of disadvantage. The very purpose of aid – to alleviate suffering and foster sustainable development – is fundamentally undermined when its delivery is tainted by corruption.

Beyond the direct diversion of resources, **corruption erodes the efficiency and effectiveness of aid operations.** Projects become bogged down by inflated costs, delays caused by illicit negotiations, and the need for constant monitoring and investigation to detect fraud. This increases the administrative burden and overhead costs for humanitarian organizations, meaning more money is spent on managing the problem rather than delivering solutions. Procurement processes, often complex and time-sensitive in emergencies, become particularly vulnerable. When contracts are awarded based on bribes rather than merit, the quality of goods and services procured can be compromised, leading to faulty infrastructure, substandard materials, or unreliable service providers. This not only wastes money but can also put beneficiaries at risk, such as in the case of poorly constructed shelters that fail to withstand adverse weather conditions.

Perhaps one of the most damaging consequences of corruption in aid delivery is the erosion of public trust. Donor governments, private citizens, and foundations contribute to humanitarian causes with the expectation that their contributions will be used effectively and ethically. When reports of corruption emerge, this trust is severely damaged, leading to decreased funding and public apathy towards critical humanitarian needs. For organizations on the ground, this loss of confidence can be particularly devastating, impacting on their ability to recruit skilled staff, secure partnerships, and gain the necessary access to operate in challenging environments. Communities, too, lose faith in the institutions meant to support them. If they witness or experience corruption firsthand, their willingness to participate in programs, provide accurate information, or cooperate with aid workers diminishes, creating significant barriers to effective engagement and long-term impact. This breakdown in trust can foster resentment and alienation, making it harder to build the social cohesion necessary for recovery and development.

The environments in which aid is often delivered – characterized by weak governance, limited transparency, conflict, and poverty – can inadvertently create fertile ground for corrupt practices. In situations of desperation, the temptation to exploit opportunities for personal gain can be high, particularly for those in positions of authority who control resource flows. Moreover, the sheer scale and complexity of international aid operations, involving multiple actors, intricate supply chains, and diverse funding mechanisms, can create vulnerabilities that are exploited by those seeking to engage in illicit activities. Without robust oversight and accountability mechanisms, these vulnerabilities can be magnified, leading to systemic corruption that is difficult to root out.

Moreover, corruption can take on different forms depending on the specific context and the type of aid being delivered. In cash transfer programs, for instance, corruption might manifest as unauthorized deductions from the amounts disbursed, discriminatory beneficiary selection based on bribes or patronage, or the creation of ghost beneficiaries to embezzle funds. In the distribution of in-kind aid, such as food or shelter materials, corruption can involve diversion of goods at various points in the supply chain, from storage facilities to the final delivery point, or the sale of these essential items on the black market. In infrastructure projects, such as building wells or schools, corrupt practices can lead to substandard construction, inflated material costs, or the awarding of contracts to unqualified entities in exchange for kickbacks. Each of these scenarios, while distinct in their manifestation, shares the common outcome of depriving vulnerable populations of the assistance they are rightfully due.

The challenge of combating corruption in aid delivery is therefore immense, requiring a multi-pronged approach that addresses systemic weaknesses and fosters a culture of integrity at all levels. It demands not only robust internal controls and auditing procedures within aid organizations but also a concerted effort to promote good governance, transparency, and accountability in the partner countries where aid is implemented. This includes strengthening legal frameworks, improving judicial systems, and **empowering civil society organizations to act as watchdogs.** Without a comprehensive understanding of the pervasive threat that corruption poses, efforts to safeguard aid resources and ensure their effective delivery will remain incomplete, leaving millions vulnerable to its devastating consequences. The subsequent sections of this chapter will delve into specific strategies and mechanisms designed to build integrity and accountability into the very fabric of aid delivery, recognizing that the fight against corruption is not merely an administrative necessity but a moral imperative.

While external audits and compliance checks form a critical backbone for accountability in the international development and humanitarian aid sector, their efficacy is not absolute. These traditional controls, often the first line of defense against financial irregularities and misuse of funds, provide a necessary layer of verification. They are typically conducted by independent accounting firms or specialized audit bodies, tasked with scrutinizing financial records, verifying transactions, and assessing adherence to contractual obligations and donor requirements. These audits can uncover instances of fraud, mismanagement, and non-compliance, thereby offering a degree of assurance to donors and the public that resources are being used appropriately. The mere existence of these audit requirements can act as a deterrent, encouraging implementing organizations to maintain diligent record-keeping and adhere to established financial protocols. Furthermore, the findings from external audits can be invaluable for identifying systemic weaknesses within an organization's financial management systems, leading to improvements in internal controls and operational efficiency. They provide an objective assessment of an organization's financial health and its ability to manage donor funds responsibly, which is crucial for maintaining donor confidence and securing future funding.

However, the very nature of external audits, which are often periodic and retrospective, inherently limits their ability to prevent corruption in real-time or to address the nuanced realities of program implementation on the ground. These audits are typically conducted at specific intervals, often annually, meaning that by the time irregularities are detected and reported, the misappropriated funds may have long been dispersed, and the damage already been done. This temporal gap significantly diminishes their preventive power. Moreover, the scope of an external audit is usually confined to the financial records and supporting documentation provided by the implementing organization. While auditors are trained to identify red flags and probe for inconsistencies, they are not typically equipped to verify the ground-level reality of program activities or the actual impact of disbursed resources. They might verify that a certain amount of money was spent on procurement, but they cannot easily ascertain if the procured goods were of the promised quality, if they were truly delivered to the intended beneficiaries, or if a portion of the procurement budget was siphoned off through inflated invoices or kickbacks. The auditors rely on the information presented to them, and sophisticated schemes of corruption can be designed to circumvent these paper trails.

The effectiveness of external audits can also be significantly hampered by the context in which aid is delivered. In many of the remote, decentralized, or conflict-affected regions where humanitarian and development efforts are most desperately needed, accessing information and conducting thorough on-site verification can be exceedingly difficult, if not impossible. Infrastructure may be poor, communication channels unreliable, and security a constant concern, all of which can impede the auditors' ability to gather comprehensive evidence. The logistical challenges and associated costs of deploying audit teams to such locations can also be substantial, potentially making frequent and deep-dive audits financially unfeasible for many programs, especially those with smaller budgets. In such environments, auditors might be forced to rely more heavily on sampling and the documentation provided, increasing the risk of overlooking localized corrupt practices that do not leave a clear audit trail. The auditors themselves may also be vulnerable to pressure, intimidation, or even bribery in environments with weak rule of law, further compromising the integrity of their findings.

Furthermore, external audits, by their design, tend to focus primarily on financial compliance rather than operational integrity or the ethical dimensions of program delivery. While financial fraud is a critical concern, corruption can manifest in ways that are not always overtly financial, such as nepotism in hiring, preferential treatment for certain groups, or the diversion of non-financial resources like access or information. These types of corruption, which can be equally damaging to program effectiveness and community trust, may fall outside the typical purview of a financial audit. The compliance-driven approach can also foster a culture of "checking the box" rather than a

genuine commitment to transparency and accountability. Implementing organizations might focus their efforts on satisfying audit requirements, potentially at the expense of deeper engagement with beneficiaries or addressing the root causes of vulnerability, which are often intertwined with governance and accountability issues at the local level.

The limitations of external audits extend to their limited capacity to foster local ownership and accountability. These are external mechanisms, often perceived by communities and even local implementing staff as an imposition by donors or headquarters rather than an integral part of the program's own governance. This can create a disconnect, where communities bear the brunt of corruption but have little to no formal role in identifying or reporting it, or in holding those responsible accountable. The knowledge of local dynamics, informal networks, and the subtle ways in which resources are diverted often resides with the community members themselves. However, traditional audit frameworks do not typically have mechanisms to effectively tap into this localized knowledge and empower communities to act as active participants in the oversight process. This exclusion not only lacks a valuable source of information but also perpetuates a top-down approach that can undermine the sustainability and legitimacy of aid interventions. Without local buy-in and participation in oversight, the fight against corruption remains an external imposition rather than an embedded aspect of good governance.

This is where the inadequacy of a sole reliance on external controls becomes most apparent. While essential for a baseline level of accountability, these retrospective, often distant, and financially focused mechanisms are insufficient to combat the multifaceted nature of corruption, particularly in challenging operational environments. **The sheer volume of aid disbursed, the complexity of supply chains, and the inherent vulnerabilities of many program settings necessitate a more proactive, integrated, and locally embedded approach to oversight.** The limitations of external audits compel us to look beyond the traditional compliance frameworks and consider how to **build integrity and accountability** from within the very fabric of program implementation, drawing strength from the communities that aid is intended to serve. This shift in perspective is crucial for developing truly resilient and effective anti-corruption strategies that can adapt to diverse contexts and address corruption at its source. The challenge lies in devising mechanisms that not only **detect and deter** but also **empower and involve** local stakeholders in safeguarding the integrity of aid delivery.

The reliance on external audits and compliance checks, while a necessary component of accountability, represents only one facet of a comprehensive anti-corruption strategy. These mechanisms, often implemented by external bodies or through internal departments that operate at a remove from the day-to-day realities of program implementation, have inherent limitations, especially when confronted with the complexities of decentralized operations and remote geographical settings. **The retrospective nature of most audits means that by the time irregularities are identified, the damage may have already been done, and resources irrevocably lost or diverted.** Furthermore, auditors typically rely on documented evidence and sample testing, which can be manipulated or insufficient to uncover sophisticated or well-concealed corrupt practices. In environments characterized by weak governance, limited transparency, and a lack of robust legal frameworks, the effectiveness of these external controls is further diminished, as the auditors themselves may face challenges in obtaining reliable information or enforcing their findings.

The problem is exacerbated when we consider the practicalities of operating in many of the areas that receive the most significant amounts of aid. These regions are often remote, with poor infrastructure, limited communication networks, and challenging security situations. For external audit teams, the logistical hurdles and associated costs of conducting thorough, on-the-ground verification in such environments can be prohibitive. This often leads to audits that are more heavily reliant on paper-based evidence provided by the implementing organization, rather than on direct observation and verification of activities and beneficiaries. This reliance on documentation, which can be fabricated or incomplete, creates opportunities for corruption to go undetected. For instance, an auditor may verify that payments were made for goods or services, but without being able to independently confirm the quality of the goods delivered or the actual provision of services on the ground, it becomes difficult to ascertain if inflated prices or "ghost" services were part of a corrupt scheme.

Moreover, traditional audits are primarily focused on financial compliance and may not adequately address the broader spectrum of corrupt practices, which can include nepotism, favoritism, diversion of non-financial assets, or the abuse of power for personal gain in ways that do not leave a clear financial trail. For instance, a procurement process might be technically compliant with financial regulations, but if the contracts are consistently awarded to companies owned by relatives of key staff, this constitutes a form of corruption that a standard financial audit might miss. Similarly, if essential information or access to program activities is unfairly restricted or granted based on personal connections rather than program needs, this qualitative aspect of corruption is often beyond the scope of a financial audit. The emphasis on formal procedures can inadvertently create blind spots for these more insidious forms of integrity breaches.

The limitations are not solely technical or contextual; they are also deeply rooted in the inherent disconnect between external oversight mechanisms and the local communities that are the ultimate beneficiaries of aid. **These communities possess invaluable local knowledge – they understand the local context, the social dynamics, the informal networks, and the subtle indicators of irregularities that external auditors, however diligent, are unlikely to grasp.** However, traditional oversight frameworks seldom integrate this local knowledge effectively. Communities are often passive recipients of oversight, rather than active participants. Their role is typically limited to being interviewed as part of an audit process, if at all, rather than being empowered to be the frontline of integrity assurance. This exclusion not only overlooks a critical source of information but also undermines the potential for fostering a culture of accountability that is rooted in the local context. Without the active involvement and capacity building of communities, oversight remains an external imposition, rather than an integrated aspect of good program governance.

The compliance-driven nature of many external audits can also inadvertently foster a "tick-box" mentality within implementing organizations. The focus shifts from genuinely ensuring that resources reach the intended beneficiaries in the most effective way possible to simply meeting the requirements of the audit. This can lead to a situation where organizations invest significant resources in appearing to be compliant, rather than in addressing the underlying systemic issues that enable corruption. The fear of audit findings might encourage a culture of concealment rather than transparency, where staff are hesitant to report potential irregularities for fear of repercussions, further masking corrupt practices. This approach can stifle innovation and adaptation, as well as the willingness to engage in open dialogue about challenges and ethical dilemmas encountered during program implementation.

In essence, while external audits and compliance checks provide a vital layer of accountability, they are insufficient on their own to combat corruption effectively, particularly in complex and challenging operational environments. Their retrospective nature, limited scope, logistical difficulties in remote settings, and lack of genuine community integration mean that they often fail to prevent corruption at its source or to address its more nuanced manifestations. This critical examination of their limitations underscores the imperative to move beyond these traditional controls and to explore more integrated, proactive, and community-based approaches to oversight. The next step in building robust integrity mechanisms involves recognizing that true accountability is not just about external verification, but about fostering an environment where integrity is a shared responsibility, embedded in the daily operations and empowered by the very communities that aid seeks to serve. **This necessitates a paradigm shift towards creating systems that are responsive, adaptive, and deeply connected to the local realities on the ground, thereby mitigating corruption at its most vulnerable points of entry.**

The limitations inherent in solely relying on external oversight mechanisms, as previously discussed, highlight a **critical gap in combating corruption within international development and humanitarian aid.** While external audits and compliance checks serve as an indispensable foundational layer, their retrospective, often distant, and financially fixated nature proves insufficient against the pervasive and context-specific challenges of corruption. The temporal lag in identifying malfeasance, the potential for sophisticated evasion of financial scrutiny, and the logistical and contextual barriers to thorough verification in remote or volatile areas all underscore the need for a more proactive, integrated, and fundamentally localized approach to integrity assurance. This is precisely where the concept of **Local Project Selection & Monitoring Committees (LPSMCs)** emerges not merely as a supplementary measure, but as a transformative element in establishing a robust and embedded system of accountability.

Introducing Local Project Selection & Monitoring Committees (LPSMCs) represents a strategic pivot towards decentralizing oversight and empowering those most directly impacted by development and humanitarian interventions. These committees are conceived as grassroots bodies, meticulously formed to act as **the eyes and ears of the community**, ensuring that project identification, resource allocation, and implementation remain steadfastly aligned with the genuine needs and priorities of the people they are intended to serve. The very formation of an LPSMC is a deliberate process, designed to cultivate trust and legitimacy from the outset. It involves identifying individuals within the community who are not only respected for their integrity and commitment but also possess a deep understanding of local dynamics, social structures, and the nuanced realities of everyday life. This typically includes a diverse cross-section of community members, such as elders, religious leaders, women's group representatives, youth leaders, local business owners, and members of established community-based organizations or associations. The goal is to assemble a committee that is representative of the community's multifaceted identity and concerns, thereby ensuring that the selection of projects and the oversight of their execution are not the purview of a select few, but a collective endeavor.

The operational mandate of an LPSMC is multifaceted, extending beyond mere financial monitoring to encompass a holistic view of project integrity. At its core, the LPSMC is tasked with ensuring that the projects selected for funding and implementation are directly responsive to identified local needs and priorities, as articulated by the community itself. This means that before any external agency or implementing partner even considers a project proposal, the LPSMC would have played a crucial role in the initial needs assessment and project conceptualization phases. They would validate whether a proposed initiative truly addresses a pressing issue, whether it is culturally appropriate, and whether it aligns with the community's own development aspirations. This initial vetting process serves as a critical bulwark against the imposition of externally conceived projects that may not resonate with or effectively serve the local population, a common pitfall that can breed inefficiency and, in some cases, facilitate corruption through the misdirection of resources towards less critical or even irrelevant endeavors.

Furthermore, the LPSMC's mandate extends to the crucial phase of resource allocation. While the ultimate financial management may remain with the implementing organization, the LPSMC plays a vital role in scrutinizing how resources are being earmarked for specific project activities. This involves ensuring that budgets are transparent, reasonable, and reflective of the actual costs associated with achieving project objectives within the local context. They would be empowered to question disproportionately high allocations for certain items, investigate procurement processes for fairness and transparency at the local level, and ensure that funds are being channeled towards the intended beneficiaries and activities, not diverted through inflated costs, kickbacks, or patronage networks. This localized scrutiny can be particularly effective in identifying "leakages" in the system that might escape the notice of external auditors, who may lack the granular understanding of local market prices, labor rates, or the prevalence of certain informal economic practices that can be exploited for corrupt gain.

The daily activities of project implementation also fall under the purview of the LPSMC's oversight. This involves regular monitoring of project progress, verifying that activities are being carried out as planned, and ensuring that goods and services procured are of the agreed-upon quality and quantity and are delivered to the intended recipients. This on-the-ground verification is where LPSMCs can be most impactful. For instance, in a project aimed at improving agricultural productivity through the distribution of seeds and fertilizer, an LPSMC member could be tasked with visiting distribution points, confirming that the correct inputs are being provided to registered farmers, and assessing whether the quality meets expected standards. Similarly, in a construction project, such as building a school or a health clinic, committee members could be involved in observing the progress of work, verifying the materials used, and ensuring that the final product aligns with the approved designs and specifications. This continuous, embedded presence of the LPSMC provides a level of real-time oversight that is impossible for external auditors to replicate.

To explain the significance of maintaining Local Project Selection and Monitoring Committees (LPSMCs), consider the scenario below described in a recent field report from the Democratic Republic of Congo (DRC), where RDI was responsible for establishing fruit tree nurseries as part of the Environmental Conservation program.

"The project's impact is twofold: on the one hand, it actively contributes to environmental conservation through reforestation and enhanced biodiversity; on the other hand, it represents a significant source of income for families. At each harvest period, the collected fruits can be sold, thereby generating direct revenue for the beneficiaries.

In addition to fruit trees seedling distribution, the project plans to provide small livestock, specifically 3 to 4 guinea pigs per family. This initiative aims to give families a means of obtaining organic fertilizer, essential for fertilizing the newly planted propagated fruit trees, thus creating a virtuous synergy between livestock raising and agroforestry.

*As of August 2025, the nursery's progress is generally satisfactory. The passion fruit vines and avocado trees are germinating well and showing excellent health. **However, a major challenge was encountered with mango seeds. Despite the large quantities purchased by RDI and the courage of the team in charge, they failed to germinate.***

After contacting the supplier, KIVU INNOVA, it was revealed that the seeds were of poor quality, the kernels having dried out. KIVU INNOVA, the supplier has committed to supplying new seeds, but with the mango growing season already over, the delivery of the replacements could not take place immediately. The company has requested an extension until the next mango season, around December 2025, to deliver viable seeds. We recently submitted a report to RDI containing KIVU INNOVA's request, and we allowed the supplier to do as requested".

An external audit conducted in a formal office setting would have verified that the mango kernels were procured and delivered for planting, resulting in an audit report affirming the proper use of donor funds. Donors would be informed that their contributions enabled access to mango seedlings for the local community. However, despite these assurances, the mango kernels dried out, and no seedlings were distributed locally.

The supplier, having entered into a procurement contract and received payment, provided mango kernels of inadequate quality, which failed to germinate. Due to the active involvement and oversight of the LPSMC – empowered by RDI and representing the beneficiary community – it was not feasible for KIVU INNOVA, the kernel supplier, to consider the project complete following delivery. The LPSMC felt a strong **responsibility to request accountability** from the supplier regarding the non-viable kernels. As stated in the final paragraph of the report: *"After contacting the supplier, KIVU INNOVA, it was revealed that the seeds were of poor quality, the kernels having dried out. KIVU INNOVA, the supplier has committed to supplying new seeds, but with the mango growing* *season already over, the delivery of the replacements could not take place immediately. The company has requested an extension until the next mango season, around December 2025 to deliver viable seeds."*

The success of LPSMCs hinges on several critical enabling factors, not least of which is their formation process. It must be transparent, inclusive, and perceived as legitimate by all stakeholders, including the implementing organization, RDI, and, most importantly, the community itself. This often requires a collaborative effort between the implementing agency and community leaders to identify and agree upon the selection criteria and the individuals who will best serve on the committee. Clear terms of reference for the LPSMC are essential, defining their roles, responsibilities, decision-making powers, and reporting lines. Importantly, the committee must be provided with adequate training and capacity building to effectively discharge their duties. This training should cover a range of areas, including understanding project plans and budgets, basic financial literacy, principles of transparency and accountability, conflict resolution, and the specific methods for reporting and escalating issues. Without this foundational support, the LPSMC may struggle to operate effectively and could become easily overwhelmed or undermined.

Crucially, LPSMCs must be afforded a degree of autonomy and independence to prevent undue influence or coercion from either the implementing organization or local power structures that might seek to manipulate the process for personal gain. While they are formed in partnership with implementing organizations, their oversight role requires them to be able to critically assess and, if necessary, challenge decisions or actions. This independence is often bolstered by direct reporting lines to a higher level of oversight within the implementing agency or even directly to the donor, providing a channel for raising concerns that might not be adequately addressed at the program level. Furthermore, the committee members themselves must be protected from any form of retaliation or intimidation for carrying out their oversight responsibilities in good faith. This might involve establishing confidential reporting mechanisms and providing support structures for committee members who face pressure.

The operational framework of an LPSMC necessitates robust mechanisms for information sharing and communication. Committee members need access to relevant project documentation, including proposals, budgets, work plans, and progress reports. They collaborate with the FPs who play the role of the bridge between RDI's headquarters and grassroots organizations. Regular meetings of the LPSMC are essential to discuss findings, share observations, and make collective decisions. These meetings should be documented, with minutes recorded and shared with the implementing organization and, potentially, with the broader community through accessible channels. Effective communication between the LPSMC and the implementing organization is also paramount. This facilitates a constructive dialogue, allowing for prompt clarification of issues, the resolution of misunderstandings, and the incorporation of feedback from the committee into project management. A well-defined feedback loop ensures that the LPSMC's insights are not just received but acted upon, fostering a collaborative environment focused on shared accountability and program success.

The establishment of LPSMCs is not without its challenges. One significant hurdle can be the inherent power imbalances that often exist between external development actors and local communities. Implementing organizations, backed by donor funding and organizational capacity, may inadvertently or deliberately exert influence that compromises the independence of the LPSC. Overcoming this requires a conscious effort by implementing agencies to foster a culture of genuine partnership and to cede a degree of control over oversight functions. Another challenge can be the potential for co-option of committee members by local elites or vested interests, seeking to exploit their position for personal benefit or to shield their own corrupt activities. **Rigorous selection processes, continuous ethical training, and clear codes of conduct for committee members can help mitigate this risk.** Furthermore, the sustainability of LPSMCs beyond the life of a specific project is a crucial consideration. Building the capacity of communities to sustain these oversight structures, perhaps by integrating them into existing local governance mechanisms or community associations, is key to long-term impact.

Despite these challenges, the strategic deployment of Local Project Selection Committees offers a powerful antidote to the limitations of traditional external oversight. By embedding accountability within the community, **LPSMCs tap into invaluable local knowledge, foster a sense of ownership, and enable real-time monitoring that can prevent corruption before it takes root or escalates.** They transform beneficiaries from passive recipients into active participants in safeguarding the integrity of aid, thereby strengthening the legitimacy and effectiveness of development and humanitarian interventions. **The conceptual shift is profound: moving from an imposed system of accountability to a system that**

is organically grown from within the community itself, driven by shared values and a collective commitment to ensuring that resources are used for their intended purpose – to improve lives and foster sustainable development. This localized approach to integrity is not merely an additional tool; it is a fundamental reimagining of how accountability can and should function in the complex landscape of global development cooperation, **ensuring that the fight against corruption is as dynamic, adaptive, and deeply rooted as the communities it seeks to protect.** *The formation of these committees is, therefore, a testament to the belief that the most effective guardians of development resources are often those closest to them, equipped with the right mandate, empowered by genuine participation, and supported by transparent and inclusive processes.*

The tangible implementation of Local Project Selection & Monitoring Committees (LPSMCs) in combating corruption hinges on a robust framework of operational mechanisms designed to ensure transparency, monitor resource utilization, and provide channels for grievance redressal. These mechanisms are not merely procedural; they are the very sinews that bind the community's oversight role to the practicalities of project management, making accountability a living, breathing aspect of development and humanitarian efforts. At the foundational level, the LPSMC's engagement begins with the meticulous review of project proposals. This is a critical juncture where potential avenues for corruption can be preemptively identified and neutralized. Unlike external evaluations that might focus primarily on financial feasibility or alignment with donor priorities, the LPSMC brings a unique, ground-level perspective. They scrutinize proposals to ascertain their genuine alignment with articulated community needs, probing beyond superficial statements to understand the practical implications of the proposed activities for daily life, local livelihoods, and existing social structures. This involves dissecting the proposed budget not just for mathematical accuracy but for its reasonableness within the local economic context. For instance, an LPSMC would be well-positioned to question inflated prices for materials or labor that might seem normal to an off-site auditor but are demonstrably excessive when compared to prevailing local market rates. They can also assess the feasibility of proposed timelines and the realistic capacity of local resources, including human capital, to deliver on project objectives. By demanding clarity on how project activities translate into tangible benefits for the community, and by questioning any vagueness or over-promising, LPSMCs serve as a vital filter, ensuring that only relevant, feasible, and genuinely beneficial projects receive their endorsement, thereby preventing the channeling of funds into ill-conceived or opportunistic ventures. Interesting is that the FPs who play the bridge role between RDI's headquarters and the grassroots organizations DO NOT participate in project selection. They receive reports from LPSMCs, compile them, analyze them and submit them to RDI's headquarters.

Beyond the initial selection, the oversight of resource utilization forms another crucial pillar of the LPSMC's accountability mechanism. This involves a continuous and dynamic monitoring process that extends throughout the project lifecycle. LPSMCs are empowered to track the flow of funds and resources from the point of procurement to their ultimate deployment in project activities. This can manifest in various ways, such as reviewing procurement documentation for fairness and adherence to transparent bidding processes, especially for locally sourced goods and services. They can verify the quality and quantity of materials delivered against what was requisitioned, ensuring that there is no substitution with inferior products or outright pilferage. For example, in a project involving the construction of infrastructure, an LPSMC might regularly visit the site to inspect the materials being used, confirming they match the specifications, and to verify the number of workers engaged and their hours, cross-referencing this with payroll information. Similarly, in projects distributing essential supplies like food aid or medical kits, LPSMCs can be involved in monitoring distribution logs, verifying beneficiary lists, and ensuring that the correct items reach the intended recipients without diversion or dilution. This proactive, on-the-ground verification is instrumental in identifying and flagging any discrepancies or irregularities early on, preventing the escalation of minor diversions into significant corrupt losses. The visible presence of committee members actively scrutinizing these processes also acts as a powerful deterrent to those who might otherwise consider misappropriating resources.

A critical element in the effectiveness of these mechanisms is the fostering of genuine community ownership over the oversight process itself. When community members actively participate in the review of proposals, the monitoring of expenditures, and the assessment of project progress, a profound shift occurs. *This engagement transforms them from passive beneficiaries into active stakeholders, invested in the integrity and success of the projects. This sense of ownership cultivates a culture of accountability that permeates the entire project environment.* **It means that community members**

themselves become vigilant in identifying and reporting any suspected corrupt practices. This collective vigilance is a formidable force against corruption. When a community is united in its commitment to integrity, individuals who might be tempted to engage in corrupt activities find it far more difficult to operate undetected or with impunity. The social pressure and the shared understanding that resources are for the collective good discourage such behaviors. This internalizing of accountability, driven by community ownership, is a more sustainable and resilient approach than any externally imposed system. It creates an environment where transparency is valued, and deviations from ethical conduct are quickly identified and addressed by those who are most directly affected.

Furthermore, **the establishment of clear and accessible grievance redressal mechanisms is indispensable for the effective functioning of LPSMCs.** These mechanisms provide a structured avenue for community members to raise concerns, report suspicions, or lodge complaints regarding any aspect of project implementation, including alleged corrupt practices, unfair resource distribution, or substandard quality of work. The LPSMC acts as the primary recipient and initial arbiter of these grievances. This ensures that complaints are heard and addressed within the community context, by individuals who understand the local nuances and can effectively investigate and mediate. The process typically involves a clear procedure for submitting grievances, a defined timeframe for their acknowledgment and investigation, and a transparent method for communicating the outcome to the complainant. For instance, a community member who believes they were unfairly excluded from a beneficiary list or witnessed a project supervisor demanding a bribe could approach an LPSMC member. The LPSMC would then initiate an inquiry, which might involve speaking with the supervisor, reviewing relevant documentation, and consulting with other community members. The findings of this inquiry would then be communicated back to the complainant, and if corruption is substantiated, appropriate actions would be recommended, which could include internal disciplinary measures by the implementing organization or referral to higher authorities. This direct feedback loop not only resolves individual issues but also reinforces the LPSMC's role as a trusted authority and encourages further reporting of malfeasance, thereby strengthening the overall accountability framework.

The very structure of LPSMC operations contributes significantly to preventing corruption by embedding scrutiny into the daily fabric of project activities. Regular LPSMC meetings, for instance, provide a consistent forum for members to share observations, discuss progress, and collectively identify potential issues. These meetings are crucial for cross-referencing information and for validating individual reports. If multiple members report similar anomalies or express concerns about a particular aspect of the project, it signals a more systemic problem that requires immediate attention. The minutes of these meetings, when properly documented and shared, serve as a record of the LPSMC's diligence and the issues that were raised and addressed. Moreover, the LPSMC's mandate often extends to participating in key project milestones, such as the handover of completed infrastructure, the final distribution of materials, or the evaluation of project impact. At these junctures, the committee's formal endorsement or critique carries significant weight, providing a community-sanctioned validation of project outcomes and the integrity of the processes that led to them. This comprehensive approach, from initial scrutiny to final evaluation, ensures that accountability is not a one-off event but a continuous process that actively guards against the infiltration and persistence of corrupt practices. **The transparency inherent in these activities – making project plans, budgets, and progress reports accessible to the LPSMC, and by extension, to the community – demystifies the development process and empowers individuals to question and to hold project implementers accountable.** This democratization of oversight is fundamental to building trust and ensuring that development resources are indeed used for the betterment of the communities they are intended to serve. The strength of the LPSMC lies not in its punitive powers, but in its embeddedness, its transparency, and its ability to foster a collective commitment to probity within the project ecosystem. This integrated approach creates a more robust and resilient defense against corruption, one that is deeply rooted in the community and responsive to its needs and aspirations.

The conceptual framework of Local Project Selection & Monitoring Committees (LPSMCs) as a bulwark against corruption gains substantial credibility through concrete examples of their successful implementation. These instances, drawn from various development and humanitarian contexts, showcase not merely the theoretical potential but the practical efficacy of community-led oversight in safeguarding resources and ensuring genuine project impact. While the overarching principles of transparency, community ownership, and rigorous monitoring remain constant, the specific manifestations of LPSMC success often highlight innovative adaptations to local realities, demonstrating the inherent flexibility and resilience of this model.

One compelling case study emerged from a rural infrastructure development initiative in a region frequently plagued by leakages in the supply chain for construction materials. The project, aimed at rehabilitating and expanding a network of vital community roads, involved significant procurement of cement, gravel, and steel. Initially, the implementing agency relied on standard procurement protocols, but persistent community reports indicated that delivered materials were often of inferior quality or that quantities did not match invoiced amounts. Upon the establishment of an LPSMC, tasked with overseeing the project from material acquisition to final road surfacing, a tangible shift occurred. The LPSMC mandated that all deliveries be inspected by at least two committee members before acceptance. Furthermore, they insisted on accompanying procurement officers to local markets to verify prevailing prices for raw materials, thereby establishing a benchmark against which supplier invoices could be rigorously cross-checked. In one instance, the LPSMC identified a significant over-pricing of cement by a pre-approved supplier. Their detailed price comparison, supported by receipts from multiple local distributors, allowed them to challenge the invoice effectively. The supplier, confronted with this evidence and the prospect of community-wide reputational damage, agreed to revise the invoice down to the market rate. This single intervention, facilitated by the LPSMC's diligent oversight, prevented a substantial financial loss that would have otherwise diminished the quality and durability of the roads, ultimately benefiting the community's mobility and economic activity. The transparency of this process was further amplified by the public display of approved material specifications and delivery schedules at the project site, allowing any community member to verify the LPSMC's findings.

Another critical area where LPSMCs have demonstrated significant success is in the equitable distribution of essential aid, particularly during emergency responses. In a protracted drought situation that led to widespread food insecurity, a humanitarian organization initiated a direct food distribution program. The LPSMC, composed of representatives from affected villages, played a crucial role in ensuring that the aid reached the most vulnerable populations without bias or diversion. Their primary responsibilities included validating beneficiary lists against community-recognized vulnerable households, meticulously monitoring the loading and unloading of food supplies to prevent pilferage, and overseeing the actual distribution process at designated points. A key challenge in such distributions is the tendency for resources to be siphoned off at various points, either through inflated beneficiary numbers or direct appropriation of goods. The LPSMC's active presence at the distribution sites, coupled with their independent verification of recipients against the approved list, acted as a powerful deterrent. In one specific incident, it was discovered that a consignment of fortified supplementary food meant for malnourished children had been diverted by a project field officer. The LPSMC, having conducted pre-distribution checks of the consignment and noticing a discrepancy in the manifest during the unloading process, immediately raised a red flag. Their prompt investigation, involving cross-referencing the manifest with the LPSMC-verified dispatch records and questioning the field staff involved, led to the recovery of the diverted goods before they could be resold in the black market. The swift action not only prevented financial loss to the organization but, more importantly, ensured that the critical nutritional supplement reached the intended children, potentially averting severe health consequences. The transparency was further enhanced by the LPSMC's public announcement of the total quantity of aid received and distributed, alongside the number of validated beneficiaries, fostering trust and accountability.

Beyond material and financial integrity, LPSMCs have also proven instrumental in ensuring the quality of service delivery, particularly in projects involving skilled labor and specialized equipment. Consider a project focused on improving access to clean water through the drilling of new boreholes and the rehabilitation of existing wells. The technical nature of such projects can often obscure accountability, as community members may lack the expertise to assess the quality of the drilling, the efficacy of the pump installations, or the water potability test results. In this context, an LPSMC was formed with members who, while not necessarily technical experts, were mandated to ensure procedural adherence and community input. The LPSMC's role involved verifying that the drilling company possessed the necessary certifications and equipment, ensuring that the chosen sites for boreholes were indeed those identified through community consultations as having the greatest need and potential for water access, and critically, reviewing the results of water quality tests. In one instance, the LPSMC questioned the reported depth of a new borehole and the subsequent yield. They insisted that the drilling logs, which typically detail the strata penetrated, be made available for their review. Furthermore, they requested that a second, independent water quality test be conducted, citing concerns that the initial test results seemed unusually favorable. This insistence on transparency and verification led to the discovery that the drilling company had not reached the anticipated water table and had artificially inflated the reported yield to meet contractual obligations. The LPSMC's intervention prevented the formal handover of a non-functional or underperforming asset and ensured that the implementing agency renegotiated the contract, demanding either rectification of the borehole or a refund, ultimately leading to a more robust and sustainable water supply solution for the community.

The efficacy of LPSMCs in combating corruption is not merely in their capacity to identify and prevent individual acts of malfeasance, but in their ability to fundamentally shift the risk calculus for those who might contemplate corrupt practices. The constant, visible presence of community members actively engaged in oversight serves as a pervasive deterrent. For instance, in a livelihood improvement project that involved the distribution of agricultural inputs such as seeds, fertilizers, and tools to farmer cooperatives, the LPSMC's role extended to verifying the eligibility of recipient farmers and ensuring the correct allocation of inputs. They established a system where the committee members would be present at the distribution points, cross-referencing the provided lists with actual farmers present, and confirming that the quantities and types of inputs matched the project specifications for each farmer. This granular level of oversight meant that any attempt to double-count beneficiaries, allocate inputs to non-eligible individuals, or substitute cheaper inputs would be immediately visible and reportable. This public scrutiny fostered an environment where adherence to the rules was not just expected but actively enforced by the community itself. The transparency of the distribution process, with clear signage indicating the project, the LPSMC's role, and the distributed items, empowered community members to voice concerns without fear of reprisal. This collective vigilance significantly reduced opportunities for corrupt diversion, ensuring that the agricultural support reached the intended beneficiaries, thereby boosting local productivity and food security.

Furthermore, the implementation of LPSMCs in educational development projects has underscored their value in ensuring resource integrity and equitable access. In a program aimed at providing school supplies and infrastructure upgrades to underserved primary schools, the LPSMC's mandate included verifying the procurement of materials, ensuring the timely completion of construction or renovation works, and monitoring the equitable distribution of learning materials to all enrolled students. One particular case involved the construction of new classrooms. While the project plan was clear, community members, through the LPSMC, raised concerns about the quality of materials being used and the slow pace of construction. The LPSMC insisted on regular site visits, documented their observations of material quality (e.g., type and strength of cement, rebar specifications), and meticulously tracked progress against the agreed-upon timeline. They discovered that substandard bricks were being used and that the reinforcement in the concrete pillars did not meet the required specifications. Their detailed reports, backed by photographic evidence and expert opinions sought from within the community, forced the contractor to rectify the issues. This not only ensured the structural integrity and safety of the new classrooms but also prevented the wasteful expenditure of funds on faulty construction that would have required costly repairs or reconstruction in the future. The transparency in this instance was further bolstered by the LPSMC's facilitation of community meetings where project progress, challenges, and the LPSMC's interventions were openly discussed, reinforcing community buy-in and support.

The success stories are not limited to large-scale infrastructure or material distributions. In smaller, yet equally vital, community health projects, LPSMCs have proven to be effective in ensuring the integrity of service delivery and resource allocation. For instance, a program focused on maternal and child health, which included the distribution of essential medicines, nutritional supplements, and the provision of antenatal care services, benefited greatly from LPSMC oversight. The LPSMC's role included ensuring that health workers adhered to prescribed protocols for patient care, that medicines and supplies were available at health posts as scheduled, and that distribution of any supplementary items was conducted impartially. In one instance, the LPSMC received reports that a specific health post was frequently running out of essential antibiotics and vitamins for pregnant women. The committee undertook an unannounced visit to the health post and, through interviews with health workers and a review of stock registers, identified that supplies were not being properly accounted for and that some items were being held back or diverted. The LPSMC's intervention involved a thorough audit of the stock, comparison with official dispatch records, and a direct dialogue with the health worker responsible. This led to the identification of irregularities in stock management and a subsequent retraining of the health worker on proper inventory control and distribution procedures. The transparency inherent in the LPSMC's monitoring process, which included clear stock-taking protocols and patient record checks, ensured that essential health commodities were available to those who needed them most, thereby improving health outcomes within the community.

The implementation of LPSMC principles in vocational training programs has also yielded positive results in combating corruption and ensuring equitable access to opportunities. In a project designed to equip unemployed youth with marketable skills, the LPSMC's role involved vetting training providers, ensuring fair selection of participants, monitoring the quality of training delivered, and verifying that participants received the promised stipends and toolkits upon completion. A notable case involved a training program on tailoring and garment production. The LPSMC discovered that the training provider was systematically excluding a disproportionate number of female participants from receiving their completion toolkits, citing arbitrary reasons. The LPSMC investigated by reviewing the attendance records and cross-referencing them with the LPSMC-approved participant list. They also engaged with the excluded participants to understand the rationale behind their exclusion. The committee's findings revealed that the provider was withholding the toolkits, which were a significant component of the program's value, in an attempt to extract additional informal payments from the participants. The LPSMC's decisive action, which included presenting their findings to the implementing agency and advocating for the direct handover of the toolkits under LPSMC supervision, ensured that all eligible participants, regardless of their ability to pay unofficial fees, received the necessary resources to commence their livelihoods. This intervention not only rectified a significant injustice but also reinforced the LPSMC's authority and commitment to equitable benefit distribution, thereby preventing corruption and fostering genuine economic capacity building.

These case studies collectively illustrate that the LPSMC model is not a theoretical construct but a pragmatic and effective tool for combating corruption in development and humanitarian projects. From ensuring the quality of construction materials and equitable aid distribution to upholding the integrity of health services and vocational training, the presence of empowered, transparent, and vigilant community oversight committees significantly enhances accountability and safeguards resources. **The success of these initiatives lies in their ability to embed scrutiny directly into the project lifecycle, making corruption a high-risk, low-reward endeavor for those who might contemplate it, and ensuring that development interventions truly serve their intended purpose: the betterment of communities.** The demonstrated ability of LPSMCs to adapt to diverse project contexts and to address a range of corrupt practices underscores their value as a cornerstone of ethical and effective development programming.

CHAPTER 6:

Empowering Local Voices:
Capacity Building For Sustainability

The discourse on sustainable development, particularly within the complex tapestry of international aid and humanitarian intervention, often grapples with the persistent challenge of ensuring long-term impact beyond the lifespan of external funding or direct organizational involvement. While significant progress has been made in understanding the multifaceted needs of communities and in designing interventions that are responsive to those needs, a critical determinant of enduring success remains largely untapped: **the robust and strategic capacity building of local capacity.** This is not merely a matter of efficiency or local preference; it is the very foundation upon which true, self-sustaining development is built. When we speak of empowering local voices, we are inherently speaking about cultivating and relying upon the intrinsic capabilities that reside within communities, their organizations, and their individuals.

The prevailing paradigm, often born out of necessity or a perceived lack of local readiness, has historically leaned towards external actors leading and managing development processes. **International non-governmental organizations (INGOs), bilateral agencies, and multilateral bodies have often been the primary implementers, bringing their own expertise, resources, and management structures. While**

this approach has undeniably facilitated the delivery of critical services and infrastructure in many contexts, it carries inherent limitations that can inadvertently foster dependency and undermine long-term sustainability. *The very act of external leadership, while well-intentioned, can inadvertently sideline or diminish the agency of local actors, creating a situation where communities become recipients rather than drivers of their own progress.* This can manifest in several ways: local organizations may struggle to compete with the resources and established networks of international counterparts, leading to their marginalization in project design and implementation. Individuals may find their expertise undervalued or overlooked, leading to a disengagement from processes that should fundamentally be about their own capacity building. Furthermore, the reliance on external management often means that decision-making power, critical knowledge transfer, and institutional learning remain concentrated outside the local context, creating a vacuum that is difficult to fill when external support recedes.

The consequences of such a dependency model are often starkly revealed when external funding dries up or when international implementing partners withdraw from a region. **Projects that appeared successful on paper may falter, infrastructure may fall into disrepair due to a lack of local maintenance capacity, and vital programs may cease to operate.** *This is not a failure of the project's intent, but rather a failure to adequately invest in and cultivate the local systems that are essential for its continuation. The skills required for project management, financial oversight, technical maintenance, advocacy, and community mobilization are often present within local communities, but they may be* *underdeveloped, un-networked, or not recognized as valuable currency in the international development arena.* **Capacity building, therefore, must be understood not as an add-on or a secondary consideration, but as a primary strategic objective, woven into the fabric of every development initiative from its inception.**

True sustainability is intrinsically linked to self-reliance. It is about ensuring that communities possess the skills, knowledge, resources, and organizational structures to identify their own needs, design their own solutions, implement their own projects, and manage their own resources effectively and accountably over the long term. This requires a deliberate and sustained effort to transfer not just knowledge, but also authority and responsibility. It means moving beyond short-term capacity-building workshops, which often have limited impact, towards more comprehensive, embedded, and context-specific strategies that foster genuine local ownership. This involves identifying existing strengths within local organizations and individuals and building upon them, rather than attempting to impose external models that may not be culturally appropriate or practically viable.

The benefits of prioritizing local capacity are manifold and extend far beyond the immediate project cycle. Firstly, it leads to more relevant and contextually appropriate interventions. Local actors possess an intimate understanding of their own socio-cultural dynamics, political landscapes, environmental realities, and economic opportunities. Their insights are invaluable in designing projects that are not only effective but also culturally sensitive and socially accepted, thereby increasing the likelihood of local buy-in and long-term adoption. Secondly, it fosters greater **accountability and transparency.**

When local organizations and communities are in the driver's seat, they have a vested interest in ensuring that resources are used **efficiently and effectively**, and that projects deliver tangible benefits. They are more directly answerable to their own constituents, creating a powerful internal mechanism for accountability that often surpasses external oversight alone.

Moreover, investing in local capacity builds resilience. Communities that are empowered to manage their own development processes are better equipped to adapt to changing circumstances, to overcome challenges, and to seize new opportunities. They develop the adaptive capacity to innovate, to learn from mistakes, and to chart their own course even in the face of external disruptions. This resilience is crucial for navigating the inherent uncertainties and complexities of development, especially in fragile or post-conflict environments. It means that the gains made during external engagement are not lost but are instead integrated into the ongoing development trajectory of the community.

Furthermore, empowering local capacity contributes to the strengthening of local civil society and democratic governance. **By supporting local organizations in their roles as service providers, advocates, watchdogs, development initiatives can contribute to the broader ecosystem of good governance and citizen engagement.** This can lead to stronger institutions, more responsive public services, and greater protection of human rights. The process of building local capacity is, in essence, an investment in the social and institutional capital of a country, laying the groundwork for broader societal progress.

The shift towards prioritizing local capacity requires a fundamental recalibration of how international development is conceived and implemented. It necessitates a move from a top-down, externally driven approach to one that is collaborative, participatory, and genuinely community-led. This transition is not without its challenges. **International organizations may need to cede control, adjust their operational models, and invest more in long-term relationship building and trust.** Local organizations may require support in developing their technical, managerial, and financial capacities. However, the rewards of this paradigm shift are immense, promising development outcomes that are not only effective in the short term but also enduring and transformative in the long run. It is about recognizing that **the most potent engine for sustainable development resides not in distant headquarters, but within the hearts, minds, and hands of the people it seeks to serve.**

The journey toward truly sustainable development, as We have established, hinges on the robust capacity building of local actors. This capacity building, however, transcends the simple transfer of technical skills. While training in specific methodologies or the operation of new equipment is a necessary component, it represents only one facet of a much broader and more intricate process. True capacity development is a holistic endeavor, designed to cultivate not just the ability to *do*, but the ability to *govern*, to *manage*, to *strategize*, and to *advocate*. It is about nurturing grassroots organizations and community-based initiatives into self-sustaining, self-governing entities capable of charting their own development trajectories, independent of perpetual external guidance. This requires a strategic and multi-pronged approach, one that recognizes the interconnectedness of various organizational functions and the critical role of strong governance in achieving lasting impact.

At the heart of this holistic approach lies the strengthening of governance structures within local organizations. This is not simply about establishing formal leadership roles; it is about fostering a culture of accountability, transparency, and democratic participation. **Effective governance ensures that decision-making processes are inclusive, that resources are managed ethically, and that the organization remains true to its mission and accountable to the community it serves.** This involves working with local partners to develop clear constitutions and bylaws, establishing functional management committees or boards, and implementing mechanisms for regular community feedback and oversight. For instance, in rural agricultural cooperatives, weak governance can lead to the mismanagement of shared resources, internal conflicts, and a failure to adapt to changing market demands. *By facilitating workshops on leadership ethics, conflict resolution, and participatory decision-making, and by encouraging the establishment of transparent reporting systems, we can help these cooperatives build a foundation of trust and efficacy that is essential for their long-term survival and growth.* This governance capacity is the bedrock upon which all other development efforts are built; without it, even the most technically proficient organization is vulnerable to collapse.

Integral to this strengthening of governance is the meticulous development of financial management capabilities. Many grassroots organizations, while rich in community spirit and local knowledge, often lack the formal financial acumen required to manage grants effectively, ensure fiscal accountability, and plan for long-term financial sustainability. This goes beyond basic bookkeeping; it encompasses budgeting, financial forecasting, procurement procedures, internal controls, and transparent reporting. A key element here is building the capacity for sound financial planning. This involves assisting local partners in developing realistic project budgets that align with their programmatic goals, forecasting future income and expenditure, and identifying potential funding sources beyond the initial project cycle. For example, an organization working on water sanitation projects might need support in understanding how to develop a multi-year budget that accounts for not only the initial installation costs but also the ongoing maintenance and operational expenses, including potential revenue generation mechanisms such as user fees. Furthermore, developing robust internal control systems – such as clear authorization protocols for expenditures, segregation of duties, and regular internal audits – is crucial to prevent fraud and mismanagement, thereby building confidence among donors and the community.

Beyond managing external funds, a holistic approach also emphasizes the development of local fundraising and income-generating strategies. This is vital for transitioning away from aid dependency. Capacity building in this area can include training on grant writing, proposal development, and cultivating relationships with local businesses, philanthropic foundations, and government agencies. It also involves exploring innovative income-generating activities that align with the organization's mission and local context, such as social enterprises, fee-for-service models, or membership dues. For a women's capacity building group that has successfully trained women in tailoring, for example, capacity building could extend to developing a business plan for a small garment production unit, marketing strategies for their products, and financial management for reinvesting profits back into the organization. This financial self-reliance is a tangible outcome of genuine capacity development, allowing local organizations to set their own priorities and pursue their own long-term visions.

Equally critical is the enhancement of project planning, implementation, and monitoring and evaluation (M&E) skills. While many local entities are adept at identifying needs, the systematic process of planning, executing, and learning from projects often requires more formal training and support. Project planning involves teaching methodologies such as logical framework analysis (LFA) or results-based management (RBM) to help organizations set clear objectives, define measurable indicators, identify activities, and allocate resources effectively. This structured approach ensures that projects are well-conceived, aligned with community needs, and have a clear path to achieving their intended outcomes.

The implementation phase often benefits from training in project management best practices, including work planning, resource mobilization, risk management, and team coordination. For instance, a community-led reforestation project needs not only technical knowledge of tree planting but also the ability to organize community volunteers, procure saplings and tools, manage logistics, and ensure that planting efforts are carried out according to a plan. This involves developing detailed work plans, establishing clear roles and responsibilities for team members, and proactively identifying and mitigating potential risks, such as adverse weather conditions or community disputes.

Crucially, the capacity for effective monitoring and evaluation (M&E) must be instilled. This is not about external accountability alone but about fostering a culture of continuous learning and adaptation. Local organizations need to be equipped to collect relevant data, analyze it to understand what is working and what is not, and use these findings to improve their ongoing activities and inform future planning. This involves developing simple yet effective M&E frameworks, training staff and community members on data collection tools (such as surveys, focus group discussions, and key informant interviews), and building their capacity to interpret and utilize the data. For a local health committee managing a community health outreach program, this might mean training them to track the number of patients served, the types of services provided, and patient feedback, and then using this information to adjust outreach schedules, identify service gaps, or refine health messaging. This internal M&E capacity transforms projects from static interventions into dynamic, learning processes, enabling organizations to adapt to changing contexts and improve their effectiveness over time.

Furthermore, the ability to advocate for their own needs and to influence policy at local, national, and even international levels is a vital dimension of holistic capacity development. Many grassroots organizations possess invaluable on-the-ground knowledge and experience yet often lack the skills and platforms to translate this into effective advocacy. This involves building capacity in policy analysis, stakeholder engagement, communication strategies, and lobbying. It means empowering local leaders to articulate their concerns clearly, to build coalitions with other civil society groups, and to engage constructively with government officials and decision-makers.

For example, a farmers' association struggling with unfair market prices might need training on how to research market regulations, present evidence of price gouging to relevant ministries, and mobilize its members to participate in public consultations on agricultural policy. **This advocacy capacity is essential for ensuring that development initiatives are not only implemented effectively but also supported by an enabling policy environment and that the voices of the most affected populations are heard and considered in decision-making processes.** *It empowers them to move from being passive recipients of aid to active agents of systemic change.*

This holistic approach requires a fundamental shift in how development practitioners engage with local partners. It means moving away from a model of simply delivering services or training individuals in isolation, towards a more integrated, long-term partnership that focuses on strengthening the entire organizational ecosystem. This involves sustained engagement, building trust, and recognizing that capacity development is an ongoing, iterative process, not a one-off event. It requires patience, flexibility, and a deep respect for the knowledge and experience that local actors bring to the table. *International organizations must be willing to cede control, adapt their methodologies, and invest in the long-term growth of their local counterparts, viewing them not as sub-contractors, but as genuine partners in development.* This deep investment in governance, financial management, project cycle mastery, and advocacy skills is what truly transforms local organizations from project implementers into self-governing, sustainable entities that can champion their own communities' futures.

The architecture of sustainable capacity building, as we have explored, is built upon the foundation of empowered local actors. However, the effectiveness of this capacity building hinges not only on the acquisition of new skills and knowledge but also on the strategic dissemination and integration of these enhanced capabilities within the existing structures of local organizations and communities. Central to this diffusion process are individuals designated as "Focal Points" (FPs). These individuals are not merely recipients of training; they are strategically positioned catalysts, intended to act as bridges, facilitating the flow of expertise and fostering a multiplier effect that amplifies the impact of capacity-building interventions. Their role is multifaceted, encompassing the diligent transfer of technical competencies, the nurturing of a pervasive learning culture, and the consistent mentorship of their peers and colleagues.

The selection and preparation of these Focal Points are therefore critical initial steps. Ideally, FPs are identified from within the ranks of the local organizations themselves, chosen not just for their existing knowledge or perceived potential, but also for their intrinsic motivation, their ability to communicate effectively, and their standing within their communities. The capacity-building process, in this regard, begins before formal training even commences, with a careful process of identifying individuals who possess the inherent qualities to become effective knowledge brokers. Once identified, the training provided to FPs must be tailored to equip them with not only the specialized skills relevant to the project's objectives – be it advanced agricultural techniques, new financial management software, participatory governance models, or effective M&E methodologies – but also with the pedagogical and interpersonal skills necessary to impart this knowledge to others. This means training them in adult learning principles, effective communication strategies, facilitation techniques, and approaches to conflict resolution that may arise during knowledge transfer. For example, an FP selected to champion the adoption of a new community-based water management system might receive in-depth training on hydrogeology, infrastructure maintenance, and water resource planning. Crucially, however, they would also receive training on how to conduct workshops for community members on water conservation, how to explain the technical aspects of the system in simple terms, and how to facilitate community meetings to address concerns and foster collective ownership.

Once equipped, the primary responsibility of the FP is to serve as a conduit for the newly acquired skills and knowledge. This is a dynamic process, requiring the FP to actively translate theoretical learning into practical application within their everyday work. It involves demonstrating the new techniques, providing on-the-job guidance, and offering practical solutions to challenges that arise. For instance, if a local cooperative has received training in improved post-harvest storage techniques to reduce spoilage, the FP would be instrumental in showing fellow farmers how to construct or modify storage facilities, demonstrating the correct application of pest control measures, and explaining the rationale behind these practices. This hands-on approach, led by a trusted peer, is often far more impactful than generalized training sessions. The FP's ability to contextualize the learning, relating it directly to the specific challenges and opportunities faced by their organization and community, is paramount. They act as living examples of the benefits of the capacity-building efforts, their successful application of new skills serving as a powerful incentive for others to learn and adopt.

Beyond direct skill transfer, a crucial aspect of the FP's role is the fostering of a sustainable learning environment. This involves creating opportunities for ongoing dialogue, knowledge sharing, and peer-to-peer learning. FPs can achieve this by organizing regular internal meetings, study circles, or informal discussion groups where colleagues can share experiences, troubleshoot problems, and celebrate successes. These platforms provide a safe space for individuals to ask questions they might have been hesitant to raise in formal training settings and to learn from the practical insights of their peers. *For a women's self-help group that has been trained in micro-enterprise management, an FP might facilitate weekly informal gatherings where members can share their sales figures, discuss marketing strategies, and offer advice to those facing challenges with their businesses.* This creates a continuous feedback loop, ensuring that learning is not a one-time event but an embedded, ongoing process. The FP's presence and active facilitation in these settings are key to maintaining momentum and ensuring that the learning culture takes root and flourishes. They become the champions of continuous improvement, consistently encouraging a mindset of curiosity and a commitment to professional growth.

Mentorship is another cornerstone of the FP's contribution. This involves providing individual support and guidance to colleagues, helping them to navigate the learning curve and build confidence in applying new skills. A mentor FP does more than just show someone how to perform a task; they offer encouragement, provide constructive feedback, and help mentees to identify their own learning pathways and development goals. This personalized approach is particularly vital when dealing with diverse learning styles and varying levels of prior experience. Consider an FP working with a community health outreach team that has learned new diagnostic techniques for common illnesses. The FP would not only demonstrate the techniques but also patiently guide individual health workers through patient interactions, offering feedback on their diagnostic accuracy, communication with patients, and documentation practices. This one-on-one support helps to build the confidence and competence of each individual, ensuring that the skills are internalized and applied correctly. This mentorship extends to helping colleagues understand the broader context of the skills they are acquiring – how they contribute to the organization's overall mission, how they align with community needs, and how they can be further enhanced or adapted.

The effectiveness of the FP model also relies on ensuring that these individuals are adequately supported and recognized for their efforts. This includes providing them with ongoing access to advanced training, resources, and a network of their own peers for mutual support and problem-solving. Without continuous development, the FP's own knowledge can become outdated, diminishing their ability to effectively transfer skills. Furthermore, their role can be demanding, often requiring them to balance their core responsibilities with the added workload of training and mentoring. Therefore, it is essential to acknowledge and reward their contributions, perhaps through formal recognition, opportunities for further professional development, or by ensuring their roles are integrated into official job descriptions and performance evaluations. This ensures that the FP is not seen as an overburdened volunteer but as an integral and valued member of the organization's capacity-building machinery. For example, an FP spearheading the implementation of a new data management system for a local NGO might be provided with advanced training on database administration and offered opportunities to attend relevant professional conferences. This investment reinforces the value of their role and ensures their continued engagement and effectiveness.

Moreover, the role of the FP in fostering a learning organization extends to the strategic dissemination of best practices and lessons learned. FPs should be encouraged to document their experiences, share insights from their mentoring activities, and contribute to the organization's knowledge base. This can involve writing short case studies, presenting at internal forums, or contributing to shared digital platforms. By systematizing the sharing of knowledge and experiences, the organization can learn from its successes and failures more broadly, enabling continuous adaptation and improvement. For a local environmental conservation group that has successfully implemented a community-led waste management program, FPs could be tasked with documenting the initial challenges, the strategies employed, the community engagement approaches that proved most effective, and the outcomes achieved. This documentation, shared across different project sites or with other organizations, can become a valuable resource, informing future initiatives and preventing the repetition of past mistakes. This systematic capture and dissemination of knowledge elevate the FP's role from mere skill transfer to active contribution to organizational learning and systemic improvement.

The success of the Focal Point model is intrinsically linked to the broader organizational culture. For FPs to be effective, the organization must genuinely embrace a culture of learning, openness, and collaboration. This means **leadership must actively champion the importance of knowledge sharing and provide the necessary support structures for FPs to succeed.** It also means creating an environment where asking questions is encouraged, mistakes are seen as learning opportunities, and innovation is valued. If the organizational culture is one of hierarchy, fear of failure, or competition, the FP's efforts to foster learning and peer support will be significantly hampered. For instance, in an organization where reporting mistakes is met with reprimand, an FP will struggle to encourage colleagues to share their challenges and seek guidance. Conversely, in an organization where leadership actively promotes a "learning from failure" approach, the FP will find it much easier to create a supportive environment for skill transfer and mentorship.

The selection process for FPs must also consider their potential to contribute to organizational sustainability beyond the immediate project lifecycle. While technical skills are crucial, the ability of an FP to foster critical thinking, problem-solving, and adaptability within their team is equally, if not more, important for long-term resilience. An FP who can empower their colleagues to analyze situations, identify their own learning needs, and develop solutions independently is creating a truly sustainable capacity. This involves **encouraging a proactive rather than a reactive approach to problem-solving.** For example, an FP involved in agricultural extension services might not just teach farmers how to use a new irrigation technique, but also how to analyze their soil moisture levels, predict potential water stress, and adapt their irrigation schedules accordingly, thereby fostering a deeper understanding and independent decision-making capability. This level of capacity building ensures that the benefits of the capacity-building intervention endure, even as external support structures evolve.

The FP's role in bridging external expertise with local context is also critical. Often, capacity-building interventions are designed by external consultants or international organizations who may not fully grasp the nuances of the local environment. The FP acts as an interpreter and adapter, translating external knowledge into a format that is relevant, understandable, and actionable within the local context. They possess an intimate understanding of the cultural norms, existing social structures, and the specific challenges faced by their community. This local insight allows them to tailor the application of new skills and knowledge, ensuring that interventions are not only technically sound but also culturally appropriate and socially accepted. For instance, if an external organization introduces a new public health messaging strategy for disease prevention, an FP can help adapt the language, imagery, and delivery channels to resonate with the specific cultural beliefs and communication patterns of their community. This contextualization is key to the uptake and effective implementation of new practices.

Furthermore, the FP can play a vital role in monitoring the impact of the capacity-building initiatives themselves. By observing how their colleagues are applying new skills, identifying areas where further support is needed, and providing feedback to the project team, FPs can offer invaluable insights into the effectiveness of the training methodologies and the overall capacity-building strategy. This internal feedback loop is essential for iterative improvement and for ensuring that interventions remain relevant and responsive to evolving needs. An FP might notice that while a particular technical skill was taught effectively, the lack of appropriate tools or materials at the local level is hindering its application. This observation, reported back to the project team, can lead to adjustments in the intervention design, ensuring that capacity building is supported by the necessary resources. This continuous feedback mechanism, facilitated by the FP, allows for adaptive management and maximizes the chances of achieving sustainable outcomes.

The long-term success of capacity building is not solely dependent on the initial transfer of skills but on the embedding of a learning culture that perpetuates growth and adaptation. Focal Points are instrumental in this endeavor, serving as linchpins in the process of knowledge diffusion and the cultivation of self-reliance. By actively sharing their expertise, fostering peer-to-peer learning, mentoring colleagues, and advocating for continuous improvement, FPs transform initial training inputs into lasting organizational and community assets. Their commitment to this multifaceted role, supported by appropriate organizational structures and a conducive learning environment, is what ultimately allows local voices to not only be heard but to gain the sustained capacity to lead their own development journeys effectively and sustainably. The investment in well-selected, well-trained, and well-supported Focal Points is therefore not merely an operational detail; it is a strategic imperative for achieving genuine and enduring local capacity building.

The efficacy of any capacity-building initiative, particularly those that rely on empowering local Focal Points (FPs), is

profoundly amplified by the provision of appropriate and accessible tools. These are not just supplementary resources; they are foundational enablers that transform potential into tangible outcomes, bridging gaps in knowledge, connectivity, and operational efficiency. In an increasingly digitalized world, understanding and strategically deploying these technological tools is paramount to ensuring that FPs are equipped not just with skills, but with the means to effectively apply, disseminate, and advance those skills within their contexts.

At the forefront of these empowering tools are the ubiquitous yet transformative laptops. For an FP tasked with managing project data, coordinating activities, or facilitating information sharing, a reliable laptop is indispensable. It serves as the central hub for accessing training materials, compiling reports, managing finances, and engaging in communication. Imagine an FP in a rural agricultural cooperative tasked with introducing climate-smart farming techniques. A laptop allows them to access up-to-date weather data, research best practices for drought-resistant crops, analyze soil reports, and create visual aids for training sessions with fellow farmers. Without this device, their ability to research, strategize, and present information effectively would be severely curtailed, limiting their impact to what could be achieved through manual methods and word-of-mouth, which, while valuable, are often less scalable and less precise. The laptop becomes a portal to a world of information, allowing the FP to bring the latest agricultural science and management strategies directly to their community, adapting them to local conditions rather than relying solely on inherited knowledge. This access democratizes information, leveling the playing field and enabling local actors to engage with global knowledge bases.

Beyond information access, laptops are critical for operational management. FPs often oversee complex activities, requiring meticulous record-keeping, scheduling, and resource allocation. Software for project management, accounting, and even basic word processing and spreadsheet applications allows them to streamline these tasks. Consider an FP coordinating a community health program focused on maternal and child health. They need to track patient visits, manage appointment schedules, record vaccination data, and monitor the distribution of essential supplies. A laptop, equipped with appropriate databases and scheduling software, enables efficient data entry, analysis of trends (e.g., identifying high-risk areas or seasonal disease patterns), and timely reporting to project stakeholders. This not only enhances the FP's personal productivity but also improves the overall accountability and effectiveness of the program. The ability to generate clear, data-driven reports fosters trust with partners and funders and provides valuable evidence for program adjustments and future planning. Furthermore, many of these project management tools can be adapted for collaborative use, allowing the FP to share progress updates and tasks with team members, fostering a sense of shared ownership and accountability.

Equally vital is access to robust communication tools. In today's interconnected world, the ability to communicate effectively and efficiently is not a luxury but a necessity. For FPs operating in remote or underserved areas, reliable communication channels are lifelines that connect them to vital support, information, and networks. This encompasses a range of technologies, from basic mobile phones to internet-based platforms and social media. Mobile phones, particularly in regions where fixed-line infrastructure is scarce, are often the primary means of communication. They enable FPs to check in with supervisors, coordinate with local government officials, communicate with community members about meeting times or urgent issues, and even access basic information through SMS services. For instance, an FP working on disaster preparedness in a coastal village can use a mobile phone to receive early warning alerts and immediately relay critical information to community leaders and residents, potentially saving lives. The ubiquity of mobile technology makes it a powerful tool for immediate reach and dissemination.

As connectivity improves, internet-based communication platforms become increasingly important. Email, instant messaging applications (like WhatsApp or Signal), and video conferencing tools (such as Zoom or Google Meet) enable FPs to engage in more complex and nuanced communication. These platforms facilitate the sharing of documents, images, and videos, allowing for richer and more detailed interactions. An FP leading a local literacy program might use email to share updated curriculum materials with volunteer tutors, use a messaging app to coordinate the logistics of community book drives, and employ video conferencing for virtual training sessions with expert educators located elsewhere. This not only saves time and travel costs but also expands the reach of specialized expertise. Video calls can be particularly impactful for mentorship and technical support, allowing an experienced mentor to visually guide an FP through a complex task or to provide real-time feedback on their presentation skills. These tools create virtual meeting rooms, breaking down geographical barriers and fostering a sense of community among dispersed FPs and their support networks.

Moreover, these communication tools are crucial for building and sustaining networks. FPs are often part of larger initiatives, and connecting with peers, mentors, and experts is vital for professional development and problem-solving. Online forums, professional social media groups, and dedicated communication channels allow FPs to share challenges, exchange best practices, and offer mutual support. Imagine an FP involved in promoting sustainable tourism in a protected area. They might join an online forum for conservation practitioners to discuss challenges related to human-wildlife conflict mitigation or to learn about innovative community engagement strategies from peers in different regions. This peer-to-peer learning is invaluable, providing practical insights and emotional support that formal training alone cannot replicate. It transforms individual FPs into members of a learning community, fostering a collective intelligence that strengthens the overall impact of their work. This interconnectivity also allows for rapid dissemination of critical information, such as policy updates, new funding opportunities, or emerging best practices in their field.

The third critical pillar of empowering tools is access to curated knowledge resources. This goes beyond simply having a laptop and internet connection; it involves providing FPs with organized, relevant, and easily accessible information that directly supports their capacity-building objectives. This can take the form of digital libraries, online databases, repositories of best practices, training modules, case studies, and research papers. For an FP working on improving local governance structures, access to a digital repository of successful decentralization models, participatory budgeting guides, and conflict resolution frameworks would be invaluable. This curated knowledge allows them to draw on proven strategies, adapt them to their specific context, and avoid reinventing the wheel. The selection of these resources is crucial, ensuring they are relevant, up-to-date, and presented in formats that are accessible to FPs with varying levels of digital literacy.

Digital libraries and online learning platforms offer a structured approach to knowledge acquisition. These platforms can host video tutorials, interactive modules, quizzes, and forums where FPs can engage with the material and with each other. For an FP involved in developing vocational training for youth, access to online courses on entrepreneurship, financial literacy, and specific trades would be highly beneficial. They could not only upskill themselves but also leverage these resources to design and deliver effective training programs for their target beneficiaries. The advantage of digital learning platforms is their flexibility; FPs can access the material at their own pace and revisit complex topics as needed, a significant benefit for individuals juggling multiple responsibilities.

Beyond formal learning resources, access to practical guides and toolkits is essential. These are often in the form of downloadable PDFs, interactive checklists, or templates that provide step-by-step instructions for specific tasks. For an FP implementing a new monitoring and evaluation (M&E) system, having access to templates for data collection forms, guidelines for conducting focus group discussions, and manuals on data analysis software would greatly enhance their ability to execute their responsibilities effectively. These practical tools demystify complex processes and provide a clear roadmap for implementation, reducing the likelihood of errors and increasing the efficiency of the FP's work. They serve as on-demand reference materials, empowering the FP to perform tasks confidently and competently.

The strategic provision and training on these tools are as important as the tools themselves. Simply handing out laptops or access codes is insufficient. FPs need to be trained not only on how to operate the devices and platforms but also on how to effectively utilize the knowledge resources available to them. This includes developing digital literacy skills, critical thinking for evaluating online information, and strategies for applying learned concepts in their practical work. Training should also focus on data security and privacy, ensuring that FPs understand how to protect sensitive information. For example, an FP managing community-level health data must be trained on anonymization techniques and secure data storage protocols. Furthermore, ongoing technical support and troubleshooting are essential to ensure that FPs can overcome any challenges they encounter with technology.

The impact of these tools on enhancing skills and operational effectiveness is profound. Laptops, as discussed, provide the platform for research, data analysis, and reporting, directly improving the quality and depth of an FP's work. Communication tools foster collaboration, facilitate timely decision-making, and build essential support networks, leading to more coordinated and responsive interventions. Curated knowledge resources equip FPs with the latest information and proven methodologies, enabling them to adapt to changing contexts and implement best practices. Together, these tools create a virtuous cycle: improved access to information leads to better decision-making, more efficient operations lead to greater impact, and stronger networks foster continuous learning and adaptation.

Consider the synergy between these tools. An FP might use their laptop to research a specific community development challenge. They then use a communication platform to connect with an expert identified through an online network to discuss potential solutions. The expert might share relevant case studies or guides from a digital library, which the FP then accesses on their laptop to adapt for their local context. Finally, the FP uses their laptop to prepare a report on the implemented solution, which they then share with their team via a messaging app. This interconnected use of tools demonstrates how they work in concert to empower the FP and amplify their effectiveness.

The sustainability of these technological interventions is also a key consideration. It is not enough to provide tools for a project's duration. Plans must be in place for maintenance, upgrades, and ongoing training. This might involve **establishing local IT support mechanisms, providing subsidies for internet access, or integrating technology usage into the long-term operational plans of local organizations.** *Without such foresight, the initial investment in tools can quickly become obsolete or unusable, undermining the capacity-building efforts. Therefore, a holistic approach that considers the entire lifecycle of technology is essential.*

Empowering Focal Points through the strategic provision of tools – laptops for processing and accessing information, communication platforms for connectivity and collaboration, and curated knowledge resources for informed practice – is a critical component of **sustainable capacity building.** These tools are not merely conveniences; they are fundamental enablers that enhance an FP's ability to **learn, adapt, implement, and lead.** By equipping FPs with these tangible means, we unlock their potential, enabling them to navigate complex challenges, connect with vital support systems, and ultimately drive meaningful and lasting change within their communities. The investment in these technological assets, coupled with adequate training and support, ensures that local voices are not only empowered to speak but are equipped with the means to effectively shape their own futures.

Measuring capacity growth is not a static or one-time event; it is a continuous process of observation, assessment, and adaptation. It requires a robust framework of indicators that can reliably track the tangible improvements in an organization's ability to manage itself, execute its programs, handle finances responsibly, and engage with its community effectively. For organizations like the Rescue Democracy International (RDI), which are deeply invested in fostering genuine local capacity building, this meticulous measurement is the bedrock upon which we build trust, demonstrate impact, and ensure the long-term sustainability of our partnerships. **Without clear metrics, capacity building can become an amorphous concept, difficult to substantiate and therefore challenging to scale or replicate.**

One of the primary areas of focus in measuring capacity growth is **organizational management**. This encompasses the internal structures, processes, and human resources that enable an organization to function efficiently and effectively. Key indicators here include the development and implementation of clear strategic plans, operational manuals, and internal policies. We look for evidence that partner organizations have moved beyond ad-hoc decision-making towards a more structured approach. For instance, an indicator might be the existence of a documented annual work plan, derived from a longer-term strategic vision, which outlines specific objectives, activities, timelines, and responsible parties. We also assess the regularity and effectiveness of internal meetings, such as board meetings or staff retreats, noting whether minutes are kept, action points are assigned, and follow-up occurs. The presence of a well-defined organizational chart, with clear lines of authority and responsibility, is another important marker. Furthermore, we gauge the level of staff development and retention. Are staff members receiving ongoing training relevant to their roles? Is there a system for performance appraisal and feedback? Is there a noticeable reduction in staff turnover, suggesting a more stable and satisfying work environment? For a local environmental advocacy group, an indicator of improved organizational management might be their ability to successfully lobby local government for stronger environmental regulations after developing a systematic advocacy strategy and building consensus among their members. This goes beyond simply having a passion for the environment; it demonstrates an organizational capacity to translate that passion into concrete policy change through structured engagement.

Another critical dimension of capacity building is project execution and implementation. This measures how well partner organizations can design, manage, and deliver their projects or programs to achieve their intended outcomes. Indicators here are often tied to the project cycle itself. We assess the quality of project proposals submitted, looking for **clear problem statements, realistic objectives, well-defined activities, and measurable indicators of success.** During project implementation, we monitor adherence to timelines and budgets. For example, a key performance indicator might be the percentage of project activities completed on schedule and within budget. We also look at the quality of outputs and outcomes. Are the services being delivered as planned? Are the target beneficiaries satisfied? Is there evidence that the project is achieving its intended impact? For a local health clinic aiming to improve maternal health services, an indicator of successful project execution could be a documented increase in the percentage of pregnant women attending antenatal care sessions, coupled with a decrease in preventable maternal complications, as recorded in their clinical data. This demonstrates not just the ability to run a program, but to run it in a way that yields positive results for the community. We also examine the organization's ability to adapt to unforeseen challenges during project implementation. Resilience and flexibility are key indicators of robust project management capacity. This might be measured by how effectively they adjust their plans or resource allocation in response to external shocks, such as natural disasters or sudden changes in funding availability, while still striving to meet their core objectives.

Financial accountability and management are fundamental to an organization's sustainability and its ability to gain and maintain the trust of its stakeholders, including donors, beneficiaries, and the wider community. Our measurement in this area focuses on transparency, accuracy, and compliance. Key indicators include the establishment and adherence to sound financial management systems, such as robust accounting software and clear internal controls. We assess the regularity and quality of financial reporting. Are organizations producing timely and accurate financial statements, including income and expenditure reports, balance sheets, and cash flow statements? Are these reports understandable to a range of stakeholders, including those without specialized financial knowledge? An important indicator is the presence of an independent audit or review process, which provides an objective assessment of financial health and compliance. We also look at the organization's ability to manage its own resources effectively, including budget planning, expenditure tracking, and prudent financial decision-making. For a community cooperative focused on agricultural marketing, a strong indicator of financial accountability would be their ability to produce transparent annual financial reports that clearly detail income from sales, expenses for inputs and operations, and distributions to members, all of which are made accessible to the cooperative's membership. Furthermore, we assess their capacity to manage grant funding responsibly, ensuring compliance with donor requirements, proper documentation of expenditures, and timely reporting. This includes their ability to develop compelling financial proposals that are realistic and well-justified, demonstrating a clear understanding of their financial needs and how funds will be utilized to achieve programmatic goals.

Community engagement and participation are at the heart of what it means to be truly empowered. This area of measurement focuses on how well partner organizations involve their target communities in decision-making, program design, implementation, and evaluation. Indicators here are more qualitative but equally crucial. We look for evidence of participatory approaches, such as community consultations, focus group discussions, and the establishment of community advisory committees. Is the organization actively seeking feedback from its beneficiaries? How is that feedback being used to inform program adjustments? An important indicator is the level of community ownership and commitment to the initiatives. Are community members actively contributing resources, whether in-kind or financial, or dedicating their time and skills to support the organization's work? For a local youth center aiming to provide vocational training, a key indicator of strong community engagement would be the active participation of parents and local employers in shaping the curriculum, mentoring trainees, and creating internship opportunities. This shows that the center is not just a service provider but a community hub, deeply integrated into the social fabric. We also assess the organization's ability to build partnerships and collaborations with other local stakeholders, including other NGOs, local government agencies, and the private sector. Strong partnerships can amplify impact and create a more enabling environment for sustainable development. This might be measured by the number of successful joint projects undertaken or the establishment of formal Memoranda of Understanding with key partners. The transparency of the organization's communication with the community is also a vital indicator; are they sharing information about their activities, finances, and achievements in accessible ways? This might include public meetings, newsletters, or the use of local media.

To ensure that these measurements are meaningful and actionable, RDI employs a multi-faceted approach to monitoring. This often involves a combination of **quantitative and qualitative data collection methods**. Quantitative indicators, such as the percentage of staff trained in a specific skill, the number of project beneficiaries reached, or the ratio of administrative costs to program expenses, provide objective benchmarks for progress. However, these numbers only tell part of the story. Qualitative data gathered through interviews with staff and community members, observations of organizational processes, and case studies of successful interventions, provides crucial context and deeper insights into the nature and sustainability of capacity growth. For example, while a quantitative indicator might show an increase in the number of community meetings held, qualitative data from those meetings could reveal whether community members feel their voices are genuinely heard and whether their input is influencing decisions.

We also recognize that capacity building is not a linear process, and progress can sometimes be uneven. Therefore, **our monitoring framework is designed to be flexible and responsive**. We work collaboratively with our partner organizations to identify the most relevant indicators for their specific context and objectives. This participatory approach ensures that the measurement process is not perceived as an external imposition but as a shared endeavor to understand and enhance their capabilities. **Regular review meetings are held with partner organizations to discuss progress against the agreed-upon indicators, identify challenges, and collectively develop strategies for improvement.** This ongoing dialogue is essential for fostering learning and adapting our support to meet evolving needs.

Moreover, RDI places significant emphasis on **building the capacity of our partners to monitor their own progress**. This involves training staff in data collection, analysis, and reporting techniques, as well as in the importance of using monitoring data for learning and decision-making. **The goal is**

to empower organizations to become self-sufficient in tracking their own development and demonstrating their impact to a wider audience. This might involve workshops on developing logical frameworks, designing data collection tools, or utilizing simple database systems. We believe that true capacity building includes the ability for local organizations to articulate their own successes and challenges, using data and evidence to advocate for their needs and to continuously improve their own effectiveness. This internal capacity for monitoring and evaluation is a critical indicator of an organization's maturity and its potential for long-term sustainability.

The ultimate aim of measuring capacity growth is to ensure that our interventions lead to **increased local autonomy and sustainability**. When partner organizations demonstrate robust management, effective project execution, sound financial practices, and strong community engagement, they are better equipped to achieve their mission independently. This means they are less reliant on external support for their day-to-day operations, more resilient in the face of challenges, and better positioned to attract diverse funding sources and build enduring relationships within their communities and with other stakeholders. An organization that can reliably measure its own progress, learn from its experiences, and adapt its strategies accordingly is an organization that has truly built its capacity. It is an organization that is not only surviving but thriving, driven by its own vision and sustained by its own strengths. This is the transformative power of capacity building when it is guided by a clear understanding of what growth looks like and how to measure it effectively.

CHAPTER 7:

Monthly Incentives and Motivation:
Sustaining Engagement

The human element is arguably the most vital component in any development endeavor. While robust organizational structures, sound financial management, and well-articulated strategies are indispensable, their effectiveness hinges on the sustained commitment and drive of the individuals who bring them to life. In the often-demanding landscape of international development and humanitarian aid, where challenges are frequent and resources can be stretched thin, maintaining a certain level of motivation is not merely a desirable attribute; it is a fundamental prerequisite for success. This commitment is the engine that powers progress, enabling individuals and teams to navigate complex environments, overcome obstacles, and ultimately achieve the transformative impact that development work strives for. Without a deeply ingrained sense of purpose and the internal and external mechanisms to foster it, even the most meticulously planned projects risk faltering, their potential unrealized due to a decline in the very human energy that drives them forward.

Motivation, in the context of development work, transcends simple job satisfaction. It is a complex interplay of intrinsic desires and extrinsic rewards, a confluence of personal values aligning with the mission, and the recognition of one's contribution to a greater good. For those on the front lines, whether they are local community organizers, field staff in remote areas, or international aid workers, the daily realities can be arduous. They often contend with limited infrastructure, cultural nuances that require careful navigation, and the emotional weight of witnessing persistent needs and systemic inequalities. In such environments, where the immediate gratification of results might be slow to materialize, sustained motivation becomes a critical buffer against burnout and disillusionment. It is the internal compass that keeps individuals oriented towards their goals, even when faced with setbacks, and the fuel that propels them to go the extra mile.

Understanding the drivers of this motivation is therefore paramount for any organization committed to effective and sustainable development. At its core, intrinsic motivation often stems from a profound belief in the mission itself. When individuals feel a deep personal connection to the cause – whether it be alleviating poverty, promoting education, protecting the environment, or ensuring access to healthcare – their work becomes more than just a job; it becomes a calling. This sense of purpose, coupled with the opportunity to make a tangible difference in the lives of others, is a powerful motivator. Development professionals are often drawn to this sector precisely because they want to contribute to positive social change. The ability of an organization to continuously articulate and reinforce this shared vision, and to demonstrate how individual contributions connect to the larger impact, is crucial in nurturing this intrinsic drive. Regular communication about project successes, highlighting the stories of beneficiaries whose lives have been positively impacted, can serve as a potent reminder of why the work matters and reinforce the value of the effort being expended.

Beyond the intrinsic satisfaction of purpose, extrinsic motivators also play a significant role, particularly in contexts where financial remuneration or professional advancement may be less competitive compared to other sectors. While often viewed with skepticism in discussions about idealism, well-designed incentives can significantly bolster engagement and performance. These incentives are not necessarily about monetary gain alone, but about creating an environment where effort is recognized, performance is rewarded, and individuals feel valued. This can manifest in various forms, from performance-based bonuses or salary increments to opportunities for professional development and career advancement. In many development organizations, particularly those operating in lower-income countries, staff may be working for modest salaries. In such scenarios, non-monetary incentives become even more critical. These might include opportunities for specialized training, attendance at international conferences, leadership development programs, or the chance to take on more challenging and impactful responsibilities. Such investments in human capital not only motivate the individual but also build the organization's overall capacity, creating a virtuous cycle of growth and engagement.

The nature of development work, especially in its more challenging manifestations, necessitates a workforce that is not only skilled and knowledgeable but also resilient and adaptable. Individuals who are highly motivated are more likely to exhibit these qualities. They are more willing to learn new approaches, embrace innovation, and persevere through difficulties. This is particularly evident in field operations, where unexpected challenges are commonplace. A motivated field officer, for instance, is more likely to proactively seek solutions to logistical hurdles, to invest extra time in building trust with local communities, and to maintain a positive attitude even when faced with setbacks. This proactive and persistent approach is invaluable in ensuring that projects stay on track and that intended outcomes are achieved, even in dynamic and unpredictable environments.

Moreover, sustained motivation is intrinsically linked to an organization's ability to retain its most valuable personnel. High turnover rates can be incredibly disruptive, leading to loss of institutional knowledge, increased recruitment and training costs, and a potential decline in program quality. **When staff feel motivated, supported, and recognized, they are more likely to remain with the organization long-term.** This stability is crucial for building strong relationships with partner communities, fostering a cohesive team environment, and ensuring the continuity of critical programs. Conversely, a lack of attention to motivation can lead to a revolving door of staff, undermining the very foundations of sustainable development efforts. Organizations that prioritize understanding and nurturing motivation create a more stable, experienced, and effective workforce, which is a significant competitive advantage in attracting and retaining talent in a sector that relies heavily on human capital.

The design and implementation of effective incentive structures require a nuanced understanding of the specific context and the diverse needs of the workforce. What motivates one individual or group may not resonate with another. Therefore, a one-size-fits-all approach is rarely effective. Organizations must invest in understanding the specific drivers of motivation within their particular operational settings. This might involve conducting regular staff surveys, holding informal feedback sessions, or engaging in one-on-one conversations to gauge satisfaction levels and identify areas for improvement. For example, in a rural setting with limited access to specialized training, offering scholarships for advanced degrees or certifications might be a highly potent motivator. In a more urban environment with greater access to educational resources, performance bonuses or opportunities for international travel for project learning could be more appealing. The key is to tailor incentives to be meaningful and relevant to the lived experiences and aspirations of the staff.

Furthermore, it is important to acknowledge that motivation is not solely an individual concern but also a collective one, deeply influenced by the organizational culture. **A supportive and collaborative work environment where teamwork is valued, where open communication is encouraged, and where mistakes are seen as learning opportunities rather than failures, can significantly boost morale and engagement.** Leaders play a pivotal role in shaping this culture. By demonstrating integrity, empathy, and a genuine commitment to the well-being of their staff, leaders can inspire loyalty and foster a shared sense of purpose. When staff feel that their leaders are invested in their success and growth, their own motivation tends to increase. This can involve anything from providing constructive feedback and mentorship to actively advocating for the resources and support that teams need to succeed.

The concept of recognition, both formal and informal, also acts as a powerful motivator. Publicly acknowledging exceptional performance, celebrating team achievements, or simply expressing gratitude for hard work can go a long way in making individuals feel seen and appreciated. This recognition does not always need to be tied to monetary rewards. A heartfelt thank you from a supervisor, a mention in a company-wide newsletter, or a small token of appreciation can have a profound impact on morale. In many development settings, where individuals might be working under stressful conditions and with limited personal comforts, such expressions of appreciation can be particularly meaningful. They signal that the organization recognizes the sacrifices and dedication of its staff, reinforcing their commitment to the cause.

The sustainability of development efforts is intrinsically linked to the sustained motivation of the people implementing them. When individuals are motivated, they are more likely to be innovative, to be resilient in the face of adversity, and to maintain a high level of commitment to their work. This translates into more effective program delivery, stronger community relationships, and ultimately, a greater likelihood of achieving lasting positive change. Therefore, investing in understanding and nurturing motivation through thoughtful incentive structures, supportive leadership, and a positive organizational culture is not merely a human resource best practice; it is a strategic imperative for any organization serious about making a difference in the world. It is the human capital, energized and committed, that transforms good intentions and sound strategies into tangible impact on the ground. The monthly incentive structures discussed in subsequent sections are designed with this fundamental understanding in mind, aiming to foster and sustain the crucial motivation that underpins all successful development work.

The provision of monthly incentives to Focal Points (FPs) is rooted in a clear understanding of the critical, often demanding, role they fulfill within development projects. It is essential to frame these incentives not as salaries, which imply a full-time employment contract and a comprehensive benefits package, but rather as performance-based stipends. This distinction is crucial for setting expectations and accurately reflects the nature of the arrangement. These modest financial recognitions are designed to acknowledge the significant commitment of time, intellectual energy, and practical effort that FPs dedicate to their responsibilities. Their roles extend far beyond mere participation; they involve active engagement, problem-solving, community liaison, data collection, and the overall facilitation of project activities within their designated areas.

The rationale for these stipends is multifaceted, directly addressing the value and the costs associated with the FP's contribution. Firstly, these incentives serve as a tangible recognition of the substantial time investment required. While FPs may not always be engaged on a full-time basis, the cumulative hours dedicated to project tasks – attending meetings, conducting field visits, compiling reports, and responding to queries – can be considerable. In many contexts, FPs are drawn from local communities and may have existing vocational responsibilities or personal commitments. The stipend helps to compensate for the hours that are directly allocated to the project, acknowledging that this time is often diverted from other potential income-generating or personal activities. This ensures that the project does not impose an undue burden on the FP's existing livelihood.

Secondly, the incentives are designed to acknowledge the inherent responsibilities and the often-complex nature of the FP's tasks. FPs are frequently the primary interface between the project team and the local beneficiaries or stakeholders. This position demands a high degree of trust, communication skills, cultural sensitivity, and accountability. They are expected to understand project objectives, translate them into local contexts, gather accurate information, and communicate project updates and feedback effectively. This intermediary role carries significant weight and requires diligent attention to detail and adherence to project protocols. The stipend acts as a validation of this critical function, recognizing that the successful execution of project activities often hinges on the FP's competence and diligence.

Furthermore, the stipends address the concept of opportunity cost. In many developing regions, skilled and motivated individuals who could serve as effective FPs may have alternative employment opportunities that offer more stable or higher remuneration. By providing a modest incentive, the project aims to mitigate the opportunity cost of engaging the FP, making their participation financially viable and attractive. This is particularly relevant when considering individuals who possess valuable local knowledge and community standing, qualities that are indispensable for project success but may not be fully captured by traditional employment metrics. The incentive acknowledges that by choosing to dedicate their efforts to the project, these individuals are forgoing other avenues for income or personal advancement.

The performance-based aspect of these stipends is a cornerstone of their design. They are not unconditional payments but are linked to the fulfillment of specific deliverables and the achievement of agreed-upon performance indicators. This approach fosters accountability and encourages a proactive and results-oriented approach from the FPs. For instance, timely submission of accurate data, successful mobilization of community members for project activities, or demonstrated progress in specific project objectives can be tied to the disbursement of the monthly stipend. This performance linkage ensures that the incentives are aligned with the project's goals and that the FPs are motivated to actively contribute to achieving them. It also provides a clear framework for evaluating their contribution and identifying areas where additional support or training might be beneficial.

Moreover, these financial recognitions can play a role in professionalizing the FP role. By offering a consistent, though modest, stipend, the project implicitly elevates the status of the FP position within the community. It signals that the organization values their contribution and is willing to invest in their involvement. This can enhance the FP's own sense of professionalism and commitment, encouraging them to approach their duties with greater seriousness and dedication. It can also contribute to building a pool of trained and experienced individuals who can be relied upon for future development initiatives, thereby strengthening local capacity and fostering a long-term engagement with development work.

The structure of these monthly incentives is also informed by the need for sustainability and equitable distribution within the project framework. The amounts are calibrated to be meaningful enough to acknowledge effort and offset costs, without becoming so substantial that they create dependency or distort local economic dynamics. This careful calibration ensures that the incentives remain a supportive mechanism rather than a primary source of income, thus preserving the voluntary and community-oriented spirit of the FP role where appropriate. The regular, monthly disbursement provides a predictable stream of support, allowing FPs to better manage their personal finances and maintain their engagement with the project over the duration of its implementation.

In essence, the rationale for monthly incentives for Focal Points is grounded in the principles of fairness, recognition, and mutual benefit. They are a strategic investment in human capital, acknowledging that the dedication and effort of individuals on the ground are pivotal to the successful implementation of development projects. These stipends are a mechanism to ensure that their valuable contributions are not only acknowledged but also adequately supported, thereby fostering sustained engagement, high performance, and ultimately, the achievement of the project's overarching development objectives. By providing these financial recognitions, the project demonstrates its commitment to valuing its human resources and creating an environment where dedicated individuals can thrive and effectively contribute to positive change.

The design of any incentive structure, particularly within the nuanced landscape of international development and community-based projects, must be meticulously crafted to ensure fairness, transparency, and efficacy. At the core of sustaining the engagement and motivation of Focal Points (FPs) lies the establishment of clear, objective, and consistently applied criteria for receiving their monthly stipends. This is not merely a procedural requirement; it is a foundational element that builds trust, reinforces accountability, and cultivates a sense of equitable contribution among all participants in the project network. The overarching goal is to create a system that is not only understood but also perceived as just by every individual serving as an FP, thereby maximizing its positive impact on their commitment and the project's overall success.

To achieve this, the incentives must be directly linked to demonstrated performance and unwavering commitment to the project's objectives. This linkage moves beyond abstract expectations and grounds the reward system in concrete actions and outcomes. The criteria for eligibility for the monthly stipend should be explicitly defined and communicated to each FP during their onboarding and at regular intervals thereafter. Ambiguity in this regard can quickly breed dissatisfaction and demotivation, leading to an erosion of trust in the project's management and its commitment to its field personnel. Therefore, the process begins with a clear articulation of what constitutes successful performance.

This clarity often translates into a set of measurable key performance indicators (KPIs) or agreed-upon deliverables. For instance, an FP's monthly stipend might be contingent upon the timely submission of accurate field reports, which could include data on community participation in project activities, local market price fluctuations for agricultural products, or the prevalence of specific health issues. The definition of "timely" and "accurate" must be precise. Is a report considered timely if submitted within 48 hours of the end of the reporting period, or within 24 hours? What constitutes accuracy – a report with no factual errors, or one that meets a predefined completeness threshold? These details, while seemingly granular, are critical to ensuring objectivity and preventing subjective interpretations that could lead to disputes.

Beyond data submission, performance can also be evaluated based on the FP's role in facilitating project activities. This might include evidence of successful community mobilization, such as consistent attendance at training sessions or active participation in community meetings. The project might define success here by the number of community members reached or engaged, or by qualitative assessments of their participation levels. Another crucial aspect could be the FP's proactive engagement in problem-solving at the local level. This could be evidenced by the identification and reporting of challenges coupled with proposed solutions or actions taken to mitigate immediate issues. The transparency in evaluating these qualitative contributions is paramount. This often requires establishing a feedback mechanism where supervisors or project coordinators can provide structured observations and assessments of an FP's performance, which are then shared with the FP.

Commitment is another vital dimension that the incentive structure should acknowledge. This can be measured through factors such as consistent availability for project-related tasks, responsiveness to communication from the project team, and the overall dedication demonstrated towards fulfilling their responsibilities. For example, an FP who consistently makes themselves available for unscheduled field visits or readily responds to urgent queries, even outside of regular working hours, exemplifies a strong commitment that warrants recognition. This aspect can be assessed through communication logs, attendance records, and feedback from project supervisors who directly interact with the FPs. The emphasis here is on recognizing sustained effort and dedication, not just isolated instances of high performance.

The principle of fairness dictates that the criteria for receiving incentives must be applied uniformly across all FPs within similar roles and contexts. This means that the performance indicators and expectations should be standardized, allowing for a level playing field. While the nature of field work may necessitate some contextual adaptations in the specific targets or benchmarks, the underlying principles of what is required to earn the stipend must remain consistent. For example, if an FP in one region is responsible for gathering data on agricultural yields, and an FP in another region is responsible for monitoring sanitation facilities, the core requirements for accurate reporting and community engagement should be comparable in their rigor, even if the specific data points differ.

Transparency in the incentive system extends to the communication of how these incentives are calculated and disbursed. FPs should have a clear understanding of the total potential stipend amount and the specific factors that influence its disbursement each month. This includes knowing which performance indicators are being assessed, what the benchmarks are, and how their performance against these benchmarks translates into their monthly earnings. Any deductions or adjustments to the stipend should also be clearly explained, along with the rationale behind them. This open communication fosters trust and reduces the likelihood of misunderstandings or perceptions of favoritism.

A critical component of this transparency involves the regular feedback loops. **FPs should receive not only confirmation of their stipend but also constructive feedback on their performance. This feedback should highlight areas of strength, acknowledge achievements, and identify areas for improvement.** When a stipend is reduced or withheld due to performance, the FP must be informed of the specific reasons, with clear links to the pre-defined criteria. Furthermore, a process for appeal or clarification should be in place, allowing FPs to discuss their assessments or present mitigating circumstances if they believe an error has been made. This ensures that the system is not only perceived as fair but also possesses mechanisms for correction, reinforcing its credibility.

The design process itself should also embody transparency. When developing or revising the incentive structure, it is beneficial to involve FPs or their representatives in the discussion. Gathering input on what they perceive as fair performance metrics, understanding the challenges they face in meeting them, and seeking their perspectives on the motivational impact of different incentive designs can lead to **a more robust and accepted system. While the final decision rests with the project management, a participatory approach can significantly enhance buy-in and ensure that the structure is practical and relevant to the realities on the ground.**

Furthermore, the financial aspect of the incentives must be managed with the utmost integrity and efficiency. The disbursement of monthly stipends should be predictable and reliable. Delays or irregularities in payment can undermine even the most well-designed incentive structure, erode morale and create financial instability for the FPs. Robust financial management systems are therefore essential to ensure that funds are available and disbursed promptly, according to the agreed-upon schedule. This reliability is a tangible demonstration of the project's commitment to its FPs.

Considerations for varying economic contexts are also vital for maintaining fairness. While standardization of criteria is important, the actual value of the stipend might need to be adjusted to reflect the cost of living and local economic conditions in different operational areas. A stipend that is adequate in one region might be insufficient in another. Therefore, while the performance expectations remain consistent, the financial value of the incentive could be benchmarked against local economic indicators to ensure it remains a meaningful, though supplementary, source of support. This requires careful research and periodic review of local economic data.

The appeal of an incentive structure also lies in its clarity regarding what *not* to do. **Explicitly stating that FPs are not full-time employees and that the stipend is performance-based, rather than salary, is crucial for managing expectations.** This prevents potential misunderstandings about benefits such as health insurance, pension contributions, or formal employment rights. Transparency here means clearly defining the boundaries of the contractual relationship and the scope of the stipend's purpose, which is to recognize and support performance and commitment within the specific framework of their role.

In practice, the implementation of a fair and transparent incentive structure often involves a tiered approach or a system of progressive recognition. For example, FPs might receive a base stipend for meeting minimum performance standards, with additional bonus amounts or honoraria for exceeding expectations or taking on additional responsibilities. This allows for differentiation based on contribution levels while still ensuring that everyone who meets the core requirements is recognized. Such a system can be particularly effective in motivating FPs to go above and beyond their basic duties.

Another practical aspect is the mechanism for collecting performance data. The tools and processes used for data collection must be simple, user-friendly, and accessible to FPs, especially those working in remote areas with limited technological access. Training on how to use these tools effectively and ensuring that the data collected is handled securely and confidentially are also key elements of a transparent and fair system. The accuracy and integrity of the performance data directly impact the fairness of the incentive disbursement.

The review and adaptation of the incentive structure over time are also essential in this shift. As projects evolve, new challenges emerge, and operational contexts change, the incentive structure may need to be adjusted to remain relevant and effective. Establishing a regular review cycle, perhaps annually or bi-annually, where the criteria, performance metrics, and financial amounts are assessed for their ongoing fairness and motivational impact, is a hallmark of a well-managed project. This review process should ideally involve feedback from FPs and project management to ensure that the system continues to serve its intended purpose effectively.

Ultimately, the success of any incentive system hinges on its perceived fairness and transparency by the very individuals it aims to motivate. When FPs understand the criteria, trust that they are applied objectively and consistently, and feel that their efforts are genuinely valued, their engagement and commitment will be significantly enhanced. This fosters a positive feedback loop, where motivated FPs contribute more effectively to project goals, leading to better outcomes, which in turn reinforces the value of the incentive system and the project's commitment to its field personnel. **The ongoing investment in clearly defining, communicating, and consistently applying these structures is fundamental to**

the long-term sustainability of any development initiative that relies on dedicated individuals at the grassroots level.

The introduction of a consistent, performance-linked monthly incentive system for Focal Points (FPs) has demonstrably catalyzed tangible improvements in project delivery across various operational domains. An analysis of project data and qualitative feedback from field supervisors reveals a pronounced positive correlation between the regular disbursement of these financial recognitions and enhanced FP performance. This impact is not merely anecdotal; it is observable in the increased reliability, timeliness, and overall quality of the tasks undertaken by the FPs. For instance, in numerous project sites, the timely submission of accurate field reports has seen a significant uptick. Where previously there might have been a degree of variability in the submission of crucial data – whether related to community needs assessments, distribution of essential supplies, or monitoring of project activity implementation – the advent of the incentive structure has fostered a greater sense of urgency and accountability. FPs, understanding that their monthly stipend is directly tied to the consistent and accurate fulfillment of these reporting obligations, are more diligent in collecting and submitting information within the stipulated timeframes. This has, in turn, provided project managers with more up-to-date and reliable data, enabling more agile decision-making and proactive problem-solving. The ability to track progress with greater accuracy allows for the swift identification of bottlenecks or emerging challenges, thereby facilitating timely interventions that can prevent minor issues from escalating into major setbacks. This improved data flow, driven by the incentive mechanism, directly contributes to the overall efficiency and effectiveness of project operations, ensuring that resources are deployed optimally and that project milestones are met with greater regularity.

Furthermore, the responsiveness of FPs to project-related communications and requests has also shown a marked improvement. In environments where FPs are often the primary interface between the project and the beneficiary communities, their availability and promptness in responding to queries or executing new tasks are critical. The monthly incentive, acting as a constant reminder of the project's value and the FP's role within it, cultivates a proactive attitude. FPs are more likely to be accessible and engaged, readily responding to calls, messages, or requests for information, even when these may arise outside of conventional working hours. This heightened responsiveness translates into smoother coordination, faster resolution of community-level issues, and a stronger sense of partnership between the project team and the FPs. Supervisors have reported a noticeable reduction in the time lag between a request being made and an action being taken at the community level, a direct consequence of the motivational boost provided by the incentive. This improved communication flow also ensures that FPs are kept abreast of any changes in project protocols or objectives, allowing them to **adapt** their work accordingly and maintain alignment with the project's evolving needs.

The quality of work undertaken by FPs has also experienced a discernible uplift. **When individuals feel that their contributions are recognized and financially compensated, they are naturally inclined to invest more effort and attention to detail in their tasks.** This is particularly evident in activities requiring meticulous data collection, careful observation, or the nurturing of community relationships. For example, in projects focused on public health outreach, FPs who receive incentives are more likely to conduct thorough community education sessions, ensuring that health messages are clearly communicated and understood. They are also more motivated to meticulously record attendance, follow-up on individuals who miss sessions, and provide detailed feedback on community reception. Similarly, in agricultural development projects, FPs may demonstrate greater diligence in monitoring crop health, recording pest infestations, or tracking the adoption of new farming techniques, knowing that the accuracy and completeness of their observations contribute directly to their monthly earnings. This increased commitment to quality not only enhances the integrity of the project's data but also improves the efficacy of the interventions themselves, leading to more sustainable and impactful outcomes at the community level. The incentive system, therefore, serves as a powerful tool for embedding a culture of excellence and accountability within the FP network.

The tangible link between motivated individuals and successful project outcomes can be quantified through various performance metrics. For instance, projects that have implemented performance-based incentives have often observed a reduction in the number of incomplete or erroneous reports submitted by FPs. A comparative analysis might show a decrease in the percentage of late reports from, say, 15% to under 5% after the introduction of the incentive scheme. Similarly, the rate of successfully completed community mobilization events, measured by attendance figures or specific community engagement indicators, can rise significantly. If, for example, a project aims to increase participation in child vaccination drives, FPs incentivized for their efforts might contribute to a 20% increase in the number of children brought to health centers, directly attributable to their persistent outreach and community engagement. The incentive, therefore, acts as a catalyst, transforming passive participation into active, results-oriented engagement. This demonstrates a clear return on investment in human capital, as the modest financial incentive yields disproportionately larger gains in project efficiency and effectiveness.

Moreover, the incentive structure fosters a sense of professional development and ownership among FPs. When their efforts are recognized and rewarded, FPs are more likely to view their role not just as a voluntary contribution but as a valued position with tangible benefits. This can lead to a greater willingness to invest time in understanding project protocols, improving their skills, and proactively seeking solutions to challenges they encounter in the field. Supervisors often observe that incentivized FPs are more likely to proactively identify areas where they can improve their performance or contribute more effectively to project goals. This self-driven initiative, nurtured by the incentive system, cultivates a more empowered and engaged workforce at the grassroots level. The financial reward becomes a symbol of appreciation for their hard work and dedication, reinforcing their commitment and encouraging them to continually strive for better results. This psychological impact of recognition, coupled with the material benefit, creates a potent combination for sustained motivation and improved performance, directly impacting the successful delivery of project objectives and the achievement of broader development goals.

The economic rationale behind such incentive systems is robust. **By providing a predictable and performance-dependent stipend, projects can ensure a more reliable and dedicated cadre of field personnel without incurring the overheads associated with full-time employment.** This is particularly crucial in resource-constrained settings where flexibility and cost-effectiveness are paramount. The incentive serves as a flexible financial support, enabling FPs to cover basic expenses related to their project work, such as transportation, communication, and small administrative costs, thereby removing practical barriers to their engagement. When FPs are not burdened by these immediate financial considerations, they can dedicate more of their energy and focus to the core tasks of the project. This optimization of human resources, driven by a well-structured incentive program, allows development organizations to maximize the impact of their limited budgets, ensuring that a larger proportion of funds directly benefits the target communities. The improved delivery of services and the more efficient implementation of activities, resulting from the enhanced performance of incentivized FPs, ultimately contribute to more sustainable and meaningful development outcomes. This financial prudence, married with a strategic investment in motivating field staff, underscores the efficacy of performance-based incentives in the complex landscape of international development.

Furthermore, the incentive system contributes to a more equitable distribution of project benefits within the FP network. By clearly linking rewards to demonstrable performance, the system helps to differentiate between those who consistently meet and exceed expectations and those who may struggle to do so. This fairness in reward allocation, provided the criteria are transparent and consistently applied, can foster a positive competitive spirit among FPs, encouraging them to improve their own performance by observing and learning from their more successful peers. It also serves to validate the efforts of high-performing individuals, ensuring that their dedication is recognized and that they remain motivated and engaged with the project. This contrasts with systems where all FPs might receive a uniform stipend regardless of their individual contributions, which can lead to demotivation among the most dedicated members and a general sense of stagnation. The performance-driven incentive structure, therefore, plays a critical role in cultivating a high-achieving team, where individual efforts are acknowledged and collective project success is driven by the aggregated performance of its dedicated FPs. This fosters a culture of continuous improvement and professional accountability, essential for the sustained success of any development initiative.

The observed improvements in consistency are particularly noteworthy. In project phases where FPs received only an honorarium or no financial recognition, there was often a pattern of sporadic engagement, with some FPs being highly active for periods and then disappearing due to competing demands or a lack of perceived benefit. The monthly incentive, however, transforms this dynamic. It provides a consistent, though supplementary, income stream that encourages ongoing and regular participation. **This regularity is crucial for building sustained community relationships, ensuring continuous monitoring of project activities, and maintaining a consistent flow of information to the project management.** For example, in a project focused on early childhood education, regular home visits by FPs are vital for parent engagement and child development monitoring. A consistent incentive ensures that FPs are more likely to undertake these visits throughout the project cycle, rather than only when they feel particularly motivated or have spare time. This regularity directly contributes to the sustained progress and positive outcomes for the children involved, demonstrating the profound impact of consistent financial recognition on the reliability of project delivery at the grassroots level. The predictability of the incentive allows FPs to plan their own activities more effectively, integrating their project responsibilities with their personal lives, thereby ensuring a more dependable commitment to their roles.

In conclusion, the impact of monthly incentives on project delivery and Focal Point performance is overwhelmingly positive and multifaceted. The evidence points towards enhanced consistency in reporting and activity execution, improved responsiveness to project needs and community issues, and a tangible increase in the quality of work performed. These improvements are directly attributable to the motivational power of a well-structured incentive system that recognizes and rewards diligent effort and tangible results. Financial recognition, when coupled with clear performance expectations and transparent application, serves not only as a tangible benefit but also as a powerful enabler of proactive engagement and dedicated service. This investment in human capital yields significant returns in terms of project efficiency, effectiveness, and ultimately, the achievement of sustainable development outcomes. The data consistently shows that motivated FPs are more effective FPs, and the incentive structure is a critical tool in fostering that motivation and ensuring the successful implementation of vital development programs on the ground.

The implementation of any incentive-based remuneration, even when designed to enhance performance and efficiency, necessitates a thorough examination of its ethical underpinnings and long-term sustainability. At Rescue Democracy International (RDI), this principle is paramount. While the efficacy of monthly incentives in galvanizing Focal Points (FPs) has been clearly demonstrated in driving improved project delivery, timeliness, and overall quality of work, it is imperative to anchor these practices in robust ethical frameworks and ensure their financial and operational viability over the long haul. This involves a delicate balancing act: **leveraging the motivational power of financial recognition without undermining the core principles of aid effectiveness, fostering genuine capacity building, and crucially, avoiding the creation of unintended dependencies.**

One of the primary ethical considerations revolves around the concept of 'aid dependency' and the potential for incentives to inadvertently create such a dynamic. The intention behind RDI's incentive model is to supplement the efforts of dedicated individuals who are deeply embedded within their communities and possess invaluable local knowledge. The incentives are designed to be a recognition of diligent service and performance, enabling FPs to cover essential project-related expenses and providing a modest financial cushion that allows them to dedicate more time and energy to their roles. It is crucial, therefore, that the incentive amount is calibrated to reflect this supplementary nature, rather than evolving into a primary source of income that could disincentivize alternative economic activities or create an unhealthy reliance on the project. Ethical practice demands that FPs remain primarily driven by a commitment to their communities and the project's development goals, with the incentive acting as a catalyst and reward for these intrinsic motivations, not a replacement for them. Regular reviews of the incentive structure are conducted to ensure it remains aligned with this principle, considering local economic conditions and the actual costs associated with carrying out project responsibilities. This involves engaging with FPs themselves to understand their financial realities and how the incentives are perceived and utilized, ensuring that the system supports, rather than supplies, their broader livelihoods.

Furthermore, the transparency and fairness in the application of the incentive criteria are non-negotiable ethical imperatives. As previously highlighted, the linkage between performance and reward is a cornerstone of the model. However, the metrics used to measure performance must be clear, objective, and communicated effectively to all FPs. Any ambiguity or perceived arbitrariness in assessment can lead to disillusionment, a decline in morale, and a breakdown of trust, negating the intended motivational benefits. **RDI is committed to establishing well-defined Key Performance Indicators (KPIs) that are directly attributable to the FPs' responsibilities and are measurable.** These KPIs are not static; they are periodically reviewed and refined based on project evolution and lessons learned, ensuring their continued relevance and achievability. For instance, if a project's focus shifts from community mobilization to post-distribution monitoring, the relevant KPIs for FPs would be adjusted accordingly. The process of performance assessment itself must be equitable, with supervisors trained to conduct evaluations impartially and to provide constructive feedback. This feedback loop is vital, not only for fair assessment but also for fostering the professional development of the FPs, allowing them to understand how they can improve their performance and, consequently, their incentives. This commitment to transparency extends to the communication of decisions regarding incentives, ensuring that FPs understand the basis for any variations in their monthly remuneration.

The sustainability of the incentive model is intrinsically linked to its financial viability within the broader RDI operational framework and its alignment with the principles of aid effectiveness. Development projects, by their nature, operate within often-constrained budgets, and any financial mechanism must be robust enough to withstand fiscal fluctuations and project lifecycle changes. RDI approaches this by integrating the incentive budget as a core component of project planning from the outset. This is not an add-on; it is a calculated investment in human capital that directly contributes to achieving project objectives efficiently and effectively. Financial sustainability is ensured through rigorous budgeting, diligent fund management, and a proactive approach to resource mobilization. It also involves scenario planning to anticipate potential funding gaps and to develop contingency strategies. For example, if there is a potential for delayed disbursements from donors, RDI may have pre-established internal financial mechanisms or reserve funds to ensure that the incentive payments to FPs are not disrupted, thereby **maintaining the trust and reliability of the system.**

Moreover, the sustainability of the incentive model is also viewed through a programmatic lens. The model is designed to complement, rather than replace, the core mission of empowering communities. The FPs are integral to this mission, acting as conduits of information, facilitators of activities, and bridges between RDI and the communities. The incentives are intended to enhance their capacity and commitment to fulfilling these roles, ultimately strengthening the community's own agency and ability to drive their development. This means that **the success of the incentive model is not solely measured by the FPs' performance in project-related tasks, but also by the extent to which their engagement leads to greater community participation, ownership, and the development of local capacities.** For instance, if FPs, motivated by the incentives, effectively facilitate community meetings where local leaders are empowered to make decisions about resource allocation, this demonstrates a sustainable impact that goes beyond individual performance metrics. The aim is to foster a self-sustaining cycle of engagement and development within the community, where the presence and support of FPs, bolstered by the incentive structure, lead to lasting positive change.

Examining the ethical dimension further, it is crucial to consider the potential for the incentive structure to inadvertently create divisions or foster an unhealthy sense of competition among FPs. While a degree of healthy competition can be beneficial, if the incentive system is perceived as unfairly favoring certain individuals or groups, it can breed resentment and undermine team cohesion. RDI's approach is to ensure that the performance metrics are applied universally and that all FPs have equal opportunity to meet or exceed them. Training for supervisors emphasizes the importance of recognizing and nurturing the strengths of all FPs, providing tailored support where needed. Peer-to-peer learning and collaborative problem-solving are actively encouraged, creating an environment where FPs can learn from each other's successes and challenges. This fosters a sense of collective responsibility for project outcomes, rather than an individualized pursuit of incentives. For example, in areas where data collection is particularly challenging due to geographical or security constraints, RDI might provide additional training or logistical support to FPs in those areas, ensuring a more level playing field.

The sustainability of the incentive model also hinges on its adaptability to different contexts and project phases. What works in a highly urbanized setting might not be appropriate for a remote rural area. RDI's approach is therefore flexible and context-specific. The design of the incentive structure, including the specific KPIs and the value of the incentive, is developed in close consultation with field teams and community representatives during the initial project design phase. This ensures that the model is relevant, practical, and aligned with the unique realities on the ground. As projects evolve, the incentive structure is subject to ongoing monitoring and evaluation, allowing for adjustments to be made as needed. For instance, if a project shifts from direct service delivery to capacity building, the nature of the FPs' activities and the metrics for their performance may change, necessitating a recalibration of the incentive system. This iterative approach ensures that the model remains effective and sustainable throughout the project lifecycle, maintaining its relevance and motivational impact.

Ethical considerations also extend to the potential impact of the incentives on the broader community. While the incentives are directed at the FPs, their actions and their enhanced capacity can have ripple effects. It is important to ensure that the increased focus and engagement of FPs do not inadvertently lead to the exclusion of other community members or stakeholders. For example, if FPs are incentivized for organizing community meetings, they should be encouraged to ensure that these meetings are inclusive and representative of diverse community groups, including marginalized populations. RDI's community engagement strategies emphasize broad participation, and the role of FPs is to facilitate this inclusivity. The training provided to FPs includes modules on gender equality, social inclusion, and participatory approaches, reinforcing the ethical imperative to serve all members of the community equitably. The financial benefit received by the FP should ultimately translate into a greater benefit for the entire community through more effective and inclusive project implementation.

The long-term sustainability of the incentive model is also tied to the perception of its legitimacy and fairness by the beneficiaries. While beneficiaries do not directly receive the incentives, they are the ultimate recipients of the project's services, and their observations of the FPs' work are crucial. If the community perceives the FPs as being well-supported, diligent, and committed, and if they witness the positive impact of this enhanced engagement on project outcomes, the model gains legitimacy. Conversely, if the community views the FPs as being motivated solely by financial gain, or if they perceive inequities in the system, it can undermine community trust and cooperation. RDI actively solicits feedback from community members through various channels, including focus group discussions and community meetings, to gauge their perceptions of the FPs and the overall project implementation.

This feedback is used to refine the incentive model and ensure that it aligns with community expectations and fosters positive relationships. The sustainability of the model, therefore, is not just about financial resources, but also about maintaining the social contract between RDI, the FPs, and the communities they serve.

In considering **financial sustainability**, RDI also explores the potential for integrating the incentive structure into local government or community-led initiatives over the long term. While the initial funding often comes from external donors, the goal of development is to foster self-sufficiency. As local institutions strengthen and community-based organizations gain capacity, there is potential for them to take ownership resource elements of the project, including the remuneration of local facilitators. This long-term vision informs the design of the current incentive model, ensuring that the processes and metrics established are transparent and replicable, and that FPs are also supported in building their own organizational and advocacy skills. The focus remains on **building local capacity and leadership**, so that the positive impacts achieved through the incentive system can endure beyond the lifespan of any specific project funding. This involves not only financial planning but also strategic capacity building for local partners, ensuring that the motivation and dedication fostered through the incentive system can be sustained through local ownership and commitment.

Ultimately, the ethical considerations and sustainability of monthly incentives for FPs are inextricably linked. An ethically sound model, characterized by transparency, fairness, and commitment to capacity building, is more likely to be sustainable in the long run. Conversely, a financially viable and well-managed system that is aligned with the core development mission provides the foundation for ethical practice. RDI's commitment is to continuously assess and adapt its incentive models to ensure they remain a powerful tool for positive change, driven by integrity and a vision for lasting development impact. This ongoing commitment involves regular internal audits, external evaluations, and a willingness to learn from both successes and challenges, ensuring that the pursuit of improved project delivery through incentives is always guided by a strong moral compass and a clear understanding of our responsibility to the communities we serve and the donors who entrust us with their resources. The aim is to create a virtuous cycle where motivated FPs contribute to empowered communities, thereby ensuring the long-term success and sustainability of our development efforts.

CHAPTER 8:

Bridging The SDG GAP:
A Scalable Solution

The global tapestry of development is woven with threads of ambition, aspiration, and, increasingly, urgency. At the heart of this intricate design lies the **Sustainable Development Goals (SDGs)**, a universal call to action adopted by all United Nations Member States in 2015 (after the failure of the Millennium Development Goals (MDGs). These seventeen interconnected goals represent an unprecedented commitment to tackling humanity's most pressing challenges and charting a course towards a more equitable, prosperous, and sustainable future for all. Their scope is breathtaking, encompassing a comprehensive agenda that seeks to eradicate poverty in all its forms, protect the planet, and ensure that all people enjoy peace and prosperity by the year 2030. This ambitious undertaking is not merely a set of lofty ideals; it is a concrete roadmap for transformation, grounded in the recognition that progress in one area is intrinsically linked to progress in others.

The sheer breadth of the SDGs speaks to the interconnectedness of global issues. They address fundamental human rights and needs, starting with the eradication of extreme poverty and hunger (SDG 1 and SDG 2). This foundational goal is inextricably linked to ensuring good health and well-being for all (SDG 3), providing quality education (SDG 4), and achieving gender equality (SDG 5).

These are not isolated issues; poverty exacerbates health problems, lack of education perpetuates cycles of deprivation, and gender inequality limits the potential of half the world's population. Beyond these core human development concerns, the SDGs also pivot towards economic progress and structural change, calling for decent work and economic growth (SDG 8), industry, innovation, and infrastructure (SDG 9), and the reduction of inequalities within and among countries (SDG 10). These economic dimensions are crucial for creating the resources and opportunities necessary to address the more fundamental human needs.

Furthermore, the SDG agenda extends to the critical need for sustainable cities and communities (SDG 11), responsible consumption and production (SDG 12), and urgent action to combat climate change and its impacts (SDG 13). The health of our planet is a prerequisite for the health of its inhabitants, and the SDGs acknowledge this vital relationship. This recognition is further amplified in goals focused on life below water (SDG 14) and life on land (SDG 15), underscoring the imperative to conserve and sustainably use our natural resources. Finally, the framework is completed by a commitment to partnerships for the goals (SDG 17) and peace, justice, and strong institutions (SDG 16). These latter goals are the enablers, recognizing that achieving all the other targets requires strong governance, the rule of law, access to justice, and collaborative action on a global scale. Without peace and strong institutions, sustainable development remains an elusive dream.

The urgency surrounding the SDGs stems from a stark reality: the clock is ticking. The year 2030, the target date for achieving these goals, is not a distant horizon but a rapidly approaching milestone. As we move further into the current decade, the window of opportunity for meaningful intervention and transformative change narrows with each passing year. The initial promise and optimism of 2015, when the goals were adopted, are now tempered by the palpable need for accelerated and more effective action. Progress has been made in certain areas, a testament to the dedication of governments, civil society, and individuals worldwide. However, the overall pace of change is insufficient to meet the ambitious targets set. Many of the most vulnerable populations, those most affected by poverty, conflict, and environmental degradation, are being left further behind.

The complexity of the challenges we face is immense. Poverty, while declining in some regions, remains deeply entrenched in others, often exacerbated by conflict, climate shocks, and economic instability. Inequalities, both within and between nations, continue to widen, undermining social cohesion and hindering inclusive development. Climate change poses an existential threat, with rising global temperatures leading to more frequent and intense extreme weather events, impacting food security, water availability, and human displacement. Access to basic services like healthcare and education remains a privilege for far too many, perpetuating cycles of disadvantage. The COVID-19 pandemic, in particular, has had a devastating impact on global development progress, reversing years of gains in poverty reduction, health, and education, and highlighting the fragility of our interconnected world.

This reality underscores the fundamental premise of the SDGs: they are not optional extras or aspirational ideals to be pursued at leisure. They are a critical imperative for the survival and well-being of current and future generations. The limited time remaining amplifies the **need for a paradigm shift in how we approach development.** Business as usual is no longer an option. We must move beyond incremental improvements and embrace bold, innovative, and scalable solutions. The SDGs represent a shared global vision but translating that vision into tangible reality requires a commensurate level of commitment, resource mobilization, and, crucially, effective implementation strategies.

The SDG agenda is inherently ambitious because the problems it seeks to solve are deeply rooted and multifaceted. **Eradicating extreme poverty, for instance, is not simply about providing aid; it requires addressing the systemic causes of poverty, including lack of access to resources, education, healthcare, and decent employment, as well as challenging discriminatory practices and promoting inclusive economic policies.** Similarly, achieving gender equality is not just about legal reforms; it involves transforming deeply ingrained social norms and power structures that perpetuate discrimination against women and girls. Addressing climate change demands a fundamental reorientation of our energy systems, consumption patterns, and economic models.

The urgency is amplified by the potential for irreversible tipping points. If we fail to act decisively on climate change, we risk crossing thresholds beyond which adaptation becomes impossible, with catastrophic consequences for ecosystems and human societies. Similarly, if we allow inequalities to fester unchecked, they can lead to social unrest, political instability, and the erosion of trust in institutions, further hindering development progress. The SDGs, therefore, are not just about achieving desirable outcomes; they are about averting existential risks and safeguarding the future of our planet and its inhabitants.

The commitment to achieving the SDGs by 2030 necessitates a profound re-evaluation of our current approaches. It demands a shift from fragmented, short-term interventions to integrated, long-term strategies that address the root causes of development challenges. It calls for a renewed emphasis on data and evidence-based policymaking, robust monitoring and evaluation mechanisms, and a willingness to adapt and innovate in response to evolving contexts. The success of the SDGs will ultimately depend on the ability of governments, international organizations, civil society, the private sector, and individuals to work together in a coordinated and impactful manner.

The scale of the undertaking is such that it requires a fundamental re-thinking of how development is financed, implemented, and governed. Traditional models of aid, while still important, are insufficient to bridge the vast funding gaps that exist. Innovative financing mechanisms, private sector engagement, and the mobilization of domestic resources are all critical components of a comprehensive strategy. **Moreover, the effectiveness of our efforts is contingent upon fostering strong partnerships and ensuring that the voices of those most affected by poverty and inequality are central to decision-making processes.** The SDGs are not a one-size-fits-all blueprint; they must be tailored to national contexts and implemented with a deep understanding of local realities and aspirations.

The narrative of the SDGs is one of both immense opportunity and critical challenge. The opportunity lies in the collective power of humanity to create a better world, a world where poverty is eradicated, the planet is protected, and every individual has the chance to thrive. The challenge lies in overcoming the inertia of existing systems, the vested interests that resist change, and the sheer complexity of the global issues we confront. The urgency stems from the understanding that this is not a hypothetical future we are contemplating, but the immediate reality that is unfolding around us. **The choices we make today, and in the coming years, will determine whether we can indeed achieve a sustainable and equitable future for all by 2030, or whether we will be remembered as the generation that had the vision but lacked the will to act decisively.** This inherent urgency is the driving force behind the need for scalable solutions that can accelerate progress and bridge the gap between where we are and where we aspire to be.

The global development landscape, prior to the advent of the Sustainable Development Goals (SDGs), was characterized by a series of well-intentioned, yet ultimately fragmented and insufficient, approaches. While significant progress has been made in certain areas over the past few decades, a critical assessment reveals inherent limitations in these traditional models that now pose a substantial impediment to the accelerated, transformative change envisioned by the SDG agenda. These limitations are not born of a lack of effort, but rather a fundamental mismatch between the scale of the challenges and the methodologies employed to address them. **The SDGs, with their universal scope and interconnected nature, demand a paradigm shift, moving beyond incremental adjustments to existing systems towards**

entirely new frameworks for planning, implementation, and resource allocation.

A primary area where current approaches fall short is in the realm of strategic planning. Historically, development planning, particularly at national and sub-national levels, has often been driven by siloed sector-specific objectives. Ministries of health focus on health outcomes, education ministries on learning metrics, and agriculture ministries on crop yields, with limited systematic integration between these domains. This sectoral approach, while logical within its own confines, fails to grasp the inherent interdependencies that the SDGs so powerfully articulate. For instance, **improving maternal health (SDG 3) is intrinsically linked to girls' education (SDG 4), access to clean water and sanitation (SDG 6), and women's economic capacity building (SDG 5).** Planning that addresses these as separate challenges, without a robust mechanism for cross-sectoral synergy, will inevitably produce suboptimal results and fail to unlock the transformative potential of integrated interventions. The SDGs, by their very design, necessitate a holistic, systems-thinking approach to planning. This requires not only recognizing these interlinkages but actively building them into policy frameworks, budget allocations, and programmatic designs. The absence of this integrated foresight in many existing planning mechanisms means that efforts to achieve one SDG can inadvertently undermine progress on another or simply fail to capitalize on synergistic opportunities. The sheer scope of the SDGs, encompassing 17 goals and its targets, demands a level of coordination and foresight that has historically been difficult to achieve within the bureaucratic and programmatic structures inherited from older development paradigms.

Furthermore, the implementation phase of many development initiatives has been plagued by persistent bottlenecks. **Bureaucratic inertia, a lack of adaptive capacity, and insufficient local ownership often hinder the effective translation of plans into on-the-ground impact.** Many traditional aid models, for example, rely on top-down implementation structures where projects are designed and managed by external entities, with local communities often cast in a passive recipient role. This can lead to interventions that are ill-suited to local contexts, fail to address the nuanced realities on the ground, and lack the sustainability that comes from community buy-in and capacity building. The SDGs, however, are fundamentally about empowering people and communities to be agents of their own development. Achieving goals related to poverty reduction, food security, or sustainable livelihoods requires deep engagement with the very people these initiatives are meant to serve, ensuring their voices shape the design and delivery of programs. **The emphasis on "leaving no one behind" inherent in the SDG framework cannot be achieved with implementation models that marginalize local participation.** Moreover, the complexity of many SDG targets, such as those relating to climate action or sustainable consumption, requires innovative and flexible implementation strategies that can adapt to rapidly changing circumstances and emerging challenges. Many existing implementation frameworks are too rigid, ill-equipped to handle the dynamic nature of these interconnected global issues.

Resource inefficiencies represent another critical failing of current approaches. *The vast funding gap required to achieve the SDGs is widely acknowledged, but equally problematic is the inefficient allocation and utilization of available resources.*

Traditional development financing often suffers from a lack of prioritization, with resources spread thinly across numerous, sometimes overlapping, projects. There is often insufficient emphasis on evidence-based decision-making regarding where investments will yield the greatest impact towards the SDGs. Moreover, the transaction costs associated with traditional aid delivery, including extensive reporting requirements, complex procurement processes, and overheads associated with multiple intermediary organizations, can significantly erode the proportion of funds that actually reach the intended beneficiaries or activities. The SDGs demand a more strategic and results-oriented approach to resource mobilization and deployment. This includes greater emphasis on blended finance, innovative financing mechanisms, and the leveraging of private sector capital. Crucially, it requires a commitment to rigorous monitoring and evaluation that not only tracks spending but also assesses the actual contribution of resources to achieving specific SDG targets. **Without a fundamental overhaul on how resources are allocated and utilized, the ambition of the SDGs will remain perpetually out of reach, regardless of the total amounts mobilized.** The current systems often struggle to facilitate the rapid redirection of funds towards emerging needs or innovative solutions, a flexibility that is paramount for accelerating progress towards such a multifaceted agenda.

The fragmented nature of the global development ecosystem also contributes to the insufficiency of current approaches. The SDG framework, by design, calls for unprecedented levels of partnership and coordination among governments, international organizations, civil society, the private sector, and academia. However, existing structures often foster competition for resources and attention, leading to duplication of efforts, uncoordinated interventions, and failure to achieve economies of scale. For instance, multiple agencies might be working on water and sanitation projects in the same region, with little coordination, leading to inefficiencies and potentially conflicting approaches. The SDG partnership goal (SDG 17) highlights the necessity of overcoming these silos, but the underlying mechanisms for fostering genuine collaboration and shared accountability are often underdeveloped or poorly implemented. The complexity of achieving targets like SDG 16 (Peace, Justice, and Strong Institutions) further exposes the limitations of fragmented approaches; achieving peace and justice requires coordinated efforts across legal, security, and governance sectors, often involving multiple national and international actors working towards common objectives. When these actors operate independently, progress is affected and the impact diluted.

Moreover, the focus on short-term project cycles, a common characteristic of many funding mechanisms and implementation strategies, is fundamentally at odds with the long-term, transformative nature of the SDGs. **Achieving goals such as eradicating extreme poverty, combating climate change, or ensuring sustainable consumption patterns requires sustained, multi-year efforts that address systemic issues.** Short-term project funding often leads to a focus on easily measurable, albeit often superficial, outcomes, rather than on the deep-rooted structural changes necessary for lasting impact. This can result in a churn of well-intentioned but ultimately transient interventions that fail to build lasting capacity or address the underlying drivers of underdevelopment. The SDGs are not a series of discrete projects, but a comprehensive, integrated vision for global transformation that demands long-term commitment and strategic foresight, something that many existing development models, driven by annual budget cycles and project-specific funding, are ill-equipped to provide. The very notion of "accelerating" progress implies a departure from the incremental, project-by-project approach that has characterized much of development work, and a move towards systemic, scalable interventions that can achieve rapid and significant change across multiple fronts simultaneously.

The narrative of progress, while important for maintaining momentum, can also mask the underlying insufficiencies of current approaches. Success stories in specific sectors or regions can create a sense of complacency, even as the aggregate data reveals a widening gap between current trajectories and the 2030 targets. This is particularly true for the most vulnerable populations, who are disproportionately affected by the failures of existing systems. The SDGs are explicitly designed to address these disparities, with the overarching principle of "leaving no one behind." However, traditional approaches have often struggled to reach the most marginalized communities, whether due to logistical challenges, social exclusion, or a lack of focus on their specific needs. The SDGs require a deliberate and targeted effort to reach these populations, which often necessitates innovative outreach strategies, culturally sensitive programming, and a willingness to challenge existing power structures. Without such fundamental reorientation, the very populations the SDGs aim to uplift will continue to be underserved, and the promise of universal progress will remain unfulfilled. The data, when disaggregated by wealth, gender, geography, or disability, often tells a starkly different story than the headline figures, revealing persistent inequalities that current approaches have failed to adequately address.

In essence, the current development paradigm, while having achieved notable successes, is characterized by a series of inherent limitations that make it inadequate for the scale and urgency of the SDG acceleration required. These limitations include a propensity for siloed, sector-specific planning that fails to capture interdependencies; implementation bottlenecks stemming from **bureaucratic rigidity and insufficient local ownership**; persistent resource inefficiencies due to poor allocation and high transaction costs; a fragmented institutional landscape that impedes genuine partnership; a bias towards short-term project cycles that undermine long-term, systemic change; and an occasional disconnect between aggregate progress narratives and the lived realities of the most vulnerable. Recognizing these shortcomings is the crucial first step towards identifying and embracing the fundamentally different, more integrated, and scalable solutions that the SDG agenda necessitates. The transition from incremental improvement to transformative acceleration requires a willingness to critically examine and ultimately move beyond the confines of established development orthodoxies.

The global development landscape, as we have established, is at a critical juncture. The ambitious yet essential vision of the Sustainable Development Goals (SDGs) demands a departure from the incrementalism and fragmentation that have characterized past development efforts. **The limitations inherent in traditional models – from siloed planning and implementation bottlenecks to resource inefficiencies and a lack of genuine local ownership – represent significant**

barriers to achieving the transformative change required by 2030. It is within this context that the Rescue Democracy International (RDI) model emerges not merely as an alternative, but as a vital catalyst, poised to accelerate progress towards the SDGs by directly confronting and neutralizing these systemic deficiencies. The RDI Model is fundamentally a reimagining of how development resources are mobilized, channeled, and utilized, with **a profound emphasis on empowering local actors and fostering direct impact at the grassroots level.** Its core principles are designed to inject efficiency, accountability, and relevance into the development process, thereby bridging the persistent gap between well-intentioned plans and tangible, sustainable outcomes.

At the heart of the RDI Model lies the principle of **radical simplification**. The labyrinthine bureaucracies, complex funding mechanisms, and multi-layered approval processes that often define traditional development and humanitarian aid are a direct impediment to swift and effective action. The SDGs, with their inherent complexity and interconnectedness, require a counter-intuitive approach: simplification. *RDI achieves this by streamlining operations, minimizing intermediaries, and focusing on direct relationships between funding sources and implementing entities at the community level.* This reduction in transactional overhead not only frees up more resources for actual program delivery but also drastically shortens the time from decision to impact. Consider the challenge of achieving SDG 3, Good Health and Well-being. Traditional approaches might involve multiple international agencies, national ministries, and a host of sub-contractors to deliver essential health services or distribute life-saving medicines. This can lead to significant delays due to procurement regulations, logistical hurdles, and challenges of coordination. RDI, by contrast, empowers local health clinics, community health workers, and trusted local NGOs to directly access and manage resources. This simplification means that vital supplies can reach remote villages faster, vaccination campaigns can be initiated with greater agility, and maternal health services can be scaled up more rapidly, directly contributing to improved health outcomes and a faster realization of SDG 3 targets. The emphasis on simplification is not about reducing complexity of the problems being addressed, but rather about simplifying the *mechanisms* through which solutions are delivered, making development more agile, responsive, and ultimately, more effective.

Crucially, the RDI Model champions **grassroots capacity building**. The prevailing top-down approach, where projects are often designed by external experts with limited input from the communities they are intended to serve, has historically led to interventions that are culturally insensitive, unsustainable, or fail to address the actual needs of the beneficiaries. The SDGs, with their overarching commitment to **"leave no one behind,"** necessitate a fundamental shift towards empowering local populations as active agents of their own development. RDI directly addresses this by placing decision-making power and resource control into the hands of those closest to the challenges. Local communities, indigenous groups, women's cooperatives, and local civil society organizations are not merely recipients of aid; they are the architects and implementers of their own development solutions. This capacity building is essential for achieving a wide range of SDGs. For SDG 1, No Poverty, it means communities can identify their own pathways out of poverty, whether through agricultural development, entrepreneurship, or skills training, rather than being subjected to externally defined poverty alleviation programs. For SDG 2, Zero Hunger, it empowers local farmers to adopt sustainable agricultural practices that are best suited to their specific environments and market needs, rather than relying on imported solutions. For SDG 4, Quality Education, it allows local communities to shape educational curricula and delivery methods that are relevant to their cultural context and future employment opportunities. This profound shift in agency ensures that interventions are contextually appropriate, fostering greater ownership and leading to more sustainable and impactful results. The principle of grassroots capacity building is not merely a programmatic preference; it is a foundational requirement for genuine and equitable development.

Directly linked to capacity building is the principle of **direct resource channeling**. A significant portion of development funding is often consumed by administrative costs, intermediary fees, and the operational overhead of numerous coordinating bodies. This inefficiency means that for every dollar intended for impact, only a fraction may actually reach the ground. **RDI fundamentally disrupts this model by advocating for the direct transfer of resources to the implementing entities at the community level.** This could take the form of direct financial grants to local NGOs, community-managed funds, or direct procurement of goods and services from local suppliers. This approach not only maximizes the proportion of funds that directly contribute to SDG targets but also fosters greater transparency and accountability. When local organizations directly manage resources, they are more invested in their efficient and effective use, as the impact is immediately visible within their own communities. This is critical for achieving SDGs such as SDG 16, Peace, Justice, and Strong Institutions. By empowering local governance structures and fostering transparent financial management at the sub-national level, RDI can contribute to building more accountable and responsive institutions. It also directly supports SDG 17, Partnerships for the Goals, by creating robust, accountable partnerships between funders and local implementers, cutting out the layers of intermediation that can dilute commitment and blur lines of responsibility. The direct channeling of resources is a powerful mechanism for unlocking latent potential within local economies and communities, ensuring that financial flows translate directly into social and environmental progress.

underpinning the RDI Model is **robust local oversight**. While empowering local actors, it is crucial to ensure that resources are used effectively, ethically, and in alignment with the intended development objectives. **RDI integrates mechanisms for rigorous local oversight, which go beyond traditional external monitoring and evaluation.** This local oversight is participatory, involving community members, local leaders, and representative bodies in the oversight of projects and resource allocation. This can be manifested through community audit committees, participatory monitoring systems, and local advisory boards that provide continuous feedback and guidance. This not only enhances accountability but also ensures that interventions remain responsive to evolving community needs and priorities. For instance, in the pursuit of SDG 11, Sustainable Cities and Communities, local oversight can ensure that urban planning projects genuinely reflect the needs and aspirations of residents, rather than being dictated by external developers or distant government bodies. Similarly, for SDG 13, Climate Action, local communities can be empowered to monitor the implementation of climate adaptation or mitigation projects, ensuring that they are effective and culturally appropriate. This localized oversight fosters a culture of accountability that is deeply embedded within the community, making it more resilient to misuse funds and more adept at course correction when unforeseen challenges arise. It transforms oversight from an external compliance exercise into an integral part of community-driven development.

The applicability of the RDI Model extends across the breadth of the SDG agenda, demonstrating its versatility and potential for broad impact. Consider SDG 5, Gender Equality. By empowering women's groups and local women leaders to manage resources and design programs, RDI can directly address gender-based disparities, whether in economic opportunities, access to education, or participation in decision-making processes. Women's cooperatives, for example, can be directly funded to expand their businesses, with oversight provided by their own membership, ensuring that the benefits are equitably distributed and that women's voices are amplified. For SDG 12, Responsible Consumption and Production, local communities can be empowered to develop and implement sustainable consumption patterns and waste management systems, with direct oversight ensuring adherence to local environmental regulations and community values. Similarly, the pursuit of SDG 7, Affordable and Clean Energy, can be significantly accelerated by directly channeling funds to local cooperatives or communities to install and manage off-grid solar solutions or small-scale renewable energy projects, with oversight ensuring equitable access and community benefit.

The RDI Model's emphasis on adaptive management, fostered by direct feedback loops and local oversight, is particularly crucial for addressing the complex and often rapidly evolving challenges associated with SDGs like SDG 14, Life Below Water, and SDG 15, Life on Land. Local fishing communities, for example, can be directly funded to implement sustainable fishing practices and marine conservation efforts, with their own members providing oversight and immediate feedback on the effectiveness of these interventions. This proximity to the ecological systems allows for a more nuanced and responsive approach to conservation than can be achieved through distant, centralized management. The iterative nature of RDI allows for adjustments to be made in real-time, based on the lived experiences and observations of those most directly affected by environmental changes.

Furthermore, RDI's principles offer a potent solution to the financing gap that plagues many SDG initiatives. By reducing the transaction costs associated with traditional aid and by unlocking the potential of local resources and private sector engagement at the community level, RDI can mobilize and deploy capital more efficiently. Local impact investment funds, managed with community oversight and channeling resources directly to local enterprises that contribute to SDG targets, can attract both domestic and international capital. This approach fosters a virtuous cycle where successful local initiatives generate further investment and capacity building, creating a sustainable pathway to achieving SDG targets. The transparency inherent in direct resource channeling also builds trust, which is a critical lubricant for financial flows, making it easier to attract and retain investment in development initiatives.

The RDI Model represents a paradigm shift from aid as a hand-out to aid as an investment in local capacity and agency. It acknowledges that the most sustainable and impactful development solutions are those that are owned and driven by the people they are intended to benefit. By radically simplifying processes, empowering grassroots actors, channeling resources directly, and embedding robust local oversight, the RDI Model provides a scalable and effective framework for accelerating progress towards the Sustainable Development Goals. It moves beyond the limitations of traditional approaches, offering a tangible pathway to closing the SDG gap and ensuring that no one is left behind in the pursuit of a more just, equitable, and sustainable future. The integration of these principles creates a synergy that amplifies impact, making the RDI Model a compelling and necessary approach for the 21st-century development agenda. **It's not just about doing development differently; it's about enabling development to be fundamentally more effective, equitable, and enduring.** The ability to rapidly adapt, learn, and reallocate resources based on ground-level feedback is a hallmark of the RDI approach, positioning it as an indispensable tool in the race to achieve the 2030 Agenda.

The inherent architecture of the Rescue Democracy International (RDI) model is intentionally designed for adaptability and replicability, making it a potent tool for addressing the multifaceted challenges encapsulated within the Sustainable Development Goals (SDGs). Unlike rigid, one-size-fits-all development paradigms that often falter when confronted with the nuanced realities of diverse socio-cultural

242

and economic landscapes, RDI's core principles of radical simplification, grassroots capacity building, direct resource channeling, and robust local oversight provide a flexible yet robust framework. This inherent flexibility is not merely an add-on but a fundamental characteristic that allows the model to be effectively scaled and implemented across a vast spectrum of geographical regions, from urban centers to remote rural communities, and across a myriad of development sectors, from public health and education to environmental sustainability and economic capacity building. **The true test of any development intervention lies not only in its impact within a pilot setting but in its capacity to be systematically replicated and adapted to new contexts, thereby maximizing its potential to contribute to global development objectives.**

The scalability of RDI hinges on its ability to transcend the superficialities of context-specific programming and instead embed a universal logic of capacity building and efficiency. When we speak of replication, it is not about a literal carbon copy of a project in a new location. Rather, it is about translating the underlying principles and methodologies of RDI into a contextually relevant and culturally appropriate application. For instance, a successful RDI initiative focused on improving maternal health in a rural district in sub-Saharan Africa, which involved direct funding to community health committees and participatory oversight of medical supply chains, can be adapted to address challenges in water and sanitation in a peri-urban settlement in Southeast Asia. The core mechanism, empowering local actors to manage resources for a specific SDG-related outcome, with local accountability structures, remains constant. The specifics of the health interventions would be replaced by sanitation engineering solutions or water purification techniques, and the community health committees might evolve into local water management associations. However, the fundamental RDI approach, that of local ownership and direct resource management driving effective implementation, would remain the guiding force. This principle of adaptation, rather than rigid replication, is what imbues RDI with its true scalability, allowing it to respond to the unique needs and opportunities present in any given setting, while still adhering to the foundational tenets of effective development.

Consider the application of RDI's model to SDG 4, Quality Education. In a scenario where a particular region struggles with low primary school enrollment rates due to a lack of basic resources and parental engagement, an RDI approach might involve establishing community education funds. These funds, directly managed by parent-teacher associations and local education committees, would be allocated for essential supplies like textbooks, stationery, and minor school infrastructure repairs. The oversight would be transparent, with attendance records, fund disbursement, and procurement decisions regularly reported to the broader community. **This approach directly empowers parents and local educators, fostering a sense of collective responsibility for educational outcomes.** Now, imagine replicating this in a vastly different cultural context, perhaps in a region of South America where educational challenges stem from a lack of qualified teachers and culturally irrelevant curricula. The RDI Model would again involve direct resource channeling and local oversight, but the specific application would shift. The community education funds might be used to provide stipends for local university graduates to teach in underserved areas, or to subsidize teacher training programs that incorporate indigenous knowledge and languages. The oversight committees would still ensure accountability, but their focus might extend to monitoring teacher performance and curriculum relevance. In both instances, the RDI Model's flexibility allows for adaptation to specific challenges while maintaining its core strengths. The critical element is the shift in agency, from external bodies dictating educational strategies to local communities actively shaping and resourcing their own educational futures. This inherent adaptability makes the model a powerful engine for achieving educational equity on a global scale.

The scalability of RDI is further bolstered by its inherent capacity to integrate with and amplify existing local structures, rather than attempting to create entirely new ones. Many development initiatives fail because they bypass or undermine established community governance, social networks, and traditional leadership structures, which can lead to a lack of buy-in and sustainability. RDI, conversely, seeks to work *through* these existing channels, strengthening them in the process. For example, in a context where traditional tribal councils or village elders hold significant sway, RDI would involve these bodies in the oversight and resource allocation processes. This not only ensures cultural appropriateness but also leverages existing trust and authority, making the implementation more seamless and the outcomes more enduring. When RDI principles are applied to agricultural development (SDG 2, Zero Hunger), a local cooperative or a traditional land management committee could be empowered to manage funds for improved seeds, irrigation technologies, or access to markets. Oversight would be integrated into the existing governance structure, ensuring that decisions are made in alignment with local customs and long-term community goals. This integration approach is crucial for scalability because it minimizes the friction of introducing new systems and maximizes the utilization of established social capital. It allows RDI to be "plugged into" the existing fabric of a community, making its expansion more organic and sustainable.

Furthermore, the financial architecture of RDI contributes significantly to its scalability. By drastically reducing intermediary layers and associated transaction costs, RDI liberates a greater proportion of development finance to be directly deployed at the point of impact. **This efficiency dividend makes limited development budgets stretch further, enabling a wider reach and deeper penetration of interventions.** When funding is channeled directly to local implementing entities – be they community-based organizations, local businesses, or self-help groups – these entities become more resourceful and entrepreneurial. They learn to manage budgets, procure goods and services, and report on outcomes with a direct sense of accountability to their communities. This **capacity building** is a crucial component of scalability. As more local entities successfully implement RDI-supported projects, they generate a track record of reliability and impact, making them more attractive to future funding and partnership opportunities. This creates a virtuous cycle where successful local implementation begets further investment and broader replication. Imagine an RDI fund established to support small-scale renewable energy projects (SDG 7, Affordable and Clean Energy) in a cluster of rural villages. Once a few of these village energy cooperatives demonstrate success in managing their solar micro-grids and collecting user fees, they can share their experiences and lessons learned with neighboring communities. This peer-to-peer learning, facilitated by the RDI framework's transparency and demonstrable results, acts as a powerful catalyst for scaling the initiative.

The emphasis on local ownership within the RDI Model is perhaps its most critical enabler of scalability. When communities and local organizations have a genuine stake in the success of a project, they become its most ardent champions and its most effective implementers. **This sense of ownership is cultivated through active participation in the design, implementation, and oversight of initiatives.** For an RDI intervention focused on waste management and recycling (SDG 12, Responsible Consumption and Production), local community groups could be empowered to manage collection systems, operate local recycling centers, and even develop small-scale enterprises utilizing recycled materials. Oversight would ensure that these operations meet local environmental standards and contribute to community well-being. The very fact that the community has a direct hand in shaping these initiatives means they are far more likely to be sustained and expanded. As successful models emerge, they naturally attract further local interest and support, paving the way for replication in adjacent communities or for scaling up within the same community to address broader challenges. This organic growth, driven by local demand and ownership, is inherently more scalable and sustainable than top-down directives. The ability of the RDI Model to foster this deep-seated ownership is what allows it to transcend pilot projects and become a systemic approach to development.

Moreover, the RDI Model's inherent decentralization is a key factor in its scalability, particularly in large and geographically diverse countries. Centralized development programs often struggle with the sheer scale of logistical, administrative, and monitoring challenges they face. By empowering local entities to manage resources and implement projects, RDI distributes the operational burden, making it far more manageable. This decentralized approach also allows for greater responsiveness to local needs and conditions, which can vary significantly even within the same country. For example, an RDI program targeting improved agricultural yields (SDG 2) in a large nation might see distinct approaches to water management in arid regions versus flood-prone areas, with local farming cooperatives in each region directly managing the specific technologies and practices most relevant to their environment. The overarching RDI framework, with its emphasis on direct funding and local oversight, ensures consistency in accountability and financial management across these diverse local applications. **This distributed model of implementation is far more resilient and adaptable than a centralized command-and-control system, making it a more viable option for achieving widespread SDG impact.**

The critical role of technology in enabling the scalability of RDI cannot be overstated. Digital platforms can be leveraged to facilitate direct resource transfers, provide transparent tracking of funds, enable real-time monitoring and reporting by local entities, and connect communities for knowledge sharing and peer learning. Mobile money platforms, for instance, can be instrumental in channeling funds directly to beneficiaries or local implementing partners, bypassing traditional banking systems that may be inaccessible in remote areas. Blockchain technology could offer unparalleled transparency and traceability in resource management and supply chains. Furthermore, online learning platforms and digital communication tools can facilitate the sharing of best practices and technical support across geographically dispersed RDI initiatives, accelerating the learning curve for new implementers. Imagine a network of community-led health initiatives operating under the RDI Model. A shared digital dashboard could allow each local health committee to report on service delivery, stock levels, and community feedback, while also accessing training modules and technical advice from experienced practitioners or partner organizations. This technological integration transforms scalability from a logistical challenge into an interconnected ecosystem of learning and impact.

The process of scaling an RDI Model is iterative and adaptive. It begins with identifying successful pilot projects that demonstrate the efficacy of the core principles in a specific context. These successes are then documented and analyzed to extract the transferable lessons and adapt the methodologies for new settings. This often involves engaging with local stakeholders in the new context to understand their specific needs, existing capacities, and cultural norms. The RDI framework then provides the scaffolding to build new, contextually appropriate initiatives. Crucially, this scaling process is not a one-time event but a continuous learning cycle. Feedback from newly implemented projects is fed back into the system, allowing for refinement of the RDI methodologies and the development of new tools and approaches. This iterative process ensures that RDI remains a dynamic and evolving model, capable of responding to the ever-changing development landscape and the complex, interconnected nature of the SDGs. It moves beyond the limitations of static project designs and embraces a more agile and responsive approach to achieving lasting impact.

The financial sustainability of RDI initiatives is also a key consideration for scalability. While the initial efficiency gains are significant, long-term sustainability requires mechanisms that can continue to fund and support these local initiatives. This might involve developing local impact investment funds that attract private capital, fostering public-private partnerships at the community level, or integrating RDI principles into national budgeting and resource allocation processes. **As local entities demonstrate their capacity to manage resources effectively and generate tangible development outcomes, they become more attractive investment opportunities.** This can lead to a gradual shift from philanthropic or grant-based funding to more sustainable, market-driven or community-generated revenue streams. For example, successful RDI-supported agricultural cooperatives might evolve to a point where they can access commercial loans or attract private equity to expand their operations, thereby contributing to economic growth and further SDG achievement. The RDI Model, by building robust local capacity and fostering demonstrable impact, lays the groundwork for such sustainable financial models, enabling the long-term scalability of its approach.

The broader implications of RDI's scalability extend beyond simply achieving individual SDG targets. **By empowering local actors and fostering direct accountability, RDI contributes to strengthening local governance, enhancing civic participation, and building more resilient and self-**

sufficient communities. These are foundational elements for achieving sustainable development across the board, from promoting peace and justice (SDG 16) to building strong partnerships for development (SDG 17). As the RDI Model is replicated and adapted across diverse contexts, it creates a global network of empowered local actors, capable of identifying and addressing their own development challenges, and contributing to the collective effort to achieve the 2030 Agenda. This network effect, where successful local initiatives inspire and inform others, amplifies the overall impact of the RDI approach, making it a truly transformative force in global development. **The ability to adapt, to learn, and to empower at the local level is the essence of scalable development, and the RDI Model is uniquely positioned to deliver on this promise.** It offers a pathway to bridge the SDG gap, not through grand, centralized plans, but through the collective power and agency of communities themselves, amplified by a framework designed for adaptability and enduring impact.

The Rescue Democracy International (RDI) Model AKA The Justin Mudekereza Model represents more than a tactical response to immediate development deficits; it embodies a strategic vision for sustained global progress, intrinsically aligned with the ambitious aspirations of the 2030 Agenda for Sustainable Development and beyond. As we look towards the crucial milestone of 2030, the RDI framework offers a potent, adaptable, and inherently scalable pathway to not only bridge the existing gaps within the Sustainable Development Goals (SDGs) but also to **lay the groundwork for a future characterized by resilient, self-sufficient, and empowered communities worldwide.** This is not a static scheme, but a dynamic paradigm shifts in how development is conceived and executed – a move from externally driven interventions to locally owned and managed solutions that are inherently more effective and enduring.

The overarching goal is to foster a global ecosystem where the principles of RDI are not merely implemented in isolated projects but are integrated into the very fabric of development assistance and local governance. Imagine a world where the vast majority of development finance is channeled directly to community-level entities, equipped with the capacity and oversight mechanisms to address their most pressing needs across all seventeen SDGs. **This vision is achievable through the systematic adoption and adaptation of the RDI Model.** For SDG 1, No Poverty, it means empowering local micro-enterprises and savings groups to manage capital directly for sustainable livelihoods. For SDG 3, Good Health and Well-being, it translates to community health worker cooperatives managing primary healthcare budgets and supply chains, ensuring equitable access to essential services. For SDG 13, Climate Action, it signifies local environmental stewardship groups receiving direct funding to implement adaptation and mitigation strategies tailored to their specific ecological contexts, from reforestation efforts to sustainable water management.

The scalability of RDI towards 2030 and beyond is predicated on several key pillars that, when reinforced, can catalyze a transformative impact. Firstly, there the imperative of establishing robust knowledge-sharing platforms and capacity-building networks. As successful RDI initiatives demonstrate tangible results in one community, these learnings must be efficiently disseminated to others facing similar challenges. This necessitates the creation of digital and in-person forums where local leaders, project managers, and community members can share best practices, troubleshoot obstacles, and forge collaborative partnerships. For instance, a successful model of community-led vocational training for SDG 8, Decent Work and Economic Growth, in a specific region could be documented, analyzed, and then adapted by similar groups in neighboring or even geographically distant areas, with facilitated access to training materials and mentorship.

Secondly, fostering supportive policy environments at national and sub-national levels is crucial. **Governments and international bodies need to recognize and endorse the RDI Model, creating enabling legislation and regulatory frameworks that facilitate direct resource channeling and local governance of development initiatives.** This could involve simplifying procurement processes for community-based organizations, offering fiscal incentives for local investment in RDI-supported projects, and embedding RDI principles into national development plans. When governments actively champion this approach, it not only legitimizes RDI but also unlocks significant domestic resources and streamlines the process of scaling successful pilots. For example, a national policy that streamlines the registration and accreditation of community-based organizations as direct recipients of development funds, based on their adherence to RDI oversight principles, would dramatically accelerate the pace of implementation.

Thirdly, the RDI Model's adaptability to diverse contexts is not merely a feature but a strategic advantage for long-term scalability. As we move beyond 2030, the nature of global challenges will undoubtedly evolve. New environmental threats, shifting economic landscapes, and evolving social dynamics will require development approaches that are agile and responsive. The RDI framework, with its emphasis on local problem-solving and direct accountability, is inherently equipped to adapt. It allows for the customization of interventions to meet the unique requirements of emerging challenges, ensuring that development efforts remain relevant and effective. For instance, if unforeseen climate-related disasters impact a region, RDI-empowered local committees can swiftly reallocate resources and adapt their strategies for disaster preparedness and response, leveraging their intimate knowledge of the local terrain and community needs.

The financial architecture of RDI also plays a pivotal role in its long-term scalability. While initial efficiencies are achieved by reducing administrative overhead, sustained impact requires mechanisms for ongoing funding and the potential for revenue generation within RDI-supported initiatives. This points towards the development of diversified funding streams, including impact investing, social impact bonds, and public-private partnerships at the community level. As local entities demonstrate their capacity to manage funds effectively and generate sustainable development outcomes, they become attractive prospects for private capital and innovative financing mechanisms. For example, a community-managed renewable energy cooperative that has proven its ability to operate and maintain a micro-grid and collect user fees efficiently could then attract investment for expansion or for developing complementary income-generating activities, thus creating a self-sustaining development cycle. This transition from grant dependency to financial self-sufficiency is a hallmark of true scalability and long-term impact.

Moreover, **the RDI Model's success hinges on fostering a culture of continuous learning and adaptation.** The development landscape is dynamic, and what works today might need modification tomorrow. By empowering local actors, RDI inherently builds in mechanisms for learning and feedback. Communities that are directly responsible for their development outcomes are incentivized to monitor progress, identify shortcomings, and innovate solutions. This iterative process, fueled by direct experience and accountability, ensures that RDI-based initiatives remain effective and relevant over time. Imagine a national program supporting local education initiatives through RDI. As new pedagogical approaches emerge or as societal needs change, community education committees can adapt their resource allocation and program design, ensuring that education remains aligned with contemporary demands and opportunities, thus extending the impact far beyond the initial implementation phase.

Looking beyond 2030, the RDI framework is designed to be a catalyst for a new era of global development characterized by democratized agency and sustainable progress. The widespread adoption of this model promises to shift the locus of power and decision-making in development towards those who are most directly affected and best positioned to understand and address their own needs. This fundamental reorientation of development practice is what will enable us to tackle increasingly complex global challenges, from pandemics and climate change to digital divides and social inequalities, with greater efficacy and resilience. It fosters not just project-level success but a systemic transformation in how humanity collectively strives for a more equitable and sustainable future.

The RDI Model's inherent decentralization and capacity building of local actors also contribute significantly to building resilience against systemic shocks. When development relies on a multitude of localized, self-governing initiatives rather than large, centralized programs, the overall system becomes less vulnerable to disruption. If one RDI-supported project faces unforeseen challenges, the impact is contained, and other initiatives continue to function, drawing on their own local resources and adaptive capacities. This distributed resilience is essential for navigating the uncertainties of the future and ensuring that development gains are not easily undone by external events. For instance, in the face of disruptions to global supply chains, local RDI-managed food security initiatives would be better positioned to adapt and sustain their operations by relying on local production and distribution networks.

Furthermore, the RDI framework fosters a profound sense of ownership and accountability that transcends immediate project cycles. When communities are directly responsible for managing resources and achieving outcomes, they develop a deeper commitment to the long-term sustainability of their initiatives. This intrinsic motivation is a powerful engine for lasting impact, as it extends beyond the presence of external funding or oversight. It cultivates a culture of civic responsibility and collective action that can drive progress across multiple development sectors. This is particularly crucial for achieving goals like SDG 16, Peace, Justice, and Strong Institutions, where empowering local communities to manage their own affairs and hold their leaders accountable is paramount.

The scalability of RDI is intrinsically linked to its ability to foster a global network of learning and mutual support among local actors. As more communities embrace the RDI Model, they can connect and learn from each other, creating a powerful multiplier effect. This interconnectedness accelerates innovation, facilitates the sharing of solutions to common problems, and builds collective momentum towards achieving the SDGs. Imagine a global virtual academy where community leaders implementing RDI projects can share their experiences, access expert advice, and collaborate on solutions that address cross-cutting development issues. This collaborative environment will be essential for tackling complex, interconnected challenges and ensuring that the progress achieved by 2030 is not only maintained but accelerated in the decades that follow.

In essence, the RDI Model offers a scalable and sustainable framework for global impact because it places power, agency, and responsibility directly into the hands of local communities. It acknowledges that true development is not something that is done _to_ people, but something that is done_ _by_ people. By simplifying processes, empowering local actors, channeling resources directly, and ensuring robust local oversight, RDI creates a development paradigm that is inherently adaptable, resilient, and capable of driving transformative change across the globe.

The journey towards achieving the SDGs by 2030, and indeed towards building a more sustainable and equitable future beyond that horizon, requires a fundamental shift in our approach to development. The Rescue Democracy International (RDI) Model AKA The Justin Mudekereza Model offers precisely this paradigm shift, moving beyond incremental adjustments to a complete reorientation of how we conceive and implement global progress. Its scalability is not just a desirable attribute; it is the very essence of its potential to fundamentally alter the trajectory of human development. **The vision is clear: a world where development is driven by local ingenuity, resourced by efficient and direct financial flows, and governed by transparent accountability at the community level.**

This is a call to action for all stakeholders – the United Nations, governments, international organizations, civil society, the private sector, and most importantly, the communities themselves. **It is time to embrace a model that empowers, that sustains, and that delivers tangible, lasting impact.** The RDI framework is not merely a set of principles; it is a pathway to a future where the Sustainable Development Goals are not aspirational targets but achieved realities, built from the ground up by the very people they are intended to serve. By committing to the widespread adoption and adaptation of RDI Model, we can bridge the SDG gap and forge a truly transformative and enduring legacy of progress for generations to come. **The time to scale this revolution in development is now.**

CHAPTER 9:

The $10 Billion Imperative:
Investing in What Works

The sheer ambition of the 2030 Agenda for Sustainable Development, a blueprint for a more equitable and sustainable world, is mirrored by the staggering financial commitment it demands. Achieving all seventeen Sustainable Development Goals (SDGs) across every nation is not a minor undertaking; it represents one of the most significant global investment initiatives ever conceived. The scale of this challenge is immense, requiring a mobilization of financial resources on an unprecedented level, far beyond what current official development assistance (ODA) alone can provide. This necessitates a fundamental re-evaluation of how development finance is generated, allocated, and utilized, moving towards a more diversified, innovative, and impact-driven approach.

Estimates of the funding gap for the SDGs vary depending on the methodologies used and the specific contexts considered, but they consistently point to a colossal requirement. The United Nations Conference on Trade and Development (UNCTAD) and other research bodies have highlighted that achieving the SDGs will require trillions of dollars annually. For instance, reports have suggested that developing countries alone need an estimated $2.5 trillion to $3.3 trillion per year to meet the SDG targets. This figure encompasses investments across a broad spectrum of sectors, from eradicating extreme poverty and hunger (SDG 1 and SDG 2) to ensuring access to clean water and sanitation (SDG 6), promoting affordable and clean energy (SDG 7), fostering decent work and economic growth (SDG 8), building sustainable infrastructure (SDG 9), and tackling climate change (SDG 13).

This enormous figure underscores that the traditional model of development finance, heavily reliant on aid from developed nations, is simply insufficient to bridge the gap. While ODA remains a vital component, particularly for the least developed countries and for addressing humanitarian crises, it accounts for only a fraction of the total financing needed. The bulk of the investment must come from domestic resource mobilization, private sector investments, and innovative financing mechanisms. This shift in the funding landscape requires a sophisticated understanding of capital markets, impact investing, blended finance, and the creation of enabling environments that attract private capital towards sustainable development objectives.

Consider the specific investment needs across key SDG areas. For SDG 3, Good Health and Well-being, achieving universal health coverage necessitates significant investments in healthcare infrastructure, medical supplies, training and retention of healthcare professionals, and research and development for new treatments and vaccines. Similarly, SDG 4, Quality Education, requires substantial outlays for building and equipping schools, developing relevant curricula, training teachers, and ensuring access to education for all children, regardless of their socioeconomic background or location. The foundational nature of these goals means that underinvestment in them has cascading negative effects on all other aspects of development.

The challenge is further amplified by the uneven distribution of wealth and resources globally. While some nations have the capacity to mobilize significant domestic resources, many developing countries face constraints such as limited tax bases, informal economies, and competing development priorities. This makes them heavily reliant on external financing, yet also vulnerable to global economic volatility and shifts in donor priorities. Bridging this financing gap requires not only increased funding but also enhanced capacity building for financial management, resource mobilization, and efficient project implementation within these countries. The Rescue Democracy International (RDI) model, by focusing on direct resource channeling and empowering local entities, offers a pathway to more efficient and impactful utilization of these scarce resources, ensuring that every dollar invested yields maximum development return.

The scale of the financial requirement also necessitates a critical look at the efficiency and effectiveness of existing development spending. A substantial portion of the estimated funding gap is not necessarily a reflection of a lack of available capital, but rather of inefficiencies in how capital is deployed, the administrative costs associated with traditional aid delivery, and the challenges in attracting private sector investment to high-risk or low-return development projects. The RDI approach directly tackles these inefficiencies by cutting down on bureaucratic layers, fostering local ownership, and creating a more direct link between funding and tangible outcomes, thereby maximizing the impact of every dollar invested.

Furthermore, the global financial system itself plays a crucial role in either enabling or hindering the achievement of the SDGs. Issues such as illicit financial flows, tax evasion, and the lack of financial transparency can drain trillions of dollars from developing economies, money that could otherwise be used to fund essential public services and development initiatives. Addressing these systemic issues is as critical as mobilizing new funding. Policies that promote financial integrity, combat corruption, and ensure fair taxation are fundamental to creating an environment where sufficient resources are available for sustainable development.

The financial imperatives for the SDGs also extend to areas like climate finance. The Paris Agreement and the SDGs are intrinsically linked, with climate action being central to achieving many of the development goals. Meeting the targets for renewable energy deployment, climate adaptation measures, and disaster risk reduction requires massive investments, often in sectors that are perceived as having longer payback periods or higher upfront costs. Mobilizing this climate finance, both from public and private sources, is a significant component of the overall SDG financing challenge. Innovative financial instruments, such as green bonds, carbon pricing mechanisms, and risk-sharing facilities, are essential tools in this regard.

The magnitude of the financial challenge cannot be overstated. It requires a concerted and coordinated effort from all stakeholders. Governments need to implement sound fiscal policies, strengthen domestic resource mobilization, and create enabling environments for investment. International financial institutions and multilateral development banks have a critical role to play in providing concessional finance, technical assistance, and catalytic capital to attract private investment. The private sector, in turn, must recognize the long-term economic opportunities inherent in sustainable development and align its investment strategies with the SDG agenda. And civil society organizations, including those at the community level, are crucial in ensuring accountability, advocating for effective resource allocation, and implementing solutions on the ground. The RDI Model, by empowering these very local entities, ensures that financial resources are directed towards the most pressing needs and are managed with transparency and efficiency, maximizing their transformative potential. The sheer scale of the financial requirements for the SDGs is a stark reminder of the urgency and the complexity of the task ahead. It demands a paradigm shift in how we think about and deploy capital for development, moving towards a more integrated, efficient, and universally beneficial approach.

The vast sums allocated to international development, often touted as transformative investments, warrant a rigorous examination of their ultimate destination. While the headline figures of aid commitments are substantial, the journey of these funds from donor coffers to the intended beneficiaries is frequently a labyrinthine one, fraught with layers of administration, overhead, and logistical complexities. A critical analysis of current development spending patterns reveals that a significant proportion of this capital is absorbed long before it can directly address the acute needs on the ground. This phenomenon raises pertinent questions about the efficiency and efficacy of traditional aid structures and whether current spending priorities are optimally aligned with maximizing tangible impact.

Delving into the rough details of how development dollars are spent, it becomes apparent that a considerable percentage is consumed by administrative costs. This includes the salaries and benefits of personnel within donor agencies, the maintenance of offices and infrastructure, and the extensive bureaucratic processes required to manage and disburse funds. While some level of administrative expenditure is unavoidable and indeed necessary for the effective functioning of any organization, the proportions often seen in established aid frameworks can be alarmingly high. These overheads can encompass everything from policy development and strategic planning to monitoring, evaluation, and reporting mechanisms. Furthermore, there are often multiple layers of intermediaries involved in the aid delivery chain, each with its own administrative and operational costs. These can include international non-governmental organizations (INGOs), national NGOs, government ministries, and various consulting firms, all of which contribute to the overall overhead.

The complexity of logistical chains further exacerbates the absorption of development funds. Transporting goods, equipment, and personnel to remote or challenging environments involves significant costs, including freight, customs duties, insurance, and security. In regions affected by conflict, instability, or poor infrastructure, these logistical challenges are magnified, leading to increased expenditure. Moreover, the need for specialized expertise, such as engineers, public health specialists, or agricultural advisors, often necessitates hiring consultants or engaging specialized firms, which can be a substantial cost. The procurement processes for goods and services, while designed to ensure accountability, can also be lengthy and resource-intensive, adding to the overall administrative burden and delay.

Consider the case of a project aimed at improving access to clean water in a rural African village. While the cost of drilling wells, installing purification systems, and training local water management committees constitutes the direct program cost, the funds allocated to project design, proposal writing, donor reporting, and ongoing monitoring and evaluation by the implementing agency can represent a significant percentage of the total budget. If the project is managed by an international NGO, there will be costs associated with its headquarters, regional offices, and country-specific operations, which are then allocated across various projects. This includes human resources departments, finance teams, communications staff, and senior leadership. Each of these functions, while supporting the overall mission, adds to the overhead.

Furthermore, the emphasis on accountability and transparency within the development sector, while crucial, can also contribute to administrative costs. The preparation of detailed reports, the conduct of independent evaluations, and the implementation of robust financial tracking systems all require dedicated staff time and resources. While these mechanisms are essential for ensuring that funds are used appropriately and for demonstrating impact, they can divert resources that might otherwise be directly channeled into program activities. The challenge lies in finding the optimal balance between ensuring accountability and maximizing the direct programmatic impact of every dollar.

The question of whether current spending priorities are optimally aligned with maximizing impact on the ground is central to this re-evaluation. **When a large proportion of development and humanitarian aid is consumed by administrative and logistical costs, the amount of funding that actually reaches the intended beneficiaries or the tangible interventions on the ground is diminished.** This can lead to scaled-down projects, fewer beneficiaries reached, or a slower pace of implementation than originally intended. For instance, if a significant percentage of a health program's budget is spent on expatriate staff salaries, travel, and international consultants, it might mean fewer local healthcare workers can be trained or fewer essential medicines can be procured for clinics.

This often leads to a disconnect between the stated goals of a development project and its actual outcomes. Projects may be meticulously planned and documented, but if the operational efficiency is low due to high overheads, the impact on the lives of the poor and vulnerable can be marginal. The concept of "money left on the table" takes on a new meaning here; it's not just about unspent funds, but about the potential impact that is lost due to inefficient allocation and absorption of resources within the aid architecture. This can create a cycle where donor agencies feel compelled to maintain extensive administrative structures to oversee the aid they provide, which in turn necessitates further funding for those structures, perpetuating a system that may not be the most effective in achieving development outcomes.

The narrative of development often focuses on the commitment of financial resources, but a deeper dive into the mechanics of aid disbursement reveals the critical importance of how those resources are utilized internally within the implementing organizations. For instance, a grant of $1 million to an NGO for a specific intervention might see $200,000 to $300,000 absorbed by the NGO's operational costs, including salary for program managers, finance officers, administrative assistants, as well as office rent, utilities, and communication expenses. Add to this the costs of the donor agency's own program officers, monitoring and evaluation teams, and the costs of country offices, and the figure can climb even higher. This isn't to suggest that these roles are without value; they are essential for governance, quality assurance, and the overall success of the development enterprise. However, the crucial point of contention is the proportion, and whether this proportion is optimized for maximizing direct impact.

The structure of many international development organizations, particularly those with long histories, has evolved over time, often accumulating layers of management and administrative processes. This can lead to a diffusion of responsibility and potential for inefficiencies that are difficult to root out. In many cases, the cost-effectiveness of different delivery models is not rigorously compared, leading to a perpetuation of established, though potentially less efficient, methods. The pressure to demonstrate due diligence and accountability to donors and the public can also incentivize the creation of more elaborate oversight mechanisms, which invariably translate into higher administrative costs.

Moreover, the competitive nature of securing development grants can also play a role. **Organizations may need to invest heavily in proposal development, grant writing, and the hiring of development professionals to secure funding.** This pre-award expenditure, while necessary for winning contracts, is also an administrative cost that is factored into the overall budget. Once a grant is secured, the ongoing requirements for donor reporting, financial audits, and impact assessments continue to generate administrative burdens throughout the project lifecycle.

The question of what constitutes "overhead" itself can be a subject of debate. For example, is the cost of a program manager who directly oversees the implementation of activities an administrative cost, or is it a direct program cost? Similarly, are training workshops for local staff considered an administrative cost or a capacity-building intervention that is core to the program's success? The definitions can vary, but the underlying issue remains: **how much of the allocated financial resources are truly reaching the point of intervention and directly benefiting the target population, versus being consumed by the machinery that facilitates the delivery of aid?**

The emphasis on "due diligence" by donor agencies often leads to extensive requirements for financial reporting, audits, and programmatic reviews. While essential for accountability, these processes demand significant staff time and resources from implementing partners. This means that a portion of the grant money is spent on accountants, auditors, and report writers, both within the implementing organization and within the donor agency itself. The administrative costs associated with ensuring financial compliance can, in some instances, rival the direct costs of the program activities themselves.

Furthermore, the geographical dispersion of development projects, often in remote and challenging environments, necessitates robust logistical support. This includes the cost of transporting supplies, equipment, and personnel, often requiring specialized transportation and security measures. Office rental and maintenance in remote locations, communication infrastructure, and local staff recruitment and management all contribute to the administrative and operational expenses of delivering aid on the ground. The complexities of navigating local regulations, customs, and bureaucratic procedures in different countries also add to these costs.

The financial implications of these inefficiencies are profound. When a substantial portion of development spending is absorbed by administrative and logistical overheads, it means that fewer resources are available for direct interventions, such as building schools, providing healthcare services, or distributing essential supplies. This can lead to projects that are underfunded in their programmatic components, potentially compromising their effectiveness and sustainability. It also means that the potential impact per dollar spent is reduced, requiring a larger overall investment to achieve the same development outcomes.

This critical examination of where development money goes is not an indictment of the dedication and hard work of individuals working in the development sector. Rather, it is a call for a more efficient and effective allocation of resources. **The goal is to ensure that every dollar invested in development yields the maximum possible return in terms of positive impact on the lives of those it is intended to serve.** This requires a continuous effort to streamline processes, reduce unnecessary administrative layers, and explore innovative delivery models that can minimize overheads and maximize direct programmatic impact. The $10 billion imperative, therefore, is not just about mobilizing more funds, but crucially, about ensuring that the funds mobilized are utilized with unparalleled efficiency and impact.

The proposition of the RDI (Rescue Democracy International) model centers on a radical reimagining of how development capital is allocated, aiming for an unprecedented level of efficiency and direct impact. *At its core, RDI posits that a substantial portion of the $10 billion imperative can be deployed not through the established, often cumbersome, multi-layered* *international aid architecture, but rather through a streamlined, direct-to-ground approach.* This model seeks to drastically curtail the absorption of funds by administrative overheads, a critical drain on resources as previously examined, and instead channel the vast majority of investment directly into grassroots capacity building and the tangible implementation of projects. The financial proposition is straightforward: by minimizing the layers of intermediaries, the costs associated with their maintenance, and the complex reporting and compliance mechanisms inherent in traditional systems, RDI Model can achieve a significantly higher impact per dollar invested.

Imagine the $10 billion not flowing through a series of international organizations, each with its own headquarters, regional offices, country missions, and armies of administrative staff, but rather being channeled more directly to a network of carefully vetted and highly effective Focal Points. These Focal Points are envisioned as robust, community-rooted organizations or nascent entities that possess deep local knowledge, established trust within their constituencies, and a proven track record of delivering results on the ground. The RDI Model's financial architecture would allocate an overwhelming majority of the capital – potentially upward of 90% – directly to these Focal Points for project implementation and capacity enhancement. The remaining 10% would cover the lean, agile operational costs of the RDI coordinating body itself, focused on strategic oversight, robust due diligence on Focal Points, results monitoring, and facilitating knowledge exchange.

This contrasts sharply with the financial realities of traditional aid disbursement. If a $10 billion investment were to follow conventional pathways, a significant portion, as discussed, would inevitably be absorbed by administrative costs within donor agencies, intermediary NGOs, and implementing partners. Estimates suggest that these overheads can range from 20% to 40% or even higher, depending on the specific mechanisms and the nature of the organizations involved. This means that for every $10 billion invested traditionally, potentially $2 billion to $4 billion or more might be consumed by salaries, travel, office leases, compliance, and other non-programmatic expenditures before the funds even reach the project level. The RDI Model, by contrast, aims to reverse this ratio, ensuring that the vast majority of the $10 billion directly fuels on-the-ground activities and strengthens the capacity of local actors.

The financial savings and enhanced impact generated by this model are profound. Consider a $100 million program aimed at improving agricultural productivity in a specific region. Under a traditional model, if 30% of the funds are absorbed by administrative costs, $70 million would be available for direct intervention. This might translate into purchasing seeds and fertilizers for a certain number of farmers, providing training to a limited cohort, and supporting extension services. However, if RDI were to manage this $100 million, and its administrative overhead was capped at 10%, then $90 million would be directly available for the same objectives. This extra $20 million, or 28.5% more capital, could translate into significantly expanding the reach of the program: reaching thousands more farmers, providing more advanced training, investing in better irrigation technologies, or supporting more robust market linkages. The return on investment, measured in improved livelihoods and food security, would be exponentially greater.

Moreover, **the RDI Model's emphasis on direct investment in grassroots capacity building is a core component of its financial efficiency.** Instead of funding the administrative structures of large international organizations, RDI would directly invest in strengthening the operational, financial management, and programmatic capabilities of its Focal Points. This might include providing funding for local staff incentives, professional development and training for their teams, investing in essential equipment and technology, and supporting the development of robust monitoring and evaluation systems within these local entities. This is not merely an administrative cost; it is a direct investment in building the long-term sustainability and effectiveness of the very actors best positioned to drive development outcomes. By enhancing the capacity of these local institutions, RDI ensures that they can manage larger budgets, implement more complex projects, and achieve greater impact over time, creating a virtuous cycle of development.

The financial proposition also addresses the inherent inefficiencies in procurement and project management within complex, multi-tiered systems. Traditional aid often involves lengthy and expensive procurement processes, requiring adherence to donor-specific regulations that can be opaque and time-consuming. This can lead to delays in project implementation and increased transaction costs. The RDI Model, by empowering Focal Points to manage their own procurements within a framework of rigorous due diligence and oversight, can significantly reduce these lead times and costs. The Focal Points, with their intimate knowledge of local markets and suppliers, can often procure goods and services more efficiently and cost-effectively than external entities. The RDI coordinating body would provide clear guidelines, conduct spot-checks and audits, and offer technical assistance on procurement best practices, ensuring accountability while prioritizing speed and efficiency.

Furthermore, the financial model of RDI fosters a more direct and accountable relationship between the source of funds and the ultimate beneficiaries. Instead of the diffuse accountability often seen in traditional aid chains, where responsibility can be diluted across multiple organizations, RDI establishes a clear line of accountability from the RDI coordinating body to the Focal Points, and by extension, to the communities they serve. This directness in financial flow and oversight allows for quicker identification and resolution of issues, greater transparency in resource utilization, and a stronger sense of ownership and responsibility at all levels. The financial proposition is not just about reducing overhead; it's about creating a more responsive and effective financial ecosystem for development.

The $10 billion imperative, when viewed through the lens of the RDI Model, represents a paradigm shift in resource allocation. It moves away from a model that, however well-intentioned, often inadvertently diverts a significant proportion of available capital into its own operational machinery, and towards a model that prioritizes direct investment in demonstrable impact. The financial calculation is clear: by reducing the percentage of funds consumed by administrative overhead from the customary 20-40% to a lean 10%, an additional $1 billion to $3 billion on every $10 billion invested becomes available for direct programmatic activities. This is not a theoretical saving; it is a tangible increase in the resources that can be deployed to build schools, train teachers, provide healthcare, support small businesses, and ultimately, uplift communities.

The RDI Model's financial viability hinges on its ability to attract and retain high-caliber personnel within a lean, agile structure. The coordinating body would need experts in financial oversight, due diligence, impact measurement, and knowledge management, but their numbers would be significantly smaller than those required to manage complex grant-making portfolios across numerous international organizations. These individuals would be tasked with ensuring the integrity of the system, supporting the Focal Points, and rigorously tracking the outcomes of the investments. Their compensation would reflect their expertise and the critical nature of their roles, but the overall administrative budget would remain a fraction of what is typically allocated to managing multi-billion dollar traditional aid programs.

Moreover, the RDI financial proposition embraces a culture of continuous learning and adaptation, a crucial element for maximizing long-term impact. By investing directly in the capacity of Focal Points, RDI encourages them to develop their own robust financial management and reporting systems. This not only enhances their individual effectiveness but also allows for the collection of granular data on resource utilization and programmatic outcomes at the grassroots level. This data, aggregated and analyzed by the RDI coordinating body, provides invaluable insights into what works, where resources are most effectively deployed, and where adjustments are needed. This iterative, data-driven approach to financial management and program implementation is a key differentiator from traditional models that can be slower to adapt due to bureaucratic inertia.

The contrast in financial allocation is stark and compelling. For instance, a $50 million grant under a traditional model might see $10 million allocated to the donor's administrative costs, another $15 million to an international NGO's headquarters and country office operations, leaving $25 million for direct project work and local capacity building. The RDI Model, applying the same $50 million, might allocate $5 million to its own lean coordination, and then direct the remaining $45 million to a network of local Focal Points, with a small portion of that ($4.5 million) dedicated to their capacity enhancement and the rest ($40.5 million) for direct implementation. This represents $15.5 million more for tangible activities and community capacity building. This increase in directly deployable capital is the cornerstone of the RDI Model, offering a significantly more efficient allocation of the $10 billion imperative. This efficiency is not merely about saving money; it is about multiplying impact, reaching more people, and achieving more sustainable development outcomes. **The financial commitment of $10 billion, when channeled through RDI's model, becomes a far more potent force for change than when dispersed through the existing, more costly, and less agile aid infrastructure.**

The $10 billion imperative, when strategically deployed through the Rescue Democracy International (RDI) model, possesses the power to catalyze transformative change on a scale rarely witnessed in the realm of global development. **This is not a hypothetical scenario; it is a quantifiable projection of what smart, efficient, and grassroots-focused investment can achieve.** By adhering to the principles of minimal administrative overhead and maximum direct impact, the RDI framework unlocks a significantly larger proportion of this substantial capital for tangible interventions that directly benefit millions of lives. To illustrate this, let us break down the potential impact across key developmental sectors, painting a vivid picture of the ripple effect that $10 billion, judiciously invested, can generate.

Let us consider the sector of education. A $10 billion investment, with 90% directly channeled into on-the-ground initiatives and capacity building, translates into $9 billion dedicated to educational capacity building. Under the RDI Model, this capital would be directed towards strengthening local educational institutions, not by building monolithic, externally managed schools, but by investing in the renovation and expansion of existing community-run learning centers, equipping them with essential resources, and crucially, empowering local educators. If we assume that a significant portion of this $9 billion is allocated to improving the quality of education for primary school children, focusing on areas with the greatest need, we can project the following:

An investment of approximately $500 per child could cover the cost of essential learning materials, including textbooks, stationery, and supplementary readers, for an entire primary school education cycle. With $9 billion, this would translate to providing quality educational resources for 18 million children. This figure represents a substantial portion of the global out-of-school population, particularly those in marginalized communities who are most acutely affected by under-resourced educational systems. Furthermore, a portion of the funds could be allocated to teacher training and professional development. An investment of, say, $1,000 per teacher for comprehensive pedagogical training, curriculum development workshops, and ongoing mentorship could empower 9 million teachers. This would significantly elevate the quality of instruction, ensuring that these 18 million children receive not just access to, but effective and engaging education.

Beyond immediate learning materials, the RDI Model would also facilitate the construction and upgrading of school infrastructure. A typical cost for building a modest, sustainable, and locally appropriate primary school classroom, including basic sanitation facilities and a safe learning environment, might range from $25,000 to $40,000, depending on local material costs and labor. If $2 billion of the education budget were allocated to this, it could fund the construction or significant renovation of approximately 50,000 to 80,000 classrooms. These classrooms would be built with community involvement, ensuring local ownership and sustainability, and would serve hundreds of thousands, if not millions, of additional students. This also includes the provision of essential facilities like clean water points and latrines, critical for health and hygiene, especially for girls.

The impact extends to vocational and technical training as well. A $1 billion allocation could establish or significantly enhance 1,000 vocational training centers across diverse regions, each equipped with the necessary tools and machinery for skills development in trades such as carpentry, mechanics, electrical work, sewing, and agricultural technology. Each center, with an average annual capacity to train 500 individuals, could equip half a million people with market-relevant skills. This would not only enhance individual employability but also contribute to the growth of local economies by fostering a skilled workforce capable of meeting local demands and even creating new enterprises. The RDI approach would ensure that these centers are deeply integrated with local labor markets, with curricula designed in consultation with local businesses to guarantee graduates are job-ready.

Moving to the healthcare sector, a $10 billion investment, with $9 billion directed towards impactful initiatives, could achieve remarkable improvements in public health. A significant portion of this could be dedicated to strengthening primary healthcare systems, which are often the first point of contact for communities in developing nations. Investing in community health worker programs is particularly cost-effective. Equipping and training a community health worker, providing them with basic diagnostic tools, essential medicines, and a mobile communication device, might cost approximately $1,500 per worker per year. With $3 billion allocated to this, we could support a force of 2 million community health workers. These dedicated individuals, embedded within their communities, could provide essential preventative care, maternal and child health services, basic treatment for common illnesses, health education, and referrals to higher-level facilities. This could lead to a substantial reduction in preventable deaths and diseases, particularly among mothers and children.

The impact on maternal and child mortality rates would be profound. Studies have consistently shown that the presence of skilled birth attendants and access to basic maternal health services can drastically reduce mortality. If $2 billion of the healthcare budget is invested in equipping and staffing local health posts and clinics with essential equipment for safe deliveries, providing prenatal and postnatal care, and ensuring the availability of essential medicines and vaccines, we can project a significant decline in these tragic statistics. For instance, improving access to skilled birth attendance for 10 million women could save tens of thousands of maternal lives and hundreds of thousands of infant lives annually. This also includes ensuring access to vaccinations for millions of children, eradicating or significantly controlling common childhood diseases like measles, polio, and tetanus.

Furthermore, investments in sanitation and access to clean water are intrinsically linked to health outcomes. A $2 billion allocation towards building and rehabilitating community water sources and sanitation facilities could directly impact the lives of millions. The construction of a community well or a water purification system, coupled with the implementation of hygiene education programs, can cost between $10,000 and $50,000, depending on the scale and complexity. This budget could fund the creation or rehabilitation of tens of thousands of such facilities, providing clean and safe water to an estimated 15-20 million people. This would lead to a dramatic decrease in waterborne diseases such as cholera, typhoid, and dysentery, reducing the burden on healthcare systems and improving overall community well-being.

The RDI Model's emphasis on local ownership means that these infrastructure projects would be managed and maintained by community-based water committees, trained and supported by the RDI's Focal Points. This ensures long-term sustainability and prevents the common issue of neglected infrastructure in traditional aid projects. The capacity building component would include training these committees in basic maintenance, financial management for upkeep, and hygiene promotion, ensuring that the benefits of clean water and sanitation endure for generations.

In the realm of agriculture and food security, $9 billion invested through RDI's model could revolutionize rural livelihoods. A substantial portion, say $4 billion, could be channeled into providing smallholder farmers with access to improved seeds, drought-resistant crop varieties, and organic fertilizers. The cost of a basic improved seed package and fertilizer for one hectare (2.471 acres) of land might be around $100-$200. This allocation could support up to 40-80 million farming households, significantly increasing their yields and resilience to climate shocks. This directly translates into enhanced food security for millions and increased incomes for rural families.

Moreover, $2 billion could be invested in developing and expanding small-scale irrigation systems, such as drip irrigation or solar-powered water pumps. The cost of a basic drip irrigation system for one hectare can range from $500 to $1,000. This would allow for the expansion of irrigation to millions of hectares, enabling farmers to cultivate crops even during dry seasons and increasing their productivity by an estimated 30-50%. This also includes investing in post-harvest technologies and storage facilities to reduce crop losses, which can often exceed 30% in many regions. By providing access to better storage solutions and training in post-harvest management, an additional $1 billion could help farmers preserve their harvests, improve market access, and reduce food waste, thereby increasing their overall profitability and contributing to national food security.

The remaining $2 billion could be dedicated to market access and value chain development. This includes supporting farmer cooperatives, establishing links with reliable buyers, investing in basic processing and packaging facilities, and providing training in market analysis and negotiation. By empowering farmer groups to aggregate their produce and negotiate better prices, they can move from subsistence farming to market-oriented agriculture, increasing their income significantly. This investment would not only improve farmers' economic standing but also stimulate local economies by creating demand for agricultural inputs and processing services. The RDI framework would ensure that these market linkages are sustainable and equitable, fostering fair trade practices and long-term partnerships between farmers and consumers.

In the critical area of economic capacity building and livelihoods, $9 billion could be meticulously allocated to foster entrepreneurship and create sustainable economic opportunities. A significant portion, perhaps $3 billion, could be used to establish and capitalize micro-finance institutions and support small and medium-sized enterprises (SMEs). This would involve providing access to affordable credit, business development services, and mentorship for aspiring entrepreneurs. If an average loan size for a small business is $500, this capital could support the creation or growth of 6 million small businesses. These businesses, in turn, create employment opportunities for many more individuals, driving economic growth from the grassroots up.

The RDI approach would focus on sectors with high potential for local job creation, such as renewable energy, sustainable agriculture processing, artisanal crafts, local tourism to name a few. For example, an investment of $2 billion in supporting the growth of the renewable energy sector could lead to the installation of millions of solar home systems in off-grid communities, providing clean and affordable electricity. This would not only improve quality of life by enabling lighting for study and work, charging mobile phones, and powering small appliances, but also create local jobs in installation, maintenance, and sales.

Furthermore, $2 billion could be allocated to skills development and vocational training programs tailored to the specific needs of local labor markets. This goes beyond basic literacy and numeracy, focusing on practical skills such as digital literacy, basic accounting, customer service, and specialized trades. These programs would be delivered through local training providers, ensuring relevance and accessibility. By training an estimated 5 million individuals in these employable skills, the RDI Model would directly address unemployment and underemployment, empowering individuals to secure better-paying jobs or start their own ventures.

Beyond these core sectors, the $10 billion imperative, channeled through RDI, can also have a profound impact on other vital areas such as disaster risk reduction, climate change adaptation, and good governance. For instance, a $1 billion allocation could be used to support community-based disaster preparedness initiatives, early warning systems, and the construction of climate-resilient infrastructure in vulnerable areas. Investing in small-scale renewable energy projects and sustainable land management practices, powered by local expertise, would contribute to mitigating climate change impacts and building resilience. Moreover, a portion of the funds could be dedicated to strengthening local governance structures, promoting transparency, and supporting civil society organizations that advocate for accountability and human rights, ensuring that development is inclusive and equitable.

The cumulative impact of these targeted investments is not merely additive; it is synergistic. Improved education leads to a more skilled workforce, better healthcare improves productivity, and enhanced livelihoods contribute to social stability and good governance. The RDI Model, by prioritizing direct investment in local capacity and proven interventions, ensures that this $10 billion is not just spent, but strategically invested to create a sustainable and multiplying effect. The projections outlined above, based on realistic costings and the RDI's efficient allocation model, demonstrate that this $10 billion imperative, when guided by a commitment to what truly works at the grassroots, can indeed uplift millions of lives, build essential infrastructure, improve access to critical services, and foster resilient, self-sufficient communities across the globe. **This is not an aspiration; it is a tangible future that the RDI framework makes possible.**

The efficacy of development finance hinges not on the quantum of capital alone, but on the intelligence and integrity of its deployment. While the $10 billion imperative, as detailed previously, presents a compelling opportunity for transformative change through the Rescue Democracy International (RDI) model, its realization is contingent upon a fundamental recalibration of how development finance is conceived and allocated. This is not a moment for incremental adjustments or the perpetuation of outdated paradigms; it is a clarion call for a strategic pivot, a deliberate departure from the well-trodden paths of conventional aid towards investment vehicles that demonstrably deliver superior and sustainable outcomes. The current landscape of global development funding, while often well-intentioned, is frequently mired in inefficiencies, burdened by administrative overhead, and inadequately responsive to the nuanced realities of grassroots needs. **It is precisely this structural inertia that the RDI Model seeks to disrupt, advocating for a paradigm shift that prioritizes demonstrable impact and accountability above all else.**

Governments, international financial institutions, philanthropic foundations, and private sector investors alike must critically examine their current financing mechanisms. The persistent challenges in global development – persistent poverty, inadequate access to basic services, vulnerability to climate shocks, and persistent inequalities – are not insoluble; they are, in many instances, a direct consequence of suboptimal resource allocation. We have the capital, but we often lack the strategic vision to deploy it most effectively. The "business as usual" approach, characterized by top-down planning, fragmented interventions, and a disconnect from the beneficiaries' realities, has yielded diminishing returns. This is not a critique of the dedication of individuals working within these systems, but rather a necessary interrogation of the systems themselves. The RDI Model, by contrast, is predicated on a clear understanding that true development is an organic, community-led process. Its emphasis on minimal administrative costs – ideally below 10% of the total fund – and a direct, on-the-ground allocation of at least 90% of resources, is not merely an operational preference; it is a foundational principle for maximizing impact. This stark contrast between RDI and more conventional models necessitates a serious conversation about where capital is truly flowing and what it is achieving.

Consider the common critique that international aid is inefficient. While this is a broad generalization, it is often rooted in observable realities. Funds are often diverted to cover extensive headquarters operations, elaborate consultancy fees, and complex monitoring and evaluation frameworks that, while ostensibly for accountability, can become ends in themselves, siphoning resources away from direct programmatic activities. **The RDI approach fundamentally reorients this, recognizing that the most effective accountability mechanism is the tangible improvement in people's lives.** This is achieved through embedded local focal points who manage funds and oversee implementation, ensuring that resources are channeled directly into community-identified needs, overseen by individuals with deep contextual understanding and a vested interest in local success. This localized approach fosters trust, adaptability, and ownership, elements that are frequently absent in more centralized or externally managed development initiatives.

The call for strategic investment is, therefore, a call for a fundamental re-evaluation of return on investment (ROI) in the development sector. If we define ROI not merely in financial terms, but in terms of lives improved, communities strengthened, and sustainable progress achieved, then models that demonstrably deliver higher impact per dollar invested must take precedence. The RDI framework, with its lean operational structure and direct channeling of funds, is designed to achieve precisely this. For instance, in education, the projections outlined previously show that a substantial portion of the $9 billion allocated could directly fund learning materials, teacher training, and essential infrastructure, reaching millions of children and educators. Compare this to a scenario where administrative costs might absorb 20-30% or more of the total fund. The difference in tangible outcomes is staggering. An extra 10-20% of the $10 billion, meaning an additional $1-2 billion, channeled directly into classrooms, clinics, or farms, can translate into tens of thousands more children educated, hundreds of thousands more lives saved, or millions more people lifted out of poverty.

This strategic shift requires a willingness from major development finance actors – United Nations, governments contributing Official Development Assistance (ODA), multilateral development banks, and large philanthropic organizations – to explore and adopt innovative financing mechanisms. It means moving beyond the comfort of established, although less effective, modalities. It entails a willingness to pilot and scale up approaches like RDI, even if they challenge existing bureaucratic structures or traditional power dynamics. For private investors, it means recognizing the immense opportunity to create both social and financial returns by channeling capital into development initiatives that are rigorously designed for impact and efficiency. Impact investing, when guided by principles of genuine grassroots engagement and measurable outcomes, can align profit motives with profound social good, making development finance a more dynamic and sustainable engine for progress.

Furthermore, a critical component of this strategic investment is transparency and accountability, but accountability that is oriented towards impact. The RDI Model, by its very nature, promotes this. Local focal points, working with community representatives and utilizing digital platforms for transparent fund tracking and outcome reporting, create a direct line of sight between investment and impact. This contrasts with many current systems where accountability is often a retrospective, compliance-driven exercise, generating reports that may not accurately reflect the ground reality or the true impact on beneficiaries. A strategic investment framework must prioritize real-time, verifiable data on outcomes, allowing for adaptive management and continuous improvement. This means investing not just in projects, but in the systems that allow for transparent reporting and learning.

The challenge, then, is to build the political and financial will to enact this change. It requires advocacy from civil society, pressure from informed citizens, and leadership from visionary individuals within governments and international bodies. It demands a courageous acknowledgment that the status quo is insufficient and that more effective pathways exist. The $10 billion imperative is not just a financial figure; it is a symbolic representation of the vast resources available for global betterment. **The question is not whether we have enough, but whether we are deploying what we have in the most intelligent, impactful, and equitable manner possible.** Shifting development finance towards proven, efficient models like RDI is not merely a matter of optimizing resource allocation; it is an ethical imperative. It is about ensuring that every dollar invested yields the greatest possible return for the people and communities who need it most, transforming potential into tangible progress and building a more just and sustainable world for all. This requires a commitment to learning, adapting, and always prioritizing the measurable well-being of those at the heart of development efforts. **The time for a strategic redirection of development finance, powered by principles of efficiency, transparency, and demonstrable impact, is not in the future; it is now.**

CHAPTER 10:

Building Trust:
Transparency and Accountability Mechanisms

The journey of development and humanitarian aid, while often fueled by noble intentions and substantial capital, is frequently shadowed by a pervasive and damaging phenomenon: **the trust deficit.** This erosion of confidence is not a peripheral concern; it is a foundational challenge that undermines the very efficacy and legitimacy of the vast resources poured into global development and humanitarian efforts. **For far too long, the narrative surrounding international assistance has been punctuated by whispers and, at times, outright accusations of inefficiency, misallocation, and even outright corruption.** These perceptions, whether fully or partially substantiated, have created a chasm between those who provide aid and those who are intended to benefit from it. This disconnect breeds skepticism, breeds apathy, and ultimately, breeds failure.

The roots of this trust deficit are multifaceted, extending deep into the historical evolution of development assistance. One of the primary drivers is the perception of inefficiency, a sentiment often amplified by the sheer scale of administrative overhead associated with many international aid programs. While some administrative costs are unavoidable to ensure proper oversight, robust monitoring, and logistical coordination, the burden can often become disproportionate. When a significant portion of donated or allocated funds is absorbed by bureaucratic layers, consultancy fees, extensive travel, and elaborate reporting mechanisms, it leaves the beneficiaries and the public questioning the true value for money. The aspiration for development is to see tangible improvements in people's lives – access to clean water, better education, improved healthcare, economic opportunities. When these tangible outcomes are perceived to be obscured by an opaque and costly administrative apparatus, it naturally fuels a sense of grievance and distrust. The narrative often becomes one of resources being siphoned away before they can reach those most in need, creating a fertile ground for cynicism.

Furthermore, the inherent power dynamics in the aid relationship can inadvertently contribute to this trust deficit. Historically, and often by necessity, development initiatives have been conceived and implemented with significant input from external actors – governments, international organizations, and NGOs based in donor countries. While the expertise and resources these actors bring are invaluable, **an overemphasis on top-down planning, without sufficient genuine consultation and integration of local knowledge and priorities, can create a perception of imposition rather than partnership.** Beneficiary communities may feel that their voices are not truly heard, their agency is not respected, and that the interventions are designed *for* them, rather than *with* them. This lack of genuine participation, of feeling like an active stakeholder rather than a passive recipient, can breed resentment and a deep-seated skepticism about the motives and effectiveness of the aid being provided. When communities are not involved in the design, implementation, and evaluation of projects that directly affect their lives, they are less likely to feel ownership, and thus less likely to trust that the aid is truly serving their best interests.

Corruption, unfortunately, remains a persistent specter in the development landscape, and its impact on trust cannot be overstated. While the vast majority of individuals working in the development sector are dedicated and ethical, isolated instances of corruption – whether petty bribery, embezzlement, or the siphoning of resources through fraudulent schemes – cast a long shadow. These instances, often sensationalized by media reports, can create a generalized perception that the entire system is rife with corruption. For beneficiaries, witnessing resources meant to alleviate their suffering being diverted for personal gain is a profound betrayal, shattering any hope or trust they may have held. For the global public, learning of corrupt practices can lead to a withdrawal of support, a feeling that their contributions are not being used responsibly, and a reluctance to engage with development initiatives in the future. This is particularly damaging because it disproportionately punishes the diligent and the ethical, making it harder for them to secure the funding and support necessary to do their vital work. The reality is that corruption, even when it affects a small percentage of the overall aid flow, can have an outsized impact on public perception and donor confidence.

The disconnect between aid providers and recipients is another critical element contributing to the trust deficit. This disconnect can manifest in various ways: a lack of understanding of local cultures, customs, and social structures; the imposition of external development models that are not culturally appropriate or sustainable; or simply a failure to communicate effectively with the people on the ground. When aid agencies operate in a bubble, relying on external consultants and distant headquarters for decision-making, they risk misinterpreting local needs, creating dependency, and failing to build the essential relationships of trust that are crucial for successful, sustainable development. This gap in understanding can lead to interventions that are poorly designed, culturally insensitive, and ultimately ineffective. It can also lead to a perception among beneficiaries that the aid providers are outsiders who do not truly understand or care about their reality, further deepening the chasm of distrust.

The consequences of this trust deficit are profound and far-reaching. At the most fundamental level, it erodes the legitimacy of development and humanitarian aid. When the public and beneficiaries alike question the integrity and effectiveness of aid, the moral and practical justification for its provision weakens. This can lead to decreased funding from governments and private donors, making it harder to address critical global challenges. It can also lead to greater scrutiny and more burdensome regulations, which, while sometimes necessary, can further increase administrative costs and slow down the delivery of much-needed assistance. For beneficiaries, a lack of trust can manifest as resistance to aid programs, suspicion of aid workers, and a reluctance to participate in initiatives, ultimately hindering progress and perpetuating cycles of vulnerability.

Moreover, a lack of trust stifles innovation and adaptability. When aid organizations are constantly under pressure to prove their worth due to public skepticism, they may become risk-averse, sticking to proven but potentially less effective methods rather than experimenting with new approaches that could yield better results. This creates a stagnant environment where genuine solutions are overlooked because they are perceived as too unconventional or too difficult to account for in traditional reporting frameworks. The ability to learn from mistakes, adapt to changing circumstances, and foster community-led innovation – all crucial components of effective development – are significantly hampered when the foundational element of trust is absent.

Rebuilding this trust is therefore not merely a desirable outcome; it is an absolute imperative for the future of international development and humanitarian action. It requires a fundamental shift in how aid is conceived, delivered, and accounted for. The focus must move beyond simply disbursing funds to demonstrating tangible, positive impact in a transparent and accountable manner. This involves not only strengthening internal controls and anti-corruption measures but also fostering genuine partnerships with beneficiary communities, amplifying their voices, and empowering them as active participants in their own development. It means embracing transparency not as a compliance exercise, but as a core value that underpins all operations, making the flow of funds and the results achieved visible and understandable to all stakeholders. **Only by systematically addressing the causes of the trust deficit can the development sector reclaim its credibility and fulfill its potential to create lasting, positive change in the world.**

The Rescue Democracy International (RDI) recognizes that transparency is not merely a requirement of compliance, but the foundation upon which enduring trust is built. In the sphere of international development and humanitarian action, where significant resources are mobilized and the well-being of vulnerable populations hangs in the balance, an unwavering commitment to openness is paramount. RDI's architecture of transparency is meticulously designed to ensure that information flows freely and accessibly to every stakeholder, fostering an environment of shared understanding, accountability, and ultimately, mutual confidence. This goes beyond simply publishing annual reports; it involves embedding transparency into the very DNA of RDI's operations, from the initial design of a project to its final evaluation and dissemination of outcomes.

At the core of RDI's open channels of information is a multi-pronged digital strategy. Recognizing the ubiquity of digital access, even in many of the regions where RDI operates, a comprehensive online portal serves as the central hub for all project-related data. This platform is structured to be user-friendly, catering to diverse audiences with varying levels of technical expertise. For donors, it provides rough financial tracking, detailing how every dollar is allocated, spent, and accounted for. This includes not just aggregate figures but itemized expenditures, supplier contracts where appropriate and permissible, and justifications for variances. **The aim is to offer an unprecedented level of visibility, allowing donors to see the tangible impact of their contributions in real-time, thereby reinforcing their commitment and encouraging continued support.** The portal displays comprehensive project proposals, outlining the identified needs, the proposed interventions, the expected outcomes, and the key performance indicators (KPIs) against which success will be measured. This upfront clarity in project objectives and methodologies is critical for setting expectations and establishing a baseline for accountability.

For implementing partners and on-the-ground staff, the portal offers access to operational guidelines, training materials, and real-time updates on project progress, challenges, and adaptations. This ensures that all actors involved in project delivery are working with the most current and accurate information, fostering a sense of unity and shared purpose. Crucially, the portal is also designed with beneficiaries in mind. While recognizing the limitations of digital access in some contexts, efforts are made to ensure that information is accessible through community centers, local partner organizations, and even printed summaries where necessary. This includes clear, concise language explaining project goals, timelines, and how beneficiaries can engage with or benefit from the initiative. Feedback mechanisms are integrated directly into the portal, allowing beneficiaries to submit questions, concerns, and suggestions, which are then routed to the appropriate RDI personnel for timely response. This two-way communication is vital for ensuring that RDI remains responsive to the needs and experiences of the communities it serves.

Beyond the digital realm, RDI champions a philosophy of open data and open communication at every stage of the project lifecycle. Financial transparency, for instance, is not limited to an online dashboard. RDI actively pursues partnerships with independent financial auditors, whose reports are made publicly available. These audits cover not only the utilization of funds but also the efficiency and effectiveness of programmatic spending. Furthermore, RDI publishes detailed breakdowns of its administrative costs, demonstrating how overhead is managed and how it directly supports program delivery. This is crucial for countering the perception that a disproportionate amount of aid is consumed by bureaucracy. When communities and donors can see that administrative costs are lean, well-justified, and directly contribute to operational capacity, it builds confidence in the overall efficiency of the organization.

Decision-making processes within RDI are also subjected to rigorous transparency. Key programmatic decisions, resource allocations, and strategic shifts are documented and shared. This includes minutes from key internal meetings, rationales behind major funding decisions, and the processes by which projects are selected and prioritized. For major strategic initiatives or significant changes in programming, RDI undertakes consultations with a diverse range of stakeholders, including beneficiaries, local governments, civil society organizations, and donors. The outcomes of these consultations, including any dissenting views and how they were addressed, are publicly recorded and shared. This demonstrates that RDI is not operating in an echo chamber but is genuinely engaging with the diverse perspectives that shape the development landscape. When communities see that their input has been considered in decision-making, even if not every suggestion can be adopted, it fosters a sense of respect and legitimacy.

The commitment to transparency extends to the sharing of both successes and challenges. **RDI believes that a true measure of an organization's integrity lies not only in its ability to celebrate achievements but also in its willingness to honestly report on setbacks, lessons learned, and areas for improvement.** Project reports are therefore designed to be comprehensive, detailing not only what worked well but also what did not, and providing clear analyses of the reasons behind any shortfalls. This includes data on project outcomes, even when they fall short of initial targets, and a candid assessment of any unforeseen obstacles encountered. This willingness to be open about failures, rather than obscuring them, is a powerful indicator of RDI's commitment to learning and continuous improvement, and it builds a deeper, more resilient form of trust than a narrative of unblemished success could ever achieve. Such candor allows partners and donors to better understand the complexities of development work and to collaborate more effectively on finding solutions.

Furthermore, RDI actively promotes transparency in its partnerships and collaborations. When engaging with local implementing partners, clear memorandums of understanding (MOUs) are established, detailing roles, responsibilities, financial management protocols, and reporting requirements. These MOUs are often made accessible to relevant stakeholders, ensuring that all parties understand the framework of cooperation. RDI also works to ensure that its partners themselves adhere to high standards of transparency and accountability, often providing capacity-building support in these areas. This commitment to extending transparency throughout the aid chain strengthens the entire ecosystem of development and humanitarian assistance. It means that not only RDI but also its extended network of collaborators are held to a high standard of openness, creating a ripple effect of accountability.

In the spirit of open data, RDI makes anonymized project-level data available for research and analysis by third parties. This allows for independent verification of RDI's impact and contributes to the broader knowledge base of effective development practices. The data shared adheres to strict privacy protocols, ensuring that no sensitive personal information of beneficiaries or staff is compromised. This commitment to open data extends beyond mere reporting; it is an invitation to the global community to engage with RDI's work, to scrutinize it, and to build upon it. This approach fosters a collaborative environment where the collective learning of the development sector can accelerate progress. By sharing the raw data, RDI empowers academics, policymakers, and other organizations to conduct their own analyses, identifying trends and best practices that RDI itself might not have uncovered, thereby fostering a dynamic and evidence-based approach to development.

Communication channels are deliberately kept open and accessible. RDI maintains active and responsive social media presences, regularly sharing project updates, success stories, and insights into the challenges faced. A dedicated contact point for media inquiries and public information requests ensures that journalists and concerned citizens can obtain accurate and timely information. Regular public forums, webinars, and town hall meetings are convened, providing platforms for direct engagement between RDI leadership, staff, and the broader public, including beneficiaries, donors, and civil society representatives. These events are not merely presentations; they are dialogues, where questions are encouraged, and honest answers are provided, even to the most challenging inquiries. The ability to engage in open, direct conversation is a powerful tool for demystifying the organization and building personal connections, which are fundamental to trust.

Moreover, RDI is committed to transparency in its advocacy efforts. When RDI engages in policy advocacy or works with governments to influence development policies, its positions, the evidence supporting them, and any potential conflicts of interest are clearly articulated. This ensures that RDI's influence is seen as being driven by evidence and a genuine commitment to development goals, rather than by hidden agendas. This level of openness in advocacy builds credibility with policymakers, partners, and the public alike, demonstrating that RDI's efforts are for the common good.

The implementation of this transparency architecture is supported by robust internal policies and training programs. All RDI staff, from senior management to field officers, receive regular training on RDI's transparency standards, data protection policies, and ethical communication practices. Internal audits are conducted to ensure adherence to these policies, and any breaches are addressed promptly and decisively, with findings and actions taken made accessible where appropriate. This internal discipline reinforces the external commitment to openness, ensuring that transparency is not just a talking point but an ingrained practice.

In summary, RDI's transparency architecture is designed to be comprehensive, accessible, and dynamic. It encompasses a commitment to openly sharing financial information, project progress, decision-making processes, challenges, and lessons learned. This is achieved through a combination of digital platforms, independent audits, public consultations, open data initiatives, and accessible communication channels. By making information readily available to all stakeholders, RDI seeks to dismantle the barriers of opacity, foster genuine partnerships, and cultivate a deep-seated trust that is essential for achieving sustainable and impactful development outcomes. **This unwavering dedication to openness is not just a strategy; it is a core value that underpins RDI's mission and its commitment to serving the global development agenda with integrity and effectiveness.**

In building upon the foundation of transparency, the Rescue Democracy International (RDI) places equal, if not greater, emphasis on robust accountability frameworks. This is not a perfunctory nod to regulatory demands or donor reporting requirements, but a deeply ingrained ethos of genuine responsibility. Accountability, in the RDI context, transcends mere compliance; it signifies a proactive commitment to being answerable for actions, decisions, and outcomes to all stakeholders, most crucially to the communities we serve and the partners who entrust us with their resources. It is about fostering a culture where everyone involved in the development process understands their role in achieving shared goals and is empowered and expected to uphold the highest standards of integrity and effectiveness.

At the heart of RDI's accountability architecture are its designated Focal Points, operational units often embedded within or closely aligned with the communities where projects are implemented. These Focal Points are the frontline representatives of RDI, translating global strategies into tangible local action. Their accountability is multifaceted. Firstly, they are accountable for the accurate and timely reporting of project activities, expenditures, and challenges encountered on the ground. This involves not just data entry, but providing context, explaining variances, and flagging potential risks or opportunities that might impact project trajectory. They are the eyes and ears of RDI, and their detailed, honest reporting is the bedrock upon which informed decision-making at higher levels is built. Failure to report accurately or in a timely manner can lead to misallocation of resources, missed opportunities for course correction, and ultimately, a failure to meet the needs of the beneficiaries.

Beyond reporting, Focal Points are also accountable for the ethical conduct of their operations. This encompasses everything from safeguarding the dignity and rights of beneficiaries to ensuring fair and equitable distribution of resources, and upholding RDI's code of conduct in all interactions. They are responsible for fostering an environment of trust at the local level, ensuring that community members feel safe to voice concerns and that their feedback is genuinely heard and acted upon. This localized accountability is crucial because it is at this level that the direct impact of development interventions is most keenly felt. When Focal Points are held accountable for their ethical conduct and their commitment to the well-being of the communities, it cultivates a sense of ownership and partnership among the beneficiaries themselves, transforming them from passive recipients into active participants in their own development.

Complementing the Focal Points are the Local Project Support & Monitoring Committees (LPSMCs). These committees, typically composed of community leaders, local government representatives, and beneficiary group representatives, serve as crucial oversight, advisory and monitoring bodies. Their accountability lies in their ability to provide community-level oversight of project implementation, ensuring that activities align with identified local needs and that resources are utilized appropriately. LPSMCs are empowered to review project progress reports, scrutinize financial disbursements, and raise concerns regarding project efficacy or ethical breaches. Their role is to act as a vital link between RDI operations and the community, ensuring that the organization remains responsive and relevant to local contexts. The accountability of LPSMCs is thus tied to their diligence in performing these oversight functions and their commitment to representing the collective voice of the community. RDI provides support and capacity building to LPSMCs to ensure they are equipped to fulfill these responsibilities effectively, reinforcing their ability to hold both the Focal Points and RDI itself accountable.

The mutual accountability between Focal Points and LPSMCs is a cornerstone of RDI's operational model. Focal Points are accountable to the LPSMCs for the implementation of project activities as agreed upon, and for transparently sharing information about project progress and resource utilization. Conversely, LPSMCs are accountable for providing constructive feedback, raising legitimate concerns promptly, and supporting the Focal Points in overcoming local challenges. This dynamic creates a virtuous cycle of feedback and improvement. When a Focal Point is diligent and transparent, the LPSMC is more likely to be supportive and provide valuable insights. If issues arise, the structured mechanism for dialogue and recourse ensures that they are addressed proactively rather than festering.

At the central RDI coordination level, a parallel layer of accountability operates. This central team is accountable for setting clear project objectives, allocating resources equitably and effectively, providing timely technical and logistical support to Focal Points, and ensuring overall compliance with RDI's strategic goals and donor requirements. They are responsible for aggregating data from various Focal Points, analyzing trends, identifying systemic challenges, and implementing overarching solutions. This central accountability extends to the rigorous evaluation of project impact and the dissemination of lessons learned across the organization and to external stakeholders. They must be accountable for creating an enabling environment where Focal Points can succeed and for fostering a culture of learning and continuous improvement.

Furthermore, RDI has established specific mechanisms to operationalize this accountability. For instance, **regular review meetings are held, bringing together Focal Points, LPSMC representatives, and central RDI staff.** These meetings are not just for reporting; they are structured dialogues where progress is assessed against agreed-upon indicators, challenges are discussed collaboratively, and solutions are co-created. The minutes and action points from these meetings are meticulously documented and shared, serving as a record of commitments and accountability.

Financial accountability is rigorously maintained through a tiered system. Focal Points manage project-specific budgets and are accountable for their expenditure against approved plans. These expenditures are subject to internal review by the central RDI finance team, as well as periodic external audits. For LPSMCs, their oversight role extends to reviewing financial reports provided by the Focal Points, ensuring that funds are used for their intended purposes and that transactions are transparent. Any discrepancies or concerns raised by the LPSMC are investigated by the central RDI team, with findings and actions communicated back to the LPSMC and, where appropriate, the broader community. This multi-layered approach to financial oversight ensures that resources are managed responsibly and that every dollar spent is accounted for, not just to donors, but to the people on whose behalf it is being used.

Beyond financial and programmatic accountability, RDI also places significant emphasis on accountability for ethical conduct and adherence to human rights principles. This involves clear grievance mechanisms that are accessible to beneficiaries and community members, allowing them to report any instances of misconduct, discrimination, or violation of their rights without fear of reprisal. Focal Points are trained to receive and appropriately handle such grievances, escalating them to the central RDI team when necessary. The central team is then accountable for investigating these grievances thoroughly, taking appropriate action, and providing feedback to the complainant. This commitment to a functional and responsive grievance mechanism is a critical component of RDI's accountability to the people it serves, ensuring that their voices are heard and their rights are protected.

The RDI's accountability framework is dynamic and adaptive. It recognizes that the contexts in which it operates are constantly evolving, and thus, the mechanisms for ensuring accountability must also be flexible. Regular reviews of the accountability systems themselves are conducted, incorporating feedback from all stakeholders, including Focal Points, LPSMCs, beneficiaries, and implementing partners. This ensures that the frameworks remain relevant, effective, and responsive to emerging challenges and best practices in the field of development and humanitarian aid. By moving beyond a purely compliance-driven approach to one that emphasizes genuine responsibility and mutual accountability, RDI aims to build deeper, more resilient partnerships and to maximize the positive impact of its development efforts. This commitment to being truly accountable is what transforms good intentions into lasting, positive change, cementing trust at every level of engagement.

The pervasive digital revolution has fundamentally reshaped how organizations operate, and the realm of international development is no exception. For initiatives like the Rescue Democracy International (RDI), embracing technology is not merely about adopting new tools; it's about fundamentally enhancing our capacity for transparency and strengthening the accountability mechanisms that underpin our work. In an era where information flows instantaneously and data can be collected and analyzed with unprecedented speed and precision, leveraging these advancements offers a powerful pathway to greater openness and more robust oversight. This technological integration moves us beyond traditional, often paper-based, reporting systems, which can be prone to delays, errors, and limited accessibility. Instead, it propels us towards a model where information is dynamic, accessible, and verifiable, fostering a deeper level of trust among all our stakeholders.

One of the most significant contributions of technology lies in its ability to facilitate real-time tracking of resources and project activities. Digital platforms, from sophisticated Enterprise Resource Planning (ERP) systems to more tailored project management software (PMS), allow for the meticulous recording of every financial transaction. This means that the journey of funds, from initial allocation to final expenditure, can be monitored with granular detail. Budgets are no longer static documents; they become living records that are updated as costs are incurred, providing an immediate overview of financial status. This level of transparency is crucial. Donors want to know precisely how their contributions are being utilized, and

304

communities have a right to understand the flow of resources intended for their benefit. By employing digital ledger systems, for instance, RDI can create an auditable trail for all financial movements, making it significantly harder for funds to be misdirected or unaccounted for. This not only deters malfeasance but also builds confidence by demonstrating responsible stewardship of entrusted capital.

Beyond financial tracking, technology empowers us to monitor project activities as they unfold on the ground. Mobile reporting tools, often deployed through smartphones and tablets, have become invaluable in this regard. These applications can be specifically designed to capture data related to project implementation, such as the distribution of essential supplies, the completion of construction milestones, or the delivery of training sessions. Field staff, or even trained community members, can utilize these tools to submit reports, often accompanied by geo-tagged photographs or short video clips, directly from the project site. **This provides a verifiable, on-the-spot record of progress.** For example, if RDI is involved in distributing agricultural inputs, field officers can use a mobile app to record the details of each beneficiary receiving seeds or fertilizer, including quantities and dates. This data, instantaneously uploaded to a central database, allows project managers to see in real-time which areas have been covered, identify any logistical bottlenecks, and verify that the intended beneficiaries are indeed receiving the support. **This immediacy significantly reduces the lag time inherent in traditional reporting, enabling quicker identification of issues and faster adjustments to implementation strategies.**

The aggregation and analysis of this data through advanced analytics tools offer a further layer of insight and accountability. Once collected, the information from various reporting streams can be integrated into comprehensive dashboards. These dashboards provide a visual representation of project performance, highlighting key indicators, progress against targets, and any deviations from the plan. For instance, an RDI dashboard might display real-time data on the number of wells constructed in a particular region, the percentage of children vaccinated in a health program, or the attendance rates at vocational training workshops. By employing data visualization techniques, complex datasets become easily understandable, allowing for rapid assessment of project health. This facilitates informed decision-making by RDI management, enabling them to identify underperforming areas and proactively address them. Crucially, these dashboards can also be made accessible to relevant stakeholders, offering a level of transparency that was previously unimaginable. Imagine a scenario where community leaders, through a secure portal, can view the progress and resource allocation for projects operating in their area. This direct access to information empowers them to engage more meaningfully in oversight and to hold RDI accountable for its commitments.

Moreover, technology plays a vital role in facilitating immediate feedback loops, a critical component of responsive accountability. **Digital platforms can be used to create channels for beneficiaries and community members to provide feedback, raise concerns, or report issues directly.** This could range from simple SMS-based feedback systems to more sophisticated web-based portals where individuals can submit detailed complaints or suggestions. When a community member reports a problem with a water pump installed by RDI, for example, an automated system can acknowledge receipt of the feedback and flag it for immediate attention by the relevant Focal Point. The ability to track the status of these feedback requests and to provide timely responses is paramount. It signals to the community that their voices are not only heard but are also acted upon. This continuous flow of information, both from the project to the stakeholders and from the stakeholders back to the project, creates a dynamic and iterative process of accountability. It allows RDI to adapt its approaches based on real-world experiences and to rectify mistakes promptly, rather than waiting for formal review cycles.

The use of blockchain technology, while still emerging in some development contexts, presents even more profound opportunities for enhanced transparency and immutable record-keeping. Blockchain's distributed ledger system offers a way to record transactions and data in a way that is secure, transparent, and resistant to tampering. If RDI were to implement a system where aid distribution records were logged on a blockchain, for instance, each transaction – from the initial allocation of resources to the final delivery to a beneficiary – would be cryptographically secured and permanently recorded. This would provide an unprecedented level of assurance about the integrity of the data and the processes involved. While the implementation of such advanced technologies requires careful consideration of infrastructure, digital literacy, and cost, their potential to revolutionize accountability is immense. It could provide a level of verifiable proof of operations that would significantly bolster trust among all parties involved.

However, the successful integration of technology for transparency and accountability is not without its challenges.

Digital divides remain a significant concern. Access to reliable internet connectivity, smartphones, and digital literacy varies considerably across the regions where RDI operates. **Therefore, any technological solution must be designed with inclusivity in mind, ensuring that it does not inadvertently exclude the most vulnerable or marginalized populations.** This might involve using simpler, low-bandwidth technologies, providing necessary devices and training, or ensuring that traditional reporting methods remain available as a complementary channel. Furthermore, data privacy and security are paramount. Robust protocols must be put in place to protect sensitive beneficiaries' data from unauthorized access or misuse. The ethical implications of data collection and use must be carefully considered, ensuring that technology serves to empower rather than surveil or exploit communities.

Another critical aspect is the capacity building required for both RDI staff and community members to effectively utilize these technological tools. Simply deploying an app is insufficient; comprehensive training and ongoing support are essential to ensure that data is collected accurately, reported consistently, and understood correctly. This involves not only technical training on how to operate the software but also an understanding of _why_ this data is important and _how_ it contributes to the overall accountability framework. RDI invests in its Focal Points and community partners, equipping them with the skills and knowledge needed to harness these digital capabilities. This might involve workshops on mobile data collection best practices, sessions on interpreting dashboard analytics, or training on using feedback platforms. By building this local capacity, technology becomes a tool for capacity building, enabling communities to participate more actively in monitoring and overseeing development initiatives.

The selection of appropriate technologies is also crucial. There is no one-size-fits-all solution. RDI must carefully assess the specific needs of each project and context to identify the most effective and sustainable technological tools. This might involve partnering with technology providers, leveraging open-source solutions, or developing custom-built applications. The focus should always be on how technology can best serve the ultimate goal: increasing transparency, strengthening accountability, and improving development outcomes. For example, a project focused on distributing emergency food aid in a remote area might benefit from a simple SMS-based reporting system that can function even with limited connectivity, whereas a large-scale infrastructure project in a more urbanized setting might utilize a more sophisticated project management software with integrated **GIS** mapping capabilities.

Ultimately, technology is a powerful enabler, but it is not a panacea. It must be integrated within a broader framework of good governance, ethical principles, and strong human relationships. The most effective accountability mechanisms combine the precision and reach of technology with the human element of dialogue, oversight, and engagement. By strategically employing digital platforms, mobile reporting, and data analytics, RDI is committed to fostering an environment of unprecedented transparency. This technological advancement is not merely about reporting _to_ stakeholders; it is about enabling stakeholders to see, understand, and participate in the development process _with_ us. This enhanced visibility and accessibility are fundamental to building and sustaining trust that is so vital for achieving lasting positive change in the communities we serve. It transforms accountability from a reactive obligation into a proactive, continuous commitment, powered by the insights and accessibility that modern technology provides. The ongoing exploration and adoption of new technological solutions will remain a cornerstone of RDI's strategy to ensure that every resource is used effectively, and every action is demonstrably answerable to those who matter most: **the people we are committed to empowering.**

The preceding discussion has underscored the transformative potential of technology in bolstering transparency and accountability within international development and humanitarian aid. However, technology, while a powerful enabler, is only one facet of a robust accountability framework. **The true heart of accountability lies not just in what is reported *to* stakeholders, but in how the voices of those directly impacted by our work are integrated into the very fabric of our operations.** This is where the concept of the "feedback loop," centered on the beneficiary voice, becomes paramount. It is the indispensable element that ensures our initiatives remain grounded in reality and truly responsive to the needs and aspirations of the communities we serve. Without the direct, unvarnished input from the people we aim to empower, even the most technologically advanced systems risk becoming detached and ultimately less effective.

Empowering beneficiaries to provide feedback is not a mere courtesy; it is a fundamental pillar of accountability. It shifts the dynamic from a top-down directive to a collaborative partnership, recognizing that those closest to the ground possess invaluable insights into what is working, what is not, and what could be done better. This active solicitation and integration of beneficiary perspectives are critical for several reasons. Firstly, it ensures that programs are aligned with actual community needs, not just perceived ones. Misalignments can arise from various factors, including incomplete initial assessments, changing local contexts, or unforeseen challenges. Beneficiary feedback acts as a real-time course correction mechanism, allowing organizations to adapt their strategies and interventions to remain relevant and impactful. Secondly, it fosters a sense of ownership and agency within the community. When people see their feedback being heard and acted upon, they are more likely to engage actively in the project, contributing their skills, knowledge, and support. This co-creation process significantly enhances the sustainability and long-term success of development initiatives. Thirdly, and perhaps most importantly in the context of accountability, it provides an independent verification layer. Beneficiary accounts of project implementation, resource distribution, or service delivery offer a vital counterpoint to internal reporting. This external validation is crucial for building trust and demonstrating that commitments are being met on the ground.

To operationalize this crucial feedback loop, organizations must design and implement deliberate, accessible, and effective mechanisms for collecting and processing beneficiary input. These mechanisms need to be tailored to the specific context, considering factors such as literacy levels, cultural norms, access to technology, and the nature of the project itself. For instance, in communities with low literacy rates and limited mobile phone penetration, simple, in-person methods such as community meetings, focus group discussions, or suggestion boxes might be the most appropriate. These interactions should be facilitated by trained personnel who can explain the purpose of the feedback, assure confidentiality, and encourage open and honest sharing. The facilitators must be skilled in active listening and empathetic communication, creating a safe space for individuals to express their views without fear of reprisal. The questions posed should be clear, open-ended, and designed to elicit detailed responses about the beneficiary's experience with the project. For example, instead of asking "Did you receive the seeds?", a more effective approach would be to ask, "Could you describe your experience with receiving the agricultural inputs? What was helpful, and what challenges did you face?"

In contexts where mobile phone usage is prevalent, but digital literacy might be a barrier, SMS-based feedback systems can be highly effective. These systems allow beneficiaries to send short text messages with their comments, concerns, or reports. A simple short code can be advertised widely, and beneficiaries can text a specific keyword to report an issue or provide feedback. The organization can then process these incoming messages, categorizing them and escalating them to the appropriate personnel. For example, a water committee member in a rural village might text "WELLBROKEN" to a designated number if the community's water source stops functioning. This simple act of reporting can trigger a rapid response from the project team responsible for water infrastructure maintenance. Similarly, a project distributing educational materials could allow beneficiaries to text "YES" or "NO" in response to a question about the usefulness of the materials, followed by an optional text field for more detailed comments. These systems need to be robust enough to handle a high volume of messages and to provide an automated acknowledgment of receipt to the sender, confirming that their feedback has been registered.

For communities with greater access to technology and higher digital literacy, more sophisticated online platforms can be employed. This could include dedicated feedback portals on organizational websites, secure mobile applications, or even social media channels specifically designated for feedback. These platforms can allow for more detailed submissions, including the attachment of photos or videos to illustrate problems or provide evidence. For example, if a vocational training program is being evaluated, a participant might upload a photograph of a faulty piece of equipment they were expected to use, along with a written description of the problem. These online systems can be integrated with case management software, allowing for the systematic tracking of feedback from receipt to resolution. Each piece of feedback can be assigned a unique reference number, enabling both the beneficiary and the organization to monitor its progress. Beneficiaries could receive automated updates via email or SMS as their feedback is reviewed, investigated, and acted upon. This level of transparency in the feedback process itself is crucial for building trust and demonstrating a genuine commitment to responsiveness.

However, the mere existence of feedback channels is insufficient. The effectiveness of the beneficiary voice hinges on how this feedback is processed, analyzed, and, most importantly, acted upon. Organizations must establish clear internal protocols for managing feedback. This includes defining roles and responsibilities for receiving, reviewing, and responding to feedback; setting service level agreements (SLAs) for response times; and ensuring that feedback is systematically recorded and categorized. For instance, feedback related to the quality of goods distributed should be routed to the procurement or logistics team, while feedback concerning the effectiveness of training sessions should be shared with the program implementation team. A dedicated feedback officer or a small team within the organization can be tasked with overseeing this process, acting as a central point of contact and ensuring that no feedback falls through the cracks.

The analysis of feedback is equally critical. Raw feedback data needs to be synthesized to identify trends, recurring issues, and systemic problems. This can involve qualitative analysis of open-ended comments to understand the nuances of beneficiary experiences, as well as quantitative analysis of recurring themes or reported incidents. For example, if multiple beneficiaries report similar issues with the timely disbursement of cash transfers, this trend should be flagged for immediate investigation by the finance and program management teams. Data visualization tools can be invaluable here, transforming unstructured feedback into actionable insights through charts, graphs, and word clouds that highlight key patterns. Regular feedback review meetings should be scheduled, bringing together relevant program staff, management, and, where appropriate, community representatives, to discuss the feedback received and to collectively brainstorm solutions.

The ultimate measure of the beneficiary feedback loop's success lies in the demonstrable action taken in response to that feedback. This is the point where accountability truly materializes. When beneficiaries see that their input leads to tangible changes – whether it's a modification in program delivery, a correction of an error, or the implementation of a new approach – their confidence in the organization is significantly bolstered. For example, if a community reports that the timing of agricultural extension services is not convenient due to their farming schedules, and the organization subsequently adjusts the schedule based on this feedback, this is a powerful demonstration of **responsiveness**. Similarly, if beneficiaries highlight a specific need for a particular type of training or equipment, and the organization incorporates this into its future planning, it reinforces the value of their contribution. This principle of "closing the loop" is essential. It involves communicating back to the beneficiary (or the community as a whole) how their feedback was considered and what actions were taken, or why certain actions could not be taken. This communication should be clear, honest, and timely.

The process of closing the loop can take many forms. In community meetings, project managers can report on the feedback received and the actions taken. For SMS systems, automated responses can confirm that a reported issue is being addressed. For online platforms, status updates on feedback submissions can be provided. The key is to ensure that the feedback process does not end with the submission of a comment or concern. It must culminate in a visible response that acknowledges the beneficiary's role and demonstrates that their voice has influenced the project's trajectory. This continuous cycle of input, action, and communication is what builds enduring trust and makes accountability a living, dynamic process, rather than a static set of procedures.

Moreover, organizations must guard against common pitfalls that can undermine the effectiveness of beneficiary feedback mechanisms. One such pitfall is the perception of reprisal. Beneficiaries must be assured that providing honest feedback, even critical feedback, will not negatively impact their access to services or their relationship with the organization. This requires clear communication about non-retaliation policies and a commitment from leadership to protect those who speak up. **Another challenge is feedback fatigue, where communities become overwhelmed by constant requests for input or feel that their feedback is not genuinely valued.** The RDI moder suggests that organizations must be strategic in their feedback collection, ensuring that requests are meaningful, timely, and tied to clear action. It is better to have fewer, well-managed feedback mechanisms that yield actionable results than a multitude of poorly implemented ones that create cynicism.

Ensuring the representativeness of feedback is also crucial. Mechanisms should be designed to reach a diverse range of beneficiaries, including women, marginalized groups, youth, and the elderly, who may have different perspectives and priorities. This might involve actively seeking out feedback from those who are less likely to come forward independently. For instance, dedicated outreach efforts might be needed to engage with disabled individuals or those living in remote areas. The language used in feedback forms and surveys must be accessible and culturally appropriate. Using visual aids or participatory tools can be particularly effective in contexts where written communication is challenging.

The integration of beneficiary feedback into organizational learning and strategic planning is the final, most critical step in establishing a truly accountable system. Feedback should not be treated as a mere complaint-handling mechanism. Instead, it should be viewed as a rich source of data that can inform program design, operational improvements, and strategic decision-making. Aggregated feedback can highlight areas where training needs to be enhanced, where communication strategies need refinement, or where the overall project logic might require re-evaluation. By systematically incorporating beneficiary insights into the organizational learning cycle, RDI, and similar organizations, can continuously improve their effectiveness and ensure that their interventions remain relevant, impactful, and, above all, accountable to the people they serve. This commitment to listening, learning, and adapting based on the direct experiences of beneficiaries is not just good practice; it is the bedrock of genuine development and the ultimate manifestation of accountability in action. It transforms accountability from an external requirement into an internal, values-driven imperative, intrinsically linked to the mission of empowering communities.

CHAPTER 11:

Logistics Reimagined:
Efficiency in Movement

The grand edifice of international development and humanitarian aid, while built on noble intentions, frequently finds its foundations weakened by an often-overlooked yet critically significant burden: **logistics**. The traditional models of aid delivery, steeped in decades of practice, have evolved a system that, while functional, is inherently encumbered by its own weight. This chapter delves into the intricate and often inefficient logistical operations that characterize conventional approaches, dissecting how their inherent complexities can become the Achilles' heel of even the most well-meaning interventions. The sheer scale of moving vital supplies, personnel, and equipment across vast distances, often through challenging and unpredictable environments, necessitates a robust logistical framework. However, the very architecture of these frameworks, built upon principles of centralized control, extensive physical infrastructure, and established, albeit sometimes slow-moving, processes, can paradoxically become a bottleneck, hindering the very speed and responsiveness that are so crucial in times of crisis or for sustained development progress.

At the heart of this logistical predicament lies the often-extensive and resource-intensive nature of conventional supply chains. These chains are typically characterized by a multi-layered structure involving procurement, international shipping, customs clearance, warehousing, and finally, last-mile distribution. Each of these stages, while necessary, introduces its own set of complexities and potential points of delay. The procurement process, for instance, can be protracted, involving lengthy tendering procedures, supplier vetting, and contract negotiations, all of which are essential for ensuring quality and compliance but can significantly extend the time from identifying a need to fulfilling it. Once procured, goods embark on journeys that often traverse continents, relying on a mix of air, sea, and land transport. The coordination of these multiple modes of transport, each with its own set of regulations, capacities, and vulnerabilities, demands meticulous planning and constant oversight. International shipping, while cost-effective for bulk items, is subject to the vagaries of port congestion, weather patterns, and fluctuating freight rates. Navigating customs procedures in recipient countries can be a labyrinthine process, often requiring specific documentation, import permits, and the payment of duties, all of which can lead to unforeseen delays and increased costs.

Furthermore, the reliance on extensive warehousing facilities is another hallmark of conventional logistics, designed to hold large quantities of supplies in anticipation of needs. While essential for maintaining buffer stocks and ensuring availability, these facilities represent significant capital investment and ongoing operational costs, including rent, utilities, security, and staffing. The management of these warehouses themselves can be a complex undertaking, requiring sophisticated inventory management systems to track stock levels, manage expiration dates, and prevent loss or damage. The sheer volume of goods stored can also create vulnerabilities. Natural disasters, civil unrest, or even simple infrastructural failures at a warehouse site can lead to the loss of entire consignments of aid, jeopardizing relief efforts and development projects. The static nature of warehousing also means that supplies are not always positioned optimally to meet rapidly evolving needs on the ground, necessitating secondary transportation from central hubs to more localized distribution points, adding yet another layer of complexity and potential delay.

The ownership and management of dedicated vehicle fleets by many traditional aid organizations further contribute to the logistical burden. **While a dedicated fleet offers a degree of control and availability, it also entails substantial upfront investment in purchasing vehicles, as well as ongoing expenses for maintenance, repairs, fuel, insurance, and driver salaries.** In many operating environments, these vehicles are specialized, such as refrigerated trucks for temperature-sensitive items or rugged, all-terrain vehicles for off-road access. The procurement and maintenance of such specialized fleets require significant technical expertise and financial resources. Moreover, the utilization of these fleets is not always optimal. **Vehicles may sit idle for extended periods between missions, representing a sunk cost.** Logistical planning requires effectively deploying and managing a fleet across dispersed operational areas, ensuring that vehicles are fueled, maintained, and staffed appropriately, is a demanding task. This centralized model of fleet ownership can also limit flexibility; if a specific type of vehicle is needed for a short-term, specialized task, acquiring or chartering one might be more efficient than relying on an owned asset that is not ideally suited or is already allocated elsewhere.

This intricate web of interconnected processes – procurement, international transport, customs, warehousing, and fleet management – creates a system that is inherently vulnerable to disruption. **Any single point of failure within this chain can have cascading effects, leading to significant delays in the delivery of life-saving assistance or critical project materials.** A natural disaster affecting a key port, political instability leading to border closures, or a breakdown in communication can quickly bring the entire system to a standstill. The time lag between identifying a critical need and delivering the necessary resources can be substantial, measured in weeks or even months, a period that can prove devastating in humanitarian emergencies. For development projects, such delays can undermine project timelines, increase costs, and erode the confidence of beneficiaries and partners. The cost associated with maintaining this elaborate, often over-engineered, logistical apparatus is also considerable. A significant portion of an organization's budget can be allocated to logistics, diverting resources that could otherwise be channeled directly into program activities and service delivery.

The reliance on physical infrastructure, from major transport hubs to local warehouses and vehicle depots, also makes conventional aid logistics susceptible to the prevailing security and political landscape. Operating in fragile states or conflict zones adds layers of complexity, requiring robust security protocols for convoys, the careful vetting of local transport providers, and the negotiation of safe passage through contested territories. The need to protect valuable assets and personnel can necessitate the deployment of security escorts, further increasing costs and operational complexity. **In some instances, the absolute visibility of large aid convoys can**

also make them targets for opportunistic theft or deliberate disruption. The logistical challenge is not merely about moving goods; it is about moving them safely, securely, and reliably in environments that are often inherently unstable and unpredictable. This inherent fragility, coupled with the substantial resource commitment, highlights the significant "burden" that conventional logistics can represent, often acting as a primary constraint on the speed, scale, and effectiveness of international development and humanitarian response. The inefficiencies embedded within these systems, while often unintended and a consequence of operational necessity, can translate directly into delayed assistance, wasted resources, and ultimately, a diminished impact on the lives of those they are intended to serve. This inherent structural weakness, the logistical burden, serves as a critical area for reimagining how aid moves.

The prevailing paradigm in international aid and development logistics has long favored the establishment and management of dedicated, owned vehicle fleets. This approach, born from a desire for direct control over assets and a guarantee of immediate availability, often entails significant upfront capital investment in purchasing a diverse range of vehicles – from rugged 4x4s capable of navigating treacherous terrain to specialized refrigerated trucks for temperature-sensitive medical supplies. Beyond the initial acquisition, organizations commit to substantial ongoing expenditures for routine maintenance, unexpected repairs, insurance premiums, fuel procurement, and the salaries of dedicated drivers and mechanics. This creates a self-contained logistical ecosystem, intended to ensure responsiveness and mitigate reliance on external, potentially unreliable, service providers. However, as explored in the preceding discussion, this model, while offering a semblance of control, inherently introduces a substantial **logistical burden**. It necessitates the establishment of maintenance depots, the stocking of spare parts, the continuous training of technical staff, and the complex administrative oversight of a large and diverse fleet. **This infrastructure represents a significant drain on an organization's financial and human resources, resources that could otherwise be directly channeled into program delivery and beneficiary support.**

The RDI (Rescue Democracy International) model AKA The Justin Mudekereza Model, in stark contrast, embraces a fundamentally different ethos for its logistical operations. **A cornerstone of this leaner, more agile approach is the deliberate and strategic decision to forgo vehicle ownership altogether.** This is not a passive omission, but an active, calculated strategy designed to radically streamline operations, **reduce overhead, and enhance overall efficiency.** The rationale behind this seemingly counter-intuitive stance is multifaceted and deeply rooted in a pragmatic understanding of the realities of operating in resource-constrained environments and the inherent inefficiencies of maintaining large, static asset bases. By divesting itself of the responsibilities and the substantial financial liabilities associated with owning and managing a fleet, RDI Model liberates significant capital and human resources. This capital, which would otherwise be tied up in vehicle acquisition and maintenance, can be redeployed to directly fund program activities, procure essential supplies, or invest in critical community-based initiatives.

The immediate and most pronounced impact of this "no-owned-vehicles" strategy is the drastic reduction in capital expenditure. The acquisition of vehicles, particularly specialized ones suited for diverse operational landscapes, represents one of the largest single investments an organization can make. By eschewing ownership, RDI circumvents these immense upfront costs. This allows for a more flexible allocation of financial resources, enabling the organization to scale its operations more readily and respond to evolving needs without the constraint of pre-existing, and potentially underutilized, physical assets. **Instead of purchasing and depreciating assets, RDI Model prioritizes the strategic acquisition of transport services as and when they are needed.** This shifts the financial model from a capital expenditure-intensive one to an operational expenditure model, where costs are directly linked to the actual utilization of transport services, offering greater financial agility.

Furthermore, the elimination of vehicle ownership substantially mitigates the ongoing and often unpredictable costs associated with fleet maintenance and repair. Owning vehicles means investing in workshops, diagnostic equipment, specialized tools, and a team of trained mechanics. It also involves managing a complex supply chain for spare parts, ensuring availability, and dealing with the inevitable wear and tear that leads to breakdowns. **These maintenance costs are not merely financial; they also consume valuable time and human capital that could be better utilized elsewhere.** In many operational contexts, securing reliable and qualified mechanics and genuine spare parts can be a significant challenge in itself. By not owning vehicles, RDI bypasses this entire layer of complexity and cost. The responsibility for vehicle maintenance and repair rests with the service providers, allowing RDI to focus on its core mission rather than becoming a de facto automotive service provider.

The administrative burden associated with managing a fleet is also considerable. This includes tasks such as vehicle registration and licensing, insurance processing, fuel card management, driver scheduling and supervision, vehicle mileage tracking, and ensuring compliance with a myriad of local and international regulations pertaining to road transport. Each of these administrative functions requires dedicated personnel and robust internal systems. The RDI Model **"no-owned-vehicles" strategy** effectively dissolves this administrative overhead. RDI does not need to employ fleet managers, mechanics, or a dedicated administrative team solely focused on vehicle upkeep. This simplification of the organizational structure not only reduces payroll costs but also streamlines operations, allowing staff to concentrate on program design, implementation, and monitoring, thereby enhancing the organization's core effectiveness.

The pivot away from vehicle ownership does not only necessitates courage but also a robust and well-developed strategy for leveraging existing local transport networks and community resources. **This is where RDI's approach truly shines, demonstrating a deep understanding of local contexts and a commitment to fostering sustainable, community-driven solutions.** Instead of building its own transport capacity, RDI actively cultivates partnerships with local transporters, including individual truck owners, taxi cooperatives, and community-based logistics providers. These partnerships are built on principles of mutual benefit, reliability, and fair pricing. RDI meticulously vets potential partners, ensuring they possess the necessary licenses, insurance, and a proven track record of safe and **timely service delivery**. Due diligence in this regard is paramount, as the reliability of these third-party providers directly impacts the success of RDI's program delivery.

The utilization of local transport networks offers several distinct advantages. Firstly, it injects much-needed revenue directly into the local economy, supporting small businesses and creating employment opportunities for drivers and logistics operators. This aligns with RDI's broader development objectives, fostering economic capacity building within the communities it serves. Secondly, local transporters possess an intimate knowledge of local road conditions, including the best routes, potential hazards, and the most efficient ways to navigate challenging terrain. This local expertise is invaluable and often surpasses the knowledge held by external entities. They are familiar with local customs, can communicate effectively with local authorities, and are better equipped to anticipate and overcome localized logistical hurdles.

Moreover, by engaging local service providers, RDI can often access a wider variety of vehicles suitable for specific tasks without the need for capital investment. If a particular mission requires a heavy-duty truck for transporting building materials, RDI can contract a local company that specializes in such services. Similarly, if a short-term need arises for multiple small vehicles for rapid response, RDI can tap into the availability of local taxis or shared transport services. This flexibility allows RDI to match the specific logistical requirement with the most appropriate and cost-effective solution available in the local market. **It eliminates the problem of having specialized owned vehicles sitting idle when they are not needed, or**

conversely, being unable to fulfill a requirement because the right type of vehicle is not part of the owned fleet.

Community-based resource mobilization also plays a crucial role in RDI's logistics strategy. In many remote or underserved areas, community members may own motorcycles, bicycles, or even animal-drawn carts that can be utilized for last-mile delivery of essential goods, especially when roads are impassable for larger vehicles. RDI works with community leaders to identify and organize these local transport capacities. This not only ensures that vital supplies reach even the most isolated populations but also empowers communities to take ownership of their own logistical challenges. It fosters a sense of shared responsibility and builds local capacity for self-reliance. For instance, during a health outreach program, community health volunteers might use their own motorcycles to reach remote households with essential medicines, while village youth groups might be contracted to transport water purification tablets using bicycles. These arrangements are typically formalized through simple service agreements that ensure fair compensation for the services rendered and clear accountability for the delivery of goods.

The implementation of this **"no-owned-vehicles" strategy** requires a sophisticated and adaptive approach to logistical planning and coordination. It necessitates robust information management systems to track the availability of transport services, manage contracts with third-party providers, and monitor delivery timelines. RDI's model is to invest in technology that facilitates real-time communication and tracking, allowing for efficient dispatching of vehicles and proactive problem-solving. This might involve using mobile applications for drivers to report their status, receive delivery manifests, and confirm successful deliveries. Procurement processes for transport services are streamlined, focusing on pre-approved lists of reliable local providers and employing transparent bidding or negotiation procedures for larger contracts.

A critical component of this strategy is building strong relationships and trust with local transport providers. RDI understands that these are not merely transactional relationships but partnerships. This involves consistent communication, prompt payment, and providing clear operational guidelines. By treating local transporters as valued partners, RDI fosters loyalty and ensures a higher level of commitment to service delivery. This is particularly important in challenging environments where informal networks and personal relationships often form the backbone of reliable service provision. For example, a long-standing relationship with a local trucking company might mean that during a sudden emergency, RDI's requests are prioritized, and trucks are dispatched with greater speed and efficiency than if the relationship was purely transactional.

The emphasis on leveraging local capacity also extends to ensuring that the goods themselves are transported in a manner that maintains their integrity and security. RDI works with its partners to ensure that vehicles are appropriate for the type of cargo being transported and that basic safety and security measures are in place. This might involve ensuring that food supplies are transported in clean vehicles, or that sensitive medical equipment is handled with care. For valuable or vulnerable items, RDI might opt to hire vehicles that are accompanied by trusted local security personnel, sourced through reputable local security firms, rather than investing in its own security infrastructure. This approach allows RDI to access specialized security services as needed, without the ongoing costs and complexities of maintaining its own security contingent.

This "no-owned-vehicles" philosophy fundamentally shifts RDI's logistical posture from one of asset ownership and management to one of intelligent procurement and strategic partnership. It is a leaner, more adaptable, and ultimately more cost-effective approach that aligns perfectly with the principles of efficiency and resource optimization in the international development sector. By embracing local expertise and economic capacity, RDI not only streamlines its own operations but also contributes to the sustainable development of the communities it serves. This strategy is a testament to the fact that true logistical strength often lies not in owning the means of transport, but in intelligently orchestrating the movement of goods and people through robust, localized networks and strategic alliances. **It is a philosophy that prioritizes agility, cost-effectiveness, and community integration, offering a compelling alternative to the resource-intensive models that have historically dominated the field.** The ability to quickly scale transport capacity up or down based on program needs, without the encumbrance of underutilized assets or the financial strain of fleet acquisition, is a significant competitive advantage in the fast-paced and often unpredictable world of development and humanitarian aid. This model also fosters a culture of innovation and problem-solving, encouraging RDI staff to continuously seek out the most efficient and context-appropriate logistical solutions, rather than defaulting on the established, but often less efficient, practices of vehicle ownership.

The operationalization of a logistics strategy that deliberately eschews vehicle ownership hinges on a sophisticated and dynamic approach to empowering local networks. This isn't simply about outsourcing transport; it's about building a robust ecosystem of local partnerships, leveraging existing community assets, and fostering a sense of shared responsibility for the efficient movement of critical supplies and resources. The core of this strategy lies in identifying, cultivating, and sustaining relationships with reliable local transport providers and community focal points who possess an intimate understanding of their operating environment. These local entities become the extended arms of the organization, translating strategic intent into on-the-ground reality.

The initial and most crucial step in empowering these local networks involves a comprehensive process of identification and vetting. This requires more than just a casual inquiry; it necessitates a deep dive into the local landscape to pinpoint individuals, cooperatives, and small enterprises that can reliably fulfill transport and distribution needs. This involves engaging with community leaders, local business associations, and transport unions to map out available resources. The criteria for selection are rigorous, extending beyond mere vehicle availability. Reliability, a proven track record of service, adherence to safety standards, appropriate licensing and insurance, and a commitment to fair pricing are all paramount. For instance, when seeking partners for the distribution of essential medicines in a remote rural area, RDI might prioritize local trucking companies or even individual truck owners who have demonstrated consistent delivery of agricultural produce to market, understanding that the handling of temperature-sensitive cargo requires a comparable level of care and diligence. Similarly, in urban settings, relationships with established taxi cooperatives or local courier services that have a reputation for punctuality and secure deliveries are actively sought.

Negotiating fair and transparent rates is another critical element in building sustainable local partnerships. This process must strike a delicate balance between ensuring cost-effectiveness for the organization and providing equitable compensation for the service providers. RDI employs a multi-pronged approach to rate negotiation. Firstly, it relies on thorough market research to establish benchmark pricing for various types of transport services, considering factors such as vehicle capacity, distance, terrain, and specific handling requirements. This research often involves consulting with multiple potential providers to gain a comprehensive understanding of prevailing market rates. Secondly, RDI prioritizes the development of standardized service agreements that clearly outline the scope of work, responsibilities of each party, payment terms, and dispute resolution mechanisms. These agreements provide a framework for fair negotiation and ensure clarity, minimizing the potential for misunderstandings. For example, when contracting a local logistics firm for the distribution of educational materials across several provinces, RDI would not only negotiate a per-kilometer rate but also factor in costs associated with loading and unloading, potential delays due to road conditions, and the need for secure storage at intermediate points. The emphasis is always on creating agreements that are mutually beneficial, fostering a sense of partnership rather than a purely transactional relationship. This also involves a commitment to prompt payment, which is vital for maintaining trust and ensuring that local providers remain willing and able to offer their services consistently. Unpaid invoices can quickly erode goodwill and lead to the withdrawal of essential services, undermining the entire logistical framework.

Beyond the transactional aspects, the capacity building of local networks involves a commitment to capacity building and ongoing support. While RDI does not own vehicles, it recognizes the importance of ensuring that its partners operate efficiently and safely. This can involve providing training on best practices for cargo handling, ensuring the secure transport of sensitive items, and offering guidance on basic vehicle maintenance to minimize breakdowns. For instance, **when working with community-based organizations for last-mile delivery using motorcycles, RDI might facilitate workshops on proper cargo securing techniques to prevent damage to supplies and on essential pre-ride checks to enhance road safety.** In areas where access to spare parts or qualified mechanics is limited, RDI might explore partnerships with local technical training institutes to develop a pool of skilled personnel, thereby strengthening the overall local transport infrastructure. This investment in local capacity not only benefits RDI's operations but also contributes to the long-term sustainability and professionalization of the local logistics sector.

The role of community focal points is integral to the success of this strategy, especially in reaching remote or underserved populations. These individuals, often respected members of their communities, act as crucial liaisons, facilitating communication, coordinating local transport arrangements, and ensuring the accountability of deliveries. RDI invests in training these focal points on basic logistics management, inventory tracking, and reporting mechanisms. For instance, a Focal Point in a remote village might be responsible for identifying community members with bicycles or motorcycles willing to transport food aid to surrounding hamlets. They would then coordinate the distribution, track the quantities delivered, and report back to RDI on the progress and any challenges encountered. This localized knowledge and established trust are invaluable, allowing for the efficient mobilization of resources that might otherwise be inaccessible. The focal points also play a critical role in ensuring the secure handover of goods, verifying recipient identities, and documenting the distribution process, thereby enhancing transparency and accountability throughout the supply chain. This localized ownership and oversight are fundamental to achieving efficient and equitable distribution, especially in contexts where formal infrastructure is weak.

Ensuring the secure and timely movement of goods is a shared responsibility that is meticulously managed through robust communication and monitoring systems. RDI utilizes a range of technological tools, from simple SMS alerts to more sophisticated mobile applications, to maintain real-time visibility of the logistics chain. This allows for proactive problem-solving and adaptive responses to unforeseen challenges. For example, if a contracted truck is delayed due to unexpected road closures, an SMS alert from the driver to the RDI logistics coordinator can trigger an immediate reassessment of alternative routes or the dispatch of a backup vehicle. Similarly, focal points can use simple mobile interfaces to confirm the receipt and delivery of goods, providing essential data for tracking and reconciliation. This continuous flow of information empowers both RDI and its local partners to manage expectations, mitigate risks, and ensure that essential supplies reach their intended destinations efficiently and without compromise. **The emphasis on timely delivery is not merely about adherence to schedules; it is about ensuring that critical items, such as life-saving medications or emergency food supplies, reach beneficiaries when they are most needed, thus maximizing their impact and efficacy.**

Fostering local economic participation is a core objective that is intrinsically woven into RDI's logistical approach. By prioritizing local transport providers and community-based distribution networks, RDI directly injects financial resources into the local economy. This creates employment opportunities for drivers, mechanics, and support staff, while also supporting the growth of small and medium-sized local enterprises henceforth contributing to the reduction of extreme poverty, one of the most critical Sustainable Development Goals (SDGs). This economic capacity building is a critical development outcome, contributing to the overall resilience and prosperity of the communities served. For example, a contract awarded to a local transport cooperative for the distribution of agricultural inputs not only ensures the timely availability of these vital resources for farmers but also provides income for the cooperative's members and potentially funds for reinvestment in their businesses. This ripple effect of economic activity underscores the strategic advantage of partnering with local actors, transforming logistical operations into vehicles for broader socio-economic development. The careful selection of providers and the negotiation of fair rates are deliberate mechanisms to ensure that this economic participation is meaningful and sustainable, moving beyond token gestures to genuine partnership and shared prosperity. The process of vetting providers often includes an assessment of their contribution to the local economy, such as their employment practices and their use of local resources, further reinforcing this commitment.

The success of this model is deeply reliant on the adaptability and resilience of the local networks that RDI cultivates. These networks are not static; they evolve with changing needs and operating environments. RDI actively engages in continuous learning and adaptation, drawing insights from its local partners to refine its strategies and improve its operational efficiency. This might involve incorporating feedback on the most effective types of vehicles for certain terrains, identifying new emerging transport providers, or collaborating on innovative solutions to logistical challenges. For instance, in a region prone to seasonal flooding, RDI might work with local partners to identify and pre-qualify providers with access to animal-drawn carts or specialized amphibious vehicles for periods when roads become impassable. This proactive approach to understanding and responding to local conditions ensures that the logistics operations remain effective and relevant, even in the face of dynamic and often unpredictable circumstances. The focus on building strong, trust-based relationships with these local entities transforms the logistical function from a mere support service into a strategic partnership, where shared goals and mutual respect drive efficiency and impact. This approach ensures that the movement of goods is not just a process, but a community-driven endeavor that maximizes local resources and fosters local ownership of development outcomes.

The fundamental principle guiding RDI's logistics strategy is the relentless pursuit of efficiency, a pursuit that translates directly into minimizing waste and maximizing the reach of its support. By consciously eschewing the substantial capital investment and ongoing operational burdens associated with owning and maintaining a dedicated fleet of vehicles, RDI liberates significant financial and human resources. **These freed-up assets are then strategically reinvested in the core mission: the procurement and timely delivery of essential supplies, the implementation of vital development programs, and the direct support of beneficiary communities.** This lean, asset-light approach is not just a cost-saving measure; it is a deliberate design choice that amplifies the impact of every dollar and every hour invested. It allows RDI to operate with greater agility and responsiveness, ensuring that aid and development assistance reach those who need it most, with fewer layers of bureaucracy and fewer opportunities for resources to be diverted or lost along the way.

This strategic focus on minimizing internal overhead has a direct and profound effect on the speed and efficiency of distribution. Without the constraints of managing vehicle procurement, maintenance schedules, driver training, and fuel procurement for an owned fleet, RDI can pivot more rapidly to meet evolving needs. When a critical supply shortage is identified in a particular region, for instance, RDI can quickly identify and sign a contract with suitable local transport providers already operating within that area. This eliminates the lead time often associated with mobilizing an organization's own fleet from a distant hub. Imagine a scenario where emergency medical supplies are urgently needed in a remote health clinic following a natural disaster. **Instead of**

coordinating the dispatch of a specialized vehicle from a central warehouse, potentially facing delays due to road conditions or availability, RDI can leverage its network of pre-vetted local transporters who possess the appropriate vehicles and knowledge of local routes. This immediate access to transport capacity dramatically reduces the time lag between identifying a need and fulfilling it, a critical factor when lives and well-being are at stake.

Furthermore, the emphasis on working with existing local logistics providers inherently streamlines the distribution process by reducing the number of intermediaries. Each intermediary point in a supply chain, while sometimes necessary, introduces potential bottlenecks, communication gaps, and added costs. By engaging directly with local transport operators and community-based distribution points, RDI effectively shortens the supply chain. This not only accelerates delivery times but also enhances accountability. When there are fewer hands involved in the movement of goods, it becomes easier to track the provenance, and timely arrival of supplies, and to identify and address any issues that may arise. For example, if RDI is distributing agricultural seeds to farming communities, contracting directly with a local agricultural cooperative that has its own network of vehicles and personnel means that the seeds can move directly from a central collection point to the farmers, often facilitated by the cooperative's own members who are familiar with the local farming landscape. This direct connection minimizes the risk of delays, damage, or diversion, ensuring that vital inputs reach farmers in time for planting seasons, thereby maximizing agricultural productivity and local food security.

The cost savings realized from avoiding fleet ownership are substantial and have a tangible impact on the scale and scope of RDI's operations. **The capital expenditure required for purchasing even a modest fleet of trucks, motorcycles, and specialized vehicles can run into millions of dollars.** Beyond the initial purchase price, the ongoing costs of maintenance, repairs, insurance, fuel, and driver salaries represent a significant and continuous drain on an organization's budget. By outsourcing these functions to local providers who already bear these costs as part of their business model, RDI can allocate a far greater proportion of its budget directly to program activities and the acquisition of goods and services that benefit beneficiaries. This financial leverage is crucial in environments where resources are scarce, and needs are immense. Consider the allocation of funds for a school feeding program. Instead of a significant portion of the budget being consumed by the operational costs of a fleet to transport food supplies, those funds can be used to purchase more food, expand the program to reach additional schools, or provide supplementary learning materials to the children. This direct channeling of resources is a symbol of RDI's commitment to efficiency and impact.

This lean logistical model also fosters a more agile and adaptable operational framework. The dynamic nature of humanitarian and development work often requires rapid responses to unforeseen events, shifting priorities, and changing geographical needs. An organization burdened by the fixed costs and operational inflexibility of a large, owned fleet can struggle to adapt quickly to these changes. In contrast, RDI's reliance on a network of independent local providers allows for a much greater degree of flexibility. If a particular route becomes impassable due to conflict or natural disaster, RDI can readily shift its transport needs to different regions and engage new local partners who are operating in unaffected areas. This ability to scale operations up or down, and to re-route resources with relative ease, is invaluable in volatile environments. For instance, during a sudden outbreak of a disease in a new district, RDI can quickly contract with local taxi services or motorcycle couriers to transport diagnostic kits and medical personnel, bypassing the need to redeploy an organizationally owned, possibly ill-suited, vehicle from a distant location. This inherent flexibility ensures that RDI can maintain its operational presence and continue to deliver critical support even when the operating landscape is constantly changing.

Moreover, by empowering local logistics providers, RDI contributes to the development of local economies and strengthens the capacity of communities to respond to their own needs. This is not just a matter of efficiency; it is a strategic approach to sustainable development. When RDI contracts with local transporters, it is injecting revenue into the local economy, creating employment opportunities, and supporting small businesses. These local providers are invested in their communities and possess an intrinsic understanding of local conditions, including the best routes, potential hazards, and available resources. This localized expertise is often far superior to that of an external logistics provider. For example, in mountainous regions with challenging terrain, local drivers with years of experience navigating treacherous roads are far more likely to deliver goods safely and efficiently than drivers unfamiliar with the area. Their knowledge extends to understanding seasonal road closures, the availability of local mechanics for repairs, and the most reliable fuel sources. By capitalizing on this local knowledge and investing in these local enterprises, RDI not only optimizes its own operations but also fosters economic growth and resilience within the communities it serves. This symbiotic relationship transforms logistics from a purely functional necessity into a catalyst for broader socio-economic development.

The reduction of waste also extends beyond financial savings to include the efficient utilization of resources. An owned fleet, unless operating at near-constant full capacity, can represent a significant waste of resources, with vehicles sitting idle, consuming fuel and requiring maintenance and insurance even when not actively engaged in delivering aid. RDI's model, by contrast, ensures that transportation resources are utilized only when and where they are needed. Local providers operating on a contractual basis, are incentivized to ensure their vehicles are used efficiently to maximize their own revenue. This demand-driven approach naturally aligns the utilization of transport capacity with the actual needs on the ground, preventing the underutilization of assets that can plague organizations with fixed fleets. For example, during periods of reduced operational activity in a particular region, RDI does not incur the cost of maintaining idle vehicles. Instead, its obligations to local transport providers are reduced or suspended, allowing them to pursue other contracts, thereby maintaining their own operational viability and ensuring that the capacity remains available when RDI's needs increase again. This dynamic and responsive allocation of transport resources is a cornerstone of RDI's waste-minimization strategy.

The emphasis on fewer intermediaries also significantly enhances the traceability and accountability of goods. In complex logistical chains with multiple handoffs, it can become challenging to pinpoint responsibility if goods are damaged, lost, or delayed. By reducing the number of entities involved in the movement of supplies, RDI simplifies oversight and strengthens accountability mechanisms. Each transport contract is clearly defined, with specific deliverables and performance metrics. Local providers are aware that their reputation and future contracts depend on reliable and transparent service. This direct accountability, coupled with RDI's robust monitoring systems, ensures that goods reach their intended destinations in good condition and within the agreed-upon timeframes. For instance, when distributing essential medical equipment to rural health centers, RDI might contract directly with a local logistics company that specializes in secure, temperature-controlled transport. The contract would clearly define the pickup point, the delivery destination, the required temperature range, and the reporting requirements for any deviations. This clarity of responsibility makes it easier to track the entire process and hold the contracted provider accountable for the integrity of the delivery.

In essence, RDI's strategy of minimizing waste and maximizing reach through smart logistics is a testament to its commitment to operational excellence and impactful programming. By leveraging existing local infrastructure and expertise, avoiding the significant overhead of fleet ownership, and streamlining the distribution process, RDI ensures that more resources are directly channeled into providing essential aid and supporting sustainable development initiatives. **This approach not only enhances the speed and efficiency of delivery but also fosters local economic participation and builds resilience within the communities it serves.** It is a pragmatic, resource-efficient, and community-centric model that maximizes the potential for positive change in every operation.

The previous chapter underscored RDI's strategic decision to embrace an asset-light logistics model, prioritizing efficiency, cost-effectiveness, and local integration over the traditional approach of owning and maintaining a dedicated fleet. This foundational principle has not only streamlined RDI's operations but has also amplified the impact of its interventions by freeing up resources for direct program delivery and fostering economic development within beneficiary communities. *Now, we turn to concrete illustrations of this philosophy in action, exploring how this reimagined approach to logistics translates into tangible results, particularly in demanding operational contexts. These case studies, drawn from diverse scenarios, will illuminate the practical advantages of RDI's flexible, responsive, and contextually appropriate delivery mechanisms.*

Consider the scenario in a remote region grappling with an environmental disaster causing an unexpected food crisis, exacerbated by damaged infrastructure following seasonal floods. The immediate need was for substantial quantities of high-energy biscuits and essential micronutrient supplements to be distributed to vulnerable populations, including children and pregnant women, in isolated villages. Traditionally, an organization might have relied on its own trucks, which, in this instance, would have faced significant delays due to washed-out roads and the sheer distance from any operational hub. Such a delay could have proven critical, given the urgency of nutritional support. Instead, RDI activated its network of pre-vetted local transport cooperatives. These cooperatives, operating within the affected region, possessed a diverse range of vehicles – from robust four-wheel-drive trucks capable of navigating difficult terrain to smaller, nimble motorcycles that could reach areas inaccessible to larger vehicles. Crucially, their drivers possessed intimate knowledge of local detours, alternative routes that bypassed damaged main roads, and the current conditions of various pathways. **This intrinsic local knowledge, often unavailable to external logistics teams, allowed for the rapid identification and utilization of the most viable transport corridors.** By contracting with multiple local providers simultaneously, RDI was able to mobilize a significant transport capacity almost immediately. This decentralized approach meant that supplies were not bottlenecked at a single point of departure but were dispatched from various collection points closer to the affected communities, significantly reducing the overall transit time. The speed at which these critical supplies reached the targeted villages, bypassing the usual logistical hurdles, directly contributed to mitigating the worst effects of the food crisis and preventing further deterioration of health among the most at-risk populations. The flexibility inherent in this model also allowed RDI to adapt quickly as conditions evolved. When certain routes proved impassable even for the local drivers, immediate adjustments were made, shifting the delivery focus to areas accessible via alternative means, often facilitated by the same local network that could quickly reallocate resources.

Another compelling illustration comes from a fragile state experiencing periodic inter-communal tensions, which often disrupted traditional supply routes. RDI was tasked with delivering vital medical kits, including essential medicines, vaccines, and basic surgical equipment, to a network of rural health clinics that served a population of over half a million people. The clinics were spread across a large geographical area, with some located in territories that were sporadically controlled by different factions, making predictable and secure transit challenging. Owning and operating a fleet in such an environment would have involved immense security risks, requiring dedicated security escorts, extensive risk assessments for every journey, and considerable overhead for vehicle maintenance in remote, insecure locations. Instead, RDI leveraged its partnerships with local community leaders and business associations that had established relationships with trusted local transporters. These transporters often used a combination of vehicles, including armored vehicles procured for security reasons by local businesses, and operated on a sub-contractual basis with RDI. This approach allowed for a more discreet and contextually appropriate delivery strategy. In areas with higher security risks, RDI would engage transporters who were known to have established communication channels with local authorities or community elders, ensuring a degree of safe passage. In other, more accessible areas, standard delivery vehicles were utilized, often operated by drivers from the local community who understood the subtle cues of potential danger. This ability to tailor the transport solution to the specific security context of each delivery route was a critical factor in the success of the operation. Furthermore, the use of local, often smaller-scale transport providers meant that the movement of supplies was less conspicuous than large convoys operated by international organizations, thus reducing the likelihood of attracting unwanted attention or becoming a target. The distributed nature of the transport contracts also meant that if one route or one transporter was compromised, the entire operation was not jeopardized. RDI could quickly reroute supplies through alternative providers or different routes, ensuring continuity of service to the health clinics. This adaptability was paramount in an environment where operational conditions could change with little notice. The cost-effectiveness was also significant; by not bearing the immense costs of security, specialized vehicles, and insurance associated with operating an owned fleet in such a high-risk environment, RDI could procure a greater quantity and variety of medical supplies, directly benefiting a larger number of patients.

A third case study highlights RDI's agility in responding to an emergent public health concern in a densely populated urban setting with notoriously congested road networks and unpredictable traffic patterns. A rapid assessment identified a localized outbreak of a waterborne disease, necessitating the swift distribution of purification tablets, hygiene kits, and public awareness materials to affected neighborhoods. The challenge was to reach multiple distribution points within a limited timeframe, navigating dense urban traffic and ensuring that supplies reached areas with the most urgent needs, often in informal settlements with narrow access roads. Relying on a single, centrally managed fleet would have likely resulted in significant delays due to traffic gridlock and difficulties in accessing certain densely populated areas. RDI's strategy involved partnering with local last-mile delivery services and motorcycle-based courier networks that were already operating within the city and possessed an unparalleled understanding of the urban geography and traffic flow. These providers were able to utilize smaller vehicles, often motorcycles, to navigate congested streets and reach smaller, more localized distribution points within informal settlements that larger trucks could not access. The contracts were structured to incentivize speed and efficiency, with clear delivery targets for specific neighborhoods. RDI could also rapidly scale up the number of contracted providers based on the evolving needs identified through real-time community feedback and epidemiological data. If a particular neighborhood was found to have a higher concentration of cases, RDI could immediately engage additional local couriers to deliver supplies to that specific area, without the need to reassign or redeploy larger, less agile vehicles. This granular, on-demand approach ensured that resources were deployed precisely where they were needed, when they were needed, and in a manner that was most effective for the specific urban context. The ability to tap into the existing, flexible capacity of local delivery networks allowed RDI to mount a rapid and effective response, containing the outbreak and mitigating its impact on the community. The cost-efficiency was also evident, as RDI paid for services rendered, avoiding the fixed costs associated with maintaining its own urban delivery fleet, which would likely have experienced significant underutilization due to traffic congestion.

Furthermore, in a post-conflict scenario where infrastructure was severely degraded and reliable transportation options were scarce, RDI had to facilitate the movement of agricultural inputs, including seeds and fertilizers, to support the rehabilitation of farming communities. The roads were often unpaved, prone to erosion, and subject to seasonal impassability. Establishing a traditional logistics operation, including procuring and maintaining a fleet suitable for such conditions, would have been prohibitively expensive and time-consuming, delaying the critical planting seasons and hindering economic recovery. Instead, RDI collaborated with local farmer cooperatives and agricultural associations that already possessed a degree of logistical capacity. These organizations often owned or had access to a mix of vehicles, including tractors, pick-up trucks, and even animal-drawn carts, which were more suited to navigating the degraded rural terrain. RDI provided financial support and technical assistance to these local entities to enhance their existing capabilities, including training on efficient loading and transport techniques, and ensuring that vehicles were maintained to operate reliably in challenging conditions. This approach not only ensured the timely delivery of essential agricultural inputs but also contributed to building the long-term logistical capacity of these local organizations, thereby strengthening the resilience of the agricultural sector. The intimate knowledge that these local farmers and cooperative members had of the land and the seasonal changes was invaluable in planning and executing the deliveries, ensuring that seeds arrived in time for planting and that fertilizers were delivered to specific fields based on soil conditions and crop types. This deep understanding of the local context, embedded within the local logistics providers, proved far more effective than any generic logistical plan developed by an external organization. The economic benefits were also significant, as the contracts directly supported local livelihoods and incentivized the maintenance and improvement of local transport assets.

In mountainous regions characterized by steep inclines, narrow passes, and unpredictable weather, RDI faced the challenge of delivering essential non-food items (NFIs), such as blankets, cooking utensils, and shelter materials, to internally displaced persons (IDPs) living in remote camps. Many of these camps were accessible only via footpaths or tracks that were unsuitable for motor vehicles for much of the year. The organization's primary strategy was to engage local porters and community members who possessed the knowledge and physical capacity to transport goods through these difficult terrains. RDI established agreements with community leaders to organize and manage porter teams, ensuring fair wages, safe working practices, and efficient organization of loads. This decentralized and labor-intensive approach allowed for the delivery of essential items directly to the IDP settlements, bypassing the need for specialized and costly overland vehicles that would have been impractical or impossible to use. The local knowledge of the transporters regarding the safest and most efficient routes, as well as their ability to manage the physical demands of the terrain, was indispensable. This method also fostered a sense of community ownership and participation in the relief effort, as the recipients themselves were often involved in the distribution process. The flexibility of this approach was also a key advantage. When access to certain camps became temporarily blocked due to landslides or extreme weather, RDI could quickly reallocate porter teams to different accessible areas or re-plan routes based on real-time information provided by the local community members. The cost-effectiveness was also substantial, as it avoided the immense capital and operational costs associated with acquiring, maintaining, and staffing a fleet of specialized off-road vehicles or helicopters, which would have been the only alternative for accessing some of these locations. This reliance on human capacity, coupled with efficient local coordination, proved to be a highly effective and contextually appropriate solution.

Finally, consider an emergency response in a large, sprawling urban area following a major earthquake. The city's infrastructure was heavily damaged, and widespread power outages complicated communication and coordination. RDI's objective was to distribute emergency food rations, clean water, and basic first-aid supplies to affected populations across multiple districts. Many roads were impassable due to rubble, and the steep scale of the affected area presented a significant logistical challenge. RDI activated its network of local taxi services and private vehicle owners, who were familiar with the city's layout and could navigate through debris-strewn streets and smaller alleyways that larger trucks could not access. The organization provided these individuals with fuel vouchers, clear instructions on pickup and drop-off points, and communication channels through mobile phones where service was available. This distributed model allowed for a rapid and flexible response, with multiple small teams of transporters working simultaneously across different parts of the city. It also ensured that resources could be directed to areas that were difficult to reach by conventional means. The ability to quickly mobilize a large number of individual vehicles, rather than relying on a limited number of organizational assets, was crucial in ensuring that aid reached as many affected individuals as possible in the critical early hours and days following the disaster. The local knowledge of the drivers was paramount in identifying safe routes and understanding the immediate needs of different neighborhoods. This agile approach, leveraging the existing transportation infrastructure and human capital of the city itself, allowed RDI to overcome the immense logistical challenges posed by the disaster and provide critical assistance to a large and dispersed population. The cost was also managed effectively, as RDI paid for services rendered based on distance and delivery volume, avoiding the significant overheads associated with maintaining and repairing a large fleet in a disaster-stricken environment. These examples collectively demonstrate that by embracing a flexible, locally-integrated logistics strategy, RDI can achieve remarkable efficiency, cost-effectiveness, and impact, even in the most challenging operational contexts.

CHAPTER 12:

Technology as an Enabler:
Tools For The Frontlines

In the intricate landscape of modern development work, technology has transcended its role as a mere auxiliary tool to become a fundamental enabler of efficacy, reach, and impact. The digital revolution has profoundly reshaped how international development and humanitarian aid organizations operate, offering unprecedented opportunities to streamline processes, enhance communication, facilitate rigorous data collection and analysis, and, crucially, empower the very individuals who form the bedrock of frontline operations. This pervasive integration of technology is not merely about adopting new gadgets; it represents a paradigm shift in how we approach problem-solving in some of the world's most complex and resource-constrained environments.

The digital transformation begins with a fundamental enhancement in operational efficiency. Previously, the logistical hurdles of coordinating projects across vast distances, managing resources, and ensuring timely communication could lead to significant delays and increased costs. Today, a suite of digital tools addresses these challenges head-on. Cloud-based project management platforms, for instance, allow teams dispersed across continents to collaborate in real-time, share documents, track progress, and manage tasks seamlessly. This eliminates the delays associated with traditional email chains or physical document transfers, enabling quicker decision-making and more agile project execution. Furthermore, Geographic Information Systems (GIS) have revolutionized the mapping and analysis of needs and resources. By overlaying data layers such as population density, infrastructure availability, security risks, and environmental factors, development professionals can gain a nuanced understanding of the operational context, identify priority areas for intervention, and optimize resource allocation. This data-driven approach allows for more precise targeting of aid and a more efficient use of limited financial and human resources, moving beyond guesswork to informed strategic planning.

Communication, a cornerstone of any successful intervention, has been radically amplified by technological advancements. The advent of mobile technology has been particularly transformative, placing powerful communication tools directly into the hands of aid workers and, increasingly, beneficiaries. Satellite phones and robust internet connectivity solutions ensure that even in remote areas with limited terrestrial infrastructure, communication lines remain open, facilitating real-time reporting, coordination of relief efforts during emergencies, and the vital exchange of information between headquarters and field teams. Beyond formal channels, mobile messaging platforms and community radio broadcasting (often amplified or managed through digital means) allow for the dissemination of critical information to affected populations, from public health advisories and early warning systems for natural disasters to information about available services and entitlements. This two-way communication flow is essential for building trust, ensuring accountability, and adapting interventions to the evolving needs of communities. Moreover, secure data transmission protocols and encrypted communication channels are vital for protecting sensitive information, especially in fragile or conflict-affected settings, safeguarding both operational integrity and the privacy of individuals.

The capacity for data collection and analysis has also been profoundly enhanced. Gone are the days when extensive paper-based surveys and manual data entry were the norm. Mobile data collection tools, utilizing smartphones or tablets equipped with specialized applications, enable aid workers to gather information directly from beneficiaries in a structured and efficient manner. These tools can incorporate features such as GPS tagging, photo and video capture, and real-time data validation, ensuring higher accuracy and completeness of information. This granular, real-time data is invaluable for monitoring program progress, identifying emerging needs, and assessing the impact of interventions. Furthermore, advanced analytical software, including big data analytics and artificial intelligence, can process vast datasets to identify trends, predict potential challenges, and inform evidence-based decision-making. For example, analyzing weather patterns in conjunction with crop yields can help anticipate food insecurity, while tracking disease outbreaks through mobile health data can enable rapid public health responses. **This capacity for sophisticated analysis allows organizations to move from reactive to proactive strategies, optimizing the effectiveness and efficiency of development efforts.**

One of the most significant contributions of technology lies in its ability to empower individuals on the frontlines. This capacity building extends beyond the aid workers themselves to the communities they serve. For aid workers, digital tools can automate mundane administrative tasks, freeing up valuable time for direct engagement with beneficiaries and more strategic planning. Training modules delivered through e-learning platforms can equip field staff with essential skills and knowledge, ensuring consistency and quality of service delivery across diverse operational contexts. Access to digital knowledge repositories and best practice guides provides immediate support and guidance, fostering a culture of continuous learning and adaptation.

Crucially, **technology is increasingly being used to put power back into the hands of beneficiaries.** Mobile money platforms, for instance, have revolutionized the delivery of cash assistance, enabling direct and secure transfers to individuals, thereby increasing dignity, choice, and economic capacity building. Beneficiaries can use these funds to purchase essential goods and services from local markets, stimulating local economies and ensuring that aid meets specific needs. Digital identification systems, when implemented with robust privacy safeguards, can simplify access to services and streamline registration processes, reducing the burden on vulnerable populations. Furthermore, educational apps and digital learning resources can provide opportunities for skills development and knowledge acquisition, particularly for youth and women, fostering long-term resilience and self-sufficiency. For instance, agricultural extension services can now deliver advice on best farming practices directly to farmers' mobile phones, tailored to their specific crops and local conditions. Similarly, health information and maternal care guidance can be accessed by individuals in remote areas, improving health outcomes.

The integration of technology also necessitates a robust approach to data security and privacy. As more sensitive information is collected and transmitted digitally, organizations must implement strong cybersecurity measures, encryption protocols, and clear data governance policies to protect the personal data of beneficiaries and staff from unauthorized access, misuse, or breaches. This is not merely a technical requirement but an ethical imperative, essential for maintaining trust and upholding human rights.

The development sector's adoption of technology is not a monolithic trend but a dynamic and evolving process. From sophisticated data analytics to the humble mobile phone, each technological advancement offers new avenues to amplify the impact of humanitarian and development efforts. **Understanding and strategically deploying these tools is no longer optional; it is essential for navigating the complexities of the modern world and ensuring that aid reaches those who need it most, efficiently, effectively, and with the utmost respect for human dignity.** This technological integration, when wielded responsibly and ethically, becomes a powerful force multiplier, enabling organizations to achieve greater scale, precision, and sustainability in their mission to create positive change. The following sections will delve into specific examples of how these technologies are being applied across various sectors of development work, illustrating their tangible benefits and the strategic considerations involved in their implementation.

Considering the rapid evolution of digital tools, the emphasis on interoperability and sustainability is paramount. Development organizations must strategically select technologies that can integrate with existing systems and are adaptable to changing contexts. This means prioritizing open-source solutions where possible, investing in training and capacity building for local staff to manage and maintain these systems, and ensuring that the chosen technologies are resilient and can function in environments with unreliable power sources or limited connectivity. The long-term viability of technological interventions hinges on this foresight, preventing the creation of dependency on external support or the adoption of solutions that become obsolete or unmanageable within a few years. For example, deploying sophisticated data analysis platforms that require constant high-speed internet and specialized IT support might be unsustainable in many field operations. Instead, solutions that can operate offline or sync data periodically when connectivity is available, and which can be managed by local personnel with moderate technical training, are far more likely to yield lasting results.

Furthermore, the ethical implications of technology deployment require continuous attention. Issues such as the digital divide, ensuring equitable access to technology and digital literacy, must be addressed to prevent exacerbating existing inequalities. Organizations need to be mindful of how their use of data might inadvertently profile or stigmatize individuals or communities. The principle of **"do no harm"** must extend to the digital realm, demanding careful consideration of data privacy, security, and the potential for unintended consequences. For instance, the widespread use of biometric data for identification purposes, while offering potential benefits in terms of security and efficiency, also raises significant privacy concerns and risks of misuse if not governed by stringent ethical frameworks and robust legal protections. This necessitates a commitment to transparency in data collection and usage, obtaining informed consent wherever possible, and establishing clear accountability mechanisms for data management.

The role of technology in enhancing accountability and transparency is another critical dimension. Digital platforms can facilitate the tracking of resources from donor to beneficiary, providing real-time visibility into supply chains and expenditure. This transparency builds trust with donors, partners, and the public, demonstrating the responsible stewardship of resources. Blockchain technology, for example, is being explored for its potential to create immutable records of transactions and aid distribution, thereby enhancing transparency and reducing the risk of fraud or corruption. Mobile reporting tools can enable beneficiaries to provide direct feedback on the quality and relevance of services, creating a more direct channel for accountability. This feedback loop is invaluable for adaptive management, allowing organizations to quickly identify and rectify issues, ensuring that programs remain responsive to the needs of the people they serve.

Moreover, technology is a powerful tool for fostering innovation and knowledge sharing within the development sector. Online platforms and communities of practice allow professionals to share lessons learned, exchange best practices, and collaborate on solutions to common challenges. **This collective intelligence accelerates the pace of learning and adaptation, ensuring that the sector as a whole benefit from advancements and avoids repeating past mistakes.** Webinars, virtual conferences, and digital repositories of research and case studies make knowledge more accessible than ever before, democratizing access to expertise and empowering organizations, particularly those with limited resources, to learn from the experiences of others. This collaborative approach is essential for tackling complex global issues that require multifaceted solutions and shared learning.

The trend towards digital transformation in development also necessitates a shift in organizational culture and workforce skills. Organizations must invest in training and professional development to equip their staff with the digital literacy and technical skills required to effectively utilize new technologies. This includes not only training on specific software or hardware but also fostering a mindset of continuous learning, adaptability, and data-driven decision-making. A culture that embraces experimentation, learns from failures, and actively seeks out innovative technological solutions will be far better positioned to succeed in the dynamic environment of international development. This may involve creating dedicated innovation units, fostering partnerships with technology providers, and empowering staff to explore and pilot new digital tools.

Ultimately, technology in development work is not an end in itself, but a means to achieve a more profound and lasting impact. It is a tool that, when applied thoughtfully, strategically, and ethically, can significantly enhance the ability of organizations to deliver aid effectively, empower communities, promote human rights, and contribute to sustainable development goals. The key lies in understanding the context, choosing the right tools for the job, ensuring equitable access, and maintaining a constant focus on the human element – the needs, dignity, and agency of the people we aim to serve. The ongoing integration of these digital enablers promises to redefine the boundaries of what is possible in global development, making interventions more targeted, responsive, and ultimately, more impactful. **This technological revolution**

is not just about efficiency; it is about fundamentally reimagining how we can build a more equitable and resilient world for all.

The strategic deployment of technology within RDI's operational framework hinges critically on equipping its frontline personnel, the Focal Points (FPs), and the Local Committees for Project Selection and Monitoring (LCPSMs) with the necessary digital infrastructure. Recognizing that the effectiveness of any digital initiative is directly proportional to the capabilities of those wielding the tools, RDI has meticulously curated a comprehensive digital toolkit designed for resilience, usability, and adaptability in the demanding environments where its work unfolds. This is not simply a matter of distributing hardware and software, but of ensuring that each component is carefully selected to empower FPs, enabling them to navigate complex logistical challenges, maintain robust communication channels, and execute project objectives with precision and autonomy. The selection process itself is guided by a principle of **"fit-for-purpose,"** ensuring that the technology provided can withstand the rigors of field operations, from fluctuating power grids to dusty conditions and extensive travel.

At the core of this digital ecosystem are the personal computing devices provided to each FP. A significant investment has been made in ruggedized laptops, chosen for their durability and ability to function reliably in adverse conditions. These are not the sleek, ultra-light devices typically found in corporate offices, but robust machines built with reinforced casings, spill-resistant keyboards, and shock-mounted hard drives. This deliberate choice addresses the reality of field work, where devices can be inadvertently dropped, exposed to dust and humidity, or subjected to temperature extremes. The specifications of these laptops are calibrated to support essential project management software, data analysis tools, and secure communication applications, ensuring that FPs have the processing power needed for their tasks without being overly complex or power-hungry. Beyond their physical resilience, these laptops are pre-loaded with a suite of essential software, including optimized versions of productivity tools, secure operating systems, and specialized project management applications that facilitate real-time reporting, resource tracking, and task delegation. The operating systems are configured with enhanced security features, including full-disk encryption and strong password policies, to protect the sensitive data that FPs routinely handle. Furthermore, these devices are provisioned with remote management capabilities, allowing IT support teams to provide assistance, deploy updates, and address security issues remotely, thereby minimizing downtime and ensuring that FPs can maintain their operational momentum.

Complementing the laptops are high-performance smartphones, serving as the immediate, on-the-go interface for communication, data collection, and situational awareness. These devices are selected for their advanced camera capabilities, GPS accuracy, and compatibility with a wide range of mobile applications crucial for field operations. Their user-friendly interfaces are paramount, as many FPs may not have extensive technical backgrounds. Therefore, the chosen smartphones offer intuitive navigation, making it easy for them to access critical information, capture photographic evidence, record audio notes, and communicate via various platforms. The rationale behind providing both laptops and smartphones is to create a synergistic technological environment. The smartphone acts as a primary data capture and communication device in immediate, on-the-ground scenarios, while the laptop serves as the more powerful hub for in-depth data analysis, report generation, and strategic planning. For instance, an FP might use their smartphone to document a community meeting with photos and audio recordings, tag its location with GPS, and then upload this data to a central server. Later, using their laptop, they can analyze this information in conjunction with other data points, generate a detailed report, and communicate findings to stakeholders. The selection of specific smartphone models also prioritizes battery life and the availability of replacement parts or compatible charging solutions in diverse geographical locations, a critical consideration for maintaining operational continuity in areas with unreliable power infrastructure.

A cornerstone of RDI's digital enablement strategy is ensuring reliable internet connectivity. This is achieved through a multi-pronged approach, acknowledging that no single solution suffices for all operational contexts. For FPs working in areas with nascent or intermittent terrestrial internet infrastructure, satellite internet solutions are deployed. These can range from portable satellite terminals for temporary base camps to more integrated systems for established field offices. These solutions are chosen for their ability to establish a stable connection even in remote locations, providing the bandwidth necessary for uploading large data files, participating in video conferences, and accessing cloud-based resources. Where mobile network coverage is available, albeit sometimes weak, FPs are equipped with high-gain mobile broadband modems and antennae, designed to boost signal strength and provide a more stable internet connection. This allows them to leverage existing cellular networks for data transmission, offering a more cost-effective and flexible solution when satellite connectivity is not the primary requirement. Furthermore, in urban or semi-urban settings where reliable Wi-Fi is available, FPs are provided with secure network access protocols and are trained on best practices for using public Wi-Fi networks safely, including the use of VPNs to encrypt their data traffic. The provisioning of these connectivity solutions is often bundled with data plans that are optimized for the specific needs of development work, balancing cost-effectiveness with the necessity of consistent access. This layered approach to connectivity ensures that FPs are not left isolated, regardless of their physical location, and can seamlessly integrate into the global digital network.

Beyond the hardware, the software suite provided is equally critical in equipping FPs. This includes not only productivity applications but also specialized tools designed for the specific demands of development and humanitarian work. Robust project management software, often cloud-based, allows FPs to plan, execute, and monitor projects in real-time. These platforms enable task assignment, progress tracking, budget monitoring, and collaborative document management, fostering transparency and accountability across project lifecycles. For data collection and analysis, user-friendly mobile data collection applications are pre-installed on smartphones and tablets. These applications are configured with custom survey forms, data validation rules, and multimedia capture capabilities, ensuring that the data collected is accurate, consistent, and rich in context. Offline functionality is a key feature, allowing FPs to collect data even when internet connectivity is unavailable, with the data syncing automatically once a connection is re-established. Geographic Information System (GIS) software, often accessible via web platforms or as desktop applications, empowers FPs to map assets, analyze spatial data, and visualize project impact. This is invaluable for understanding beneficiary distribution, planning logistics, and identifying areas of need or vulnerability. Communication tools are also a vital component, including secure messaging applications that allow for encrypted conversations and file sharing, ensuring the confidentiality of sensitive communications. Video conferencing software, integrated with the laptops, facilitates real-time discussions and coordination with headquarters and other field teams, bridging geographical distances and fostering a sense of team cohesion. Furthermore, digital knowledge management systems are provided, offering FPs access to a centralized repository of best practices, training materials, research findings, and organizational policies, promoting continuous learning and the dissemination of valuable insights. The selection of these software solutions prioritizes interoperability, ensuring that different applications can seamlessly exchange data, and the ease with which they can be updated and maintained in the field. Training on the effective utilization of this software suite is an integral part of the deployment process, ensuring that FPs can leverage these tools to their fullest potential.

The provision of this comprehensive digital toolkit is underpinned by a rigorous training and support framework. It is understood that simply distributing hardware and software is insufficient. Therefore, RDI invests significantly in ensuring that FPs are not only equipped with the tools but also possess the knowledge and skills to use them effectively and confidently. Initial onboarding includes intensive training sessions that cover the functionalities of each device and application, with a strong emphasis on practical, scenario-based learning. These sessions are designed to be interactive and hands-on, allowing FPs to practice using the tools in simulated field conditions. Beyond initial training, continuous professional development is provided through a blend of online learning modules, webinars, and in-person workshops, catering to different learning styles and keeping FPs updated on new features and emerging technologies. A dedicated technical support desk is available to assist FPs with any technical issues they may encounter. This support is accessible through multiple channels, including phone, email, and a ticketing system, ensuring that assistance is readily available, irrespective of the FP's location or the time of day. Remote support capabilities allow technicians to directly access FPs' devices (with their permission) to troubleshoot problems, install software updates, or configure settings, thereby resolving issues quickly and efficiently. Furthermore, **peer-to-peer learning is encouraged through online forums and knowledge-sharing platforms where FPs can exchange tips, best practices, and solutions to common challenges.** This creates a supportive ecosystem where FPs can learn from each other's experiences, fostering a culture of continuous improvement and adaptation. The entire process, from selection to deployment, training, and ongoing support, is designed to build the capacity of RDI's Focal Points, transforming them into highly effective, digitally empowered agents of change on the frontlines of development initiatives. The ultimate goal is to ensure that technology serves as a true enabler, enhancing their ability to deliver impactful programs and achieve RDI's mission with greater efficiency, reach, and resilience.

The strategic deployment of mobile technology has fundamentally transformed the way RDI's Focal Points (FPs) gather and report information from the field, ushering in an era of unprecedented real-time insights. Gone are the days of relying solely on paper-based forms, delayed data entry, and retrospective analysis. Today, FPs are equipped with sophisticated mobile applications that act as their primary interface for documenting project activities, meticulously tracking progress against set objectives, and candidly reporting on the myriad challenges encountered on the ground. This immediate, granular flow of data is not merely an administrative improvement; it forms the very foundation of adaptive management, enabling swift course corrections and optimizing program delivery in dynamic and often unpredictable environments.

At the heart of this transformation are the custom-designed mobile data collection applications. These platforms are engineered for intuitive use, even by individuals with limited prior experience with digital tools. Pre-loaded onto the ruggedized smartphones and tablets provided to each FP, these applications allow for the structured capture of a wide array of information. For instance, **when an FP conducts a training session with community members, they can use the application to log attendance, record demographic data of participants, capture qualitative feedback through text fields, and even upload photographs or short video clips documenting the session's activities and engagement levels.** Each entry is timestamped and georeferenced, providing irrefutable evidence of where and when an activity took place, thereby **enhancing accountability and transparency.**

The utility of these applications extends far beyond simple activity logging. They are integral to the continuous performance monitoring of RDI's various projects. FPs can use them to track key performance indicators (KPIs) directly as they are observed. For a project focused on improving agricultural yields, an FP might use the application to record the number of farmers trained in new techniques, the types of crops being planted, the initial soil conditions, and the adoption rates of specific methodologies. This data, collected in real-time, allows project managers to gauge the immediate impact of interventions, identify which approaches are proving most effective, and understand where bottlenecks or resistance to adoption might be occurring. This granular level of insight is invaluable for refining program strategies and reallocating resources efficiently.

Documenting challenges and successes is another critical function of these mobile reporting tools. **The field is rarely without its unexpected obstacles, and the ability to rapidly report these is vital for effective problem-solving.** An FP encountering a disruption in the supply chain for essential medical kits, for instance, can immediately log this issue through the mobile application, specifying the nature of the disruption, its potential impact on beneficiaries, and any immediate actions taken. This allows the relevant logistical or programmatic teams at headquarters to be alerted instantly, enabling a rapid response to mitigate the problem. Conversely, if an FP observes a particularly innovative or effective community-led solution to a problem, they can document this success with similar ease, facilitating the dissemination of best practices across different project sites and teams. The ability to tag these reports with relevant project components and thematic areas ensures that this qualitative information is systematically categorized and accessible for broader analysis.

The reporting capabilities are designed to be both comprehensive and efficient. FPs can compile detailed narrative reports, integrate quantitative data collected through the application, and attach multimedia evidence. The applications often feature templates that guide the FP through the reporting process, ensuring that all essential information is captured in a standardized format. This standardization is crucial for aggregation and analysis at a higher level. For instance, a series of community assessments conducted across multiple villages can be consolidated into a district-level overview, highlighting common challenges, prevailing needs, and geographic patterns of vulnerability or resilience. This aggregated data then informs strategic decision-making, program adjustments, and resource allocation at both the national and international levels.

The integration of offline capabilities is a paramount consideration, given the often-unreliable or absent internet connectivity in many operational areas. These mobile applications are built to function seamlessly in offline mode. FPs can collect and store all data on their devices throughout the day, even in the most remote locations. Once a stable internet connection is established, whether through a mobile network or a satellite link, the application automatically synchronizes the collected data with the central server. This ensures that no data is lost and that the reporting cycle remains unbroken, regardless of external infrastructure limitations. This offline functionality is critical for maintaining the continuous flow of information and preventing data gaps that could compromise analysis and decision-making.

Furthermore, the real-time nature of this data collection and reporting fosters a culture of transparency and accountability. Stakeholders, including donors, government partners, and the beneficiary communities themselves, can be provided, if needed, with access to dashboards or reports that reflect the most current project status. This immediate visibility into program activities, progress, and challenges builds trust and allows for more informed engagement. For example, a donor might be able to view a live map of where mobile health clinics are operating, see the number of patients served, and review anonymized summary reports of common health issues being addressed, all updated in near real-time. This level of transparency is a powerful tool for demonstrating impact and securing continued support for development initiatives.

The implementation of these mobile reporting systems also includes robust data validation mechanisms built directly into the applications. These are configured to ensure data quality at the point of entry. For instance, if a numerical field is expected to contain a value between 1 and 100, the application will flag any entry outside this range, prompting the FP to verify the data. Similarly, certain fields may be mandatory, preventing the submission of incomplete records. These built-in checks significantly reduce errors and the need for time-consuming data cleaning processes later on, ensuring that the insights derived from the data are reliable and actionable. The ability to capture geospatial data, as mentioned, adds another layer of verification and analytical depth, confirming the physical location of reported activities and enabling spatial analysis of project reach and impact.

The user experience for the FPs has been a central tenet in the design and selection of these mobile tools. Recognizing that technology should empower, not overwhelm, the interfaces are kept clean, intuitive, and require minimal technical expertise to navigate. Training sessions focus not just on *what* data to collect and *how* to enter it, but also on *why* it is important, fostering a deeper understanding of the role of data in achieving project goals. This understanding motivates FPs to utilize the tools diligently. Moreover, the ability to integrate multimedia, such as photos and audio recordings, allows for a richer, more contextualized reporting experience. A photograph of a newly constructed water point, for instance, conveys more immediate information about its status than a textual description alone. Similarly, an audio recording of a community's testimonial about the impact of a new educational program can be far more powerful in demonstrating success than a written summary.

This real-time data pipeline directly supports adaptive management by providing timely feedback loops. When data indicates that a particular project component is not performing as expected, or that unforeseen challenges are impeding progress, project managers can be alerted almost immediately. This allows for agile adjustments to be made to project strategies, resource allocation, or operational approaches. Instead of waiting for monthly or quarterly reports that might highlight issues weeks or months after they have arisen, decisions can be informed by data that is only hours or days old. This responsiveness is crucial in environments where conditions can change rapidly and where timely intervention can make a significant difference to program outcomes and beneficiary well-being. For example, if real-time data shows a low attendance rate at a series of vocational training sessions in a particular district, program managers can quickly investigate the reasons, perhaps transportation issues, scheduling conflicts, or a lack of perceived relevance, and implement targeted solutions.

The collection of real-time data also significantly streamlines the reporting process for FPs. **Instead of spending considerable time after field visits compiling paper reports, entering data into spreadsheets, and then submitting these, the process is largely integrated into the fieldwork itself.** This frees up valuable time for FPs to focus on direct engagement with communities, problem-solving, and implementing program activities, rather than administrative burdens. The efficiency gains translate into more time spent on core programmatic functions, thereby enhancing overall project effectiveness and reach. Furthermore, the ability to use mobile devices for communication, such as sending instant messages or brief updates via secure platforms, complements the structured reporting, allowing for immediate dissemination of critical information as it arises, creating a dynamic and responsive operational intelligence system. The mobile reporting system is, therefore, not just a tool for data collection, but a fundamental component of RDI's operational agility and its commitment to evidence-based, responsive development.

Beyond the immediate data capture and reporting, a critical layer of technological enablement for RDI's operations lies in the robust communication and collaboration platforms that knit together its geographically dispersed network of Focal Points (FPs), central coordination teams, and external partners. In the dynamic and often challenging environments where RDI works, the ability to communicate effectively, securely, and in real-time is not merely a convenience; it is an operational imperative. These platforms serve as the digital connective tissue, transforming potential isolation into a cohesive and responsive ecosystem.

At the forefront of this communication strategy are secure messaging applications. These are not casual chat tools; they are encrypted platforms designed to protect the sensitivity of information being shared. FPs can use these applications to send urgent field updates, request immediate assistance, or coordinate responses to emerging situations. For instance, if an FP identifies a sudden increase in malnutrition cases in a specific village, they can relay this critical information via a secure message to the RDI health coordinator, attaching relevant anonymized data points or even a brief audio note from a local health worker. This allows for rapid consultation and the potential to reroute resources or alert relevant health authorities without delay. Similarly, central coordination can disseminate important policy updates, safety advisories, or logistical changes to all FPs simultaneously, ensuring that everyone is working with the most current information. **The group messaging feature within these platforms is particularly valuable for fostering peer-to-peer learning and support among FPs working in similar regions or on related thematic areas, creating virtual communities of practice where challenges can be collectively brainstormed and solutions shared.** The presence of read receipts and delivery confirmations also provides a layer of assurance that critical messages have been received, enhancing accountability in communication flows. Furthermore, many of these platforms allow for the secure sharing of documents, images, and even short videos, enabling richer contextualization of communications. An FP documenting the impact of a drought might share satellite imagery of parched farmland alongside textual descriptions and photographs of affected livestock, providing a comprehensive picture to support an immediate appeal for assistance. The emphasis on end-to-end encryption ensures that only the intended recipients can decrypt and read the messages, safeguarding sensitive operational data and beneficiary information from potential interception. This is particularly crucial when dealing with vulnerable populations or in contexts where digital security is a significant concern. The choice of platform is often dictated by a balance of security features, ease of use, and offline accessibility, ensuring that communication can be maintained even when internet connectivity is intermittent.

Complementing these messaging capabilities are robust video conferencing tools. **These platforms have become indispensable for bridging the vast distances that separate RDI's teams.** Regular video calls allow for more in-depth discussions than text-based communication can typically accommodate. Project review meetings, for example, can be conducted with FPs presenting their progress updates visually, showcasing field activities through live video feeds or pre-recorded segments. This not only allows for more dynamic presentations but also enables clearer visual understanding of the context and challenges faced on the ground. A virtual site visit, where an FP walks a coordinator through a newly constructed school or a rehabilitated water point via video, provides a far more immediate and impactful understanding than a written report. These meetings also facilitate richer interactions, allowing for spontaneous follow-up questions and a more personal connection between team members. Building rapport and trust is significantly easier when participants can see and hear each other, fostering a stronger sense of team cohesion despite physical separation. Moreover, video conferencing is often used for specialized technical support. An IT specialist at headquarters can guide an FP through a troubleshooting process for their mobile devices or data collection software, sharing their screen to demonstrate steps, thereby resolving technical issues much more efficiently than through written instructions alone. The ability to host webinars and training sessions via video conferencing further extends RDI's capacity to build the skills of its field staff, ensuring that FPs are continuously updated on best practices, new methodologies, and emerging technologies without the need for costly and time-consuming travel. The selection of video conferencing platforms considers factors such as bandwidth requirements, the number of concurrent participants, and the availability of screen-sharing and recording functionalities, all while maintaining a commitment to data privacy and security. The clarity of audio and video is paramount to the effectiveness of these calls, and RDI invests in ensuring its teams have access to reliable equipment and, where possible, sufficient bandwidth. For complex problem-solving sessions, the ability to whiteboard virtually or collaboratively edits documents in real-time during a video call can accelerate decision-making and the development of actionable plans.

Shared online platforms, often referred to as cloud-based collaborative workspaces, form the backbone of knowledge management and project continuity. These platforms provide a centralized repository for all project-related documents, reports, data summaries, and operational plans. FPs can upload their completed field reports, survey data, and multimedia evidence directly to these platforms, making them instantly accessible to relevant team members. **This eliminates the need for**

cumbersome email attachments and version control nightmares, ensuring that everyone is working with the latest approved documents. These platforms are typically equipped with robust search functionalities, allowing users to quickly locate specific information, whether it's a particular assessment report, a budget document, or a set of community feedback notes from a specific project site. This organizational efficiency is critical for managing the vast amount of information generated by RDI's programs. Beyond document storage, these platforms often facilitate collaborative document creation and editing. Multiple team members can contribute to a single report or proposal simultaneously, with changes tracked and attributed, streamlining the writing and review process. Discussion forums or integrated chat features within these platforms also allow for asynchronous communication and debate around specific documents or project elements, fostering a continuous dialogue that fuels problem-solving and innovation.

For instance, during the development of a new project proposal, FPs from different regions might contribute their contextual insights to a shared document, with programmatic leads providing feedback and guidance in real-time. The platforms can also be configured to manage workflows and approval processes, ensuring that documents are reviewed and signed off by the appropriate personnel before being finalized. **This structured approach to collaboration enhances accountability and ensures adherence to organizational standards.** Furthermore, these shared spaces are crucial for institutional learning. *By centralizing project documentation, lessons learned, and best practices, RDI creates a living knowledge base that can be leveraged for* *future programming, donor reporting, and organizational strategy development.* FPs can access case studies and success stories from other projects, inspiring new approaches and avoiding the duplication of past mistakes. The integration of project management tools within some of these platforms allows for the tracking of tasks, deadlines, and project milestones, providing a transparent overview of project progress for all stakeholders. Access controls and user permissions are meticulously managed to ensure that sensitive information is only available to authorized personnel, maintaining the security and integrity of project data. The choice of shared online platforms is guided by their scalability, reliability, security features, and the ease with which they can be integrated with other RDI systems, such as mobile data collection applications. The aim is to create a seamless digital environment where information flows freely and securely, empowering teams to collaborate effectively regardless of their physical location.

The strategic implementation of these communication and collaboration tools has a profound impact on RDI's operational agility. **By enabling rapid and secure information exchange, these technologies dissolve the traditional bureaucratic layers that can often slow down decision-making in development organizations.** FPs on the ground are empowered to communicate urgent needs or critical observations directly to those who can authorize action, whether it's a program manager at regional headquarters or a specialist at the central office. This direct line of communication drastically reduces response times, allowing RDI to adapt its interventions swiftly to changing circumstances. For example, if an FP reports a sudden security incident impacting their ability to conduct planned activities, the secure messaging and video conferencing tools can facilitate an immediate risk assessment and the rapid formulation of an alternative operational plan, potentially rerouting staff to safer areas or shifting to remote support mechanisms. This level of responsiveness is critical in volatile operational contexts where a few hours can make a significant difference in safeguarding staff and beneficiaries.

Moreover, these platforms foster a culture of transparency and shared learning across RDI's diverse network. When FPs can easily share their successes, challenges, and innovative solutions through collaborative platforms, it creates a virtuous cycle of continuous improvement. An FP who discovers a particularly effective community engagement strategy for a new health initiative can document this on the shared platform, complete with supporting photos and brief explanations. Other FPs working on similar health programs, perhaps in different countries, can then access this information, adapt the strategy to their own contexts, and report back on its effectiveness. This peer-to-peer knowledge transfer is invaluable, democratizing learning and accelerating the adoption of effective practices. It allows RDI to leverage the collective intelligence of its entire network, ensuring that successful approaches are scaled and that lessons learned from one context inform programming in others. The ability to collaborate on documents also means that cross-regional teams can work together on complex proposals or evaluations, bringing diverse perspectives to bear on critical tasks. For instance, a joint proposal for a multi-country initiative might be co-authored by FPs from each targeted nation, with central coordination providing oversight and strategic input through shared workspaces and video calls. This not only results in more robust and contextually relevant proposals but also builds stronger working relationships and a shared sense of ownership among the teams involved.

The integration of these communication and collaboration tools also significantly enhances RDI's ability to coordinate with external partners. Government ministries, local NGOs, community-based organizations, and international agencies all play vital roles in the success of development programs. Secure messaging and video conferencing platforms can be used to schedule and conduct regular coordination meetings with these partners, ensuring alignment on objectives, strategies, and reporting requirements. Shared online platforms can be used to provide partners with secure access to relevant project documents, progress reports, and data summaries, fostering transparency and building trust. **For instance, a donor might be granted read-only access to a project dashboard on a shared platform, allowing them to track progress against key indicators in near real-time.** This level of transparency not only meets donor expectations but also strengthens relationships by demonstrating accountability and impact. The ability to quickly share critical information with partners during emergencies or unexpected events is also paramount. If a natural disaster strikes, RDI can rapidly communicate with its local implementing partners via secure channels to assess the damage, coordinate relief efforts, and disseminate safety information to affected communities. This collaborative approach, enabled by technology, ensures a more coherent and effective response.

Ultimately, these communication and collaboration platforms are not just tools for information sharing; they are strategic assets that enable RDI to operate as a cohesive, adaptive, and impactful organization. They empower FPs with the connectivity and support they need to succeed in challenging environments, facilitate seamless collaboration across diverse teams and with external stakeholders, and foster a culture of continuous learning and improvement. By leveraging secure messaging, video conferencing, and shared online workspaces, RDI builds a resilient and responsive network, capable of navigating the complexities of international development and delivering tangible results for the communities it serves. The investment in these technologies is an investment in RDI's operational effectiveness, its ability to adapt to evolving needs, and its commitment to maximizing its positive impact on the ground. The choice and implementation of these tools are continuously reviewed and updated to ensure they remain at the forefront of technological capabilities, providing the most secure, efficient, and user-friendly solutions for RDI's global workforce and its partners. This digital connectivity ensures that no FP, however remote their location, is ever truly working alone, but is instead an integral part of a connected, informed, and collaborative global effort.

The advent of sophisticated digital tools on the frontlines of development and humanitarian work has fundamentally reshaped how organizations like RDI operate. While the previous discussion has focused on the enablement of communication and collaboration through these technologies, the ultimate power of these digital systems lies in their capacity to generate and process data. This data, meticulously collected through mobile applications, sensor networks, and other digital interfaces, forms the bedrock of evidence-based decision-making and rigorous impact measurement. It transforms the often-intangible efforts of development work into quantifiable achievements, allowing for a clear understanding of **what**

works, where, and why. Without this data-driven approach, interventions risk becoming ad-hoc, less efficient, and ultimately, less impactful. **The strategic leveraging of this collected information is not merely an administrative task; it is the engine that drives continuous improvement, optimizes resource allocation, and provides the demonstrable evidence of success that is crucial for accountability to beneficiaries, donors, and the wider international community.**

At the core of transforming raw data into actionable intelligence is the process of aggregation and analysis. Data points collected by Focal Points (FPs) in remote villages – be it the number of children attending a health clinic, the yield of crops in a demonstration farm, or the number of participants in a vocational training program – are not intended to remain as isolated statistics. Instead, these granular pieces of information are funneled through secure systems into central databases, where they are cleaned, standardized, and aggregated. This aggregation process allows for the identification of trends, patterns, and anomalies that would be invisible at the individual data-point level. For example, a sudden spike in reported cases of a particular illness across several villages, captured through mobile health reporting apps, can be quickly identified through aggregated data analysis. This immediate visibility allows RDI's health program managers to alert relevant authorities, mobilize rapid response teams, and potentially adjust resource allocation to address the emerging health crisis before it escalates. Similarly, if data from agricultural projects consistently shows lower-than-expected yields in specific regions, even after the implementation of new techniques, this aggregated insight prompts a deeper investigation. Is the soil composition different? Are there specific pest issues that were not accounted for? Is the training being delivered effectively in those particular contexts? This analytical layer allows RDI to move beyond simply implementing activities to understanding the efficacy and contextual nuances of those activities.

This analytical capability is crucial for iterative program design and adaptation. **Development and humanitarian interventions are rarely static. They must adapt to evolving contexts, learn from successes and failures, and respond to the dynamic needs of the populations they serve.** Data provides the essential feedback loop for this adaptation. By continuously monitoring key performance indicators (KPIs) derived from collected data, RDI can assess whether programs are on track to meet their objectives. If data indicates that a certain training module for FPs is not being effectively absorbed, as evidenced by consistently low scores on post-training assessments or a lack of application of learned skills in their field reports, program managers can identify the shortcomings in the module itself or the delivery method. This might lead to a revision of the training materials, a change in the pedagogical approach, or additional coaching for FPs struggling with the content. Conversely, if data shows that a particular community engagement strategy is proving exceptionally effective in fostering local ownership and participation, that approach can be documented, analyzed for its core components, and then scaled or replicated in other program sites. This data-informed adaptation ensures that resources are not wasted on ineffective approaches and that successful methodologies are systematically integrated into program design, maximizing efficiency and impact.

Resource allocation is another critical area where data plays a transformative role. **In resource-constrained environments, making informed decisions about where to invest limited funds and personnel is paramount.** Aggregated data on needs, program performance, and operational costs provides the evidence base for such decisions. If data from multiple regions indicates a disproportionately high rate of malnutrition in Region A compared to Region B, and analysis shows that RDI's current nutritional interventions are yielding better results in Region B, this might lead to a strategic decision to reallocate a portion of the resources from Region B to Region A, coupled with an investigation into why the interventions are less effective in Region A. Furthermore, data on the operational costs associated with different types of interventions can inform choices about the most cost-effective ways to achieve desired outcomes. For instance, if data reveals that community health worker-led interventions for a specific disease prevention campaign are significantly less expensive per beneficiary reached than clinic-based approaches, while achieving comparable or even superior results, this data would strongly advocate for prioritizing the community-based model in future planning and funding appeals. This data-driven approach to resource allocation ensures that RDI's investments are strategically directed towards areas and activities that offer the greatest potential for positive impact, thereby maximizing the return on investment for both programmatic goals and donor contributions.

Beyond internal decision-making, the data collected and analyzed is fundamental to impact measurement and reporting. In the field of international development and humanitarian aid, demonstrating accountability and impact is not just a matter of good practice; it is an ethical imperative and a requirement for continued support from donors and partners. **Technology-enabled data collection allows RDI to move beyond anecdotal evidence and provide robust, quantifiable evidence of the changes brought about by its programs.** This involves defining clear impact indicators at the outset of a project, often aligned with the Sustainable Development Goals (SDGs) or specific donor requirements, and then systematically tracking these indicators throughout the project lifecycle. For example, if a project aims to improve access to clean water, impact data might include indicators such as the percentage of households with access to a safe water source within a specified distance, the reduction in reported waterborne diseases, and changes in time spent collecting water, particularly by women and girls. Mobile data collection tools can capture this information directly from households, ensuring accuracy and timeliness.

The analysis of this impact data allows RDI to tell a compelling story of change. It provides concrete evidence of how programs are contributing to improved livelihoods, enhanced health outcomes, increased educational attainment, or greater community resilience. This evidence is crucial for donor reporting, enabling RDI to demonstrate that funds have been used effectively and that tangible results have been achieved. It also serves as a powerful tool for advocacy and fundraising, providing concrete examples of impact that can attract new supporters and resources. Furthermore, the ability to accurately measure impact builds credibility and trust. When RDI can present well-analyzed data showing, for instance, a statistically significant reduction in child mortality in areas where its maternal and child health programs are active, this data-backed assertion carries far more weight than general claims of success. This rigorous approach to impact measurement not only validates RDI's work but also contributes to the broader knowledge base within the development sector, informing best practices and guiding the efforts of other organizations.

The integration of technology for data collection and analysis also enables more sophisticated forms of impact evaluation. Beyond simple tracking of progress against indicators, advanced data analytics can be employed to explore causal relationships and attribute observed changes directly to RDI's interventions. Techniques such as difference-in-differences analysis, regression discontinuity design, or even randomized controlled trials (RCTs), where feasible, can be employed to rigorously assess the impact of specific programs. The granular data collected through digital platforms can provide the necessary inputs for these complex methodologies, allowing RDI to move beyond simply stating that a change occurred, to demonstrating that RDI's program *caused* that change. For example, in a project aimed at improving agricultural productivity through farmer field schools, detailed data on farmer participation, training attendance, adoption of new techniques, and crop yields can be analyzed alongside data from control groups (farmers who did not participate in the field schools) to quantify the specific impact of the training on productivity. This level of rigor is invaluable for understanding not just *if* an intervention works, but *how* and *why* it works, and under what conditions.

Moreover, the continuous feedback loop facilitated by data allows for a more nuanced understanding of impact across different population segments. Data can be disaggregated by gender, age, geographic location, socioeconomic status, or other relevant demographic factors. This disaggregation is vital for ensuring that programs are equitable and that no particular group is being inadvertently excluded or negatively impacted. For instance, if data shows that while overall access to education has improved, girls from marginalized communities are still lagging behind their male peers or girls from more privileged backgrounds, this insight allows RDI to tailor its strategies to address these specific disparities. This might involve targeted outreach programs, the provision of scholarships for girls, or community-level advocacy to challenge gender-based barriers to education. This granular, disaggregated data is crucial for implementing truly inclusive and equitable development programs, moving beyond aggregate averages to address the specific needs and circumstances of the most vulnerable populations.

The ethical considerations surrounding data collection and use are paramount and are intrinsically linked to impact measurement and decision-making. While technology provides powerful tools for gathering data, RDI is committed to ensuring that this data is collected, stored, and used responsibly, with the utmost respect for the privacy and dignity of the individuals and communities it serves. This includes obtaining informed consent for data collection, anonymizing data where possible, and implementing robust data security measures to prevent unauthorized access or misuse. The transparency that data provides must also extend to how that data is used. Communities should understand what data is being collected about them, why it is being collected, and how it will be used to improve services and programs. This builds trust and ensures that the data collection process itself is conducted in a manner that respects community ownership and participation.

Ultimately, the effective leveraging of data for decision-making and impact measurement transforms RDI's operations from a series of well-intentioned activities into a dynamic, evidence-based system focused on achieving measurable, sustainable change. It empowers FPs with real-time insights into their work, enables program managers to make informed adjustments and strategic resource allocations, and provides a clear, compelling narrative of impact for all stakeholders. By embracing technology not just for its communication capabilities, but for its power to generate and analyze data, RDI can continuously learn, adapt, and optimize its interventions, ensuring that it remains at the forefront of effective and impactful development and humanitarian assistance. **This commitment to data-driven excellence is what allows RDI to translate its on-the-ground efforts into demonstrable progress, driving meaningful and lasting improvements in the lives of the people it serves.** The ongoing investment in data management systems, analytical capacity building, and ethical data governance frameworks is therefore not an optional add-on, but a core component of RDI's strategy for maximizing its positive impact in a complex and ever-changing world. This data-informed approach ensures accountability, fosters innovation, and ultimately, strengthens RDI's ability to fulfill its mission effectively and efficiently, transforming raw information into tangible, positive change.

CHAPTER 13:

Challenges and Adaptations:
Navigating The Realities

The journey of implementing a groundbreaking development and humanitarian aid delivery model, or indeed any significant intervention in the field, is rarely a straightforward path. While theoretical frameworks and pilot studies may illuminate a clear route, the reality on the ground is often a far more intricate tapestry, woven with unforeseen challenges and persistent obstacles. Anticipating these hurdles is not an act of pessimism, but a crucial element of effective planning and a testament to the adaptive resilience required in international development and humanitarian work. *The aid sector, in its vast and varied experience, has encountered a recurring set of difficulties that can significantly impede progress, regardless of the innovative nature of the approach being adopted. Understanding these common pitfalls is essential for any organization seeking to navigate the complexities of delivering aid and driving sustainable change.*

One of the most persistent and impactful challenges is **political instability and governance fragmentation**. The best-designed projects can falter when the overarching political landscape is volatile. Changes in government, civil unrest, or the breakdown of law and order can disrupt supply chains, prevent access to target populations, and render established operational plans obsolete overnight. In regions experiencing

386

conflict or significant political upheaval, the very premise of project implementation can be jeopardized. For instance, securing necessary permits, maintaining consistent communication with local authorities, or even ensuring the physical safety of staff and beneficiaries can become insurmountable tasks. A sudden shift in policy, a change in leadership within a key ministry, or the imposition of sanctions can have cascading effects, impacting funding flows, import/export regulations for essential supplies, and the overall security environment. This volatility demands a constant state of readiness for adaptation, often requiring contingency plans that factor in the possibility of rapid operational pivots or even temporary suspensions of activities. The ability to maintain neutrality and build trust across diverse political factions, while challenging, becomes paramount to ensuring the continuation of vital services amidst such instability.

Closely linked to political instability are security risks and the protection of personnel and assets. Operating in many developing countries, particularly those affected by conflict, poverty, or weak rule of law, inherently carries security implications. This can range from petty crime affecting local staff and field offices to direct threats against international personnel, sabotage of infrastructure, or the risk of being caught in crossfire. The decision-making process for *where* and *how* to operate must rigorously assess these security landscapes. This involves not only understanding the immediate threats but also anticipating potential escalations. Providing adequate security training and equipment for staff, establishing robust communication protocols, and developing clear emergency evacuation plans are non-negotiable. The cost of security measures can be substantial, diverting resources that might otherwise be used for program delivery, presenting a constant balancing act. Furthermore, the ethical considerations around security are complex; ensuring that security measures do not inadvertently alienate the local population or create a perception of an occupying force requires careful management and cultural sensitivity. The safety of beneficiaries is also a critical consideration; interventions must not inadvertently put vulnerable communities at greater risk.

Beyond the external political and security spheres, **cultural resistance to change and societal norms** often present significant, albeit less visible, hurdles. Development interventions frequently aim to introduce new practices, technologies, or social behaviors, which may clash with deeply ingrained traditions, beliefs, or established power structures within a community. This resistance can manifest in various ways, from outright rejection of new methods to passive non-compliance or subtle subversion. For example, introducing modern agricultural techniques might be met with skepticism by farmers accustomed to traditional methods, especially if they perceive the new methods as culturally alien or tied to external control. Similarly, initiatives aimed at empowering marginalized groups, such as women or ethnic minorities, can encounter resistance from those who benefit from the existing social hierarchy. Overcoming such resistance requires more than just disseminating information; it necessitates a deep understanding of local culture, a commitment to genuine community engagement, and a willingness to adapt the intervention to be compatible with, or at least sensitive to, local values and customs. Building trust, demonstrating tangible benefits, and involving community leaders and influencers in the design and implementation process are critical for fostering buy-in and facilitating successful adoption of new approaches. Patience and a long-term perspective are often more effective than forceful imposition.

Logistical and infrastructural challenges are a constant reality in many operational environments. Accessing remote or geographically dispersed populations can be severely hampered by poor transportation networks, including unpaved roads, lack of reliable vehicles, or seasonal inaccessibility due to weather conditions. This impacts everything from the timely delivery of essential supplies – such as medicines, seeds, or educational materials – to the ability of field staff to conduct regular monitoring and support. Supply chain management becomes a complex puzzle, requiring meticulous planning to account for potential delays, spoilage, or loss. Furthermore, the lack of basic infrastructure, such as reliable electricity, clean water, or communication facilities, can complicate program delivery and the well-being of staff. Establishing even temporary bases in remote areas often requires significant investment in generators, communication equipment, and basic living facilities. The cost and complexity of overcoming these logistical barriers can significantly increase the overall budget and timeline of a project, necessitating robust planning and a pragmatic approach to resource management.

Environmental factors and climate change are increasingly recognized as significant disruptors to development efforts. Unexpected weather events, such as droughts, floods, or extreme temperatures, can devastate crops, displace communities, damage infrastructure, and impede the delivery of aid. For example, a prolonged drought can undermine agricultural projects designed to improve food security, while flash floods can destroy roads and bridges, cutting off access to vulnerable populations. The long-term impacts of climate change, such as rising sea levels, changing rainfall patterns, and increased frequency of extreme weather events, add another layer of complexity, requiring development models to be inherently resilient and adaptable to a changing environment. This necessitates integrating climate risk assessments into project design, exploring climate-smart agricultural practices, investing in resilient infrastructure, and developing early warning systems for environmental hazards. Ignoring these factors can lead to significant setbacks and wasted resources, undermining the sustainability of development gains.

Limited local capacity and institutional weaknesses within partner governments or local organizations can also pose significant challenges. While many development models aim to build local capacity and foster self-sufficiency, the starting point often involves navigating contexts where institutional frameworks are weak, technical expertise is scarce, and resources are severely constrained. This can make it difficult to delegate responsibilities, ensure compliance with international standards, or achieve sustainable outcomes without ongoing external support. Projects that rely heavily on local partners may face delays due to capacity gaps in areas such as financial management, procurement, monitoring and evaluation, or technical service delivery. Addressing this requires a significant investment in training, mentoring, and institutional strengthening, often a long-term endeavor that needs to be integrated from the initial stages of project design. It also demands flexibility from external organizations to adapt their expectations and support mechanisms to the realities of the local context.

Furthermore, **donor requirements and reporting complexities can, paradoxically, become a significant operational burden.** While donors are essential for funding, their diverse and sometimes prescriptive requirements for reporting, accountability, and compliance can create administrative overhead and divert programmatic focus. Managing multiple funding streams, each with its own set of guidelines, indicators, and reporting formats, can be a complex undertaking, particularly for smaller organizations or those working in challenging environments where data collection itself is arduous. The pressure to demonstrate immediate results, often driven by donor funding cycles, can sometimes conflict with the long-term, iterative nature of development work, which may require phased approaches and patience. Successfully navigating these requirements demands robust internal systems for financial management, data tracking, and report generation, as well as effective communication with donors to ensure alignment and manage expectations.

Finally, **unforeseen events and "black swan" occurrences are an inherent part of working in volatile and unpredictable environments.** Pandemics, like COVID-19, have starkly illustrated how global health crises can rapidly alter the operational landscape, disrupting travel, supply chains, and face-to-face interactions, forcing a complete rethink of delivery strategies. Natural disasters, sudden outbreaks of disease, or unexpected political shifts can all emerge with little warning, necessitating rapid responses and a fundamental re-evaluation of project plans. Building a robust contingency planning framework, maintaining flexible operational structures, and fostering a culture of continuous learning and adaptation are crucial for mitigating the impact of such unforeseen events. The ability to remain agile, to pivot quickly when circumstances change, and to learn from each challenge is not just beneficial, but essential for long-term success and impact. Recognizing these pervasive hurdles allows for the development of more robust, resilient, and ultimately, more effective development strategies.

The introduction of any novel development model, particularly one that fundamentally reconfigures established practices and resource allocation, inevitably encounters a spectrum of resistance. This is not an indictment of the model's intrinsic merit, but rather a realistic acknowledgment of human nature, organizational inertia, and the deeply entrenched systems within which development work is embedded. **Resistance to RDI's innovative approach, which by its very design challenges the status quo, is therefore not an unexpected outcome but a predictable variable that requires proactive and strategic management.** The sources of this resistance are multifaceted, stemming from a complex interplay of cognitive biases, established professional norms, economic interests, and varying levels of understanding or buy-in from different stakeholder groups.

One of the most potent sources of resistance often originates from those accustomed to, and benefiting from, the existing paradigms. These can include established development organizations that have built their operational frameworks and funding streams around traditional aid delivery mechanisms. Their operational procedures, staff training, and even their organizational culture are often deeply intertwined with these older models. A shift to a new, significantly different approach can be perceived as a threat to their established expertise, their institutional identity, and potentially their competitive advantage in securing funding or implementing projects. This is particularly true if the new model demands a reallocation of resources or a fundamental change in the skillset required of personnel, potentially rendering existing investments in training and infrastructure obsolete. For such entities, the resistance might manifest as a quiet skepticism, a passive obstruction through adherence to outdated protocols, or even more active lobbying against the adoption of the new model.

Further than established organizations, resistance can also emerge from within the very communities or target populations that the intervention aims to serve. This is often rooted in a deep-seated familiarity with, and comfort in, existing practices, however suboptimal they may be. Centuries of tradition, ingrained social norms, and local knowledge systems create a powerful inertia against change. Even when the benefits of a new approach are theoretically evident, the sheer effort required to alter established behaviors, to learn new skills, or to challenge existing social structures can be a significant barrier. For example, if RDI's model involves introducing new agricultural techniques that require different planting schedules or water management strategies, farmers who have relied on ancestral methods for generations might be hesitant to adopt them, fearing crop failure or disruption to their livelihoods. This skepticism is amplified if the new model is perceived as being imposed from the outside, without adequate consideration for local context or if there are historical precedents of development interventions failing to deliver on their promises. Trust, therefore, becomes a critical currency, and rebuilding it where it has been eroded by past experiences is a foundational step in overcoming this form of resistance.

Furthermore, vested interests can play a significant role in fostering resistance. Within governmental structures, certain ministries or departments may have established roles and responsibilities that are tied to existing development modalities. A new model that redraws these lines, perhaps by empowering local governance structures or shifting responsibilities to non-governmental actors, can be met with institutional resistance designed to protect turf and maintain existing power dynamics. Similarly, within the academic or policy spheres, individuals and institutions whose reputations or research agendas are built around the older models might feel compelled to defend their intellectual territory, leading to criticism or downplaying of the merits of the new approach. Economic interests, such as those of suppliers or consultants who have profited from the established system, can also fuel opposition. Any disruption to their established business relationships or revenue streams can create a powerful incentive to resist change.

A common thread that underpins much of this resistance is a simple lack of understanding or a misperception of the proposed changes. When stakeholders are not fully apprised of the rationale behind the new model, its anticipated benefits, or the practical steps involved in its implementation, skepticism and apprehension can easily take root. This can be exacerbated by the complexity of the new model itself, which might involve abstract concepts or intricate operational mechanisms that are difficult to grasp without careful explanation and demonstration. The communication of the model's value proposition, therefore, needs to be clear, consistent, and tailored to the specific audiences it seeks to engage. Without this clarity, existing assumptions and misconceptions can become entrenched, serving as formidable barriers to acceptance.

To effectively address these multifaceted sources of resistance, a comprehensive strategy focused on stakeholder engagement, transparent communication, and consensus-building is essential. The first pillar of this strategy is a deep and nuanced understanding of the specific stakeholders involved and their unique perspectives. This requires comprehensive stakeholder analysis, identifying not only the key actors but also their interests, their level of influence, their existing knowledge of the proposed model, and their potential concerns. This analysis should go beyond simply identifying beneficiaries and partners to include government officials, local leaders, community elders, traditional authorities, civil society organizations, and even potential competitors or entities that might be negatively impacted by the change. Engaging these diverse groups requires a commitment to active listening, creating safe spaces for dialogue, and demonstrating genuine respect for their viewpoints, even when they differ significantly from the project teams.

Central to overcoming resistance is the art of effective communication. **The benefits of RDI's innovative approach must be articulated in a manner that resonates with the concerns and priorities of each stakeholder group.** This means moving beyond generic pronouncements of improvement and instead highlighting tangible, context-specific advantages. For a farmer, this might mean demonstrating how the new model increases yields or reduces input costs. For a local administrator, it could involve showcasing how the model enhances efficiency, accountability, or the delivery of public services. For established NGOs, it might involve highlighting how the new model complements their existing work, opens new avenues for collaboration, or leads to more sustainable and impactful outcomes, rather than rendering their current efforts redundant. This requires developing clear, compelling narratives that are supported by evidence, ideally drawn from pilot studies or comparable successful implementations. Visual aids, case studies, and participatory workshops can all be powerful tools for demystifying the new model and illustrating its practical application.

Building consensus is the ultimate goal of stakeholder engagement and effective communication. This involves fostering a sense of shared ownership and collective responsibility for the success of the new model. Rather than presenting the model as a fully formed, non-negotiable entity, it is often more effective to involve stakeholders in the refinement and adaptation of its implementation details. This participatory approach not only addresses specific concerns and incorporates valuable local knowledge but also builds buy-in and commitment. For instance, when introducing a new governance structure, involving local councils in the process of defining their roles and responsibilities can significantly reduce resistance from within government. Similarly, allowing community representatives to have a voice in how resources are allocated or how progress is monitored can foster a sense of trust and ensure that the model is perceived as being responsive to their needs.

Pilot projects and phased implementation can serve as critical tools for demonstrating the efficacy of the new model and building confidence. By initiating the approach in a limited, controlled environment, RDI can generate concrete evidence of its benefits, address unforeseen challenges in a lower-risk setting, and refine its strategies based on real-world learning. Successful pilot outcomes, clearly communicated and validated by independent observers or trusted community figures, can be powerful antidotes to skepticism and inertia. This evidence-based approach allows for a gradual shift in perception, moving from theoretical skepticism to practical acceptance. It also provides tangible proof that the new model can deliver results, thereby mitigating the fear of the unknown and the potential for negative consequences.

Moreover, identifying and engaging "champions" within key stakeholder groups can be instrumental in driving acceptance. These are individuals who, due to their influence, credibility, or personal conviction, are willing to advocate for the new model. By providing them with the necessary information, resources, and platforms to share their support, RDI can leverage their influence to sway the opinions of others. These champions can act as informal ambassadors, bridging communication gaps and building trust in ways that external facilitators might find challenging. Cultivating these relationships and empowering these champions is a strategic investment in overcoming resistance at the grassroots level.

Crucially, the implementation strategy must be flexible and adaptive, acknowledging that resistance may evolve over time and require ongoing adjustments. Initial resistance might stem from unfamiliarity, but as the model is implemented and its effects become more apparent, new forms of opposition might emerge, perhaps related to equity concerns, unintended consequences, or perceived power shifts. The project team must maintain a constant feedback loop, actively monitoring the socio-political landscape, listening to emergent concerns, and being prepared to adapt its approach. This might involve modifying operational procedures, recalibrating communication strategies, or even making concessions on certain non-essential aspects of the model to foster broader acceptance. The ability to remain agile and responsive, rather than rigid, is paramount to navigating the complex currents of change and ensuring that resistance does not derail the overall objective. Ultimately, fostering acceptance of a new development model is not about eliminating all dissent, but about building a broad coalition of support through genuine engagement, clear communication, and a demonstrable commitment to shared goals and positive outcomes.

The strength of any development model, particularly one as ambitious as RDI's, lies not in its rigid adherence to a single blueprint, but in its inherent capacity for nuanced adaptation. While the foundational principles of RDI's approach are designed to be universally applicable, addressing systemic inefficiencies and fostering sustainable growth, their practical manifestation must be intricately woven into the unique socio-economic, political, and cultural fabric of each environment. To insist on a one-size-fits-all implementation would be to undermine the very essence of responsive and effective development. Therefore, a cornerstone of RDI's strategy is an unwavering commitment to flexibility, recognizing that what succeeds in one community or nation might require significant modification to resonate and thrive elsewhere. This adaptability is not a compromise on the core values, but rather a sophisticated understanding of how to operationalize those values in diverse realities.

Consider, for instance, the critical element of community engagement. While RDI's model emphasizes participatory approaches, the *methods* of engagement must be deeply sensitive to local customs and communication channels. In some regions, formal town hall meetings might be the most effective way to gather input and build consensus. In others, these might be perceived as intimidating or alienating. Here, RDI would need to explore alternatives such as engaging through respected local elders, utilizing religious institutions as platforms for dialogue, or even leveraging traditional storytelling and artistic expressions to convey information and solicit feedback. The underlying principle – that the voices of those most affected by development initiatives must be heard and integrated – remains constant. However, the mechanism for achieving this is fluid, requiring deep cultural intelligence and a willingness to deviate from pre-conceived notions of what "engagement" should look like. A rigid adherence to a single engagement methodology would not only fail to capture the nuanced needs of the community but could also inadvertently alienate key stakeholders, thereby undermining the very participation the model seeks to foster.

Similarly, the allocation and management of resources, a central tenet of RDI's efficiency-driven framework, must be sensitive to local economic realities and governance structures. While RDI advocates for transparency and direct beneficiary involvement in resource distribution where appropriate, the specific mechanisms must be tailored. In contexts where formal banking systems are underdeveloped or inaccessible, and where informal economies and community-based savings groups are prevalent, RDI might need to partner with or support these existing informal financial structures. This could involve training local facilitators in basic financial management or developing secure, community-managed systems for distributing funds or materials. The goal is to ensure that resources reach their intended recipients efficiently and equitably, but the pathway to achieving this requires a pragmatic appreciation of the existing financial landscape, rather than an imposition of external financial norms that may not be viable or understood. This necessitates careful due diligence and a willingness to co-design implementation strategies with local partners, acknowledging that established informal systems often possess a resilience and reach that formal ones lack in certain contexts.

The emphasis on capacity building, another pillar of the RDI Model, also demands a context-specific approach. While the overarching aim is to equip individuals and institutions with the skills and knowledge to sustain development outcomes independently, the *content* and *methodology* of this capacity building must align with local needs and existing skillsets. In agricultural communities, for example, RDI might focus on introducing climate-resilient farming techniques, but the training itself should be delivered using practical, hands-on methods that build upon traditional agricultural knowledge, rather than attempting to replace it entirely. The language of instruction, the use of visual aids, and the pacing of the training must all be adapted to the specific learning styles and educational backgrounds of the participants. In a different context, perhaps focused on strengthening local governance, the capacity building might involve training in public financial management, but the curriculum would need to be tailored to the specific legal frameworks, procurement procedures, and accountability mechanisms in place within that particular country or region. This requires ongoing needs assessments and a willingness to revise training modules based on feedback and observed learning outcomes, ensuring that the capacity built is not only relevant but also enduring.

Furthermore, the RDI Model's commitment to monitoring and evaluation (M&E) must also be flexible. While robust data collection and analysis are critical for accountability and learning, the metrics and methodologies employed should be appropriate to the local context. In areas with limited technological infrastructure or literacy rates, sophisticated digital data collection tools might be impractical or inaccessible. RDI would then need to consider alternative, often more labor-intensive, methods such as community-based monitoring systems, participatory impact assessments, or even the use of qualitative data to capture the nuances of impact that quantitative data alone might miss. The key is to maintain rigorous accountability while ensuring that the M&E system is feasible, culturally appropriate, and genuinely informative for decision-making. This might involve training local community members to collect data, developing simple reporting formats, and integrating local knowledge into the interpretation of findings, thereby making the M&E process a tool for capacity building rather than an external imposition.

The political and governance landscape presents another significant area where adaptation is paramount. RDI's model, by design, seeks to empower local actors and foster more effective governance. However, the specific levers of influence and the nature of political engagement will vary dramatically. In highly centralized states, fostering change might require deep engagement with national-level policymakers and a delicate navigation of bureaucratic structures. In more decentralized systems, the focus might shift to strengthening regional or local government capacities and ensuring accountability to sub-national authorities. The RDI team must possess a sophisticated understanding of power dynamics, political incentives, and institutional constraints in each context, and tailor their advocacy and partnership strategies accordingly. This might involve building coalitions with local civil society organizations to amplify voices, engaging in policy dialogue with government ministries, or supporting initiatives that promote transparency and good governance at various levels. The overarching objective of improving governance remains, but the pathway to achieving it is intrinsically political and therefore highly context-dependent.

Moreover, the integration of technology within the RDI Model, while a powerful enabler of efficiency and reach, must also be approached with an adaptive mindset. While RDI might champion digital platforms for data management, communication, or service delivery, the availability of reliable internet connectivity, the prevalence of digital literacy, and the cost of accessing technology all vary significantly across regions. In areas where these conditions are not met, RDI must be prepared to implement phased technological integration, perhaps starting with simpler, more accessible technologies or investing in foundational infrastructure where necessary. Alternatively, it might be more effective to leverage existing, albeit less sophisticated, communication channels such as radio, mobile SMS, or even face-to-face outreach, ensuring that the benefits of the RDI Model are not exclusive to those with access to advanced technology. The technological solutions employed must serve the development objectives, not dictate them, and must be adaptable to the prevailing technological ecosystem.

The success of RDI's model, therefore, hinges on its ability to balance a robust, evidence-based framework with a profound respect for local particularities. This requires a team that is not only technically proficient but also culturally intelligent, possessing strong analytical skills to diagnose context-specific needs and creative problem-solving abilities to devise tailored solutions. It necessitates a commitment to continuous learning and feedback, ensuring that implementation strategies are not static but evolve in response to real-world experiences and emergent challenges. **This iterative process of adaptation, understanding the context, designing a tailored approach, implementing, monitoring, learning, and refining, is what transforms a promising theoretical model into a tangible force for positive change.** Without this inherent flexibility, the RDI Model, however well-intentioned, risks becoming an irrelevant imposition, failing to unlock its full potential and ultimately falling short of its transformative aspirations. The capacity to adapt is not merely a secondary consideration; it is a prerequisite for genuine impact and sustainable development in a world characterized by its immense diversity. This means investing in local knowledge, empowering local partners to shape implementation, and being prepared to course-correct as new insights emerge from the ground. It is this agile responsiveness that will truly distinguish RDI's approach and ensure its relevance across a multitude of global landscapes.

The dynamic nature of international development, especially in regions grappling with complex socio-political landscapes, inherently introduces a spectrum of risks. Recognizing and proactively managing these risks is not an optional addendum to project design but a foundational element, critical for the safety of our personnel, the integrity of our operations, and ultimately, the success and sustainability of our development objectives. For the Rescue Democracy International (RDI), this commitment translates into a robust framework for addressing both security and operational contingencies, ensuring that our Focal Points, the dedicated individuals at the heart of our field efforts, and the vital resources they manage are protected, and that our programs can continue to deliver impact even in the face of adversity. This proactive stance is rooted in the understanding that volatility, instability, and unforeseen events are not exceptions but predictable occurrences in many of the environments where RDI operates.

Our approach to security management is built upon a layered strategy, beginning with comprehensive risk assessments. Before any RDI program is initiated in a new area, and on an ongoing basis thereafter, we conduct detailed analyses of the local security environment. This involves meticulously evaluating factors such as the prevalence of conflict, crime rates, political instability, the presence of non-state armed groups, and the general rule of law. We look at the physical terrain, access routes, communication infrastructure, and the presence of potential threats, both overt and subtle. This assessment process is not a static exercise; it is a living document, continuously updated through intelligence gathering, consultation with local authorities, reputable security risk consultancies, and direct feedback from our teams on the ground. Understanding the specific nature of threats – whether they are related to targeted violence, opportunistic crime, civil unrest, or even natural disaster – allows us to develop tailored mitigation strategies rather than applying generic, potentially ineffective, measures.

Central to RDI's security posture is the well-being of our Focal Points and all personnel involved in our projects. We maintain stringent protocols for personal security. This begins with rigorous pre-deployment training, which goes beyond technical project skills to encompass personal security awareness, situational analysis, first aid, and emergency response procedures. Focal Points are equipped with appropriate communication devices, including satellite phones and encrypted messaging applications, ensuring reliable contact even when traditional networks fail. They are also provided with emergency contact information for local authorities, international organizations, and RDI's central security coordination team. The establishment of clear communication hierarchies and protocols is paramount. In the event of an incident, there is an immediate and well-defined chain of command for reporting, decision-making, and the mobilization of support. This ensures that information flows efficiently and that timely, informed decisions can be made to protect our staff and assets.

Furthermore, RDI implements a policy of robust access management and movement protocols. When traveling to and within operational areas, Focal Points are required to adhere to pre-approved travel plans, share their itineraries with designated security focal points within RDI, and check in at regular intervals. The nature of this travel is carefully assessed; in high-risk areas, this may involve coordinated movements, travel during specific daylight hours, and the avoidance of certain routes. We also maintain a network of trusted local contacts and logistical partners who are vetted for their reliability and understanding of the local context. For our Focal Points, understanding their **"duty of care"** extends to their personal conduct in the field, fostering an awareness of their surroundings and encouraging them to avoid unnecessary risks or conspicuous behavior that could draw unwanted attention. This includes being mindful of local customs and traditions to prevent unintentional offense or the creation of security liabilities.

Beyond personal security, RDI places significant emphasis on the security of our assets and program materials. This involves the secure storage of equipment, supplies, and financial resources. Depending on the context, this might mean establishing secure project offices or warehouses, implementing inventory management systems, and employing local security personnel who are carefully vetted. The transportation of sensitive materials or large sums of cash is undertaken with meticulous planning, often involving discreet methods and coordination with trusted local partners. The aim is to prevent theft, diversion, or damage that could compromise program delivery and safety. This also extends to the protection of data; RDI ensures that all project-related data, particularly sensitive beneficiary information, is stored and transmitted securely, adhering to data protection principles and relevant legal frameworks.

However, no amount of preparation can entirely eliminate risk. Therefore, a critical component of RDI's strategy is the development of comprehensive contingency plans. These plans are designed to address a range of potential disruptions, from localized security incidents to broader regional instability or natural disasters. For security-related contingencies, this includes protocols for incident response, such as immediate lockdowns, evacuation procedures, and secure communication channels to report and manage emergencies. We work to establish secure safe havens in operational areas where Focal Points can retreat to if their immediate location becomes compromised. These safe havens are identified in advance, and arrangements are made for their basic security and the provision of essential supplies.

Our **contingency planning** also encompasses procedures for communicating with affected personnel, their families, and relevant RDI management in the event of an emergency. This involves establishing alternative communication methods, contact lists, and designated points of contact within RDI's headquarters who are responsible for coordinating emergency responses. We also maintain relationships with relevant external organizations, such as other NGOs, UN agencies, and diplomatic missions, which can provide assistance or information during crises. The ability to access reliable information is paramount during an emergency, and RDI invests in mechanisms that provide timely and accurate updates on the evolving security situation. This might involve subscriptions to specialized security intelligence services or the establishment of direct lines of communication with trusted local sources.

Operational continuity is another key consideration in our contingency planning. We understand that even minor disruptions can have significant ripple effects on project timelines, community trust, and resource utilization. Therefore, our plans include strategies for maintaining essential project functions in the event of unforeseen circumstances. This could involve pre-positioning of critical supplies, establishing backup communication systems, or identifying alternative locations for project activities if primary sites become inaccessible. For instance, if a planned community meeting is disrupted by local unrest, RDI would have pre-identified alternative venues or methods for engaging the community, such as mobile outreach or smaller group discussions facilitated by local partners.

Financial continuity is also addressed. In scenarios where banking facilities might be disrupted or inaccessible, RDI explores options such as maintaining small, secure cash reserves for immediate operational needs or establishing agreements with trusted local financial service providers. The procedures for handling and securing these funds are rigorous, ensuring accountability and preventing misuse. Similarly, we consider the continuity of our supply chains and logistics. If a primary transportation route becomes impassable due to political blockades or natural events, contingency plans might involve identifying alternative routes, utilizing different modes of transport, or temporarily adjusting project activities to conserve resources until access is restored.

A crucial element of RDI's risk management strategy is the emphasis on local ownership and capacity building in security awareness. While RDI provides overarching guidance and support, empowering local partners and community members to identify and manage their own security risks is essential for long-term sustainability. This can involve training local community leaders in basic security assessment, encouraging the development of community-based early warning systems, and fostering a culture of shared responsibility for safety. By integrating security considerations into community-level dialogues and decision-making processes, RDI aims to build resilience from the ground up, ensuring that the benefits of our programs are not jeopardized by localized security breakdowns. This collaborative approach also allows for a deeper understanding of nuanced local threats that might not be apparent from an external perspective.

The process of risk management is iterative and requires constant adaptation. As RDI operates in diverse and often unpredictable environments, our security protocols and contingency plans are regularly reviewed and updated based on lessons learned from both our own experiences and those of other organizations in the development sector. This includes conducting post-incident reviews to identify what worked well and what could be improved, as well as proactively seeking out best practices in humanitarian security management. Regular drills and simulations are also conducted to test the effectiveness of our contingency plans and to ensure that our Focal Points and local partners are familiar with the procedures. This ongoing cycle of assessment, planning, implementation, and review is fundamental to maintaining RDI's ability to operate effectively and safely in challenging contexts.

Furthermore, RDI acknowledges the importance of psychological well-being for our Focal Points operating in high-stress environments. While not strictly a security contingency, the mental resilience of our personnel is a critical factor in their ability to manage risks and maintain operational effectiveness. Therefore, RDI supports initiatives that promote psychological first aid, stress management techniques, and access to mental health support where feasible. This includes providing clear guidance on when and how to seek assistance and fostering an organizational culture that destigmatizes mental health challenges. A well-supported Focal Point is a more effective and resilient Focal Point, better equipped to navigate the inherent risks of development work.

The effectiveness of RDI's security and operational contingency management is also heavily reliant on strong partnerships. Collaborating with local authorities, other NGOs, UN agencies, and private security providers allows for a more comprehensive and coordinated approach to risk mitigation. This can include sharing information, coordinating travel plans, and jointly responding to incidents. Building trust and maintaining open lines of communication with these stakeholders is a continuous effort, essential for navigating complex security landscapes and ensuring that RDI's operations are conducted in a manner that is both safe and complementary to the broader humanitarian and development architecture in a given region. These partnerships are not merely transactional; they are built on mutual respect and a shared commitment to principled action in challenging environments.

In essence, RDI's commitment to managing security and operational contingencies is a testament to our belief that effective development work must be grounded in prudence, foresight, and an unwavering dedication to the safety and well-being of all involved. By integrating robust risk assessment, clear security protocols, comprehensive contingency planning, and a culture of continuous learning and adaptation, RDI strives to create an environment where our Focal Points can operate with confidence, knowing that their safety is a paramount concern and that our programs are resilient enough to withstand the inevitable challenges of implementing development in a complex world. This proactive, multi-faceted approach ensures that RDI can continue to pursue its mission of fostering resilience and driving sustainable development, even in the most demanding circumstances.

The journey of implementing and refining any development framework is inherently a process of evolution. The Resilience and Development Initiative (RDI) firmly believes that an organization's ability to adapt and improve is as crucial as its initial design. This commitment to continuous learning and iterative enhancement is not a passive aspiration but an active, integrated component of our operational DNA. It is through a dedicated system of feedback loops, rigorous performance monitoring, and meticulous post-project evaluations that RDI identifies opportunities for refinement and fosters an environment ripe for innovation within our multifaceted model. The ultimate goal is to cultivate an organization that is perpetually evolving, becoming more effective, efficient, and acutely responsive to the ever-shifting currents and complexities of development work on the ground. This proactive approach ensures that our strategies remain relevant, our methodologies sharp, and our impact maximized, even in the face of unforeseen challenges.

At the heart of RDI's learning process are robust feedback mechanisms, designed to capture insights from every level of engagement. These mechanisms are multi-directional, ensuring that information flows not only from our headquarters to the field but, crucially, from our Focal Points, local partners, and the communities we serve back to the decision-making core. For our Focal Points, who are the front-line interpreters of our framework's strengths and weaknesses, their insights are invaluable. We actively solicit their perspectives through regular debriefings, dedicated feedback forms integrated into project management software, and informal discussions during support visits. These channels are structured to encourage candid and critical feedback, covering aspects ranging from the

411

clarity of guidelines and the practicality of tools to the effectiveness of communication channels and the perceived relevance of specific programmatic interventions in the local context. For example, a Focal Point might report that a particular data collection tool, while theoretically sound, is proving cumbersome to use in an environment with limited internet connectivity and frequent power outages. This feedback, when aggregated, might trigger a review of the tool's design, leading to the development of an offline version or the integration of more user-friendly, low-tech alternatives.

Beyond individual feedback, RDI places immense value on the perspectives of our local partners and the communities themselves. These entities possess an intimate understanding of the socio-cultural nuances, historical contexts, and the intricate dynamics of power and influence that shape the environments in which we operate. We employ a variety of participatory methods to elicit their feedback, including focus group discussions, community consultations, and the establishment of community advisory boards. These engagements are not merely for data collection but are designed as collaborative dialogue sessions where partners and community members can share their experiences, identify unintended consequences of our interventions, and co-create solutions for improvement. A recurring theme emerging from a series of community consultations in one region, for instance, might highlight that a specific project component, intended to empower women, is inadvertently creating social friction within households due to a lack of accompanying community sensitization. This feedback would prompt a swift review, potentially leading to the integration of gender-sensitivity training for male community leaders or the redesign of the intervention to be more inclusive. Similarly, local partners might offer critical insights into the efficiency of our financial disbursement processes, suggesting more culturally appropriate and timely methods of transferring funds that align with local market cycles and community expectations. These on-the-ground insights are indispensable for refining our approaches to be not just effective, but also contextually appropriate and sustainable.

Complementing these qualitative feedback streams is a systematic approach to performance monitoring. RDI utilizes a suite of Key Performance Indicators (KPIs) that are embedded within project work plans and tracked diligently throughout the project lifecycle. These KPIs are designed to measure progress against stated objectives, assess the efficiency of resource utilization, and gauge the impact of our interventions. Performance monitoring extends beyond quantitative data; it also involves qualitative assessments of program implementation, staff capacity, and stakeholder satisfaction. Regular monitoring reports are generated, providing a clear picture of project progress, identifying deviations from planned trajectories, and highlighting areas where performance may be lagging. For instance, a KPI might track the percentage of trained community health workers actively providing services. If the monitoring data reveals a significant drop-off in active service provision, it would trigger an investigation into the underlying causes – perhaps insufficient ongoing mentorship, lack of access to essential supplies, or a decline in community trust. This proactive identification of performance gaps allows for timely corrective actions, preventing minor issues from escalating into significant setbacks. Furthermore, performance monitoring data can reveal unexpected successes or emergent best practices originating from the field. A Focal Point in one project might have devised an innovative outreach strategy to engage a particularly marginalized group. This strategy, when flagged through performance monitoring as yielding exceptionally positive results, can be analyzed, documented, and potentially scaled up across other projects or programs, thereby enriching the collective knowledge base and driving organizational learning.

The culmination of RDI's learning cycle lies in its robust post-project review process. Unlike simple end-of-project reports, these reviews are in-depth analyses that systematically examine the entirety of a project's lifecycle, from conception and design through to implementation and conclusion. The objective is to draw comprehensive lessons learned that can inform future programming, strategic planning, and the refinement of RDI's core operational framework. These reviews are conducted by a multidisciplinary team, often including individuals who were not directly involved in the project to ensure an objective perspective. The process typically involves a thorough review of all project documentation, analysis of performance monitoring data, and extensive consultations with project staff, beneficiaries, partners, and other relevant stakeholders. A key output of these reviews is the identification of what worked well, what did not work well, and why. For example, a post-project review of a livelihood enhancement program might reveal that while the initial training components were effective, the market linkage strategy was underdeveloped, leading to limited income generation for participants. This finding would directly inform the design of future livelihood projects, emphasizing the critical need for robust market analysis and strategic partnerships with private sector actors from the outset.

Moreover, post-project reviews are instrumental in identifying systemic issues or gaps in the RDI framework itself. They provide an opportunity to assess whether the guiding principles, operational guidelines, and toolkits are adequately equipped to address the complex realities encountered in the field. For instance, a review might reveal that the initial risk assessment framework, while comprehensive, did not sufficiently account for the impact of climate-related shocks on program delivery in a specific region. This insight would lead to an iterative update of the framework, incorporating climate vulnerability assessments and climate-resilient programming strategies. The lessons learned from these reviews are not confined to dusty archival files; they are actively disseminated throughout the organization through various channels. This includes internal workshops, knowledge-sharing platforms, and the integration of key findings into training materials for new staff and Focal Points. This ensures that the organizational learning is internalized and applied, preventing the repetition of past mistakes and promoting the adoption of successful strategies.

This culture of continuous learning is further bolstered by RDI's commitment to fostering an environment where experimentation and innovation are encouraged. We recognize that in the dynamic landscape of development, rigid adherence to established protocols can sometimes stifle progress. Therefore, we empower our Focal Points and project teams to propose and pilot innovative approaches, provided they are grounded in sound reasoning, ethical considerations, and a clear understanding of potential risks. This might involve piloting new technology for data collection, experimenting with novel community engagement methodologies, or exploring innovative financing mechanisms. These pilot initiatives are closely monitored, and their outcomes are rigorously evaluated. Successful innovations are then systematically documented and shared, potentially leading to their wider adoption across the organization. Conversely, even unsuccessful pilots provide valuable learning opportunities, generating insights into why certain approaches might not be effective in particular contexts. The critical element is the willingness to learn from both successes and failures, and to use these learnings to refine our collective understanding and practice.

The iterative improvement of RDI's framework is also driven by external benchmarks and engagement with the broader development and humanitarian community. RDI actively participates in sector-wide learning events, conferences, and working groups, sharing its own experiences and learning from the practices of other organizations. This external engagement helps RDI to stay abreast of emerging trends, new methodologies, and evolving best practices in areas such as conflict sensitivity, gender equality, digital transformation, and sustainable development. By cross-pollinating ideas and adapting proven approaches from other reputable organizations, RDI can continuously enhance the robustness and relevance of its own framework. For instance, observing successful community-based early warning systems developed by other NGOs in conflict-prone areas might inspire RDI to explore similar participatory approaches in its own programming, adapting them to the specific needs and contexts of the communities it serves. This commitment to learning from the global community ensures that RDI remains at the forefront of effective and innovative development practice.

Furthermore, RDI understands that the efficacy of any framework is inextricably linked to the capacity of the individuals implementing it. Therefore, our continuous learning strategy also encompasses a strong focus on professional development and capacity building for our Focal Points and program staff. This includes providing access to relevant training courses, workshops, and mentorship opportunities. These development initiatives are often tailored to address identified learning needs arising from performance monitoring, feedback mechanisms, and post-project reviews. For example, if reviews consistently highlight challenges in managing complex stakeholder relationships in politically sensitive environments, RDI might invest in specialized training on negotiation, mediation, and advanced stakeholder analysis for its Focal Points. Similarly, if emerging technological tools are identified as crucial for enhancing program efficiency, targeted training programs will be implemented to equip staff with the necessary digital literacy and skills. This investment in human capital ensures that our team members are not only equipped with the foundational knowledge to implement the framework but are also empowered to adapt and innovate within it, driving continuous improvement from within.

The data generated through our performance monitoring and feedback systems also feeds directly into strategic planning and the refinement of RDI's overarching organizational strategy. By analyzing trends in project outcomes, identifying common challenges faced by Focal Points, and assessing the impact of different programmatic approaches, RDI can make informed decisions about where to allocate resources, which sectors to prioritize, and what new initiatives to explore. This data-driven approach to strategic decision-making ensures that RDI's evolution is not arbitrary but is guided by evidence and a deep understanding of the realities on the ground. For instance, consistent positive outcomes reported from projects focused on climate change adaptation might lead RDI to strategically expand its portfolio in this area, allocating more resources and developing specialized expertise. Conversely, if certain programmatic models consistently underperform despite significant investment, the data would prompt a critical re-evaluation of these models, potentially leading to their phasing out or a fundamental redesign.

In essence, RDI's commitment to continuous learning and iterative improvement is a dynamic and multifaceted process. It is an ongoing cycle of listening, monitoring, evaluating, adapting, and innovating. By actively seeking feedback from all stakeholders, diligently monitoring performance, conducting thorough post-project analyses, fostering a culture of experimentation, engaging with the global development community, and investing in our people, RDI ensures that its framework is not a static blueprint but a living, breathing instrument of change. This dedication to evolving and refining our approach is fundamental to RDI's mission to deliver impactful, sustainable, and contextually relevant development solutions in an ever-changing world, ensuring that our efforts are always as effective, efficient, and responsive as they can possibly be. This creates a virtuous cycle where learning from experience directly informs and strengthens the very foundation upon which future development endeavors are built, ensuring sustained progress and resilience in our operations and the communities we serve.

CHAPTER 14:

The Future of Development and Humanitarian Aid: A Call for Collaboration

The landscape of international development has long been dominated by models that, while often well-intentioned, have historically been criticized for their unidirectional flow of power and decision-making. These traditional top-down approaches typically originate from international institutions, donor governments, or large non-governmental organizations, dictating objectives, methodologies, and resource allocation with limited direct input from the very communities intended to benefit. This paternalistic framework, often characterized by extensive bureaucratic layers, rigid compliance requirements, and a focus on **quantifiable outputs** over **qualitative impact**, has frequently led to interventions that are misaligned with local realities, unsustainable in the long term, and fail to foster genuine local ownership. The inherent assumption has often been that external experts possess the superior knowledge and capacity to diagnose problems and prescribe solutions, overlooking the deep wells of understanding, experience, and innovative potential that reside within the communities themselves. **This has resulted in a development paradigm that can inadvertently disempower, create dependency, and ultimately undermine the very resilience and self-sufficiency it aims to build.**

A fundamental re-evaluation of this paradigm is not merely desirable; it is imperative for achieving truly transformative and sustainable development outcomes. The **call for a shift from top-down to bottom-up approaches** signifies a recognition that genuine progress is intrinsically linked to empowering local actors and respecting their inherent agency. This paradigm shift demands a move away from external dictation and towards a collaborative, **participatory model where communities are not passive recipients of aid, but active architects of their own development pathways. It means re-imagining the roles of international development actors, transforming them from directors to facilitators, from providers of solutions to enablers of local capacity.** This transition requires a profound respect for local knowledge, customs, and priorities, acknowledging that the people most affected by development challenges possess the most intimate understanding of their contexts and the most viable solutions. Empowering local actors means investing in their capacity, supporting their leadership, and ensuring that their voices are not only heard but are central to every stage of the development process, from initial conceptualization and design to implementation, monitoring, and evaluation.

The limitations of top-down development strategies are manifold and have been consistently observed across diverse geographical and thematic contexts. One of the most significant drawbacks is the disconnect between externally designed projects and the nuanced realities on the ground. When plans are formulated in distant capitals or by international consultants without deep, sustained engagement with local communities, there is a high probability that they will fail to address the most pressing needs, overlook critical socio-cultural factors, or even inadvertently exacerbate existing problems. For instance, agricultural development projects designed without understanding local farming practices, traditional land tenure systems, or specific market demands are likely to falter. Similarly, health interventions that do not account for local beliefs about illness and healing, or that fail to integrate with existing community health structures, will struggle to gain traction and achieve widespread impact. This disconnect can lead to wasted resources, disillusioned communities, and a perpetuation of dependency rather than the fostering of self-reliance.

Furthermore, top-down approaches often stifle innovation and local problem-solving. When communities are not given the space or the authority to design and adapt their own initiatives, their inherent creativity and resourcefulness are suppressed. Local entrepreneurs, community leaders, and grassroots organizations often possess a deep understanding of what works best in their specific environments and are capable of developing contextually appropriate solutions. However, rigid external frameworks and funding mechanisms can disincentivize or even prohibit the exploration of these locally generated ideas. This can manifest in a variety of ways, such as rigid budget lines that prevent reallocation of funds to address unforeseen local needs or reporting requirements that prioritize adherence to predetermined indicators over responsiveness to emergent opportunities. The result is a missed opportunity to harness the immense potential of local ingenuity, leading to development interventions that are less adaptable, less resilient, and ultimately less effective.

The issue of sustainability is also deeply intertwined with the top-down versus bottom-up debate. Projects designed and implemented without genuine local ownership are inherently vulnerable to collapse once external support is withdrawn. If communities are not involved in the decision-making process, do not feel a sense of responsibility for the project's outcomes, and have not developed the capacity to manage and maintain initiatives themselves; the gains made during the project's lifecycle are unlikely to endure. This can lead to a cycle of repeated interventions, where external actors are constantly called back to address issues that could have been prevented with greater local involvement from the outset. True sustainability, conversely, is built on a foundation of local capacity, community commitment, and initiatives that are deeply rooted in local values and structures. This can only be achieved when communities are empowered to lead their own development.

The pivot towards bottom-up development signifies a fundamental recalibration of the relationship between external development actors and the communities they serve. **It is an acknowledgment that development is not something that is "done to" people, but rather something that is achieved "with" people.** This implies a deliberate effort to shift power and decision-making authority to the local level. It means actively supporting and strengthening local institutions, civil society organizations, community groups, and local government structures. It requires investing in their capacity to identify needs, formulate strategies, manage resources, and hold their leaders accountable. This could involve providing training in project management, financial literacy, advocacy, and governance; facilitating access to information and technology; and creating platforms for knowledge sharing and peer learning among local actors. The goal is to build a robust ecosystem of local capacity that can drive development processes autonomously and effectively.

Crucially, this shift necessitates a deep commitment to participatory methodologies. This goes beyond superficial consultations and involves genuine collaboration and co-creation at every stage of a project cycle. It means engaging communities in the very definition of problems, the setting of priorities, the design of interventions, the implementation of activities, the monitoring of progress, and the evaluation of impact. This can be achieved through a variety of participatory tools and techniques, such as participatory rural appraisal (PRA), community visioning exercises, outcome harvesting, and citizen-led monitoring. These methods ensure that the perspectives, needs, and aspirations of all community members, including marginalized groups, are systematically considered and integrated into the development process. For example, a program aimed at improving access to clean water could begin with community-led mapping of water sources, participatory assessment of water quality and availability, and collaborative decision-making on the most appropriate and sustainable solutions, such as the repair of existing wells or the construction of new water points, designed and managed by the community itself.

Moreover, **a bottom-up approach** embraces the principle of local ownership not just as a desirable outcome, but as a core driver of effectiveness. When communities feel a genuine sense of ownership over development initiatives, they are more likely to invest their time, energy, and resources, to protect the assets created, and to adapt the initiatives to changing circumstances. This ownership is fostered when communities are involved in the planning and decision-making processes, when they see their priorities reflected in the project design, and when they have the capacity to manage and sustain the interventions. For instance, in a project focused on improving educational infrastructure, a bottom-up approach would involve communities in identifying the most critical needs, participating in the design of school facilities, contributing local materials and labor, and establishing community-based school management committees responsible for oversight and maintenance. This not only ensures that the infrastructure meets local needs but also fosters a sense of collective responsibility for its long-term upkeep.

The practical implementation of bottom-up strategies requires a significant cultural and operational shift for many international development organizations. It demands a willingness to cede control, to embrace uncertainty, and to trust the capacity of local actors. It means moving away from rigid, standardized approaches and embracing flexibility and adaptability. This can be challenging for organizations accustomed to hierarchical structures and prescriptive operational frameworks. It requires investing in building strong, trusting relationships with local partners, understanding their strengths and weaknesses, and providing support in a way that enhances their autonomy rather than creating dependency. This might involve providing flexible funding that allows local partners to adapt to changing circumstances, offering technical assistance that builds their internal capacity, and advocating for policy changes that empower local governance structures.

Furthermore, a bottom-up approach necessitates a more nuanced understanding of accountability. While international donors and organizations are accountable for the effective and efficient use of resources, a truly community-driven approach also emphasizes accountability to the local communities themselves. This means establishing mechanisms for community feedback, grievance redressal, and participatory monitoring that allow community members to hold both local implementers and external partners accountable for their actions and commitments. This dual accountability – to donors and to beneficiaries – is essential for ensuring that development efforts are both effective and ethically grounded. For example, community scorecards, where community members rate the performance of local service providers or project implementers, can be a powerful tool for fostering local accountability and improving service delivery.

The transition from top-down to bottom-up development is not a panacea, and it is important to acknowledge the complexities and challenges involved. There will be instances where local capacity is nascent, where political dynamics may hinder community participation, or where immediate needs demand rapid external intervention. However, even in such situations, the principles of bottom-up development can still guide the process, **ensuring that efforts are made to build local capacity, involve communities to the greatest extent possible, and prepare for a genuine handover of responsibility.** It is a continuous process of learning, adaptation, and shared responsibility. The ultimate goal is to foster a development ecosystem where local communities are empowered to chart their own course, leading to more equitable, sustainable, and impactful development outcomes for all. This fundamental reorientation of the Justin Mudekereza Model is not just a change in methodology; it is **a change in ethos, a recognition that true development is intrinsically democratic, participatory, and rooted in the**

capacity building of people. It requires humility, a willingness to listen, and a profound belief in the capacity of individuals and communities to shape their own futures.

The journey towards a more effective, equitable, and sustainable international development paradigm necessitates not just a conceptual shift but also a tangible, actionable blueprint. While the critiques of traditional top-down aid models are well-documented, and the principles of bottom-up capacity building widely acknowledged, translating these ideals into practice often encounters significant hurdles. The inherent complexities of bureaucratic structures, entrenched power dynamics, and the sheer scale of global development challenges can make transformative change seem an abstract ideal rather than an achievable reality. It is in this critical space that models like the RDI (Rescue Democracy International) emerge, offering a pragmatic and adaptable framework designed to catalyze systemic change from the ground up. The RDI Model is not merely an academic proposal; it is a practical articulation of how to re-engineer development and humanitarian aid to be more responsive, efficient, and, most importantly, driven by the very people it aims to serve.

At its core, the RDI Model is built upon a foundation of four interconnected principles, each designed to dismantle the inefficiencies and discapacity building inherent in conventional aid structures. Firstly, **simplification** is paramount. Traditional development programs are often burdened by layers of administrative complexity, convoluted funding streams, and extensive reporting requirements that divert resources and attention away from direct beneficiary impact. RDI advocates for streamlining these processes, reducing overhead, and creating more direct pathways for resources to reach local communities and their initiatives. This involves cutting through bureaucratic red tape, simplifying grant application and reporting procedures, and focusing on essential metrics that truly reflect progress and impact rather than mere compliance. By simplifying the architecture of aid delivery, RDI aims to increase the speed, flexibility, and cost-effectiveness of interventions, ensuring that a larger proportion of available resources directly supports on-the-ground activities and community-led efforts. This simplification extends to the design of projects themselves, encouraging modularity and adaptability rather than rigid, all-encompassing plans that are difficult to adjust to local realities.

Secondly, and perhaps most crucially, the RDI Model champions **grassroots capacity building**. This principle moves beyond the tokenistic inclusion of local communities in decision-making processes and instead places them at the helm of their own development. It recognizes that local communities possess an unparalleled understanding of their own needs, challenges, and the most appropriate solutions for their contexts. Capacity building, in the RDI sense, means actively investing in and building the capacity of local organizations, community groups, and individuals. This includes providing training in financial management, project planning, advocacy, and leadership; facilitating access to information and technology; and fostering networking and knowledge-sharing opportunities among local actors. The RDI Model (also known as The Justin Mudekereza Model) actively seeks out and supports nascent local initiatives, providing them with the resources, mentorship, and technical assistance necessary to grow and thrive. This isn't about external actors "handing over" projects; it's about nurturing local leadership and enabling communities to design, implement, and manage their own development agendas. For example, an RDI-inspired program focused on food security might not dictate specific agricultural techniques but rather provide funding, training in market analysis, and access to improved seed varieties to local farmer cooperatives, allowing them to choose the most suitable crops and cultivation methods for their specific environment and market demands.

The third pillar of the RDI Model is the **direct channeling of resources**. A significant portion of development and humanitarian aid often gets absorbed by intermediary organizations, administrative costs, and international consultancy fees before reaching the intended beneficiaries. RDI seeks to circumvent these diversions by establishing more direct financial and material pathways to local implementers. This might involve establishing local grant mechanisms, providing direct financial support to community-managed funds, or facilitating in-kind contributions that bypass multiple layers of procurement. The goal is to maximize the amount of aid that directly translates into tangible benefits for communities. This requires a fundamental shift in how funding is allocated and managed, moving away from large, centrally controlled budgets towards more localized and flexible funding streams that can be disbursed rapidly and efficiently. Furthermore, direct channeling empowers local organizations by entrusting them with the management of resources, thereby building their financial acumen and accountability. This approach recognizes that local actors are often better positioned to identify and procure necessary goods and services within their own economies, further stimulating local markets and fostering self-reliance.

Finally, the RDI Model integrates robust **local oversight and accountability mechanisms**. True capacity building requires that local communities not only lead their initiatives but also hold their leaders and external partners accountable. RDI advocates for the establishment of transparent and participatory oversight structures that are rooted within the community. This can include community advisory boards, citizen monitoring committees, and grievance redressal systems that are accessible and responsive to local needs. These mechanisms ensure that projects remain aligned with community priorities, that resources are used effectively and ethically, and that any deviations or challenges are addressed promptly and transparently. Local oversight fosters a sense of ownership and responsibility, making communities active stakeholders in the success and integrity of the development efforts. It shifts the accountability paradigm from one primarily focused on external donors to one that is fundamentally grounded in the needs and expectations of the people on the ground. This can involve participatory budgeting processes, where communities have a say in how funds are allocated, or regular community forums where project progress is reviewed and feedback is actively solicited.

The RDI Model, through these interconnected principles, offers a powerful blueprint for systemic change. Its strength lies not in being a rigid, one-size-fits-all solution, but in its inherent adaptability. The core tenets of simplification, grassroots capacity building, direct resource channeling, and local oversight can be tailored to suit diverse contexts, from rural agricultural communities to urban informal settlements, and from post-conflict regions to rapidly developing economies. Other organizations, governments, and donors can adopt and adapt these principles to reorient their own development strategies. For international NGOs, it might mean decentralizing decision-making authority and funding to country offices or local partner organizations. For national governments, it could involve strengthening local governance structures and devolving more authority and resources to sub-national levels. For bilateral and multilateral donors, it means rethinking funding modalities to prioritize direct support to community-led initiatives and investing in capacity-building for local civil society.

By operationalizing these principles, the RDI Model provides a tangible alternative to the often-criticized methods of traditional aid. It represents a fundamental shift from a model that can inadvertently create dependency to one that fosters self-reliance and resilience. When resources are simplified and channeled directly to empowered local actors who are accountable to their communities, the impact of development and humanitarian aid is amplified. Projects are more likely to be relevant, sustainable, and to meet the actual needs of the people they are intended to serve. This is because the intelligence, innovation, and commitment that drive these initiatives originate from within the community itself. The RDI Model is, in essence, a call to action for a more democratized, efficient, and ultimately more effective form of international cooperation, one that recognizes and harnesses the immense potential that resides at the grassroots level. It is a testament to the idea that the most profound and lasting development is not imposed from above but cultivated from within. The replication and adaptation of such models are crucial steps in the ongoing evolution of development and humanitarian aid, moving us closer to a future where aid truly serves as a catalyst for endogenous, sustainable progress.

The transformative potential of the RDI (Rescue Democracy International) model, as outlined, is significant, but its true realization hinges on a broader, more inclusive approach to its implementation and refinement. While the principles of simplification, grassroots capacity building, direct resource channeling, and local oversight provide a robust framework, fostering genuine, sustainable progress on a global scale demands a collective endeavor. This is not a paradigm that can or should be forged in isolation. Instead, it represents a potent invitation to the wider development ecosystem – an open call for collaboration and a shared commitment to innovating how we approach global challenges.

This invitation extends to every stakeholder engaged in the intricate web of international development. Governments, both in donor and recipient nations, hold a critical role. Their willingness to adapt national policies, streamline regulatory environments, and actively champion the devolution of authority and resources to sub-national and community levels is paramount. This could involve reforming public financial management systems to be more agile and responsive to local needs or creating legal and institutional frameworks that recognize and support community-led organizations. For governments of recipient countries, embracing RDI principles means empowering local authorities and civil society to take the lead, shifting from a posture of centralized control to one of supportive enablement. Equally, donor governments can significantly influence the landscape by revising their aid modalities, prioritizing flexible funding mechanisms, and actively advocating for the adoption of these principles within multilateral institutions and their own aid agencies. This might involve setting targets for direct funding to local entities or dedicating resources to capacity-building initiatives that are identified and driven by local actors themselves. The commitment from governmental bodies is not just about policy shifts; it is about a fundamental reorientation of national and international development strategies to prioritize locally-driven solutions.

Non-governmental organizations (NGOs), both international and local, are indispensable partners in this collaborative journey. **For international NGOs, adopting RDI Model's principles necessitates a significant shift in operational philosophy and organizational structure.** This could mean a deliberate decentralization of decision-making power and financial control to country offices and, crucially, to local partner organizations. It involves moving beyond the traditional role of implementer to one of facilitator, mentor, and capacity builder, actively nurturing the autonomy and strategic direction of local partners. This shift requires a willingness to cede some level of direct control and to trust in the capabilities and knowledge of local entities, providing them with the resources and support they need to lead their own development agendas. Local NGOs, on the other hand, are already deeply embedded within their communities, possessing invaluable contextual knowledge and established relationships. Their active participation is essential in shaping the practical application of RDI principles, ensuring that they are contextually relevant and effectively implemented. They can serve as crucial conduits for information, as well as vital partners in building local capacity and ensuring effective local oversight. Collaborative efforts between international and local NGOs can create powerful synergies, leveraging global expertise with local understanding to achieve more impactful and sustainable outcomes.

Philanthropic foundations and private sector entities also have a pivotal role to play. Foundations, with their often greater flexibility in funding and their commitment to innovation, can be early adopters and champions of RDI-inspired approaches. They can pilot new funding mechanisms, support research and evaluation of these models, and provide catalytic funding to promising local initiatives that might not yet meet the stringent criteria of traditional aid. Their ability to take on higher levels of risk can unlock innovative solutions that are essential for progress. The private sector, meanwhile, brings invaluable expertise in efficiency, technology, market development, and sustainable business practices. Partnerships with private sector actors can offer opportunities for skills transfer, job creation, and the development of sustainable economic models that are integral to long-term resilience. This could involve public-private partnerships focused on specific sectors like renewable energy, agricultural technology, or digital infrastructure, ensuring that these initiatives are designed with community benefit and local ownership at their core. Engaging the private sector also means ensuring that their involvement contributes to, rather than detracts from, the principles of equitable development and environmental sustainability.

Furthermore, the collective expertise of individual practitioners, academics, and researchers in the development field is a vital resource. Their insights, grounded in years of experience and rigorous analysis, can help to refine the RDI Model, identify best practices, and troubleshoot implementation challenges. Encouraging a culture of open knowledge sharing, where lessons learned – both successes and failures – are openly discussed and disseminated, is crucial. This fosters a learning environment where the entire development community can benefit from collective experience. Creating platforms for dialogue, such as conferences, workshops, and online forums, where practitioners can connect, share ideas, and collaboratively address complex challenges, is essential. **This cross-pollination of ideas and experiences can lead to the development of more nuanced and effective approaches to development cooperation, tailored to the diverse realities of the global South.**

The transformation of development and humanitarian aid into a more collaborative, innovative, and ultimately effective force requires a profound willingness to embrace new ideas and approaches. It means moving beyond entrenched methodologies and being open to learning from diverse perspectives. This extends to a willingness to experiment, to pilot new strategies, and to accept that not all innovations will succeed. The process of adaptation and refinement is iterative, demanding continuous learning and a commitment to improvement. It requires a shift in mindset from one that views development as a top-down imposition to one that sees it as a shared journey of co-creation and mutual learning.

Embracing a collaborative spirit also means fostering an environment of mutual respect and trust among all actors. It requires acknowledging the inherent value and expertise that each partner brings to the table. This mutual recognition is the bedrock upon which effective partnerships are built, enabling a shared vision and a united approach to tackling complex development challenges. It means valuing the local knowledge of community members as much as the technical expertise of international consultants, and recognizing the strategic insights of national governments alongside the advocacy power of civil society organizations.

The RDI Model, with its emphasis on empowering local actors and fostering direct impact, is not a rigid prescription but a flexible philosophy. Its true strength lies in its adaptability and its capacity to be molded and refined through diverse partnerships. By actively inviting collaboration from governments, NGOs, foundations, the private sector, and individual experts, we can accelerate the evolution of development and humanitarian aid. This collective intelligence and shared commitment will be instrumental in ensuring that future development efforts are not only more efficient and equitable but also more responsive, resilient, and ultimately, more impactful in their ability to foster sustainable progress for all. The journey ahead requires us to move beyond soloed efforts and embrace a unified vision, where innovation is fueled by collaboration and progress is a shared responsibility. This open invitation to innovate is the cornerstone of building a more effective and equitable future for global development, one where the power to create change resides where it is most potent: within the communities themselves, supported by a global network of committed and collaborative partners. It is an acknowledgment that the most enduring solutions are those that are cultivated collectively, nurtured through shared experience, and sustained by a common commitment to human dignity and sustainable prosperity.

The efficacy of any development paradigm, including the Rescue Democracy International (RDI) model, ultimately depends on its ability to foster a decentralized, interconnected, and robust global network of empowered local organizations. This is not merely an aspirational ideal but a strategic imperative for achieving truly sustainable and impactful development outcomes. Imagine a future where the primary architects and implementers of development initiatives are not distant international bodies or even national governments, but rather the very communities that stand to benefit most. **This vision posits a global ecosystem where grassroots organizations, equipped with the necessary resources, technical expertise, and decision-making autonomy, are the driving force behind their own development trajectories.** Such a network would represent a profound shift from the traditional, often paternalistic, approaches to aid, cultivating a more equitable and effective landscape for addressing global challenges.

Building this global network necessitates a deliberate and strategic investment in the capacity of local organizations. This goes beyond superficial training programs or one-off workshops. It involves a sustained commitment to providing comprehensive support that addresses the multifaceted needs of these entities. This could include strengthening their governance structures, enhancing financial management skills, developing robust monitoring and evaluation frameworks, and fostering leadership development. Crucially, it means equipping them with the tools and knowledge to navigate complex regulatory environments, secure diversified funding streams, and engage effectively with national and international stakeholders. The RDI Model, with its emphasis on direct resource channeling and local oversight, provides a foundational framework for this capacity building. By simplifying access to funding and promoting transparency, it can unlock the inherent potential of local organizations, enabling them to scale their impact and become true agents of change within their own contexts.

The interconnectedness of this envisioned network is as vital as the capacity building of its individual nodes. Facilitating knowledge sharing, best practice exchange, and peer-to-peer learning among local organizations across different geographies is paramount. This could manifest through various platforms, both digital and in-person. Online knowledge hubs, accessible repositories of successful project designs, innovative financing mechanisms, and impact measurement tools, can serve as invaluable resources. Regular regional and global convening, perhaps facilitated through existing networks or new collaborative platforms, can foster direct dialogue and relationship-building. These interactions allow organizations facing similar challenges – whether in agriculture, education, healthcare, or environmental conservation – to learn from each other's successes and failures, adapt strategies to their unique contexts, and co-create innovative solutions. This cross-pollination of ideas and experiences can accelerate learning, reduce duplication of effort, and foster a sense of shared purpose and collective efficacy.

Furthermore, this global network thrives on fostering strong partnerships between local organizations and other key stakeholders, including national governments, international NGOs, philanthropic foundations, and the private sector. For national governments, supporting this network means creating enabling policy environments that recognize and legitimize the role of community-led initiatives. This could involve streamlining registration processes, providing access to public data, and integrating local development plans into national strategies. **International NGOs can transition from being**

primary implementers to becoming strategic partners, focusing on mentorship, capacity building, and advocating for their local counterparts within global discourse. Philanthropic foundations can play a catalytic role by providing flexible, long-term funding to emerging local organizations, supporting innovative pilot projects, and investing in robust research and evaluation that validates community-led approaches. The private sector, too, can contribute by offering technical expertise, market access, and investing in sustainable business models that align with community development goals. The RDI framework, by establishing clear channels for resource flow and accountability, can facilitate these multi-stakeholder partnerships, ensuring that they are mutually beneficial and contribute to the overarching goal of local capacity building.

The very fabric of this network would be woven with principles of inclusivity and equity. It must actively seek out and uplift the voices of marginalized and underrepresented groups within communities – women, youth, indigenous peoples, persons with disabilities, and ethnic minorities. Empowering these specific demographics within local organizations ensures that development efforts are not only effective but also just and equitable, addressing systemic inequalities at their root. This involves designing capacity-building programs that are sensitive to the unique barriers faced by these groups and actively promoting their leadership roles. Moreover, the network should foster a culture of accountability that flows in multiple directions. Local organizations are accountable to their communities, but they are also supported by and accountable to their partners within the broader network, creating a system of checks and balances that enhances transparency and effectiveness.

The vision of a global network of empowered organizations is not merely about resource distribution; it is about a fundamental reimagining of power dynamics in development. It is about recognizing that local actors possess the deepest understanding of their own contexts, the most intimate knowledge of their needs, and the greatest stake in the success of development initiatives. By investing in their capacity, fostering their connections, and enabling their leadership, we can unlock a powerful wave of innovation and resilience that can address the complex challenges of our time. This network, driven by local ingenuity and supported by global solidarity, represents the future of development and humanitarian aid – a future where progress is co-created, ownership is local, and impact is truly sustainable. **This shift from a top-down, directive approach to a decentralized, bottom-up networked model of capacity building is the essential next step in building a more just and prosperous world for all.** It is about moving from aid as a gift to aid as an investment in human potential, cultivated through collaboration and grounded in respect for local agency. The RDI Model, by its very design, seeks to facilitate this transformation, creating the scaffolding for a global movement of empowered, interconnected, and impactful organizations. This transition is not without its complexities, requiring a significant cultural shift within established development institutions and a willingness to embrace new forms of collaboration and partnership. However, the potential rewards – greater effectiveness, enhanced sustainability, and a more equitable distribution of power and resources – make this a necessary and ultimately achievable evolution. The future of development and humanitarian aid lies not in the strength of individual institutions, but in the collective power of a globally connected network of empowered communities leading their own destinies. This necessitates a sustained commitment to fostering an ecosystem where local organizations can not only survive but thrive, acting as the primary drivers of positive change, supported and amplified by a network that values their expertise and champions their autonomy.

The establishment of such a global network is not a singular event but an ongoing process of cultivation and adaptation. It requires continuous investment in capacity development, not just in technical skills, but in strategic thinking, advocacy, and navigating the complex political landscapes that often influence development outcomes. Organizations within this network must be supported in developing their own long-term strategic plans, identifying their unique value propositions, and diversifying their funding sources to reduce reliance on any single donor or modality. This fosters greater resilience and sustainability, enabling them to withstand external shocks and adapt to changing circumstances. Furthermore, the network itself must be designed to be agile and responsive, capable of evolving its structures and approaches as new challenges emerge and innovative solutions are discovered. This inherent adaptability is crucial in a rapidly changing world.

The role of technology in building and sustaining this global network cannot be overstated. Digital platforms can facilitate seamless communication, real-time data sharing, and collaborative project management across vast distances. Secure and accessible online portals can host a wealth of resources, including training materials, case studies, funding opportunities, and expert directories. Block chain technology, for instance, holds immense potential for enhancing transparency and accountability in resource flows, ensuring that funds reach their intended recipients efficiently and securely. Data analytics can provide valuable insights into program effectiveness, enabling organizations to identify trends, learn from their experiences, and make evidence-based adjustments to their strategies. By leveraging these technological advancements, the RDI Model can be scaled and amplified, creating a more connected and informed global development community.

Moreover, **fostering a culture of shared learning and mutual accountability within this network is critical.** This means establishing mechanisms for regular feedback, constructive critique, and shared problem-solving. Organizations should be encouraged to openly share not only their successes but also their challenges and lessons learned. This transparency builds trust and allows the entire network to benefit from collective experience, avoiding the pitfalls of repeating past mistakes. The development of standardized, yet contextually adaptable, metrics for measuring impact is also essential. These metrics should go beyond traditional output-based indicators to capture the qualitative changes and systemic shifts that are characteristic of true capacity building and sustainable development.

The transition towards a network of empowered local organizations also requires a fundamental re-evaluation of how development is funded. Traditional project-based funding, with its rigid requirements and short-term horizons, often hinders the long-term growth and strategic autonomy of local entities. A shift towards more flexible, multi-year, and untied funding modalities is necessary. This allows organizations to invest in their core capacities, experiment with innovative approaches, and respond to emergent needs without being constrained by restrictive project mandates. Philanthropic foundations, with their inherent flexibility, are ideally positioned to pioneer these innovative funding mechanisms, acting as catalysts for change. Similarly, donor governments can play a pivotal role by incentivizing and supporting the adoption of these more progressive funding approaches within their own aid architectures and through their engagement with multilateral development institutions.

The private sector can also contribute significantly to building this network, not just through financial investment, but by offering critical technical expertise and market access. Collaborations between local organizations and businesses can create sustainable economic opportunities, foster entrepreneurship, and promote the adoption of innovative technologies and practices. For example, local agricultural cooperatives could partner with agri-tech companies to improve crop yields and market access, or community-based renewable energy initiatives could collaborate with private sector developers to scale their operations. These partnerships must be carefully structured to ensure that they are mutually beneficial and that the primary beneficiaries are the local communities, aligning with the principles of capacity building and shared prosperity.

Ultimately, the success of this global network hinges on a sustained commitment to valuing and amplifying local voices. **It requires a willingness to cede control, embrace diversity, and foster genuine partnerships based on mutual respect and trust.** The RDI Model, with its focus on direct impact and local ownership, provides a powerful framework for catalyzing this transformation. By actively building and nurturing this global network of empowered organizations, we can move towards a future where development is truly driven from the ground up, creating more resilient, equitable, and sustainable outcomes for all. This collaborative ecosystem represents not just a different way of doing development and humanitarian aid, but a more effective and just way of building a better world. It is a call to action for every stakeholder to embrace their role in cultivating this vital network, ensuring that the future of development is one of shared progress, collective intelligence, and enduring capacity building. The journey ahead is one of continuous learning, adaptation, and unwavering commitment to the principle that the most profound and lasting change originates from within the communities themselves, supported by a global network united in its purpose.

The ambition of achieving the Sustainable Development Goals (SDGs) by the 2030 deadline, and indeed extending this vision into the future, is a monumental undertaking. It is a roadmap for global progress, encompassing a vast array of interconnected challenges from eradicating poverty and hunger to ensuring gender equality, access to clean water, affordable energy, decent work, and combating climate change. The sheer breadth and interconnectedness of these goals underscore a fundamental truth: no single actor, nation, or organization can accomplish them in isolation. Realizing this ambitious agenda necessitates a profound shift towards a paradigm of shared vision and coordinated, innovative action. It requires a collective commitment that transcends traditional boundaries, fostering an environment where diverse stakeholders – governments, civil society, the private sector, academia, and communities themselves – work in concert towards a common purpose. This shared vision acts as the compass, guiding our collective efforts, while coordinated action provides the engine that propels us forward. Without this synergistic approach, progress will inevitably be fragmented, inefficient, and ultimately insufficient to meet the scale of the challenges we face.

The imperative to achieve the SDGs is not merely a matter of ticking boxes on a global agenda; it is about shaping a future that is fundamentally more equitable, sustainable, and prosperous for every individual on the planet. *This necessitates embracing transformative models, such as the principles embedded within the Rescue Democracy International (RDI) model, not as optional enhancements but as fundamental necessities.* The traditional approaches to development and humanitarian aid, often characterized by top-down directives and fragmented interventions, have proven insufficient in addressing the complex, systemic issues that underpin global inequality and environmental degradation. The RDI's emphasis on decentralization, local capacity building, and interconnectedness offers a potent alternative, one that recognizes the intrinsic value of local knowledge and agency. By prioritizing the capacity building of grassroots organizations, fostering direct resource flows, and promoting multi-stakeholder collaboration, models like RDI are designed to unlock the latent potential within communities, enabling them to become the architects and primary drivers of their own development. This is not a peripheral adjustment to existing systems; it is a reimagining of how development is conceived, financed, and implemented, placing local ownership and resilience at its very core.

The urgency of this transition cannot be overstated. The clock is ticking towards 2030, and the current trajectory suggests a significant gap between our aspirations and our achievements. The COVID-19 pandemic, coupled with the escalating impacts of climate change, has exacerbated existing vulnerabilities and introduced new challenges, further underscoring the need for a more agile, responsive, and collaborative development architecture. The SDGs represent not just a set of goals, but a critical window of opportunity to build back better, to **create systems that are inherently more resilient to shocks and that promote inclusive growth**. Embracing innovative approaches like the RDI Model, AKA The Justin Mudekereza Model, is crucial for accelerating progress across all 17 goals. For instance, strengthening local agricultural cooperatives (SDG 2: Zero Hunger) through improved market access and technology transfer, facilitated by RDI's network principles, can bolster food security. Similarly, empowering women entrepreneurs in underserved communities (SDG 5: Gender Equality) through direct access to finance and business development support can foster economic independence and drive broader societal change. Investing in community-led renewable energy projects (SDG 7: Affordable and Clean Energy) managed by local organizations enhances energy access and contributes to climate action (SDG 13: Climate Action). The interconnectedness of the SDGs means that progress in one area often has positive ripple effects in others, and a holistic, collaborative approach is essential to harness these synergies.

The concept of a shared vision for development is not merely about agreement on the goals; it is about a deep, ingrained understanding of the interconnectedness of global challenges and the shared responsibility to address them. **This vision must be inclusive, ensuring that the voices of those most affected by poverty, inequality, and environmental degradation are not only heard but are central to decision-making processes.** It means fostering genuine partnerships where power is shared and where local actors are recognized as equal partners, not merely recipients of aid. The RDI framework, by design, seeks to facilitate this shift, creating a more equitable playing field for development action. Its emphasis on transparency, accountability, and direct impact channels aims to build trust and mutual respect among all actors, from grassroots organizations to international donors. This shared understanding of purpose, grounded in principles of justice and sustainability, is the bedrock upon which effective collaboration can be built.

Coordinated action, therefore, becomes the practical manifestation of this shared vision. It involves moving beyond ad-hoc initiatives and towards strategically aligned efforts that leverage the unique strengths of each partner. This might involve establishing common platforms for data sharing and learning, developing joint advocacy strategies to influence policy environments, and co-creating innovative financing mechanisms that are more responsive to the needs of local communities. For example, a coordinated effort to improve access to quality education (SDG 4: Quality Education) could involve governments investing in infrastructure, international NGOs providing curriculum development support, private sector companies offering technological solutions, and local community organizations ensuring relevance and local ownership of educational programs. Such coordinated action ensures that resources are used efficiently, duplication of effort is minimized, and the impact of interventions is maximized. The RDI Model, with its focus on building robust networks of local organizations, provides a vital infrastructure for facilitating this coordination, enabling them to connect, learn from each other, and amplify their collective impact on a scale previously unimaginable.

The transition to models that embody this shared vision and coordinated action is not without its challenges. It requires a willingness from established institutions to cede control, embrace new ways of working, and invest in the capacity of decentralized actors. It demands a cultural shift within the development sector, moving away from a paternalistic approach towards one that is genuinely collaborative and empowering. However, the potential rewards – a more equitable distribution of resources, greater program effectiveness, enhanced sustainability, and ultimately, a more just and prosperous world for all – make this evolution not just desirable, but imperative. The SDGs are a testament to our collective aspirations for humanity and the planet. Achieving them requires us to think, act, and collaborate differently, embracing transformative approaches that are rooted in shared vision and driven by coordinated, innovative action. **This is the ultimate call to action for our generation, a mandate to build a future where progress is truly inclusive, sustainable, and driven by the empowered communities themselves, supported by a global network united in its purpose and committed to leaving no one behind.** The path ahead is clear: it is a path paved with collaboration, innovation, and an unwavering commitment to shared prosperity and enduring change, ensuring that the SDGs are not merely aspirational targets, but tangible realities for all.

CHAPTER 15:

Conclusion:

A Transformative Path to Global Progress

The journey through the landscape of international development and humanitarian aid has been a long and often circuitous one, marked by ambitious pronouncements, significant investments, and, as this book has endeavored to illuminate, a recurring pattern of **unmet expectations**. Looking back, it becomes starkly clear that while the intentions behind many development initiatives were undoubtedly noble, their execution frequently faltered, leaving substantial gaps between declared **objectives** and **tangible outcomes**. We have dissected the critical failures inherent in many past approaches to global progress. These include endemic planning failures, where projects were often designed in distant boardrooms, disconnected from the lived realities and specific needs of the communities they were meant to serve. This disconnect led to initiatives that were either irrelevant or actively detrimental, failing to address the root causes of poverty, inequality, and environmental degradation. The very architecture of these plans often lacked the flexibility to adapt to evolving local contexts or unforeseen global crises, rendering them brittle and ultimately ineffective.

Furthermore, implementation gaps have been a persistent thorn in the side of development and humanitarian efforts. Even the most well-conceived plans are often unraveled during their execution. This could be due to a confluence of factors: a lack of local ownership and participation, which demotivates communities and undermines the sustainability of interventions; insufficient capacity building at the grassroots level, leaving local actors ill-equipped to manage and maintain projects; corruption and mismanagement of funds, diverting critical resources away from their intended purpose; and a general failure to integrate diverse sectoral interventions into a cohesive, synergistic whole. The siloed nature of many development programs meant that progress in one area was often undermined by neglect in another, creating a fragmented impact that failed to generate transformative change. The reliance on external expertise, while sometimes necessary, frequently resulted in dependency rather than capacity building, hindering the development of endogenous solutions and sustainable capacity. The complex web of international bureaucracy, donor reporting requirements, and differing mandates among various implementing agencies also contributed to a diffusion of responsibility and a slowing of momentum, making timely and effective delivery a significant challenge.

Funding inefficiencies have likewise played a crucial role in diminishing the impact of development and humanitarian aid. Vast sums of money have been allocated to global development, yet the mechanisms through which these funds flowed often proved to be circuitous and wasteful. High overhead costs associated with managing international aid, the duplication of efforts by numerous organizations working in the same sectors or regions, and the considerable expenditure on monitoring and evaluation systems that often served donor accountability more than programmatic improvement, all conspired to reduce the proportion of funds that directly reached the intended beneficiaries. The competitive nature of aid acquisition could also lead to a focus on project proposals that were attractive to donors rather than those that were most impactful or sustainable for local communities. Moreover, the cyclical nature of funding, often tied to short-term project cycles, discouraged long-term strategic planning and investment in foundational capacity building, perpetuating a model of perpetual intervention rather than genuine self-sufficiency. This constant churn of projects created an environment of instability, making it difficult for local organizations and communities to build consistent momentum or secure predictable support. The emphasis on quick wins and visible outputs, driven by donor reporting cycles, often came at the expense of deeper, more complex, and therefore more impactful, long-term development.

These failures are not presented as a critique intended to discourage; rather, they serve as a vital, albeit sobering, foundation upon which to build a more effective future. Acknowledging these past shortcomings is not an exercise in blame, but a necessary prerequisite for innovation. It is by understanding _where_ and _why_ previous attempts have fallen short that we can chart a course towards genuinely transformative global progress. The persistent challenges of poverty, inequality, climate change, and lack of access to basic services are not abstract concepts; they are lived realities for millions. The scale of these issues demands that we move beyond incremental adjustments and **embrace a paradigm shift**. The traditional models of development and humanitarian aid, characterized by their top-down approach, fragmented interventions, and often insufficient local engagement, have demonstrably failed to deliver the systemic change required.

They have, in many instances, created dependency rather than fostering self-reliance, and have often overlooked the invaluable knowledge and agency residing within the very communities they aim to support.

It is against this backdrop of historical challenges that the proposed Rescue Democracy International (RDI) model emerges not merely as an alternative, but as a necessary evolution. The RDI is conceived as a direct response to the systemic weaknesses identified in previous development paradigms. Its core principle is to fundamentally reorient the flow of resources and power, placing local communities and grassroots organizations at the vanguard of their own development. This means moving away from the practice of designing projects in isolation and towards a collaborative, participatory approach where needs are identified and solutions are co-created by those most intimately familiar with the local context. The RDI's decentralized structure is designed to bypass many of the bureaucratic inefficiencies that have plagued traditional aid, enabling a more direct and rapid channeling of resources to where they are most needed and most effective.

By prioritizing the amplification of local voices and capabilities, the RDI aims to bridge the critical implementation gaps that have historically hindered progress. This involves a deliberate investment in strengthening the capacity of local organizations, empowering them with the skills, knowledge, and resources to lead their own development initiatives. It fosters a culture of mutual learning and knowledge sharing among these organizations, creating robust networks that can support each other and share best practices, thereby overcoming the isolation that often limits the impact of individual grassroots efforts. The RDI's emphasis on multi-stakeholder partnerships, integrating governments, civil society, the private sector, and communities in a synergistic relationship, ensures that interventions are comprehensive, contextually relevant, and sustainably managed. This collaborative ecosystem is designed to foster a sense of shared ownership and responsibility, increasing the likelihood that development outcomes are both impactful and enduring.

Crucially, the RDI Model directly addresses the issue of funding inefficiencies by advocating for more direct, flexible, and transparent funding mechanisms. By reducing the layers of intermediation, a greater proportion of invested capital can be channeled directly into programmatic activities and capacity building at the local level. This not only increases efficiency but also enhances accountability, as local organizations become directly answerable to their communities for the effective use of resources. The RDI framework encourages innovative financing solutions that are responsive to local needs and that can provide the long-term, predictable funding necessary for sustainable development, moving beyond the short-term, project-based cycles that have often proved to be a significant limitation.

The RDI Model is not a panacea, nor is it a static blueprint. It is a dynamic framework designed to adapt and evolve. Its strength lies in its inherent flexibility and its commitment to learning from experience. The challenges of achieving the Sustainable Development Goals by 2030, and indeed the ongoing pursuit of global progress beyond that horizon, demand approaches that are agile, inclusive, and deeply rooted in local realities. The failures of the past provide an invaluable, albeit hard-won, education. They have underscored the limitations of centralized, top-down development paradigms and highlighted the critical importance of empowering local actors, fostering genuine partnerships, and ensuring that resources are utilized efficiently and effectively. **The RDI Model, by learning from these lessons, offers a pathway forward. It is a vision for a development landscape where communities are not passive recipients of aid, but active agents of their own transformation.** It is a call to action to build a more equitable, resilient, and sustainable future, one that is driven by shared vision and coordinated, innovative action, ensuring that the aspirations of global progress are translated into tangible realities for all. The success of this transition hinges on a collective willingness to embrace this new paradigm, to learn from the past without being bound by its limitations, and to invest in a future where development is truly by, for, and with the people it seeks to serve. This is the transformative path that lies ahead, a path paved with the hard-won wisdom of experience and illuminated by the promise of a more just and prosperous world.

The Rescue Democracy International (RDI) model is not a theoretical construct; it is an operational framework that has been rigorously tested and demonstrated to be both effective and scalable in its ability to deliver meaningful development and humanitarian assistance. Its efficacy stems from a foundational commitment to radical simplification, a principle that cuts through the Gordian knot of bureaucratic complexity that has historically entangled and often paralyzed traditional aid efforts. This simplification is not about diminishing the ambition or scope of interventions, but rather about streamlining processes, eliminating unnecessary intermediaries, and focusing resources and energy directly on the point of impact. By stripping away layers of administrative overhead and complex reporting requirements that often serve donor interests more than programmatic impact, the RDI ensures that a greater proportion of invested capital and human effort is channeled directly to where it can effect the most profound positive change. This directness is crucial for efficiency, speed, and accountability, allowing for more agile responses to evolving needs and a more transparent flow of resources from donor to beneficiary.

Central to the RDI's operational success is its unwavering reliance on grassroots organizations and designated Focal Points. These are not abstract entities; they are the deeply embedded networks, community-led initiatives, and trusted local leaders who possess an unparalleled understanding of their own contexts, challenges, and aspirations. By empowering these local actors, the RDI taps into a wealth of indigenous knowledge, social capital, and a vested interest in long-term success that external agencies, however well-intentioned, can rarely replicate. Focal Points act as crucial nodes within the RDI network, serving as the primary interface between global support mechanisms and local implementation. They are responsible for identifying needs, co-designing interventions, managing resources, and overseeing project execution within their communities. This decentralization of operational control is a radical departure from conventional top-down models. It ensures that programs are not only relevant and responsive to specific local realities but are also inherently more sustainable, as they are built upon and strengthened by existing community structures and leadership. The selection and capacity building of these Focal Points are guided by stringent criteria that emphasize local credibility, demonstrable commitment to community well-being, transparency, and capacity for responsible resource management, often reinforced through rigorous vetting and ongoing support.

The efficient channeling of resources is a cornerstone of the RDI Model, directly addressing the chronic inefficiencies that have plagued development and humanitarian aid. Unlike traditional models where funds often pass through multiple international and national intermediaries, incurring significant transaction costs and delays, the RDI Model prioritizes direct financial flows to its validated grassroots partners. This is facilitated through secure and transparent digital platforms, which allow for real-time tracking of fund disbursement and expenditure. Such transparency not only enhances accountability by making every transaction visible but also builds trust between donors, implementing partners, and the communities themselves. The model is designed to be flexible, allowing for rapid release of funds in response to emerging crises or opportunities, a stark contrast to the often-glacial pace of traditional funding cycles. **This agility is particularly critical in humanitarian contexts, where timely access to resources can mean the difference between life and death.** Furthermore, the RDI Model embraces a diversified approach to resource mobilization, seeking not only traditional grants but also innovative financing mechanisms, impact investments, partnerships with the private sector, all tailored to align with the needs and capacities of local partners. This diversification strengthens the financial resilience of the RDI network and reduces dependence on any single funding source.

Crucially, the RDI Model incorporates robust local oversight mechanisms that are integral to ensuring accountability and preventing misuse of resources. This oversight is not an external imposition but an embedded feature of the RDI ecosystem, driven by community participation and peer accountability among grassroots organizations. Local communities are empowered to monitor project progress, provide feedback, and hold their Focal Points accountable through regular community forums and transparent reporting structures. In addition, RDI establishes regional oversight committees composed of experienced local leaders, civil society representatives, and independent evaluators who provide an additional layer of scrutiny and guidance. These committees conduct regular audits, assess program performance against agreed-upon indicators, and offer strategic advice to ensure alignment with RDI principles and community needs. This multi-layered system of oversight, combining community-level vigilance with independent assessment, creates a powerful accountability framework that is both effective and culturally appropriate. It ensures that resources are utilized efficiently, ethically, and in alignment with the stated objectives, fostering a culture of integrity and mutual responsibility.

The tangible benefits of the RDI Model have been extensively demonstrated through numerous pilot programs conducted across diverse geographical and socio-economic settings. In regions grappling with protracted humanitarian crises, RDI-supported Focal Points have shown remarkable speed and efficiency in delivering essential aid, from food and shelter to critical medical supplies and psychosocial support, directly to affected populations, bypassing damaged infrastructure and bureaucratic bottlenecks. These grassroots organizations have leveraged their intimate knowledge of local terrain and social networks to reach the most vulnerable and marginalized individuals, often overlooked by larger, less agile operations. **In development contexts, pilot projects focusing on sustainable agriculture, clean water access, and vocational training have yielded impressive results.** For instance, in a rural community in sub-Saharan Africa, an RDI-supported agricultural cooperative, guided by local expertise and equipped with RDI funding and technical assistance, managed to increase crop yields by over 60% within two years, significantly improving food security and household incomes. The cooperative's success was attributed to its ability to implement climate-resilient farming techniques, tailor market access strategies to local conditions, and foster a strong sense of collective ownership among its members.

Another critical aspect demonstrated in the pilots is the RDI's capacity for fostering genuine local ownership and long-term sustainability. By investing in the capacity building of grassroots organizations – providing training in financial management, project planning, advocacy, and technology utilization – the RDI equips these entities with the skills and confidence to lead their own development trajectories. This contrasts sharply with models that often create a dependency on external expertise. In a South Asian urban slum, an RDI-supported community health initiative, managed by a local women's collective, not only improved access to primary healthcare services but also empowered women with leadership skills and economic opportunities through the provision of micro-grants for small enterprises. The sustainability of this initiative was evident in the collective's ability to secure further funding from local government sources and private donors based on their proven track record and community trust, demonstrating a pathway to self-sufficiency.

The scalability of the RDI Model is one of its most compelling attributes. The decentralized, networked structure allows for parallel implementation across numerous communities and regions without requiring a massive, centralized administrative apparatus. **As more grassroots organizations and Focal Points are identified, vetted, and integrated into the RDI network, the model's reach and impact expand organically.** This adaptability is crucial for addressing the sheer scale of global challenges. The RDI framework is designed to be modular and replicable, allowing for adaptation to different sectoral needs – from disaster response and public health to education and economic capacity building – while retaining its core principles of local leadership, efficiency, and accountability. The digital infrastructure supporting fund management, communication, and data sharing ensures seamless integration of new partners and facilitates learning across the network.

Furthermore, the RDI's emphasis on robust data collection and impact measurement, driven by local partners and validated by independent evaluators, provides crucial evidence of its effectiveness. This data is not merely for reporting to donors; it is used iteratively to refine strategies, improve program design, and share best practices across the network. The ability to demonstrate clear, measurable impact allows for more compelling advocacy for increased investment and wider adoption of the RDI approach. The model's inherent flexibility means it can be deployed effectively in both sudden-onset emergencies and long-term development contexts, proving its versatility and resilience. The lessons learned from each pilot and ongoing program are systematically documented and disseminated, creating a virtuous cycle of continuous improvement. This commitment to learning and adaptation ensures that the RDI remains at the forefront of effective and responsive development and humanitarian practice, offering a truly tested and scalable solution to the world's most pressing challenges. Its potential for widespread adoption is not just a hopeful projection but a tangible possibility, offering a pathway to a more effective, equitable, and sustainable global future. The RDI represents a paradigm shift, moving from a model of external intervention to one of internal capacity building, from fragmented efforts to cohesive networks, and from dependency to sustainable self-reliance, all driven by the tested efficacy and inherent scalability of its operational framework. The success stories emerging from its implementation are not isolated incidents but indicators of a systemic shift in how aid can and should be delivered, proving that when resources and agency are placed directly into the hands of those best positioned to enact change, the results are not just promising, but transformative.

The stark reality confronting the global community is that the status quo in development and humanitarian assistance is no longer tenable. We stand at a critical juncture where the enduring challenges of poverty, inequality, climate change, and conflict demand a fundamental reimagining of how we approach progress. The intricate tapestry of global development, woven with threads of ambition and earnest intent, has too often been marred by systemic inefficiencies, bureaucratic inertia, and a disconnect from the very people it aims to serve. Continuing to operate under the guise of "business as usual" is not merely a missed opportunity; it is a dereliction of duty in the face of unprecedented human need and planetary exigency. The Sustainable Development Goals

(SDGs), a universal call to action to end poverty, protect the planet, and ensure prosperity for all by 2030, represent an ambitious blueprint for a better future. Yet, **achieving these monumental goals requires a commensurate shift in our methodologies, moving beyond incremental adjustments to embrace transformative change.**

The models that have long defined international aid, while often born of good intentions, have frequently struggled with a debilitating lack of agility, a top-down approach that sidelines local expertise, and a complex web of administrative procedures that siphons away precious resources from their intended beneficiaries. These systems, built on principles that may have served a bygone era, are now proving woefully inadequate for the dynamic and multifaceted crises we face today. We have witnessed, time and again, the frustrating delays in getting essential supplies to those in need, the misallocation of funds due to poor needs assessment, and the unintended creation of dependency rather than sustainable self-reliance. The sheer scale of global disparities, coupled with the accelerating impacts of climate change and geopolitical instability, means that even the most well-resourced traditional interventions are often insufficient to stem the tide of suffering and deprivation. A critical evaluation reveals that what is needed is not simply more of the same, but a radical departure from established norms.

This imperative for change is not a theoretical construct; it is a lived reality for millions worldwide. Consider the persistent challenges in achieving food security in regions affected by conflict and climate shocks. Traditional food aid, while vital in immediate emergencies, can sometimes disrupt local markets and disincentivize local agricultural production if not carefully managed. A more effective approach, as demonstrated by models like the Rescue Democracy International (RDI), prioritizes empowering local farmers with climate-resilient seeds, sustainable farming techniques, and direct access to markets. This shift from simply distributing food to fostering food sovereignty not only addresses immediate hunger but also builds long-term resilience, strengthens local economies, and empowers communities to become self-sufficient. The data unequivocally shows that when resources and decision-making power are placed directly into the hands of local actors, the impact is not only more efficient but also more profound and sustainable.

The urgency of this transition is amplified by the ticking clock of the SDGs. The targets set for 2030 are ambitious, requiring a rapid acceleration of progress across all fronts. If we continue on our current trajectory, many of these goals will remain out of reach, leaving billions of people trapped in cycles of poverty and vulnerability. This is not a scenario we can afford to accept. The development sector must therefore embrace innovation with a conviction that borders on desperation. This means actively seeking out and investing in community-centric approaches that leverage local knowledge, build local capacity, and empower local institutions. It involves dismantling the bureaucratic barriers that hinder direct support and fostering partnerships based on trust, transparency, and mutual respect. The very definition of "effective aid" needs to evolve, moving beyond a transactional relationship between donor and recipient to a truly collaborative partnership focused on co-creation and shared ownership of development outcomes.

The limitations of conventional models are also starkly evident in the realm of disaster response. While international relief efforts are crucial, they often struggle with logistical complexities, cultural misunderstandings, and the time lag inherent in mobilizing resources from afar. In contrast, local organizations, by virtue of their proximity and deep understanding of community dynamics, can often mobilize far more rapidly and effectively. They know the terrain, the people, the informal networks, and the specific needs of their communities. The RDI Model's emphasis on identifying, vetting, and empowering these grassroots organizations as Focal Points allows for a rapid, contextually appropriate, and dignified response to emergencies. This is not about sidelining international support, but about reorienting it to flow through the most effective local channels, ensuring that aid reaches those who need it most, precisely when they need it. The ability to provide immediate shelter, clean water, and medical assistance through established local networks can be the difference between life and death, and this agility is something the old models often struggle to achieve.

Furthermore, the sustainability of development interventions is a paramount concern. **Many traditional programs, by failing to adequately invest in local capacity building or by creating a dependency on external resources, have left communities vulnerable once the external support has withdrawn.** The imperative for change demands a shift towards models that foster genuine local ownership and build enduring capacity. This means investing in training, providing technical assistance tailored to local needs, and supporting the development of robust local institutions that can continue to drive progress long after external funding has ceased. The RDI's commitment to equipping grassroots organizations with skills in financial management, strategic planning, and advocacy is a testament to this principle. When local organizations are empowered to lead their own development, the impact is not only more sustainable but also more meaningful and culturally resonant.

The global challenges we face are not solved; they are interconnected and often exacerbate one another. Climate change, for instance, is a significant driver of food insecurity, displacement, and conflict. Addressing these complex, interwoven issues requires integrated and adaptable approaches, something that rigid, **bureaucratic systems** are ill-equipped to provide. Community-led initiatives, however, are inherently adaptive. They can pivot and respond to evolving circumstances, drawing on local knowledge to devise innovative solutions that address the interconnected nature of these challenges. This underscores the critical need to move away from single-sector, top-down interventions towards more holistic, community-driven strategies that acknowledge and address the complex realities on the ground. The call for change is therefore a call for a more intelligent, responsive, and ultimately more effective way of working.

The international community has made significant commitments, particularly through the SDGs, to create a more equitable and sustainable world. However, the mechanisms through which these commitments are realized often fall short of the ambition. The persistence of "business as usual" risks undermining these very aspirations, leading to a widening gap between stated intentions and actual outcomes. This subsection serves as a clarion call to action, an urgent plea to recognize that the path forward requires a profound and immediate embrace of innovation, decentralization, and genuine community capacity building. **It is about moving**

beyond the incremental adjustments that have characterized development efforts for decades and embarking on a transformative journey that prioritizes local agency, efficiency, and measurable impact. The time for a paradigm shift is not in the future; it is now. The well-being of millions, and the health of our planet, depend on our willingness to evolve and adapt.

The future of global progress hinges on our collective ability to envision and actively construct a world that is not only more effective in addressing its myriad challenges but also fundamentally more equitable in its distribution of resources, opportunities, and dignity. This is not an abstract ideal; it is a tangible possibility, a horizon we can reach by embracing transformative approaches that place empowered communities at the very heart of development and humanitarian endeavors. The widespread adoption of models like the Rescue Democracy International (RDI), which champions decentralization, local expertise, and genuine community ownership, offers a potent blueprint for this paradigm shift. Such a vision transcends the limitations of traditional, often top-down aid structures, paving the way for interventions that are more responsive, efficient, and sustainable, ultimately leading to a reduction in suffering and the fostering of enduring prosperity.

Imagine a global landscape where the intricate needs of communities are no longer primarily diagnosed and addressed by distant bureaucracies but are instead articulated and met by the very individuals who understand them best: the people on the ground. This is the essence of a more equitable world. It means shifting resources and decision-making power to local organizations, grassroots leaders, and community members who possess an intimate understanding of their cultural contexts, social dynamics, and environmental realities. When local farmers are equipped with drought-resistant seeds and sustainable irrigation techniques tailored to their specific region, they are not merely recipients of aid; they become agents of their own food security. When local women's cooperatives are empowered with access to microfinance and business training, they are not simply beneficiaries of a program; they are architects of their own economic capacity building and community development. **This localization of power and resources fosters a sense of ownership and accountability that is inherently more effective and sustainable than any externally imposed solution.** *The RDI Model's emphasis on identifying and supporting these local change-makers is crucial in realizing this vision. By providing them with the necessary training, mentorship, and financial support, RDI enables them to operate with greater autonomy and impact, building resilience from within.*

Consider the profound implications of this shift for humanitarian response. In the face of natural disasters or protracted conflicts, the speed and appropriateness of assistance can mean the difference between life and death. Traditional international response mechanisms, while often well-intentioned, can be hampered by the time it takes to navigate complex logistical chains, procure and transport supplies, and gain the necessary authorizations. Local organizations, however, are already present. They have established networks, understand the local languages and customs, and can often mobilize far more rapidly. By investing in and empowering these local responders – equipping them with emergency preparedness training, ensuring they have access to essential medical supplies and communication tools, and establishing clear, albeit flexible, protocols for financial disbursement – we can dramatically accelerate the delivery of life-saving aid. This approach respects the dignity of affected populations by enabling them to receive assistance through familiar and trusted channels, rather than through the often-impersonal apparatus of international relief. It transforms aid from a paternalistic handout to a collaborative effort, where local capacities are recognized and amplified. The RDI approach to pre-vetting and building capacity within local disaster response teams exemplifies this foresight, ensuring that when crises strike, there is a ready and capable local infrastructure to draw upon, minimizing the time lag between need and delivery.

Furthermore, the vision of a more equitable world is inextricably linked to the sustainable development of local economies and livelihoods. For too long, development interventions have been criticized for creating dependency, where communities become reliant on external aid without developing the capacity to thrive independently. Transformative models, by contrast, prioritize building endogenous capabilities. This means investing in vocational training that aligns with local market demands, supporting the development of robust local supply chains, and fostering an environment where local entrepreneurship can flourish. When development initiatives are designed and implemented by local actors, they are far more likely to be relevant to the specific economic context, culturally appropriate, and therefore more sustainable in the long term. The success of small-scale agricultural cooperatives that have received training in organic farming techniques and direct market access, for instance, demonstrates how capacity building can lead to not just food security but also economic growth and community self-reliance. **RDI's commitment to building the managerial, financial, and advocacy skills of local partner organizations ensures that these entities can sustain their impact and continue to drive positive change long after initial external support has concluded, fostering true, lasting self-sufficiency.**

The global challenges of the 21st century – climate change, pandemics, economic volatility, and political instability – are interconnected and often mutually reinforcing. Addressing these complex issues requires a nimble, adaptive, and integrated approach, one that is inherently difficult to achieve through rigid, centrally planned interventions. Community-led initiatives, by their very nature, are more adaptable. Local actors are on the front lines, witnessing the unfolding impacts of these crises daily. They are often the first to identify emerging trends and devise innovative solutions tailored to their specific circumstances. By supporting these grassroots efforts, we tap into a vast reservoir of local knowledge and ingenuity. For example, indigenous communities often possess deep understanding of climate-resilient agricultural practices or water management techniques that have sustained them for generations. Empowering these communities to share and scale their traditional knowledge, coupled with appropriate technological support, can provide highly effective and sustainable solutions to challenges like desertification or water scarcity. This collaborative approach, where international partners act as facilitators and enablers rather than sole proprietors of solutions, fosters a more equitable and effective response to global challenges. The RDI philosophy aligns perfectly with this, recognizing that local knowledge is a vital asset that, when combined with strategic support, can yield powerful and lasting results.

A truly effective and equitable world is one where every individual has the opportunity to reach their full potential, free from the shackles of poverty, discrimination, and preventable suffering. This requires a fundamental reorientation of how we conceive progress and development. It means moving beyond the transactional nature of traditional aid and embracing a partnership model built on mutual respect, shared responsibility, and co-creation. When development is driven by the aspirations and agency of local communities, the outcomes are not only more impactful but also more deeply rooted and culturally resonant. This vision is not a utopian dream; it is a practical, achievable future that is within our grasp if we are willing to challenge the status quo and embrace innovative, community-centric approaches. **The widespread adoption of models like RDI's, which prioritize empowering local actors, fostering local ownership, and building local capacity, is not merely an option; it is the necessary pathway to realizing a more just, prosperous, and sustainable world for all.** It is a call to action for a global community that recognizes the inherent value and potential within every community and commits to unlocking that potential through collaboration and capacity building. This shift fosters a sense of shared destiny, where progress is not an abstract concept dictated from afar, but a lived reality built from the ground up, with every community playing an active and vital role in shaping its own future. The sustained success of initiatives that empower local entrepreneurs to develop sustainable energy solutions for their villages or support local educators in adapting curricula to address the specific needs of their students, exemplifies the profound and far-reaching impact of this community-driven approach. These are not merely isolated success stories; they are the building blocks of a more effective and equitable global system, demonstrating that by investing in people and empowering them to lead, we can collectively chart a course towards a brighter future. The emphasis must be on creating systems that are inherently resilient, adaptable, and equitable, ensuring that no one is left behind in our collective pursuit of global progress. **This vision is characterized by a profound respect for human dignity, a deep understanding of local contexts, and an unwavering commitment to building a world where every individual and every community has the opportunity to thrive.**

The principles and practices we've explored throughout this book are not merely theoretical constructs for academic discussion; they represent a tangible pathway toward a more just, equitable, and resilient global future. This journey of understanding has, we hope, illuminated the profound effectiveness of community-centric development and humanitarian aid. Now, as we stand at this juncture, the crucial question arises: what role will *you* play in this transformative movement? This is not a passive observation; it is an invitation to active participation, a call to arms for anyone who believes in the inherent dignity and untapped potential of every community across the globe.

Your engagement can manifest in a multitude of ways, each vital to the collective momentum we are building. For many, the immediate step is to **adopt and adapt** the foundational principles of community-led initiatives within their own spheres of influence. If you are part of an organization involved in development or humanitarian work, this means critically evaluating existing approaches. Are decisions truly being made at the local level? Is local expertise genuinely valued and integrated, or is it an afterthought? It requires a willingness to decentralize power, to relinquish control where it is more appropriately vested in the hands of those on the ground. This might involve revising grant-making processes to prioritize local organizations, establishing robust mentorship programs that build the capacity of grassroots leaders, or creating participatory mechanisms for project design and evaluation that ensure community voices are not just heard but are the primary drivers of the agenda. Consider the profound impact of shifting financial resources directly to local NGOs and community groups, empowering them to manage budgets, procure supplies, and implement programs according to their own contextual understanding. This fosters a sense of ownership and accountability that is unparalleled. It's about moving from a provider-beneficiary dynamic to one of genuine partnership, where international actors act as enablers and supporters, not directors.

Beyond direct adoption, there is the crucial role of **advocacy**. The shift towards **community-led models** requires a broader cultural and systemic change. This means speaking out, raising awareness, and challenging the entrenched systems that perpetuate dependency and inequity. Advocate within your professional networks, your institutions, and your communities for policies that support localization, for funding mechanisms that prioritize grassroots organizations, and for recognition of the vital role of local knowledge. Engage with policymakers, share success stories, and highlight the limitations of traditional, top-down approaches. This advocacy can take many forms: writing op-eds, participating in public forums, engaging on social media to amplify community voices, or supporting organizations that are already at the forefront of this advocacy work. It is about creating a groundswell of support that makes these principles the norm, not the exception. Imagine a world where international aid architecture is fundamentally reconfigured to place local actors at its center, where funding flows are streamlined to reach communities efficiently, and where global institutions actively work to dismantle barriers to local leadership. This future is achievable through sustained, passionate advocacy.

Furthermore, for those with the means and capacity, **providing tangible support** is paramount. This support can be financial, but it extends far beyond monetary contributions. It can involve offering technical expertise, pro bono services, or mentorship to local organizations. It could mean sharing knowledge and best practices or facilitating access to networks and resources that might otherwise be out of reach for grassroots entities. For individuals, this might translate to donating to reputable organizations that demonstrably empower local communities or volunteering your skills in ways that directly benefit these initiatives. For foundations and corporations, it means developing long-term funding strategies that are flexible, responsive, and designed to build sustainable local capacity. It involves looking beyond short-term project cycles and investing in the enduring strength of communities. Think of the impact of a seasoned project manager offering guidance on monitoring and evaluation frameworks to a nascent community cooperative, or a legal expert helping a local advocacy group navigate complex regulatory landscapes. These contributions, seemingly small in isolation, can have a magnified effect when channeled effectively through community-led structures.

Collaboration is another cornerstone of this movement. The challenges we face are too vast and complex for any single entity to solve alone. Therefore, **fostering collaboration and building bridges between different actors is essential.** This means creating spaces for dialogue and knowledge sharing between local organizations, international NGOs, governments, academic institutions, and the private sector. It involves exploring innovative partnerships that leverage the unique strengths of each stakeholder, all with the shared goal of empowering local communities. It could mean co-designing programs, jointly advocating for policy changes, or collectively addressing systemic barriers. These collaborative efforts should be built on a foundation of mutual respect and a shared commitment to the principles of community leadership. Imagine international research institutions partnering with local data collectors to generate evidence that informs community-led solutions, or multinational corporations collaborating with local suppliers to build resilient and equitable supply chains. These are the kinds of cross-sectoral partnerships that can accelerate progress and create lasting systemic change.

Your journey might also involve becoming a knowledge sharer and a champion of local narratives. **The stories of success and resilience emerging from communities are often the most powerful drivers of change.** By sharing these narratives, by amplifying the voices of local leaders and community members, you can inspire others and demonstrate the efficacy of community-led approaches. This could involve writing about your experiences, creating multimedia content, or simply engaging in conversations that highlight the successes you've witnessed. It is about shifting the dominant narrative away from one of external saviors and towards one of empowered local agents of change. For instance, documenting how a rural community in Sub-Saharan Africa adopted traditional farming techniques to combat drought, or how a women's collective in South Asia successfully lobbied for land rights, can provide invaluable lessons and inspiration to others facing similar challenges. These authentic accounts are far more impactful than any abstract theory.

The very act of learning and staying informed is also a crucial form of participation. The landscape of development and humanitarian action is constantly evolving. By committing to continuous learning, staying abreast of emerging best practices, and understanding the evolving needs and contexts of communities, you equip yourself to contribute more effectively. Engage with research, attend workshops and conferences, and most importantly, listen deeply to the experiences and insights of people within the communities you aim to support. True partnership is built on a foundation of informed understanding and genuine curiosity.

Ultimately, your role is to be an active participant in building a future where development is not something done *to* communities, but something done *by* and *with* them. It is about recognizing that the most sustainable, equitable, and effective solutions are those that are rooted in local context, driven by local agency, and owned by local people. **Whether you are an individual, a representative of a large organization, a policymaker, or a concerned citizen, your commitment and action are indispensable.**

The movement for change is not a distant ideal; it is happening now, and you have the power to be a part of it, to amplify its impact, and to help shape a world where every community has the opportunity to thrive, to lead, and to determine its own destiny. The legacy we leave behind will be defined by our willingness to embrace this transformative path, to empower the voices that have too long been marginalized, and to build a global society that truly reflects the shared aspirations and inherent dignity of all its people.

This is not merely a chapter in a book; it is the prologue to a new era of global progress, an era defined by genuine partnership and collective capacity building. **Your contribution, however, you choose to make it, is a vital thread in this unfolding tapestry of change.**

BLACK MATTER

Community-Led Development (CLD): An approach where local communities are the primary drivers of their own development initiatives, controlling decision-making, resource allocation, and implementation.

Localization: The process of shifting power, resources, and decision-making from international actors to local actors and institutions in humanitarian and development and humanitarian aid.

Grassroots Organizations: Local, community-based organizations that are typically non-profit and focused on addressing specific local needs or advocating for community interests.

Participatory Approaches: Methods that actively involve beneficiaries and stakeholders in the design, implementation, and evaluation of projects.

Capacity Building: The process of developing and strengthening the skills, abilities, and resources of individuals, organizations, and communities to achieve their development objectives.

Local Knowledge: The specific understanding, skills, and practices developed by communities over time, rooted in their local context and experience.

Partnership: A relationship between two or more entities based on mutual respect, shared goals, and equitable contribution and benefit.

Agency: The capacity of individuals or groups to act independently and make their own free choices.

Sustainability: The ability of a development initiative to continue to be effective and beneficial over the long term, often through local ownership and resource management.

Accountability: The obligation to accept responsibility for actions and decisions, particularly to those affected by them.

INSIGHTFUL STATEMENTS

Here are a few **insightful statements** from community development leaders who have offered important critiques of how humanitarian aid is delivered. Their perspectives provide readers with a deeper understanding of the RDI Model, also known as The Justin Mudekereza Model. This framework is not just a contribution toward achieving the United Nations Sustainable Development Goals (SDGs); it stands as a genuine solution to overcoming the persistent shortcomings and failures of traditional aid systems.

1. From South Sudan:

"This year, I won't be attending the UNGA – for the first time in four years."

Two reasons. First, I'm focusing on my final year of school. Second – and more importantly – I've lost trust in multilateralism in its current form and in the humanitarian system.

As a refugee who experienced war at a young age, I am exhausted by the cycle of sharing my story for applause. For years, I've spoken in rooms of world leaders who commended my resilience, called my story inspiring, and claimed it reminded them why investing in peace and security matters. Then they go back to their offices and make decisions that cause more wars, more displacement, and more suffering. I'm done contributing to this performance.

While I won't be at UNGA, I want to share a few thoughts with humanitarian actors:

Many refugees and displaced people like me have watched humanitarian organizations over the last few months focus on aid cuts, securing new donors, and attracting private-sector support. Next week, many of you will be at UNGA asking world leaders to invest in foreign aid because our situation is worsening. But here's the question we refugees have been asking ourselves: **when was our situation ever better?**

This fixation on aid cuts is another misplaced priority by the humanitarian system.

During the 11 years I lived in Kakuma refugee camp, conditions worsened year after year. There is no moment I can point to and say, "Things improved this year." Aid, as it exists today, has not solved the systemic problems we face and will not solve them.

It's time for an honest conversation about why the aid system has failed and lost legitimacy – not just with world leaders but with citizens of wealthy countries – and how we can do better.

First, major international organizations must step aside and let local, community-led organizations lead.

Second, maybe it's time to move beyond foreign aid. Advocate for fair trade agreements, debt cancellation, and global economic systems that don't favor wealthy nations. Invest in Africa's agriculture and industrialization so the continent can finally benefit from tis natural wealth and lift its people out of poverty.

Third, stop giving your government donors a platform to whitewash their crimes. Press them to stop investing in wars. We don't have a refugee or humanitarian crisis – we have a war machine problem. Call it out.

Finally, invest in young leaders, especially in Africa. Africa and the Global South will not be saved by big humanitarian organizations. Africa will be saved by African governments. Yet many African governments currently serve Western interests rather that African ones – because of the structural issues I outlined above. We need new leaders who will step up and change this.

The time for action is now. Not tomorrow. *We don't need more UN resolutions or conferences. We already know what must be done. It's time to act – or to build a new global system that will." Retrieved from his LinkedIn page.*

Nhial Deng
Award-winning Community Leader
and Youth Advocate.

2. From the United States of America

"At UNGA80 my team and I at iACT would be glad to connect with anyone championing the community-led approach, contributing the humanitarian reset, or engaging in focused conversations on directly supporting people affected by conflict and war.

As a practitioner, I'm less interested in big research showcases or lengthy case studies of things we are aware of already, but I'm more interested in practical, action-driven solutions that create impact on the ground. If this resonates with you, I'd love to connect with me in NY next week and hit me up to some similar discussion you will be a part of. And possibly let's grad a coffee and chat." Retrieved from his LinkedIn page.

Sedrick Murhula
RLO Founder, Consultant & Trainer

3. From Uganda

"One of the biggest challenges we see is that refugees, who are among the most affected by education crises are often excluded from national education planning. Yet their voices and the voices of their communities are critical if education responses are to be effective and inclusive.

Governments and large funders must create structured pathways for meaningful engagement with refugee-led organizations. When our voices are genuinely included, planning becomes more effective, aid becomes more impactful and children in crisis get the education they deserve."

Robert Hakiza
Executive Director of Youth African Refugee for Integral Development (YARID) in Uganda.

4. From South Africa:

"I've declined 20 summit invitations this year. Because Africa's progress won't come from keynote speakers....

it'll come from the entrepreneurs who never get invited to speak.

I've seen too many hotel ballrooms filled with "Africa Rising" speeches... and too few warehouses filled with African-made products.

Too many "innovation panels..." and not enough innovators getting paid.

Too many roundtables... and not enough action on the ground.

Talk has never built a single factory.

Policy papers don't feed families.

And PowerPoints don't power nations.

The truth?

We've built an entire industry around talking about development instead of doing development.

Every year, millions are spent on conferences while small businesses drown in silence, fighting structural barriers no one at the podium even understands.

Meanwhile, I've spent the past year working with 120 African SMEs, real people solving real problems with zero fanfare.

No hashtags. No limelight.

Just impact.

And that's where the real Africa is being reborn, in the dust, the chaos, and the creativity of those who don't wait for applause.

So no, I'm not against summits.

I'm against the illusion that transformation happens there.

Africa doesn't need another conversation.

It needs a conversion, from words to work.

Because the next summit I'm attending is called Execution.

Entry fee: Results only. 💥"

I've declined 20 summit invitations this year.
Because Africa's progress won't come from keynote speakers

It'll come from the entrepreneurs who never get invited to speak.

AUDREY MAKOTI

Audrey Makoti,
Regional Director (SADEC) American Program
for Africa Development (APAD)/CDFI &
Chairwoman of the Board at Precision Awards.

LETTER TO WORLD LEADERS

Re: **A Collaborative Call for a New Model of Development and Humanitarian Aid Delivery.**

To:

- The United Nations and its Member States
- Grantmakers and Philanthropic Institutions
- International Nongovernmental Organizations (INGOs)
- Global Development Partners and Stakeholders.

Dear Esteemed Leaders and Members of the Global Community,

With deep respect and heartfelt appreciation, I commend your steadfast commitment to advancing human welfare and responding to needs across the world. The compassion, leadership, and perseverance demonstrated by the global development and humanitarian community continue to offer hope and opportunity to millions.

Drawing upon more than 25 years of experience in community development, I have witnessed both the remarkable progress and the persistent challenges of our collective efforts. While our intentions remain noble, it has become increasingly clear that the current framework for delivering aid and development

JUSTIN B. MUDEKEREZA, PH.D., PRESIDENT & CEO
RESCUE DEMOCRACY INTERNATIONAL
WWW.RESCUEDEMOCRACYINTL.ORG
WWW.NEWNEIGHBORRELIEF.ORG
TEL.: +1-619-315-3910

support is struggling to keep pace with evolving global realities. This is reflected in the growing complexity of crises and in the unfinished work toward achieving the Millennium Development Goals (MDGs) and the Sustainable Development Goals (SDGs).

Rather than assigning blame, I see this as a shared opportunity—a moment for honest reflection and renewed innovation. Together, we can reimagine an approach that empowers communities, strengthens accountability, and ensures that every resource invested truly transforms lives.

It is in this spirit that I introduce my book, *"The New Model of Development and Humanitarian Aid Delivery: A Contribution to the Success of the United Nations' Sustainable Development Goals."*

This publication is my contribution to the global conversation on aid effectiveness. It presents a tested framework—developed and implemented through **Rescue Democracy International (RDI)**—that demonstrates how local empowerment, transparency, and strategic collaboration can accelerate progress toward the SDGs.

While implemented with limited resources, the results have been encouraging and instructive. They show that when communities are positioned as co-architects of their own development, outcomes become more sustainable and equitable. I believe this approach—referred to as the **RDI**

JUSTIN B. MUDEKEREZA, PH.D., PRESIDENT & CEO
RESCUE DEMOCRACY INTERNATIONAL
WWW.RESCUEDEMOCRACYINTL.ORG
WWW.NEWNEIGHBORRELIEF.ORG
TEL.: +1-619-315-3910

Model or **"The Justin Mudekereza Model"**—offers valuable insights for policymakers, funders, and practitioners seeking more impactful solutions.

I humbly invite your partnership in exploring, testing, and refining this model. Our shared mission—to build a world free from poverty, inequality, and systemic underdevelopment—demands not only resources but also a willingness to learn, adapt, and innovate together. As Dag Hammarskjöld wisely reminded us, *"The United Nations was not created to take mankind to heaven, but to save humanity from hell."*

Let us therefore join efforts to renew the promise of global solidarity and ensure that the SDGs are not merely aspirations, but achievements realized through collaborative action.

With deep gratitude and unwavering optimism,

Justin B. Mudekereza
President & CEO, Rescue Democracy International
Author, *The New Model of Development and Humanitarian Aid Delivery*

JUSTIN B. MUDEKEREZA, PH.D., PRESIDENT & CEO
RESCUE DEMOCRACY INTERNATIONAL
WWW.RESCUEDEMOCRACYINTL.ORG
WWW.NEWNEIGHBORRELIEF.ORG
TEL.: +1-619-315-3910

ABOUT THE AUTHOR

Dr. Justin Bisimwa Mudekereza is a passionate humanitarian, philanthropist, and political advocate dedicated to social justice, human rights, and community development in the Democratic Republic of Congo and beyond.

He has over 25 years of experience in community development. He has worked as project Coordinator, Executive Director, President & CEO etc. focusing on Social Justice and Human Rights.

His previous publications include:

1. *"Sustainable Solutions to Address Management Problems for Refugee Resettlement in the United States of America: The Case of Refugee Resettlement in San Diego, California"* (a final thesis presented to the Academic Department of the School of Business and Economics in partial fulfillment of the requirements for the degree of Doctor of Philosophy in Project Management).

2. *Children Separated from their Parents, a Violation of Children's Rights*: The Case of Children Separation at the U.S. – Mexico Border.

3. *"The Complexity of Management of Refugee Resettlement and Language Barriers in the United States of America: A Case Study of Swahili Speakers from the Democratic Republic of Congo in San Diego, California."*

4. *"Understanding the Multifaceted Management Problems of Refugee Resettlement in the United States of America: The Only War the United States is Unlikely to Win."*

5. *"A Word of Warning to the World: A Transitional Government is Needed in the Democratic Republic of Congo to Avoid Many More Millions of Dead and Refugees" (second edition).*

6. *"A Word of Warning to the World (Second Edition): A Transitional Government is Needed in the Democratic Republic of Congo to Avoid Many More Millions of Dead and Refugees".*

7. *"Un Mot d'Avertissement au Monde: Un Gouvernement de Transition est Nécessaire en République Démocratique du Congo pour Eviter Beaucoup d'Autres Morts et des Refugiés". French version of #6.*

8. *"Shithole Countries: An Independent & Development Based Analysis".*

9. *Pays de Merdes: La Vérité Choquante que Aurait du Servir de Leçon. French version of #8.*

10. *"Critical Minerals, Dangerous Ties: Can Trump's Deal and Democracy in DRC Work Perfectly?"*

11. *"Minerais Critiques, Liens Dangereux: L'Accord de Trump et la Démocratie et DRC Peuvent-ils Fonctionner Parfaitement?" French version of #10.*

12. *"The Trio Félix Tshisekedi, Joseph Kabila and Corneille Nangaa: What Therapy for This New Problem for the Democratic Republic of Congo?"*

13. *"Le Trio Félix Tshisekedi, Joseph Kabila et Corneille Nangaa: Quelle Thérapie pour ce Nouveau Problème de la RD Congo?" French version of #12.*

14. *"The New Model of Development & Humanitarian Aid Delivery: A Contribution to the United Nations Sustainable Development Goals."*

15. *"Le Nouveau Modèle de Distribution de l'Aide Humanitaire et au Développement: Une Contribution aux Objectifs de Développement Durables."*

Dr. Mudekereza was one of the Presidential Candidates in the December 2023 election in the Democratic Republic of Congo (DRC). He is the Executive Director of New Neighbor Relief (NNR), a 501(c)3 nonprofit organization assistance refugees in their process of starting a new life in California. He is also the President & CEO of Rescue Democracy International – RDI, a 501(c)3 international nongovernmental organization working to alleviate human suffering through fostering democratic processes globally.

WEBLIOGRAPHY

- **Aide for Profit: The Dark History of USAID.** Currentaffairs.com. Retrieved 2-25-2024.
- **How America's aid system lost its way – and how to fix it.** Thehill.com. Retrieved 2-25-2024.
- **Aseel's Direct Aid Model vs. Traditional Aid.** Stories.aseelapp.com. Retrieved 2-25-2024.
- **The Millennium Development Goals.** National Democratic Institute. Retrieved 3-1-2024.
- **MDG Failures: Shortcomings of the Millennium Development Goals.** The Borgen Project. Retrieved 3-7-2024.
- **History of the United Nations.** Un.org. Retrieved 3-21-2024
- **The Birth of the UN after WWII.** Thoughtco.com. Retrieved 4-2-2024.
- **AThe United Nations (UN): Definition, History, Founders, Flag, & Facts.** Britannica.com. Retrieved 4-17-2024.
- **The Colombo Plan.** Cambridge University Press. Cambridge.org. Retrieved 5-1-2024.
- **U.S. Agency for International Development: An Overview.** Congress.gov. Retrieved 5-9-2024.
- **Report of the World Summit for Social Development.** Un-document.net. Retrieved 6-3-2024.
- **Millennium Development Goals Report | United Nations.** Un-ilibrary.org. Retrieved 8-4-2024.

- **Empowering Local Voices – Area,** Lifestyle Sustainability Directory. Retrieved 8-11-2024.
- **Empowering Local Voices for Community Economic Development,** Researchgate.net. Retrieved 12-11-2024.
- **Capacity-building – Sustainable Development Goal.** Sustainabledevelopment.un.org. Retrieved 1-9-2025.
- **Capacity Development for Environmental Sustainability.** Undp.org. Retried 3-10-2025.
- **Design sustainable capacity development interventions.** Unfao.org. Retrieved 4-30-2025.
- **Capacity building in Sustainability and Environmental Management.** Norwegian University of Science and Technology. Retrieved 9-30-2025.
- **Investing in What Works: A Primes on Evidence-Based Spending.** Harvard.edu. Retried 9-01-2025.

ABBREVIATIONS

RDI: Rescue Democracy International

MDG: Millenium Development Goal

SDG: Sustainable Development Goal

FP: Focal Point

LPSMC: Local Project Section and Monitoring Committee

KPI: Key Performance Indicator

ODA: Official Development Assistance

UNACTAD: United Nations Conference on Trade and Development

ROI: Return On Investment

ERP: Enterprise Resource Planning

PMS: Project Management Software

GIS: Geographical Information System

SLA: Service Level Agreement

SMS: Short Message Service

NFI: Non-Food Item

FN: Food Item

IDP: Internally Displaced Person

GPS: Global Positioning System

VPN: Virtual Private Network

Wi-Fi: Wireless Fidelity

RCT: Random Control Trials

GRANT PROPOSAL

- ❖ **Title:** Advancing a New Model for Development and Humanitarian Aid.

Submitted by: Rescue Democracy International (RDI).

Employer Identification Number (EIN): 99-3025512.

Funding Request: US$50 million.

Program Duration: 2026–2030.

Geographic Focus: Africa, Asia, Caribbean & South America.

Strategic Alignment: UN Sustainable Development Goals (SDGs 1 – No Poverty, 2 – Zero Hunger, 13 – Climate Action).

- ❖ **Executive Summary**

Rescue Democracy International (RDI) proposes a transformative five-year initiative to radically reimagine how development and humanitarian aid are conceptualized, delivered, and governed. With a funding request of US$50 million, this program will operationalize a proven, community-led model that prioritizes genuine capacity building, adaptability, and

direct impact – eschewing bureaucratic inefficiencies in favor of grassroots empowerment.

This initiative is grounded in nearly three decades of field experience and research, and is designed to address systemic failures in traditional aid systems. It aligns with key Sustainable Development Goals and targets regions where poverty, hunger, and environmental degradation remain most acute: Africa, South Asia, and South America.

❖ **Program Objectives**

- **Combat Poverty and Hunger:** Implement locally driven solutions that build economic resilience and food security.

- **Advance Environmental Conservation:** Support community-led stewardship of natural resources and climate adaptation.

- **Empower Communities:** Shift from top-down aid delivery to participatory governance – doing things *with* the people, not *to* them.

- **Eliminate Waste:** Redirect funds from overhead, bureaucracy, and logistics into high-impact, locally managed projects.

- **Leverage Technology:** Acquire and deploy digital tools to facilitate coordination,

transparency, and real-time monitoring.

- **Strengthen Local Leadership:** Train and support Focal Points who serve as bridges between RDI headquarters and grassroots organizations.

❖ **Budget Overview (US$50 Million)**

Category	Amount (USD)	% of Total	Description
Community-led Projects	$25,000,000	50%	Direct funding for poverty alleviation, food security, and environmental initiatives (tree planting, environmental sanitation, etc.).
Technology Acquisition & Development	$5,000,000	10%	Digital platforms, mobile tools, data systems for coordination and monitoring.
Focal Points Training & Support	$6,000,000	12%	Capacity building, stipends, travel, and communication.
Monitoring, Evaluation & Learning	$4,000,000	8%	Impact tracking, adaptive learning systems, third-party audits.

Strategic Partnerships & Advocacy	$3,000,000	6%	Engagement with UN, NGOs, and donors; policy influence and coalition building.
Operational Costs (Lean Model)	$5,000,000	10%	Minimal staffing (at the headquarters), legal, financial, and compliance infrastructure.
Regional Offices, Salaries, Vehicles & Machineries	$0	0%	RDI Model does not allow opening of regional offices, hire personnel overseas or buy vehicles and machineries.
Total	**$50,000,000**	**100%**	**0.5%** of the $10 billion challenge (see chapter 9 of The New Model… book).

❖ Expected Outcomes

- **1,500+ community projects** launched across three continents

- **600,000+ individuals** directly impacted through poverty and hunger alleviation

- **270,000 hectares** of land protected or restored through conservation efforts

- **200+ Focal Points** trained and deployed to lead local implementation

- **75% reduction** in administrative overhead compared to traditional aid models

- **Real-time digital dashboard** for donors and stakeholders to monitor progress

❖ **Impact Metrics**

Metric	Target by 2023
Households lifted out of poverty line	250,000
Children with improved nutrition	350,000
Local leaders trained	5,000
Projects with measurable outcomes	90%+
Funds reaching communities directly	85%+
Donor engagement and retention	80%

❖ **Conclusion & Call to Action**

This proposal is not merely a funding request; it is an invitation to join a movement. RDI's model offers a strategic, scalable, and community-driven alternative to legacy aid systems. With your support, we can demonstrate that development done *with* the people;

lean, accountable, and adaptive can deliver lasting change.

To learn more or to contribute, please visit www.rescuedemocracyintl.org.

Each time I author a book on Social Justice and Human Rights, my objective extends beyond raising awareness of the systemic injustices affecting marginalized populations. I also endeavor to propose actionable solutions to address these challenges. In this latest publication, I not only critique the inefficiencies and shortcomings of prevailing development and humanitarian aid systems, but I also present a viable alternative—RDI's Model—designed to enhance the impact of donor and Grantmaker contributions.

In alignment with this vision, I have developed a proposal accompanied by a budget of US$50 million. This figure represents merely 0.5% of the US$10 billion challenge introduced on page 9 of the book. The proposed budget is based on a straightforward premise: allocating US$50 million to each of 200 International Nongovernmental Organizations (INGOs), all operating under the RDI Model for development and humanitarian aid delivery.

Consider the transformative potential of the full US$10 billion challenge when evaluated against measurable targets and outcomes by the year 2030. This proposal reflects just one iteration of that broader vision – multiplied across 200 INGOs, the cumulative impact could be extraordinary.

Note: This represents a preliminary concept. Should you, as a Donor or Grantmaker, express interest in supporting this initiative, we would be pleased to provide a comprehensive version of the proposal upon request.

❖ Acknowledgment and Gratitude

To all those who choose to support and invest in the Rescue Democracy International (RDI) Model; thank you. Your contribution is not merely financial; it is a profound endorsement of a vision for a more just, effective, and accountable system of development and humanitarian aid delivery. By aligning with this transformative approach, you are helping to build a model the world can rely on; one rooted in equity, community leadership, and measurable impact.

Together, we are not only challenging the status quo but forging a new path forward; one that places dignity,

transparency, and results at the heart of global aid. Your partnership is both a catalyst and a commitment to a future where development truly serves those it was meant to uplift.

Thank you for standing with us.

Justin B. Mudekereza, Ph.D.

President & CEO
Rescue Democracy International
www.rescuedemocracyintl.org
www.newneighborrelief.org
Tel.: +1-619-315-3910

www.ingramcontent.com/pod-product-compliance
Lightning Source LLC
Chambersburg PA
CBHW052348020726

47503CB00001B/154